PRAISE FOR RACHEL HOWZELL HALL

"A fresh voice in crime fiction."

—Lee Child

"Devilishly clever . . . Hall's writing sizzles and pops."

—Meg Gardiner

"Hall slips from funny to darkly frightening with elegant ease."

—*Publishers Weekly*

PRAISE FOR *FOG AND FURY*

"This captivating blend of angst, mystery, and page-turning suspense delivers a top-notch reading experience."

—*Kirkus Reviews* (starred review)

"Enough nuance and complexity to make things feel fresh. Readers will be eager to return to this series soon."

—*Publishers Weekly*

"A gripping series debut."

—*Booklist*

"Of immense appeal for readers with an interest in mysteries and thrillers featuring a female sleuth, a myriad of unexpected plot twists, and a memorably 'big reveal' finale. Unreservedly recommended."

—*Midwest Book Review*

"A new Rachel Howzell Hall thriller is always call for celebration, and this one may be her very best. *Fog and Fury* is a PI page-turner, full of investigative twists, deeply rendered characters, and lush, evocative writing that could come from no one else. Pick this book up now."
—Jess Lourey, Edgar Award–nominated author of *The Taken Ones*

"Rachel Howzell Hall once again proves why she's one of the best crime fiction authors writing today. *Fog and Fury* combines whip-smart observations about race and class with a twisty mystery and cliff-hanger ending that'll have you already wanting to put the next book on your TBR list. It's a must-read for noir fans, especially if you loved her Lou Norton series."
—Kellye Garrett, award-winning author of *Missing White Woman*

"Rachel Howzell Hall has done it again with *Fog and Fury*. This is a story with depth, heart, and terror, and it cements her as one of the strongest voices in crime fiction today. Newly minted PI Alyson 'Sonny' Rush is a character to root for. Add in her extended family, the dark secrets in the town of Haven, the messy relationships and social growing pains, all at once familiar and frightening, and you have the recipe for a stellar thriller. Don't miss it!"
—J.T. Ellison, *New York Times* bestselling author of *A Very Bad Thing*

Praise for *What Fire Brings*

"Rachel Howzell Hall is a master of the psychological-suspense thriller. *What Fire Brings* delivers shocking secrets, surprises on every page, and a killer twist that will leave you breathless. A must-read!"
—Melinda Leigh, #1 *Wall Street Journal* bestselling author

"This one will keep you guessing! Hall's considerable talent is on full display as she expertly deploys misdirection and subterfuge in a riveting tale of intrigue and suspense where nothing is as it seems. The past collides with the present to forever alter the future while the twists keep coming until the final shocking reveal. If you love an intricate plot with well-crafted prose, incisive insight, and complex characters, do not miss this propulsive mystery by a superb storyteller!"
—Isabella Maldonado, *Wall Street Journal* bestselling author

"Crackling wildfires, dark secrets, and a serial killer on the loose. Rachel Howzell Hall's *What Fire Brings* is a captivating and creepy thrill ride through the California canyons, right up to the final and fiery twisty end."
—Wanda M. Morris, award-winning author of *All Her Little Secrets* and *Anywhere You Run*

"Rachel Howzell Hall is simply one of the finest crime writers of her generation, and *What Fire Brings* is her most assured novel yet . . . and one that hits a little close to home for everyone who puts pen to paper or finger to keyboard. Tense, illuminating, and filled with surprises on every page. A masterwork that will leave you flipping pages to see what you might have missed."
—Tod Goldberg, *New York Times* bestselling author

PRAISE FOR *WHAT NEVER HAPPENED*

"Rachel Howzell Hall does it again. *What Never Happened* blends blade-sharp writing and indelible characters with a suspenseful story that pulls you in and won't let go, as a seeming paradise grows dark with storms, suspicion, and murder. I couldn't put it down."
—Meg Gardiner, #1 *New York Times* bestselling author

"*What Never Happened* opens with a gut punch and doesn't let up from there. Rachel Howzell Hall's twist on the you-can't-go-home-again story is smart, dizzying, and thrilling. She not only handles the mystery elements expertly, but she honors the grief and rage of our past and present."
—Paul Tremblay, bestselling author of *The Cabin at the End of the World* and *The Pallbearers Club*

"Rachel Howzell Hall has crafted her own genre of slow-boiling, powerfully emotional thrillers. Her realistic characters are ordinary people, haunted by past horrors that won't stay buried, forcing them to face pure evil to find their own redemption."
—Lee Goldberg, #1 *New York Times* bestselling author

"In *What Never Happened*, Rachel Howzell Hall seamlessly weaves together the past and the present, decorating her breakneck plot with dark secrets and unexpected reveals that glitter like jewels. I couldn't turn the pages fast enough."
—Jess Lourey, Amazon Charts bestselling author of *The Quarry Girls*

"*What Never Happened* is superb. Beautifully and smartly written, it is an engrossing thriller with an ending that will leave your head spinning. It is deliciously creepy and perfectly crafted. In a word, stunning! Don't miss this one!"
—Lisa Regan, *USA Today* and *Wall Street Journal* bestselling author

"Rachel Howzell Hall's *What Never Happened* is a spine-tingling twist of a roller coaster that keeps you on the edge of your seat to the very last page and will have you saying 'Thanks a lot, Rachel, for my lack of sleep.'"
—Yasmin Angoe, award-winning author of the critically acclaimed Nena Knight series, *Her Name Is Knight* and *They Come at Knight*

"Rachel Howzell Hall continues to prove why she's one of crime fiction's leading writers. *We Lie Here* is a psychological-suspense fan's dream with both a heroine you'll want to root for and a story you'll want to keep reading late into the night. A must-read!"
—Kellye Garrett, Agatha, Anthony, and Lefty Award–winning author of *Like a Sister*

Praise for *These Toxic Things*

An Amazon Best Book of the Month: Mystery, Thriller & Suspense

"This cleverly plotted, surprise-filled novel offers well-drawn and original characters, lively dialogue, and a refreshing take on the serial killer theme. Hall continues to impress."
—*Publishers Weekly* (starred review)

"A mystery/thriller/coming-of-age story you won't be able to put down till the final revelation."
—*Kirkus Reviews*

"Tense and pacey, with an appealing central character, this is a coming-of-age story as well as a gripping mystery."
—*The Guardian*

"The mystery plots are twisty and grabby, but also worth noting is the realistic rendering of a Black LA neighborhood locked in a battle over gentrification."
—*Los Angeles Times*

"Rachel Howzell Hall . . . just gets better and better with each book."
—CrimeReads

"Rachel Howzell Hall continues to shatter the boundaries of crime fiction through the sheer force of her indomitable talent. *These Toxic Things* is a master class in tension and suspense. You think you are ready for it. But. You. Are. Not."

—S. A. Cosby, author of *Blacktop Wasteland*

"*These Toxic Things* is taut and terrifying, packed with page-turning suspense and breathtaking reveals. But what I loved most is the mother-daughter relationship at the heart of this gripping thriller. Plan on reading it twice: once because you won't be able to stop, and the second time to savor the razor's edge balance of plot and poetry that only Rachel Howzell Hall can pull off."

—Jess Lourey, Amazon Charts bestselling author of *Unspeakable Things*

"The brilliant Rachel Howzell Hall becomes the queen of mind games with this twisty and thought-provoking cat-and-mouse thriller. Where memories are weaponized, keepsakes are deadly, and the past gets ugly when you disturb it. As original, compelling, and sinister as a story can be, with a message that will haunt you long after you race through the pages."

—Hank Phillippi Ryan, *USA Today* bestselling author of *Her Perfect Life*

Praise for *And Now She's Gone*

"It's a feat to keep high humor and crushing sorrow in plausible equilibrium in a mystery novel, and few writers are as adept at it as Rachel Howzell Hall."

—*Washington Post*

"One of the best books of the year . . . whip-smart and emotionally deep, *And Now She's Gone* is a deceptively straightforward mystery, blending a fledgling PI's first 'woman is missing' case with underlying stories about racial identity, domestic abuse, and rank evil."
—*Los Angeles Times*

"Smart, razor-sharp . . . Full of wry, dark humor, this nuanced tale of two extraordinary women is un-put-downable."
—*Publishers Weekly* (starred review)

"Smart, packed with dialogue that sings on the page, Hall's novel turns the tables on our expectations at every turn, bringing us closer to truth than if it were forced on us in school."
—Walter Mosley

"A fierce PI running from her own dark past chases a missing woman around buzzy LA. Breathlessly suspenseful, as glamorous as the city itself, *And Now She's Gone* should be at the top of your must-read list."
—Michele Campbell, bestselling author of *A Stranger on the Beach*

"One of crime fiction's leading writers at her very best. The final twist will make you want to immediately turn back to page one and read it all over again. *And Now She's Gone* is a perfect blend of PI novel and psychological suspense that will have readers wanting more."
—Kellye Garrett, Anthony, Agatha, and Lefty Award–winning author of *Hollywood Homicide* and *Hollywood Ending*

"Sharp, witty, and perfectly paced, *And Now She's Gone* is one hell of a read!"
—Wendy Walker, bestselling author of *The Night Before*

"Hall once again proves to be an accomplished maestro who has composed a symphony of increasing tension and near-unbearable suspense. Rachel brilliantly reveals the bone and soul of our shared humanity and the struggle to contain the nightmares of human faults and failings. I am a fan, pure and simple."
—Stephen Mack Jones, award-winning author of the August Snow thrillers

"Heartfelt and gripping . . . I'm a perennial member of the Rachel Howzell Hall fan club, and her latest is a winning display of her wit and compassion and mastery of suspense."
—Steph Cha, award-winning author of *Your House Will Pay*

"An entertainingly twisty plot, a rich and layered sense of place, and most of all, a main character who pops off the page. Gray Sykes is hugely engaging and deeply complex, a descendant of Philip Marlowe and Easy Rawlins who is also definitely, absolutely her own woman."
—Lou Berney, award-winning author of *November Road*

"A deeply human protagonist, an intricate and twisty plot, and sentences that make me swoon with jealousy . . . Rachel Howzell Hall will flip every expectation you have—this is a magic trick of a book."
—Rob Hart, author of *The Warehouse*

"*And Now She's Gone* has all the mystery of a classic whodunit, with an undeniably fresh and clever voice. Hall exemplifies the best of the modern PI novel."
—Alafair Burke, *New York Times* bestselling author

Praise for *They All Fall Down*

"A riotous and wild ride."

—Attica Locke

"Dramatic, thrilling, and even compulsive."

—James Patterson

"An intense, feverish novel with riveting plot twists."

—Sara Paretsky

"Hall is beyond able and ready to take her place among the ranks of contemporary crime fiction's best and brightest."

—*Strand Magazine*

NO ONE KNOWS YOU'RE HERE

OTHER TITLES BY RACHEL HOWZELL HALL

Haven Thrillers

Mist and Malice

Fog and Fury

Vallendor

The Cruel Dawn

The Last One

Detective Elouise Norton

City of Saviors

Trail of Echoes

Skies of Ash

Land of Shadows

Stand-Alones

What Fire Brings

What Never Happened

We Lie Here

These Toxic Things

And Now She's Gone

They All Fall Down

The View from Here

NO ONE KNOWS YOU'RE HERE

RACHEL HOWZELL HALL

Published by Thomas & Mercer, Seattle

www.apub.com

Amazon, the Amazon logo, and Thomas & Mercer are trademarks of Amazon.com, Inc., or its affiliates.

EU product safety contact:
Amazon Media EU S. à r.l.
38, avenue John F. Kennedy, L-1855 Luxembourg
amazonpublishing-gpsr@amazon.com

ISBN-13: 9781662539008 (paperback)
ISBN-13: 9781662538995 (digital)

Cover design by Lisa Amoroso
Cover image: © A-photographyy / Shutterstock; © Alexander Ramos / Shutterstock; © PhotodriveStudio / Shutterstock; © Marta Nogueira / Shutterstock; © rai106 / Shutterstock

Printed in the United States of America

The way of the wicked is like darkness;
they don't know what makes them stumble.

—Proverbs 4:19

PART I

Wednesday, October 1
5:05 a.m.

I pulled off Western Avenue and into the empty parking lot of Great Redeemer Church of God in Christ.

The Dodge Neon was parked in the alley, near the dumpsters, almost transparent in the fog. The car's windows were white with condensation—it had been sitting there all night.

I parked in a space a few feet away and waited to meet "T. H."

No one exited the Neon.

Western Avenue . . . This South Los Angeles street was always mentioned in the papers and on the six o'clock news.

Four killed on Western in a gang-related shooting.

76-year-old grandmother raped in her home off Western.

And so on.

And yet here I was.

I didn't rush to leave my car—I barely hit five four and have the muscle mass of a Rice Krispies Treat. Besides, my car has a robust heater, seat warmers, satellite radio, and an SOS satellite system in the event of car trouble. Why leave that, especially with all the fog and all those crime stats—*seventeen rapes and six murders in the last five months.*

Maybe T. H. left to get coffee.

I plucked my iPhone from the cupholder and sent T. H. a text message. I'm here now. Parked across from you. I hit "send" but the bar above the message stalled.

Ah.

No reception. A dead zone.

At five fifteen, I opened the car door.

The rank odor of urine assaulted me. That and the stench of spilled beer and sour-sweet rotting meat.

I threw a few nervous glances up and down the alley. Cold, dead air pushed me from all sides. Nothing will happen to me. I'm at a church. I'm protected by angels with swords and . . .

Rustling sounds, and buzzing, lots of buzzing, came from the dumpsters just ten yards away from me. To my left and a block away, mechanical squeaking, like a shopping cart wheel that needed oil, pierced the air.

Something brushed against my ankle.

I yelped, hopped, and scanned the wet asphalt with wide eyes.

There it is!

A rat the size of a rabbit waddled past me, and headed to the trash bins.

The mechanical squeaking sounded closer than before. A bright white light flashed—I saw it out of the corner of my eye. Wasn't much. Small. Quick.

I continued to peer in that direction but saw nothing.

Just my imagination.

I turned back to the Neon.

No one had left the car.

I waved in its direction to let T. H. know that I was Syeeda McKay, the writer who had answered the text message and had driven in the dark to this neighborhood to meet someone I didn't know.

The Neon's door didn't open.

I muttered, "Crap," and waited with my keys held between my knuckles.

Once upon a time, my father had been a bus driver, and his route had been up and down Western, passing car washes, elementary schools, chicken joints, Baptist churches, Laundromats, motels, motor inns, pawn shops, Koreatown, Little Armenia. Over the course of his thirty-year career, he had been jumped and shot at countless times. He had broken up fights, rescued abandoned babies, and prevented late-night rapes, all of which happened on his bus. The violence didn't kill my father. The cigarettes did.

I glanced at the phone's clock—5:25—then mumbled, "This is crazy." I stomped over to the Neon and into a cloud of flies, the source of that crazy-loud buzzing. I tried swatting them away but there were too many.

"Hey!" I shouted at the driver's-side window. "You in there?" I swiped the glass with my jacket sleeve.

Empty seat. No T. H.

Are you kidding me? I've been waiting out here since—

I glanced over the top of the car, to the giant dumpsters filled with trash. My gaze dropped to the wet asphalt.

Rats. An ocean of rats swarming over a pair of brown legs. A woman's legs.

I quick-stepped around the Neon, heart in my throat, and darted to the woman on the ground. "Hey! Hey!" A wave of nausea washed over me as I kept swatting at those flies. The rats bumped and crawled over my shoes, skittered and scratched against my bare ankles. I screamed in my head, and held my breath to block those rotting alley smells. Tried to avoid the puddle of goopy liquid oozing toward the toes of my sneakers, knowing that it was blood. Her blood.

I pulled off the trash bag that had been dumped on top of the woman, and shrieked.

Blood everywhere.

Her face was shattered. One glassy, dead eye stared at the dark sky. The other eye no longer existed.

God help me.

1

On April Fool's Day, one hundred thirty *Los Angeles Times* staffers were laid off due to "steep revenue declines." Two crime reporters were a part of that number and I was one of those two. Initially, I hadn't been too upset—I wouldn't have to visit dark alleys in the worst parts of town when the sky was still wet. So, yeah. Cool. I had already published two novels, and had written and sold the screenplay of novel number two to my movie-director big brother, Kenny. With the film's release and my severance package, I had enough money to forge a freelance writing career. I could chase my own stories. Make my own hours. But at one twenty-eight this morning, a text message had pulled me from sleep.

Have info re Phantom Slayer. Meet @ 6561 Western 5 am. Im in the silver neon. T. H.

My first thought? *Who the hell is T. H.?*

My second thought? *A meeting at five freakin' o'clock in the morning?* I had just finished hosting a spa party, and my friends had trudged out of my house a little after midnight.

But T. H. had information about the Phantom Slayer. And since no one, including me, knew much about the Slayer, I needed to make this meeting with T. H., whoever the heck that was.

I did know that in 1990, the Slayer murdered a sex worker named Angie Kane in an alley off Western Avenue. He had left DNA in her mouth—semen. But forensic investigators could not match his DNA profile with anything in the state or federal databases. So, Angie's killer eluded the police—blame budget cuts and backlog.

In 2005, some paper-pushing numbers cruncher in the city council's finance department found money in the couch cushions, and detectives scored twenty extra dollars to put more effort into solving Angie's and other cold cases. Investigators studied backlogged bullets as well as hair and skin fragments from unsolved murders. They found matches in bullet striations from homicides committed in 1990, 1991, 1994, 1995, 2000, and 2001. The same gun had been used in all six crimes, and each victim had worked as a sex worker on Western Avenue.

The Slayer then murdered two more sex workers—one in 2006 and another in 2007.

I had been the investigative reporter who broke the story of these murders. A deputy medical examiner in the coroner's office (and a family friend) tipped me to a string of body dumps off Western Avenue going back eighteen years. With his help, I discovered those matching bullets and the identities of the victims.

Los Angeles had a new serial killer.

No one in the police department shared this information with the public. Not one press conference was held. Not one press release was written and distributed. The police chief refused to discuss these deaths with the public and ignored each of my interview requests. Guess he didn't appreciate me telling *Times* readers about the secret task force of detectives that had been formed to find the monster. Guess he didn't like that I had named the killer the "Phantom Slayer."

We don't discuss ongoing cases. That's what his press officer told me.

People should know. That's what I told him. And I would publish my stories with or without the LAPD's help.

With great reluctance, detectives offered me a deal. They'd share bits of information about the case only if I heeded to certain conditions. Like, "you can't mention any weapon specifics" and "you can't mention any current suspects."

I took the deal.

Profilers, including my sister, Eva, who worked for the FBI, believed that the Slayer knew this part of the city well. They hypothesized that he was an educated Black man now in his forties (but he killed twenty years ago?). That he succeeded because he blended in with the community. His MO was simple: He killed in the alleys of South Los Angeles, left filled trash bags over his victims—always sex workers—then disappeared into the shadows.

I now stood in one of those alleys off Western Avenue, behind Great Redeemer Church of God in Christ, as police officers armed with ribbons of yellow crime scene tape swarmed the church parking lot. I pulled at the dry skin on my bottom lip and waited for someone to shoo me away, but no one seemed interested enough. The detectives were clustered together near the victim's car. Patrol cops had finished cordoning off the murder site and were now monitoring the small crowd.

My eyes darted to the dumpsters, to the gawkers, to the spaces between the patrol cars and emergency vehicles. Couldn't shake that feeling of being watched.

Someone tapped my shoulder.

I startled and spun around.

"Ma'am, you need this?" A redheaded paramedic offered me the blanket in his hands.

I whispered, "No, thanks," then watched him amble back to the ambulance.

Clean, white light burned from the forensic team's halogen lamps. Those lights and that fog made it hard to see the church's bright white cross. The large storage containers and dumpsters looked like elephants huddled in the mist. The bars atop the patrol cars lost their urgency—soft pink, no longer blood red. That yellow tape had no bite, those black words CRIME SCENE DO NOT CROSS suggesting and not demanding.

I glanced at my phone: 6:02.

Too early in the day to think about NASH reports.

Natural, accident, suicide, or homicide?

Jeez, officer, I wanted to say to the first cop on the scene, *I don't know. I'm just a writer, and she was like that when I got here. Got a cigarette?*

I snapped at the rubber band around my left wrist (an intervention to kick my two-packs-a-day habit) and winced as the elastic popped against my skin.

Cigarettes: bad.

I glanced at my car, a late-model Mercedes-Benz now part of a crime scene. In early September, two weeks after my breast cancer surgery, I had purchased it with money left from the movie deal. I considered the Benz a "life" gift . . . or a "death" gift . . . My perspective shifted every day.

"Sweet, sweet Sy."

I turned to Detective Adam Sherwood. He held a blanket in one hand and a small steno pad in the other.

Today he looked more like his Black mother than his white father. Maybe it was the strange morning light. Maybe it was the way he said, *Sweet, sweet Sy.* More Barry White than Barry Manilow.

Adam was a detective in the Robbery-Homicide Division of the Los Angeles Police Department, specifically the division's Homicide Special Section. HSS detectives spent the bulk of their careers working the city's high-profile cases, like the Manson family murders, the Hillside Strangler case, and the O. J. Simpson fiasco. He now headed the formerly secret 320 Task Force charged with finding the Slayer, the third detective to lead the investigation. His predecessors had abandoned the hunt without much luck or much hair.

But Adam had a law degree and a 90 percent success rate in solving cases. If he couldn't unravel this mystery, then we were all SOL.

"You can't be here right now," Adam said as he draped the wool blanket across my shoulders. At a solid six three, he towered over me, a green-eyed biracial Superman wearing an off-the-rack Armani suit.

My hands shook as I held up the faded press pass dangling from the cord around my neck. It belonged to Steve Tupper, a journalist (and ex-boyfriend) now working the AP desk in Frankfurt. No one had ever cared to check the validity of the pass—*Why is a Black woman wielding a white man's ID?* But if someone studied it too long, I would smile and ask what cologne he wore. I'd compliment her shoes, her handbag, or his deep, deep voice. Drops of flattery that blurred the eyes of the Keepers of the Gate and got me all I needed.

Adam peered at the photo on the pass and chuckled.

"Couldn't find mine," I said, pulling the blanket closer. "And it was too early in the morning to look."

"Not that your pass means anything now," he said.

"I'm still on payroll until December."

"Great. But you gotta move behind the—"

"I'm not moving from this spot. I found her and I sure as hell ain't letting some bitch from the *Sentinel* steal my story."

"I'm not tryin' to break your crayons, Sy, but this is a crime—"

"I know what it is. I'm not moving."

"You look a little pale," he said with a cocked eyebrow. "And you're shaking." He reached to touch my face. "Are those dried tears on your—"

I swatted his hand. "Make fun of me all you want, but I'm not moving."

He turned to look at the cadre of detectives clustered together. They all stood back as forensic investigators from the coroner's office processed the crime scene. By the cops' sideway glances at the lab techs, and the lab techs' glares at the cops, I could tell that the LAPD had touched too much.

My gaze moved past them and back to the trash bins, to the church and those empty spaces. Still searching for those eyes that had been trained on me since my arrival here.

"If you make me leave," I said to Adam, "I'll write the most explosive story yet to be written about the Slayer. And I'll organize a press conference for the victims' families, too. You know those families: They're the ones you continue to keep in the dark—"

"Just stop, okay? Let me think." He swiped his long pointy nose, and clicked his teeth.

"I won't publish the next article until I run it past you first," I said, tamping down the desperation in my voice.

He grinned. "Same song, different verse."

"I'll acknowledge you in the book, just like I've done in the articles." I paused, and added, "Well, I'll acknowledge you once you solve the crime and give me an ending so that I can finish the book. Again, solving the crime is imperative here."

Adam rolled his eyes. "I know you're frustrated, and I know you wish I would wrap everything up by the end of the year, but if wishes were fishes . . . As for acknowledging me, you've already used that bribe."

"And I've never broken my word. Professionally."

He smiled, but said nothing.

"If I come across any new information that advances the investigation, I'll pass it on to you immediately." I arched an eyebrow. "You'll be one step closer to solving a case that's kicking your ass."

He peered at me. "Who says it's kicking my ass?"

I shrugged. "Just an observation. Just another dead woman in an alley."

A blue-and-white coroner's van rumbled to the perimeter and parked. Three morgue attendants hopped out and hustled to the van's back doors.

Adam pointed to me. "Don't touch anything and don't leave."

I nodded, exhaled. "I'll stay out of your way."

He strode toward the Neon, and whistled to his team. "All right, fellas. Let's do this."

2

The driver's-side door of the Neon was now open. A lab tech had clicked off the dome light, and a photographer now snapped a series of pictures. *Pop, pop, pop.* The flash looked dangerous, atomic. The guy with the camera moved away to let a videographer record the scene. *Blood now the color of chocolate on the church's stucco and on the asphalt. Plastic yellow evidence cones poking from the pavement like dandelions. The young woman in the middle of it all. Still and soulless . . .*

Adam snapped his fingers in front of my face. "—won't talk to me now, then I'll have to drive you downtown."

I blinked and said, "Huh?"

"I'm talking to you and you're ignoring me."

"I didn't see you." My eyes returned to those yellow evidence cones, to that dried blood. "It's just . . ." I swallowed, then closed my eyes.

He took my elbow and guided me to his black Crown Victoria. He opened the passenger door and motioned for me to get in.

It was as cold inside the car as it was outside. Even with the blanket wrapped around me, the leather seat stole my body heat and made me shiver. I could see the crime scene from the windshield—detectives stood next to the Neon as they pointed to the dead woman on the ground, then pointed north.

The photographer had moved his lens away from the Neon and now trained it on the group loitering behind the yellow tape.

Some murderers return to the crime scene to enjoy the aftermath of their depravity. So, crime scene investigators take pictures of any bystanders, and then they study each face to identify possible suspects.

Was the Slayer here?

Adam climbed into the driver's seat, a hulking figure even in a ginormous American car. He pulled that steno pad and a pen from his pocket and grabbed a small tape recorder from the car's utility tray. He sat the machine on the dashboard, and pushed its red "record" button. After a preamble that included my name and the date and time, he asked, "When did you get here?"

I took a cleansing breath, and slowly exhaled. "A little past five."

"And you called 911 . . . ?"

"Around five twenty." The willies were returning. Trembling. Breathlessness. The urge to weep. When I had reached an emergency operator to report the dead body, the dispatcher had started speaking to me in Spanish—my words had refused to fall into the proper sequence of an English speaker.

"Syeeda," Adam said, touching my hand, "just relax and focus, okay?"

"Yeah." I waggled my head to shake it off. "Okay."

"Why did you take so long to call?"

I stared at the gold detective badge hanging around his neck. "I didn't think anyone was in the car."

"That's not what I asked."

"I was scared. I couldn't move. I froze."

I had staggered away from the victim, ran back to my car, and lunged behind the steering wheel. I was crying so hard I gagged, and to keep from choking, I jammed my hand in my mouth. Calmer, I had pawed through my messy glove compartment and found a can of pepper spray. I held it out before me, certain that I'd blind myself first since I couldn't hold the can steady. My eyes had skirted the alley for the murderer. Fear froze my blood, my limbs, all of me. I couldn't reach for the keys to turn the ignition. Couldn't use my phone to call for help. Couldn't do anything. I sat in the car, don't know for how long, until my fingers thawed enough to tap the "emergency call" icon on my cell phone.

"Were you here by yourself?" Adam asked me now. "Could there be other witnesses?"

"I was alone. I think . . . Don't know."

He offered me a stick of Juicy Fruit.

I shook my head and snapped at the rubber band on my wrist more times than necessary.

"A weird place to find a dead body," he said, slipping gum into his mouth. "Who kills somebody at a church?"

"But she was killed in an alley off Western like the other victims." I grabbed the door handle. "Can I go now?"

"I'm not finished."

"Can we catch up later?" I asked, titanium now replacing the Jell-O in my backbone.

"In a hurry?"

"I need to move on this before some other reporter does."

Adam gasped and clutched his imaginary pearls. "Well, gee whiz. I thought you wanted the whole world to know about these murders."

"Of course, I do."

"Then why should you care if some other reporter tells it?"

"I broke the story, and today's murder could be the case that ends the Slayer's reign of terror and I don't want to share the credit since I'm selfish." I took a breath and slowly exhaled. "Comes from being a middle child. May I go now?"

He pressed the "stop" button on the recorder. "Just because we're involved—"

"We're not," I said. "Not really."

Adam and I met a year ago, when he had been chosen by the chief of detectives to head the Slayer investigation. Our first kiss happened this past June, on the first day of summer, literally one of the longest days of my life. A week before my surgery, I ended our relationship.

Adam wasn't thrilled with my decision, but my mind had turned to tumors, pain . . . death. I didn't want him staying with me out of pity—even with a partial mastectomy, I'd still be disfigured, and he hadn't come into our love affair to grope a gimpy boob. When I told him this, he had spat, "I'm forty years old. I'm not some superficial jerk that drools over double-Ds and scratches his crotch in public. I'm insulted that you think I am."

Didn't matter. I wanted Adam to have a way out, so I forced our separation. I focused on my treatment, no longer worrying about inconveniencing him, or anticipating the weirdness that comes when one party wants to bail but doesn't want to hurt the other party's feelings. But on the eve of my surgery, Adam stayed overnight. For dinner, he cooked ahi tuna steaks and sautéed asparagus. Then we made love. Afterward, I crumpled in tears next to the bathtub and he kneeled beside me and held me and told me that I would be okay, that my surgeons were the best in the world, that my operation would be successful. The next morning, he drove me to the hospital and sat in preop with Mom and me. He held my hand until I was rolled away to the operation room.

"No matter what we are or aren't," Adam said now, "I'm still required to follow procedure. Even if it jacks up your busy schedule."

I slumped in my seat. "I'm not here because I like kickin' it with dead people."

He smirked. "Yeah? Why are you here? Other than to advance your own agenda?"

"'The dead cannot cry out for justice; it is the duty of the living to do so for them.'"

He lifted an eyebrow. "You just make that up?"

"Lois Bujold. Award-winning sci-fi writer. Met her once. Don't change the subject. Why you trying to regulate?"

"It's my job."

"I want to find this guy as much as you do."

He nodded. "Wanna know the difference between you and me, though? I don't wanna make him a star."

"Fuck you, Adam," I muttered. "What the hell is that supposed to mean?"

"Tristan Small."

Successful drug dealer (and my junior high school friend) Tristan Small had let me trail him on a piece I was writing, "How Good Boys Turn Bad." I had wanted to understand how a former valedictorian from an overprotective, well-to-do family could reject an engineering scholarship to Stanford and instead sling weed and crack for a living. I learned where Tristan's marijuana and cocaine supply originated, discovered how and who he recruited to distribute his wares, the types of guns he owned, even the type of women he dated (which had included a brief, postdivorce fling with my best friend Lena). In exchange, Tristan had asked me to keep his name and territory a secret. And I had agreed, to Adam's chagrin.

"I didn't make Tristan a star," I said. "I only informed the public about a drug dealer's methods without threat of arrest—"

"And that's a problem," Adam said.

"People deserve to know what can hurt them."

He rubbed his eyes, then surveyed the crime scene. "The public shouldn't know every single detail, okay? People already think they understand how shit works because they watch *CSI* on Thursdays. Let's say the Slayer is reading your stories. He then tracks the progress we've made, which means he can cover his tracks or worse: He can send me on another wild-goose chase to fuckin' Nova Scotia where I discover that he lived in a hostel for three days in 1967, and when I return from fuckin' Nova Scotia, he's either changed the location of where he dumps the bodies or he's changed his MO. *Again.*"

Adam had chased leads all over the country. No suspects' DNA had matched the DNA found on Angie Kane.

I crossed my arms and glared at the dashboard. "I had nothing to do with the Slayer changing his MO. He had sex with the first victim back in '90, and that's the only time. He hasn't changed his style since. I've written four huge features about the Slayer this year alone. I don't glorify the murders nor do I glorify the murderer. This detective who reads my stories agrees. He calls my pieces clearheaded and heartbreaking, factual and—"

"I know what I said," he snapped. "It's just . . . The nuts who have nothing to do all day wanna play these mind games and I don't have the time or the interest. And you—"

"And *I* haven't told the public everything. Nor can I keep people from sending me stupid emails and tips and crap. And that one time you had to fly to some swamp in Florida wasn't my fault—I thought it was a hoax, and I *told* you that the guy wanted attention. You said that it didn't matter, that you were obligated to check it out. That was all you right there."

He gazed at me without saying anything else. He tapped his pen against his teeth as he thought—a habit that drove me crazy—then pushed the "record" button on his machine. "The victim's name was Tamar Haist. Did you know her?"

"Nope." I pulled my own notebook from my pocket, and flipped to a clean page.

Adam was staring at me, waiting for more.

I raised an eyebrow. "I answered too quickly? Want me to think about it?" I cast my eyes to the car's ceiling, then shook my head. "No clue who she was. I've never met her."

"What did she know about the Phantom Slayer?"

I shrugged. "She didn't say anything specific in her message."

"And why did she send you a message?"

"Maybe she read one of my articles."

"And why meet so early in the morning?"

"Maybe she wanted to work me in before yoga."

He stared at his notepad, pen to teeth again.

I winced. "Can you stop doing that?"

"What? The pen thing? Is it bothering you?"

"Yes."

He tapped his pen against his teeth, then winked at me. "Strange, how you just . . . *stumbled* on a dead woman, a stranger, in an alley at five in the morning."

"I didn't *stumble*. She texted me and I came. Reporters do that, you know."

He held out his hand. "Can I see that message?"

I handed him my phone.

"I can't believe you came here, Sy," he muttered.

"I know."

"Why the hell would you follow an anonymous text message—"

"Adam," I said. "I know. It was stupid. I'll be more careful in the future."

He shook his head. "No, you won't." He scribbled into his pad, looked out the windshield, then muttered, "Why meet here? It's what? Three blocks north . . ."

The coroner's team was rolling a gurney holding an empty body bag toward the Neon.

Still talking to himself, Adam turned off the tape recorder and stuck his notepad back into his pocket.

"You're doing a hell of a lot of mumbling," I said. "Is there something I should know? Shit you're not telling me?"

He snorted. "Of course there is, but I can't share any of that with you right now."

I lifted an eyebrow, then touched his knee. "You've turned off your little recorder." I moved my hand up to his thigh and squeezed. "You can tell me. We're off the record."

We stared at each other until he said, "Sorry. Can't share. Maybe if you move your hand higher and to the left . . ."

I laughed and slapped his leg. "Fine. Keep your little task force secrets. I don't give a damn." I slipped my phone and notepad back into my pockets, then grabbed his wrist. "Please? Pretty please? Just give me something. *Anything.* It's been a hell of a morning."

"The guys are probably finished taking pictures of your car," Adam said, ignoring my pleas. "I'm gonna wrap all this up and head down to Mission. Act contrite as the good doctor lectures me about crime scene contamination."

"I'll be right behind you," I said, and shrugged off the blanket.

"You and Brooks speaking now?"

Yes, Spencer Brooks and I were now speaking. Until we weren't.

3

My heart hammered as I walked back to my car.

The crowd standing at the perimeter of Great Redeemer Church had swollen to twice its original size. Most onlookers held up their cell phones and were taking pictures of the madness. Nurses in scrubs, a UPS guy, a security guard, school kids—everyone wanted to see.

Is the Slayer here?

I scanned the faces—no one resembled a lunatic who had killed eight women. They all looked "normal." Brown-skinned, thick-lipped, flattops, weaves, overweight, jeans, cheap dresses, pantyhose. They were a little too gleeful being this close to a crime scene, but maybe "gleeful near death" was the new standard.

Now that the sun had broken through the fog, I could clearly see the dark crimson gore splashed across the base of the building. Had it been a typical October morning with bright Los Angeles sunshine and clear blue skies, I would've known immediately that a dead woman lay beneath that splatter, her body hidden beneath a heavy trash bag, and her face—what was left of her face—blasted into a pulpy mess.

Who was Tamar Haist?

I plucked my iPhone from my pocket—maybe a quick search on the internet could tell me more about the young woman. Except that the icon showing the phone's battery life was near red, and the charger was in my bag at home, and I still hadn't wandered out of the dead zone. Learning about Tamar would have to wait.

I shivered and glanced at the crowd again. The heaviness of being watched had returned.

Of course people are looking at me. I'm on the exciting side of the yellow tape.

I took several breaths until that sensation eased.

The techs had covered Tamar's hands with paper bags to preserve any evidence. If she had fought the murderer, his skin, hair, or blood would be lodged beneath her nails.

Unless he chopped off her fingertips to keep us from finding his DNA.

The gun had to be on the smaller side. A .25 or a .38. Anything bigger would've blown her head off.

What would they do with the Neon after dusting for prints, after plucking every stray fiber off the seat and carpet? Would they hand it over to the family and let them junk it?

And when would the church's pastor send out a deacon with a paintbrush and a can of butter-yellow enamel to hide the blood?

I thought of pulling out my notepad and interviewing one of the forensic techs. But I didn't. Instead, I turned away from the Neon and faced my car.

Breathe. Just breathe.

Too many people. Too much noise. Air's too wet. Too much light.

My sweaty T-shirt stuck to my body, so tight it forced me to sip air. Face tilted, I exhaled and blew imaginary smoke to the sky. I told myself to shake it off, to go home, to shower and make a pot of coffee . . .

But I couldn't ignore that feeling.

Someone in that crowd was watching me. Watching me and waiting. *Who?*

4

He can't believe it—*she's here!*

Digital camera in hand, he zooms in for a better view.

She's prettier in person than on the internet, than in those photographs on the back of her books. She's smaller, too.

He presses the silver button on top of the camera.

Beep. Another perfect shot for his collection.

What are the odds?

He hadn't planned to come here—he had to be at his day job by nine. To type a report. To enter data. To answer the phone. Repeat. But the Spirit had spoken to him as he showered and told him that he needed to stop by the church. *Now?* he had thought. *It's not the right time.*

But the Spirit is never wrong.

He obeyed and there she is.

What are the odds?

He touches the small Bible in the shirt pocket over his heart. *It's not about chance. My steps are ordered.*

He is so close that he can poke her and tell her that he's here. But he won't.

Not that she will ever see him. He's not Detective Asshole Sherwood, all height, square jaw, and swagger. Always the center of attention. Always "the man."

Think you're so smart. Fuck you, Sherwood. I'll show you smart.

He grinds his teeth until his head vibrates. It takes every atom of self-control to stay put and not break past that yellow tape to shoot Sherwood in the face, then push past the cops to see the body. Just one peek. That's all he wants. Just to see what death looks like in the light.

He gazes at the writer, and coolness washes over him.

She's been writing about him since the beginning—the first person to tell the world he existed. That had meant so much to him—*we all want to be seen.* To be noticed is to be real. And now he is real. All because of her.

He googles her each day and visits her Facebook page every hour. Back in July, he had found the courage to send her a friend request. She had accepted and responded to every message he left on her wall.

The Phantom Slayer will be found, she had once assured him. *Now that we know that the monster exists.*

He watches her all the time now. Daydreams about her. Nothing sexual. At least, not all the time.

The internet told him where she lived. A beautiful house on Vista Street. He drives past it a few times a week. Not to spy on her. Just to get a feeling of . . . things.

He started following her more once she and the detective became a "couple." They would go out to dinner and Sherwood would kiss her neck and grope her ass and who knows what else he did to her.

He didn't like that, his writer acting like Sherwood's whore.

Sometimes, he stands behind her in line, at the Starbucks not far from her house. She never notices him, not once has she acknowledged his existence. She never detects him sniffing her hair or staring at the mole on her left cheek beneath her eye.

She smiled at him once, at the grocery store, by accident most likely. She said, "Excuse me" as she reached around him to grab a package of paper towels from the shelf. A wonderful moment. Intimate. Just the two of them in that aisle. But then the detective came upon them with a grocery cart filled with bottles of wine and fancy cheese and boxes of cereal and condoms, even. He kissed her, right there in paper goods. And she let him. They didn't give him a second glance, even as he followed them around the store.

How could she act like that? Like a slut? And in public?

That night, he thought about doing to her what he had done to the others. She deserved it.

He has started taking pictures of her. She is now a part of his collection. A rarity. Unlike the junkies, the writer has a protector and friends who will miss her if she disappears. No worries. Catching her is just a matter of time . . . and careful planning.

And that time is nearing, he thinks now while watching her behind that yellow tape.

Because my steps are ordered.

Twenty years ago, God had led him to South Los Angeles, to Western Avenue, to Great Redeemer Church of God in Christ. Here, he had found the answers, had made sense of it all, had learned to direct his anger in productive ways. As a church leader, he performed his job with pride and a sense of purpose. *Take pictures of all the sex workers in the area. Get rid of them, one by one. Don't rush it.*

And he hasn't rushed. And they are dying, one by one. Led by the Spirit, he is not under the Law.

And now, *he* controls that corridor of Western Avenue. Sometimes, before he kills them, he talks to the sex workers, but he always stops listening: Their stories sound the same. Alcoholic mother. No father. Raised by a grandmother. Raised by the city. Weed to heroin to crack. From bad daddies to abusive boyfriends to murderous pimps. Don't know what to do. Sex is all I got.

And death is all he can offer them.

He touches his sternum and the words tattooed there. *To fear the Lord is the beginning of freedom.*

He will never forget the women—their initials are tattooed all over his body. And one day, S. M. will go on that swatch of skin above his heart. He'd saved it just for her. Even when he didn't know her, right as he started his mission so long ago, he knew that one day, she would come.

And now, she considers the crowd and frowns.

He sees disappointment and disgust in that grimace.

He catches her gaze, and she nods slightly. *It is sickening, isn't it? How people are laughing, pointing, trying to see more. This is serious,* he wants to shout. *One of God's children has been taken, and His heart aches for her, and you're laughing?*

Yes, he has his camera, but he is not like the others. He isn't reveling in the streets as though he's waiting for a Mardi Gras parade to pass. He doesn't post his pictures on the web as jokes or curiosities. No. He prints out his shots on the best photo paper available, frames and hangs his favorites on the wall in the basement.

The writer shakes her head before turning away from the clamor.

He prays that she doesn't drop him for some heart-lifting story about an orphan getting a heart transplant or a ninety-seven-year-old Holocaust victim earning a high school diploma. She is his prophet, like Moses who brought down the law from the mountains, the only man to see the physical manifestation of God. And like Moses was to the Father, Syeeda McKay will be to him. She, too, will die after she glimpses the Promised Land.

Because sin is sin, and the wages of sin is death. Death for prostitutes on Western. And death for cleaned-up whores, like the writer.

5

On Mission Road, right outside of downtown Los Angeles, there is a beautiful Victorian building that looks out of place so close to a Chevron service station across the street. Each time I visit, I always imagine that in another town, in another era, an Atticus Finch–type in a three-piece suit and fedora climbed those stone steps, prepared to fight for his "colored" client who had been framed for the rape of a little white girl. But this gorgeous piece of old-LA architecture, with its brickwork, and wrought-iron gas lamps, and on-site souvenir shop that hawks toe-tag key chains and T-shirts, is no courthouse. This is the office of the County of Los Angeles Medical Examiner, and home to more than four hundred and eighty unclaimed dead bodies.

Back in March, I had been assigned to write a story about a posse of rats that had chewed into the department's crypt and started to gnaw on a dozen of the dead stored there. As I walked those corridors to research my article, I witnessed corpses lying everywhere, frozen in whatever position they had been in at the time of their death—arms poking up, arms stretched out, legs bent in prayer. Bodies piled in the hallways, in refrigerated crypts, in examination rooms . . .

Let's just say that some folks—including my friend Spencer Brooks—were not thrilled with my comprehensive investigative report.

In a city as big as Los Angeles, almost 59,000 deaths are reported each year. Of those, the coroner investigated close to 10,000 cases. On average, a medical examiner conducts ten to twenty autopsies a day.

Most exams consist of opening the body and examining the heart. A "half-topsy."

So many bodies. So little time. And not a lot of money.

In the subsequent "kiss and make up" piece, I wrote about the serious efforts investigators in the coroner's office make to contact a decedent's next of kin. Sometimes, they succeed—some families rescue their beloved from the gurneys, the maggots, and marauding rodents. Others refuse to pay for autopsies or can't afford to pay the fees to have the body released—it takes thousands of dollars to receive, transport, and bury the dead. So, they leave auntie, cousin, or grandma at the coroner's office. Four months later, the Left Behind are cremated, packed into brown plastic boxes, and buried at Evergreen Cemetery in a public grave, courtesy of the people of Los Angeles.

Spencer Brooks and I stood together again in his cold autopsy room. Spencer had nodded at me as I entered, and after peering at me in silence for several seconds, he had said, "Good seeing you."

I had muttered, "Yeah. It . . . Yeah."

This was my sixth time observing an autopsy. By the way I trembled, it felt like my first.

The air stank of formaldehyde, cadaverine, and pine cleaner. The aggressive sourness stuck to your clothes, to the pages of your notebook, to the lining of your nostrils.

Soon, Adam joined us. We all wore green scrubs, our eyes protected by goggles, our mouths protected by masks.

At five six and a hundred forty pounds, Spencer looked too delicate to wield a bone saw. His taut, russet skin didn't seem thick enough to handle the scars, nicks, and bruises made by fumbling scalpels and moving dead-weight from stretchers to steel tables. Psychologically, though, he was the strongest man I knew. He worked with the dead, so his resolve was as solid as petrified wood.

People always assumed Spencer was shy. "Your friend doesn't talk much, does he?" Adam had once observed. No, he didn't. He never had in the thirty years I'd known him. His mother Sue (my mother's best friend) was a human steamroller and never let anyone speak more than a paragraph. So, Spencer didn't talk. Instead, he'd stare at you with those bourbon-colored eyes, and dissect you with that gaze, searching for your pathology.

Tamar Haist lay before us on the stainless steel table. She had stiffened during the ride downtown. Before my arrival, Spencer's assistant, Big Ruben, had cut her tendons, allowing her to recline. Big Ruben had removed Tamar's dress, panties, bra, shoes, and jewelry, one piece at a time, pausing to take pictures of each article. Then, he had washed the body of dead flies and larvae. I had talked to the six six, 270-pound coroner's assistant a few times before. He hated his job, and had considered quitting more than once. "Ain't never thought this would be my life," he had confided. Then, he had shrugged. "But this . . . It's my home."

Spencer took his place at the head of the table and switched on the bright overhead light. He looked at Adam and said, "Did any of your guys touch her?"

Adam shook his head. "No."

Spencer stared at him a moment longer, letting Adam twist, giving the detective a chance to amend his statement.

Adam said, "None of my guys touched her."

Spencer eyed me.

"I touched the trash bag, but I didn't touch her."

Spencer then pressed a pedal on the floor that was connected to the small microphone hanging above us and to a digital recorder hidden in the room. "Wednesday, October 1, 2008, 1:30 p.m.," he stated, starting the preliminary examination.

According to Spencer, the victim was a Black female, around nineteen or so. Tall. Five eight. Long chestnut hair—not hers. Thin body. Massive trauma to her face. Both breasts augmented with silicone implants.

"The victim's been dead ten to fifteen hours." Spencer peered at her arms. No track marks from needles. A cut on the left forearm. An abrasion the size of a quarter on her left hand. Another abrasion near the base of her left ring finger. The rats had torn away chunks from her biceps, thighs, and abdomen.

He stooped to study her head. "Entrance wound to the face, over the right regional mandible . . . Wound is surrounded by powderlike, dark-gray particles . . ." He lifted Tamar's head and peered at the back of her skull. "No exit wound."

His eyes skipped down to her groin. "No knife markings. No bruised thighs typical of sexual assault. But I'll do a rape kit to confirm."

He moved to the end of the table to consider her feet. Pedicured toenails painted cotton-candy pink. Eggplant-colored heels from pooled postmortem blood. No calluses.

Spencer pressed the pedal to stop the tape recording. "I can tell by just looking at her that she's not like the Slayer's other victims. She's well nourished, although a little on the thin side. I see no evidence of drug use. She had enough money to buy those breast implants."

Adam cocked his head. "Just because she's not like the others physically or economically doesn't mean that he *didn't* kill her. She's connected—she wanted to meet Sy to talk about the Phantom Slayer. Maybe he's changed the type of victim he usually targets in order to throw us off."

Spencer shrugged. "Maybe. Maybe not."

Adam asked, "How long will she take?"

Spencer shrugged again. "One hour or ten hours. Don't know yet."

"So what's next?" Adam said.

Spencer's eyes flitted back to the young woman on the table. "Next? I cut her."

6

I drove west on Wilshire, ignoring the Korean BBQ joints, the hole in the ground formerly known as the Ambassador Hotel, and the six million coffee shops that lined the boulevard. The sun had reached its two o'clock position in the sky, and the light had transformed that strip of highway into fiery glass and copper. It was the perfect moment for a dirty martini with three jumbo olives and a cigarette, just to burnish the edges. My eyes burned from the smog in the air and from exhaustion—thought I'd be watching *Judge Judy* now, sweeping away the remains of last night's spa party. Instead, I was driving back home after the brief exam of a dead source and whining into my cell phone to Lena Meadows, my sorority sister from college.

Lena and I had been roommates all four years at University of California at Santa Cruz. She was originally from New York, and during our freshman year, she'd never shut up about it. Every sentence started with "Back in New York," or "Growing up in Brooklyn." She came to California because it was the farthest she could go in the continental United States to escape her mother.

Lena had married well, but had divorced better. Last year, she divorced Dodgers superstar Chauncey Meadows after he appeared on *Oprah* without telling Lena first—about his appearance on *Oprah*, or about him being gay. At first, Lena had been embarrassed, but millions of dollars helped her to heal. She had been married to her husband for twelve years—in

California, ten was the magic number. It was a tragic number for rich men like Chauncey who had married without a prenuptial agreement.

After her divorce, Lena began dating men with extra helpings of Y chromosome, rich men built like boulders who earned their wealth in quotation marks. Sergey, her newest, had made millions in "electronics" and "technology." His wife, a doughy woman with dead eyes, had remained in Russia as her husband dabbled in "green energy."

Because Lena and I were best friends, and since I took on more projects than I could handle, and since she had nothing else to do all day except eat, shop, and sun on the big Russian's yacht, I had enlisted her to proof and type whenever boredom drove her to utilize her college degree. Since I had been laid off, she had refused pay and declared herself the "Phantom Slayer Intern." And she now sat somewhere in my house, proofreading a chapter for the Slayer book.

Now on the other end of this call, she listened in silence as I told her about Tamar Haist's murder.

"Damn," she finally said. "You really need to find a new job."

I chuckled. "You think?"

"Are you almost home? I've reached capacity for reading sick, twisted shit that good Christian girls like me shouldn't even know about."

"I'm stopping to get lunch first. I haven't eaten all day and I'm about to pass out." I made a left into the Whole Foods parking lot. My scar throbbed beneath my bra and my stomach growled—I had only fed it coffee and Doritos all day. As soon as I pulled into a parking space, I grabbed the Advil bottle from the beverage holder and dumped two pills into my palm.

"I know I shouldn't ask," she said, "but are there any new leads on the Slayer's identity?"

"Nope. He could be anybody." I swallowed the pills, slumped in my seat, and willed the ibuprofen to instantaneously dissolve into my bloodstream.

"Maybe I'll visit a few of the working girls on Western," she said.

"I've talked to them already. They didn't see nothing, they didn't hear nothing."

"Did you flash some cash?"

"I don't pay sources."

She laughed. "And that's why you don't know nothing."

"It's rough down there," I warned. "You may break a nail. Get soot in your eyes."

"I'll make Sergey and his administrative assistant go with me. I'll let you know."

Beyond my windshield, I watched a nun in a lemon-colored habit push a filled shopping cart toward her minivan. A woman with curly red hair transferred her towheaded son into his car seat. A man wearing aviator sunglasses sat on the hood of his Subaru, texting on a Sidekick and smoking a cigarette. Normal, law-abiding citizens who recycled their plastic and glass, paid their taxes by April fifteenth, and obeyed every speed law.

They're all probably hiding something.

You think you know people. Because they smile at you and wave, they're so nice. Because they direct the children's choir at church, they're so good. Because they've been married for forty-five years and have never thrown loud parties and they watched your Labrador retriever while you were away on vacation that time, you think, *Wow, what great neighbors.*

But how do you reconcile that person with a lunatic accused of rape and murder?

No one suspected Dennis Rader to be the BTK Killer. He had been so sweet. So caring. His wife never thought he'd bind, torture, and kill. That he'd wear his female victims' clothes and take pictures of himself lying partially covered in a grave intended for one of his chosen.

No one looked twice at the nutjob potato farmer in Maine *(Maine!)* who had laced the church potluck dinner with arsenic. "Probably the nicest person you'll ever meet," said one of Daniel Bondeson's high school classmates. Two people died because he had a grudge against the church.

Chester Turner, considered the most prolific Los Angeles–based serial killer, beat up everybody he met, but no one thought he'd strangle and kill ten women he didn't know. Who would ever believe that he'd attend the funeral dinner of one of his victims? Yeah, he had a temper, but he'd never *kill* people. And then eat platefuls of macaroni and cheese with the victim's family days later?

Some psychotics you see thundering toward you like a flaming jumbo jet. Richard Ramirez. Ed Gein. David Berkowitz. Others sneak up on you like curls of smoke and you have no freakin' clue who they really are until they explode. And those—the sneaky ones—are more frightening than anything because you *just don't know*. Wasn't it Ted Bundy who told the judge, "I am disguised as an attorney today"?

And the Phantom Slayer . . . This monster shot prostitutes in the face and left their bodies in alleys. Who was he? Someone's father? A beloved son? Eighteen years of this, and he had yet to send boastful notes to the newspapers or to the police. After that first murder, he never left behind DNA. He didn't rape, he didn't suffocate, and he didn't torture. He killed in the shadows, a methodical demon seeming not to care if people knew he existed.

Why?

7

I knew the layout of Whole Foods well. Fruit and vegetables to the east. Seafood and poultry to the south. Snack foods in Aisle 3. I still crept through the store—it would not be the first time I'd come across my stalker standing in beverages, pretending to buy a six-pack of Hansen's sodas.

That stalker was Deon Jackson. He used to work as one of Tristan Small's slingers until he broke the cardinal rule of drug dealing: *Don't get high off your own supply.* Built like a spark plug, he had a bald head and almond-colored skin. He wore a chinchilla fur vest and gold fronts on his teeth. He had a "thang" for me, and followed me around the city in his ancient minivan. He also gifted me with red roses and gourmet muffin baskets on obscure holidays, like International Forgiveness Day.

After the publication of my first Phantom Slayer article, he had sent me chocolate-covered strawberries and a note:

> I know the Slayer, Miss Syeeda, and you probly met him too. Yall just refuse to beeleve that he is a murderer because he smart and good at his job. I bump into him at the fish market and we talk for a while about you and your newspaper article. I didn't get his real name but he told me things that will blow your mind. He said he stuffed a $50 bill in that first girl's

mouth. He is in a powerful position and no one would think he is who he is. He uses laytex gloves at work but they come in handy for his late-night missions too. He lived in New Orleans for a while after Katrina since there is no police down there. I know all kinds of stuff. We can be a good team. Let me know when we can talk. Your Number 1 Fan, Deon J.

I kept the note, tossed the fruit, and ignored his offer of help. According to Spencer, the Slayer hadn't stuffed anything in the victim's mouth. So "I know all kinds of stuff?" Hardly.

Adam brought in Deon Jackson, grilled him about the Phantom Slayer, discovered that he knew nothing, and then released him.

Deon Jackson still needed to talk to me, though, and back in June, he found me in the parking lot of Whole Foods.

"I saw you back on La Brea," he had explained, "and I followed you on over."

I did not stop in my step—I needed to surround myself with as many people as possible.

He followed me to the store's sliding doors. "When can we talk, Miss Syeeda?"

"I'll email you," I had shouted back as I rushed toward the security guard.

Deon gave me a thumbs-up and tromped back to his minivan.

After ten minutes of stalling at the coffee bar, I had glanced out the store's plate-glass windows.

Deon Jackson was pacing near my car and scribbling on a piece of paper. When he looked in the store's direction, I ducked behind the recycle bin.

I had wandered the aisles of the grocery store for an hour before gaining the courage to return to the parking lot.

A pot of lavender orchids sat on the hood of my car. A piece of paper was trapped beneath the windshield wiper.

Dear Syeeda.

Roses are red, vilets are blue. These orkids are pretty and so our you. With love, Deon.

All that evening, Deon Jackson had emailed me:

> Miss Syeeda, the Slayer is a killing machine just like the Terminator.

> Miss Syeeda, maybe yall should arrest all the pimps on Western.

> Dearest Syeeda, you a gift from God. I dreamt about you last nite and we could be so good together. I am thankful for the Slayer. Without him, there would be no me and you.

With a shaky hand and tears in my eyes, I dragged that last message into my "Notes from a Loon" folder. I was straining so hard to keep it together that I shuddered uncontrollably. I pushed away from the computer and wandered over to the window. I stared into my backyard just to force those messages out of my mind's eye.

That's when I saw it.

An orange flicker of flame in the darkness. A shadowy face briefly lit. A small circle of burning blue and red.

I squinted . . .

Deon Jackson was sitting in my Adirondack chair, watching me and smoking a cigar.

I screamed and spun away from the window. I grabbed the phone from my desk and called 911. "Please send the police," I had shouted to the emergency dispatcher. "Please, hurry!"

Then, I called Adam. "He's here! Oh shit—"

Deon Jackson started banging on the window. "Let me come in, Miss Syeeda," he shouted. "I just wanna talk."

"You hear him?" I yelled into the phone. "What if he breaks in?"

"Find a weapon," Adam shouted. "A knife or . . . or something heavy. Lock yourself in a room somewhere. I'm on my way."

"Miss Syeeda," Deon Jackson boomed. "Don't be this way!"

I dropped to my knees and pulled my father's wooden baseball bat from beneath the couch.

The knocking stopped.

The house fell silent.

I bowed my head to listen. An icy bead of sweat trickled down my spine.

The quiet was almost worse than his voice and that banging.

I crawled to the window and peeked out into my backyard.

Empty.

Someone banged on the front door. All fist—a cop knock.

I ran to the foyer and kept the chain on as I opened the door.

Two patrol officers stood on my porch.

Thank God.

I described Deon Jackson to the cops, then escorted the men to the backyard.

Soon, beams of light from flashlights wandered across the bougainvillea.

I called Lena. As soon as I had finished telling her about Deon Jackson, and right after she stopped screaming and cursing, and after she threw her BlackBerry at some unfortunate glass object, she picked up that mobile device, took a deep breath, and slowly exhaled. "I'll take care of it."

Usually, I would have demanded Lena to take the higher road, to let the police do their job, *blah blah blah.* But on this night? Ha. Justice knew what part of me to kiss.

I returned to the living room as Adam stormed in with a black box under his arm. I grabbed his hand and pulled him to the backyard, showed him where Deon Jackson had sat and the window he had hit. My words came quick until they jammed together. Tears came next and I couldn't talk.

"It's okay," Adam said, pulling me into a hug. He held me as I cried, until his shirt was wet with tears.

I pulled away from him and swiped at his chest. "Sorry for mucking up your shirt. I'll pay the dry cleaning bill."

He shook his head, then tilted my chin. "Better now?"

My eyes continued to skip around the yard.

He pulled me into another hug, and this time, the tension in my body left as quickly as it had come.

And then he kissed me. It was our first kiss.

We had just returned to the living room when the patrol cops joined us.

No Deon Jackson.

Adam had sighed. "I'll have a car patrol the area for the rest of the night." Then, he used a long silver key to unlock the small black case he had brought with him. "Syeeda, I'm giving you this because you need it." He handed me the box.

A gun was nestled in cones of gray foam. It was sleek. Black. Sexy as hell.

I shouted, "I can't shoot a gun."

"It's just a Glock," Adam said, matter-of-factly. "Very easy to use. Even for a writer."

"*Just* a Glock?" I screeched.

"You need protection," Adam said, still nonplussed.

"And you're giving me *this*?"

"What do you wanna use? A potato peeler?"

I placed the case back on the table, then hugged myself to resist temptation. "I have a bat. I keep it under the couch. And I'll file a restraining order."

He gawked at me. "Your solution is a piece of paper? Good luck with that, sweetheart." When I didn't respond, he swiped his hand across his mouth and slowly exhaled. "I'll help expedite a TRO but you need a real weapon, Sy, not a bat. Do you wanna be that close to Deon Jackson? I don't think you do. And don't worry. This ain't one of those black-market guns that blow up in your face. It's my backup piece. And I promise you: It's easy to use."

I reached for the Glock. "I hate guns."

"I know."

In my childhood neighborhood, guns had been more plentiful than roaches. My brother had been mugged at gunpoint twice in tenth grade. While driving his route, my dad had been shot at regularly. The family that lived in the apartment below us had shot at each other every full moon. My elementary and middle school yards had been peppered and pocked with bullets. A few of my friends had been, too.

I. Did. Not. Like. Guns.

Still, I pulled the weapon out of the box. It was lighter than I had expected. And I didn't see any moving parts, only a trigger. Good. I had never held a gun in my life, not even a fake one. And now, I felt heavier, in control, the power of God captured in steel and polymer.

"I'll help you get a license," Adam said. "And I'll teach you to shoot. How to load it, how to clean it . . . Where's Lena?"

I blinked at him. "I . . . don't know."

"You tell her about what happened tonight?"

I nodded.

He waited a beat, then said, "You need to control her."

Yeah. Okay. Controlling Lena was like controlling the tide or nuclear energy.

Minutes later, Adam and I walked to the front door. He held my face in his hands. "I have shit to do downtown but I'll come by later."

I nodded.

We kissed again, and my heart pounded and my knees lost all strength. I had waited so long for this, but damn. On this night? After a nut in fur had tried to break in my house? *Really?*

"Lessons start tomorrow," Adam had shouted as he left the house.

"I'll buy the coffee," I said with a wave, then closed the door.

So, in his own sick and twisted way, Deon Jackson brought Adam and me together.

And as I passed the bread aisle in Whole Foods, I saw my stalker out the corner of my eye. I froze in my step.

He was stooping to grab a pack of bagels from the bottom shelf. He wore a blue tracksuit and white Nikes. He straightened and turned in my direction.

I stood there, bug-eyed, unable to move.

He nodded at me.

No.

That's not him. That's not Deon.

Just a Black man buying bagels. He had regular white teeth, a sharp nose . . . just a man.

I sagged some, relieved, and swiped at my clammy forehead.

The man pushed his shopping cart down the aisle. "How you doin' today?"

I forced a smile. "I'm great."

Alone again.

I took a deep breath, then held it.

What's that?

I sniffed—death lined my nostrils. Rotting soft tissue and globules of disintegrated body fat stuck to me like sweat.

Fantastic. I stink.

After Tamar Haist's autopsy, Adam had tossed me a bottle of saline to rinse my nose. And it had worked. In my nose. But my nostrils hadn't been the only part of me that had been exposed to the dead woman.

Can the other customers smell me?

I quick-stepped down toiletries and grabbed a bottle of cucumber and pear body lotion. Slathered the cream on my arms and hands, then rubbed some above my top lip. *Better.*

I hurried to the deli bar before the lotion's scent wore off.

A woman stood behind me, waiting her turn to pluck a container from the stack. She whiffed the air. Then, she whiffed again and tapped my shoulder. "Excuse me?"

I turned to her.

"Is that you, smelling like that?"

"Umm . . ."

"Like cucumber and—" She wiggled her nose. "And something else. Smells good."

I held up the bottle of lotion, then directed her to toiletries.

All around me, customers filled their to-go boxes with curried chicken, stir-fried tofu, and sushi. No exotic meals for me today—just good ol' organic black-eyed peas on white rice, vegetarian collard greens, and chicken breast smothered with gravy and onions. Comfort food for the Buppie.

"Is that Syeeda McKay?"

I peered over my shoulder to attach the woman's voice to her face. My nerves jumped, and I dropped the collard greens spoon back into the pot.

Toni Fortune towered over me in Christian Louboutin stilettos. She wore a long-sleeved pink tee and a quirky, mismatched-patterned miniskirt that showed off skinny, caramel-colored legs. She had tried to hide an angry scratch on her cheek with makeup, but the foundation had melted. Diamonds—at least three carats each—sparkled in both earlobes as well as around her neck and wrist. Toni stood out, even in this well-heeled, True Religion–wearing crowd.

She smiled to show off perfect white teeth. "Sy, it *is* you." She paused. "You look . . ." Her toffee-brown eyes flicked down my body to take inventory. "You look good."

I glanced down at my baggy nylon track pants and wrinkled What the Frak? T-shirt stained with coffee and nacho cheese dust.

"It's been, what? Sixteen years since we've seen each other?"

I nodded. "Feels like . . . less."

"It's amazing that we live in the same city and haven't bumped into each other since graduation." She fake smiled again. "Isn't that amazing?"

"Wondrous."

"I read both of your books," she said, a twinkle in her eye. "Saw the movie, too."

I closed my food container. "Want your eight dollars back?"

"Twelve dollars," she said. "We saw it at the fancy theater in Hollywood. Leather seats and a concierge."

"I'll buy your lunch then," I said, "and we'll be square."

Toni and I met during our first year at UC Santa Cruz. During those first weeks of school, she had ignored me as well as the other Black girls on campus. Fear of competition, I suppose, since she had already hooked up with Joey Fortune, a gorgeous basketball-playing freshman from Compton. Spring quarter, she and I became friends. We pledged the same sorority, shared each other's clothes and countless bottles of Bartles & Jaymes wine coolers.

Meanwhile, Joey slept with any attractive female that flirted with him.

Toni would learn about his dips in other women's swimming pools, and she'd dump his punk ass. But he'd apologize and swear that he'd never sleep with another woman again, and she would believe him and take him back, and they'd be fine . . . until the next girl.

For four years, they did this. Break up to make up.

As Toni's sorority sisters, we had all found this hard to take. Toni deserved better. She didn't have to stay with a loser when there were hundreds, nay, thousands of men in the world. So, a week before graduation, we converged in Lena's and my apartment to hold a "Girlfriend, Wake Up!" intervention for our misguided soror. Topics included "Joey is a Dog Today and Will Be a Dog Tomorrow," "All the Girls He's Banged Since 1988," and "Final Appeal—Leave Him Now or Else!"

Over that hour, Toni had whimpered, "What?" and "I can't believe it!" She had shaken her head in disbelief, and had hidden her face in her hands.

Even as I pled with Toni to leave Joey, even as my friends admitted to sleeping with him, I had remained a coward. I never told her that once, during junior year, Joey came to my room after a dorm party. Lena had gone to the library to study while Joey and I talked about classes, parties, and homelife.

"What's up with you and Toni?" I had asked.

"We're just kicking it," he had claimed. "Nothing serious."

Moments later, we were naked in my bed, my gaze trained on the Bo Jackson poster taped to the ceiling.

Only Lena knew what I had done, and during the intervention, she kept elbowing me to confess. I had ignored her jabs to my ribs.

After we had presented our case, the living room fell silent. No one had wanted to speak again, and we had held our collective breath and prayed that this forced wake-up call worked.

Toni had straightened in her seat, had dried her face with tissues, and slowly exhaled. She held my gaze for several seconds, then met the eyes of everyone else, including Lena. "I don't believe one word y'all are saying," she had said. "Not one damn word." Then, she cussed us out with the dexterity of a middleweight boxer. Told us we were jealous hos and that we were nothing but backstabbing bitches, a bunch of bitter dykes who didn't want to see anyone else happy.

All this time, Lena had squirmed on the couch beside me. Her fists had clenched into tiny balls, her palms almost bleeding from the bite of her acrylic nails. "You need to chill out," she had kept warning Toni. "Chill the hell out." She had grabbed my copy of *Anna Karenina* from the coffee table to keep her hands busy.

Toni did not chill, and she concluded her rant with, "Y'all are some shady, vindictive bitches. You ain't my friends. You ain't ever been my friends. Don't call me after we cross that stage tomorrow. *Ever.*" She stormed out of the apartment.

Lena had followed her, a mongoose after a cobra, while the rest of us had sat in quiet amazement. "Let your ass get heartbroken then!" Lena had shouted, hurling my book in Toni's direction. She threw her hands in the air, called on the Lord, then turned back to us with a smile. "Who wants pizza?"

I didn't contact Toni after graduation *per her request*. I did hear through the grapevine, though, that she and Joey had married that August and had moved back to Los Angeles. He had entered the police academy, and she had enrolled in paralegal school. Happily ever after.

Toni and I carried our meals to a window booth at the front of the store. I had wanted to take my food home and eat as I typed my notes from today's drama, but she was on a mission to let bygones be just that, and had insisted that we eat together.

"I could've been offended reading *Pledged*," she said as she drizzled Italian dressing across her field greens. "And for a hot minute, I was."

Pledged, my second novel, followed a group of sorority sisters on a road trip to a party at UC Berkeley. En route, the girls argued, made heartbreaking confessions, and ended friendships.

"And then, last year, here comes the movie," Toni said. "I told myself not to get mad. That the woman up on the movie screen wasn't me. I kept saying to myself, 'Don't let Syeeda's inaccurate portrayal ruin your life.'" She plucked a cucumber from her salad and chomped it in half. "I mean, who are you? Just a cleaned-up drunk with too much time and money on her hands."

I shot a look at my old college friend. "You always say the sweetest things. I miss that the most." I swallowed my mouthful of chicken, no longer tasting it. "I've had a few challenges since college, but being a drunk ain't one of them."

She squinted at me. "Weren't you supposed to accept the truth during your . . . retreat?"

"What truth? And what retreat?"

"I heard that you went to rehab this summer," she said. "I didn't want to use that word. *Rehab.* You're much . . . *cleaner* than that word. *Rehab.* But I think that it's great—"

"I haven't been to rehab," I said, frowning. "Who told you that?"

"Oh . . ." She shrugged. "People talk. I don't remember who said what exactly." She waved her hand, then wielded her fork to *stabstabstab* at the bed of lettuce. "Your addiction is none of my business." *Stab.* "But I'm glad you got to tell your very important story." *Stabstab.* "Must be nice having a movie director for a brother."

I squared my shoulders, then said, "First of all, I don't have an addiction—someone lied to you. I had surgery back in August, and had some complications afterward. Stayed in the hospital for a few days."

Toni said, "Oh," then dropped her eyes to the box of greens.

"Cancer," I added, twisting the knife in Toni's gut. "Not bourbon. Second, Kenny didn't direct the movie because we share the same DNA. We're interested in the same stories, so we've forged a partnership, like Joel and Ethan Coen, or the siblings who did the Matrix movies. Not so weird, right?"

Kenny had bought the rights to every Slayer-related article I had written, and he planned to buy the rights to the book once I landed a publishing deal. With two MTV Awards, one Golden Globe, and an Oscar nomination, he could choose any project he wanted. "I wanna return to Western Avenue," he had told me last year over coffee. "That quintessential Los Angeles street. That street of our childhood bus rides, where men hunt prostitutes, either for sex or for death."

After he promised to pay me a decent option, I had agreed to write the screenplay. But I needed an ending.

"What else is going on?" Toni asked me now. "Are you married?"

Here we go. I pushed my fork through the mound of black-eyed peas and rice. "Nope. Not married."

"Dating?"

"Not really."

She raised an eyebrow. "Kids?"

I clicked my fingernails against the table. "Kinda want the husband before the kids."

"What are you, thirty-eight years old?" She paused to let her acid burn into my psyche. "I guess you can adopt. You'd be a great candidate since you're older and single."

In some ways—okay, only one way—Toni was like the Savior. The same yesterday, today, and tomorrow. Except that Jesus was love, and Toni was a bitch. But then she had been a bitch yesterday, was definitely a bitch today, and most certainly would be a bitch at the crack of dawn tomorrow.

"Incredible," she said with a smile. "You have your books, and I have . . . everything else. Funny how life works, huh? Remember how we all thought you'd be the one married to a lawyer? Living in a big house with two kids and a Volvo?"

"I do have the house," I pointed out.

Seven years ago, I had bought a gorgeous three-bedroom Spanish-style a stone's throw from CBS Studios and the Farmers Market. It had a courtyard, a flagstone driveway, and a backyard lined with dusty-pink and fuchsia bougainvillea. The inside boasted original tile, hardwood floors, and built-in bookshelves. The gorgeous fabric couches were spotted with ink. Books and pens were crammed between the cushions. Post-it notes were crumpled in the French porcelain bowl on the coffee table. After growing up in apartments with mismatched couches, milk crates, and cinder blocks, I had promised myself that if I hadn't married by thirty, I'd buy my dream home. My parents hadn't sent me to every lesson under the sun just for me to wait on a man to buy me an ottoman. Put simply: I didn't need someone else to start my life. And after my thirtieth birthday, I decided that I shouldn't waste any more time waiting.

"You better find yourself a husband before you gain any weight," Toni said with a good-natured laugh. "You know, once you pass that forty-year mark, men don't see you anymore. Invisible, just like that." She snapped her fingers and offered a devilish smile.

I cocked my head. "Yes, I've heard that rumor."

"You weren't part of those layoffs at the paper, were you?" she asked.

I smashed a few peas with my fork, then let the fork drop to the plate. "Alas, I was."

She winced. "Wow. It's tough out there right now. But you shouldn't worry—you have skills. If you can read and write, you can do anything. Maybe I'll talk to Joey. See if we have any open writing positions at the company."

"That would be *swell*," I snarked, not feeling swell at all.

"And if you ever need any type of security service, let me know. Fortune Security does it all. Bodyguards, security systems, personal investigations, you name it."

My eyebrows lifted. "You all have access to the state and national crime files? Social security and identity verifications? Credit histories?"

She smiled, nodded. "Yep."

"I may take you up on that," I said, my pissy mood fading fast.

"And in exchange, maybe you could do a piece on us," she said. "Joey won't believe this, me and you hanging out at Whole Foods."

"Of all places. Are you still working?"

"I ran the company's research department, but I'm retired now. Don't have to work anymore. Our company made a two-million-dollar profit last year. So I do mostly volunteer stuff. Sit on a couple of boards, fundraise for my favorite charities. You know, 'ladies who lunch' stuff." She dropped her eyes to her salad and started again with the lettuce stabbing. "Are you planning to write another novel about your ridiculous college friends?"

"You all weren't ridiculous *every* day," I said. "And no one else had a problem. In fact, seven of the girls were over last night for one of Lena's infamous theme parties. They knew that *Pledged* was a novel, a work of fiction, that any resemblance to a living person was purely coincidental."

"So the bitchy Antoinette . . . ?"

"Completely made up. Cuz your name is An-*tonia*."

"Speaking of Lena, I heard through the grapevine that she went off on Chauncey."

I nodded. "She's lucky he didn't press charges."

"What did she throw?"

"The perfume bottle hit his temple, and the fall *Vogue* . . . that broke his nose."

Toni smiled and shook her head. "I've read some of your articles about the serial killer. Dead sex workers, right?"

"Yep. I've actually started a book about the Phantom Slayer murders."

Her smile faltered as she sat back in the booth. "Of all the issues in the world to write about." She scrunched her nose and twisted her lips. "Tsunamis, kidnappings, Iraq . . . Who cares about *those* women? Not to be harsh, Syeeda, but they're . . . *prostitutes*. Do they really deserve an entire book?"

"*Those women* need help," I said. "Human beings we ignore even when they're murdered."

"Or they're grown-ass women responsible for their own actions," Toni said, squinting at me. "Women who risk their lives every time they drop to their knees for a buck. I didn't force them to sell sex to get by, so don't include me in that 'we' nonsense." She flicked her hand, not caring anymore. "How do you live with all that in your head? Death and murder?"

I shrugged, then stuffed my mouth with black-eyed peas. My mother asked that same question all the time. *How do you live with all that in your head?* I offered her the same response, usually stuffing my mouth with Nutter Butters.

Toni's cell phone rang from her purse. She plucked it out and glanced in the display. "It's Joey. Probably wondering where I am." She slipped the phone back into her handbag. "We're going to Disney Hall tonight, to that big fundraiser for the Museum of Contemporary Art. It's black tie."

"Wow. Fancy."

"It's all about who you know and how many zeros you put on the check," she said. "Since Joey won that contract for those new lofts downtown, we stay dressed up." She tilted her head and winked at me. "And you all thought he'd never amount to anything."

"Gosh. Guess we were wrong."

She stood from the table. "Incredibly wrong, but all that's behind us, right? You and I were friends once upon a time, and we're adults now. All that mess from college? Water under the bridge. Forgive and forget. I mean that."

"Done," I said. "Too much has happened in my life for me to hold grudges. Sucks that we didn't get to talk more about you."

"I didn't want to brag," she said. "I'll tell you about my very exciting news later. It involves possibly being cast on a reality TV show. One of those 'Housewives of Wherever' deals. I don't wanna jinx it, though. Just keep your fingers crossed."

We exchanged phone numbers and email addresses, and gave each other tight hugs.

"Let's have dinner," she said, moving away from the table. "I'll call you sometime this week, okay? And really: Anything you need for your story, just hit me up."

I did miss Toni. Before the "Girlfriend, Wake Up!" intervention, we had fun together in that small town by the sea. Toni had always been down for a party, always drove us around in her purple Honda Prelude, always bought drinks, always took us to her family's time-share in Jamaica because she had been an only child and her parents had been able to pay the way for her poor friends like me.

I watched her sashay to the store's exit and out to the parking lot.

She climbed into a purple Bentley that straddled two parking spaces.

I chuckled to myself, feeling normal for the first time all day. Just another thirty-something eating a grocery-store lunch and chatting with an old girlfriend. No different from any of the other women around me.

My phone chimed, and I pulled it from my pocket.

A text message from Spencer.

Hope you're okay after today. RE: Tamar H. Autopsy completed. Come back ASAP.

8

"A single shot to the right side of the face," Spencer said as Adam and I settled into our chairs. "Fractured the regional mandible and the base of the skull. And that's where I found the bullet."

Spencer's desk was covered with folders and notebooks filled with glossy photographs of corpses. His office had no windows, and the overhead fluorescent light made everything, even the dingy-white linoleum floors, look purple.

"The ballistic tests aren't completed yet," Spencer continued, "so I don't know if it's the same gun. I do know that it's a .38 caliber. Just like the others."

"But you could be wrong," I said. "Since the ballistics . . ."

He gazed at me for several seconds as if to say, *Wrong? I'm never wrong.*

I flushed and my eyes retreated to the pages of my notebook.

"And Syeeda?" Adam said.

I looked at him. "I know: Don't mention the gun's caliber in the article. We don't want him ditching his weapon for another."

Adam nodded. "He'll slip up. They always do. They get arrogant and start thinking that they're smarter than we are."

"In some ways, they are," Spencer said. "How many serial killers have been caught this year?"

"I've personally caught two," Adam said. "Not to blow my own horn, but that's a big fuckin' deal."

"Those two serial killers," Spencer said. "How long had they been killing before you lucked up?"

Adam's smile didn't reach his eyes. "Luck? Please. I think differently—I go balls out every case I work. Technology's better than before, and the city's throwing me a few more dollars. So, luck? Don't think so."

I said, "You only caught the old Black guy who raped and killed all those women back in the seventies because you were searching for the Slayer."

Adam tossed me a glare—*thanks a lot, Sy.*

"Los Angeles is the perfect place for killing," Spencer continued. "It's big. Overcrowded. No one knows you exist unless you want them to. And it's diverse—no one type of person lives here. This guy can be your next-door neighbor and you'd never know."

Adam folded his arms. "Can't ignore the wonder in your tone, Dr. Brooks."

Spencer leaned back in his chair. "And I can't ignore the arrogance in yours, Detective. Overconfidence allows crazed murderers to roam the streets for years. And it has been years with the Slayer, right? About twenty?"

"He will be caught," Adam said. "I'm still in control of this investigation."

"But you're not in control of this monster," Spencer said. "You have no clue who he is or who he'll target next."

Adam laced his fingers behind his head. "You know, I read something interesting the other day. Back in the medieval times or whenever, surgeons were also barbers. They used to perform enemas and yank out soldiers' teeth. Drain boils, shit like that."

I held up my hand. "Guys, can we skip this part so I can hear the rest of the report? Right now, I couldn't care less whose dick is bigger."

"Anything for you, Sy," Adam said with a wink.

"Tamar Haist fought her murderer," Spencer said, his voice tight. "I found tissue beneath her fingernails. We'll run the DNA—"

"After you analyze the samples you all took back in 1977?" I asked with a smile.

Adam laughed. "Good one."

Spencer did not. "You don't need my help, then."

"Spencer, it was a joke." I giggled, then added, "The corpse-chewing rats ate all those samples from '77, bumping Tamar Haist to the front of the line. Works for me."

A withering glare from the pathologist wiped the grin off my face. "First of all," he said, "the rats came from the outside and we fixed the hole immediately. You misreported that and made it a bigger deal than it was. And maggots. Yes, there are maggots. The people who come here are *dead*. Flies land on dead things and they lay eggs. You may recall that from second grade science."

After the publication of my rat story, Spencer had stopped taking my phone calls.

I had continued to email him about the Phantom Slayer murders, and surprisingly, he answered my queries, but in as few words as possible:

Still no test results.

I doubt there'll be DNA.

No one's claimed her yet.

Death haiku.

We had corresponded like this, both driven by the need to understand why some people abandoned the regular world for alleys and drugs, and why some types of people died more than others.

"Can we get back to the case?" Adam asked. "What about the time of death?"

Spencer held his frown a moment longer, then scanned the report in front of him. "Sometime between 10 p.m. on Tuesday night and 1 a.m. early Wednesday morning."

Adam turned to me. "What time did she send the text?"

"Around 1:28."

Adam turned back to Spencer. "If she died around one o'clock, then . . . ?"

Spencer shrugged. "There's a slim margin of error when it comes to predicting time of death. She could've died at 1:30."

Adam's phone chirped from his jacket pocket. He opened the cell and said, "What's up?" He looked at Spencer and me and said, "Gotta take this." He hopped up from his chair and stepped out of the office, closing the door behind him.

Spencer and I were alone.

He watched me with flat eyes.

I didn't want to say the wrong thing, so I quietly flipped through my pages of notes and popped the rubber band around my wrist.

"What's that for?" he asked. "The elastic band."

I scrutinized the band as though I'd never seen it before. "It's a hypnotism technique to stop smoking. Anytime I think about a cigarette, I'm supposed to snap the band. The brain then associates pain with the thought of smoking. The brain doesn't like pain."

"Is it working?"

I rubbed my neck. "Let's just say that I should've chosen a less stressful time to quit."

There was a knock on the door, and a man with rosacea poked his head in. "Sorry for interrupting, Dr. Brooks."

"It's okay," I said, gathering my things. "I'm gonna go find Adam." I offered my friend a weak smile. "As always, thank you for your time."

Spencer stared at me like he would stare at a bone saw.

I brushed past the red-faced man and slammed into a wall of stink. After taking several deep breaths, I hustled down the hall to the exit, and back out into fresh air.

9

I was so happy to finally get home that I almost dropped to my knees and kissed the driveway. My house still reeked from the spa party—paraffin wax, fermented grapes, and lemon-pepper chicken wings. Lena had retrieved her stilettos from the living room floor, but had forgotten to pull her black-lace bra out of the armchair's cushion. Next time she wanted to throw one of her parties—spa party, passion party, shoe party and the rest—I'd tell her to host it at her own house.

My sister Eva hadn't left my office. She had tucked in the mattress of my sleeper sofa but had remained on the couch, her deep-set brown eyes fixed on *Jeopardy*. Guess she was still recovering from her deep-tissue massage and pitcher of raspberry mojitos. She had pulled her thick, tar-black hair into a bun, and had slipped on a gray LAPD sweatshirt I had stolen from Adam. The seams of her pink leggings strained from thighs no longer size eights. "Baby weight," Eva had continued to claim, even though Josie was now in kindergarten.

A plate filled with red grapes and chunks of smoked Gouda sat on the coffee table alongside a gift basket of fruit. "I started washing the dishes," Eva said, eyes on Alex Trebek, "but I got tired and remembered that I was on vacation. Oh. Lena said to call her. And that basket was delivered just before you walked in."

I plucked the small white card from the cellophane.

You are the apple of my eye. The cherry on top. Eat
this and think of me.
Yours for all time, Deon

"Crap on a cracker." I grabbed the basket and marched out of
the office.

"Who sent it?" Eva shouted after me.

"My stalker." My stomach now ached and cicada-like buzzing filled
my head as I passed through the kitchen to the service porch. I opened
the door, dumped Deon Jackson's fruit basket in the trash can, returned
to the kitchen, and grabbed the spray bottle of Mr. Clean and a bunch
of paper towels from the counter.

"Hate to say this," Eva said when I returned, "but I almost want
him to ignore the restraining order and stop by just so the cops can
arrest him."

I sprayed the table with cleaner and swiped the spot with paper
towels. "And maybe, just maybe, I'll get to shoot his ass before they haul
him away." I sighed and sat back on my haunches. "I thought I saw him
at Whole Foods today."

"If you were Lena, whoever he was wouldn't have made it home."

On the night of Deon Jackson's visit, Lena had called Tristan
Small. She told him that his ex-slinger had crossed the line, that he
had tried to break in my house. Tristan had sent his "administrative
assistants" to First King, a strip club located deep in the hood. They
waited in the parking lot, and around two that morning, a man
found himself bloodied and toothless on the asphalt. Dude's name
was Kendall Hogan, not Deon Jackson. No one thought there would
be *two* Black men in this city who favored chinchilla vests.

After trashing the used towels, I collapsed into the adjoining armchair.
"Your moment of being young and single ended at midnight. Why aren't
you with Ben and Josie?"

Two years after graduating from Columbia University, Eva had
married Ben Kantar, an environmental lawyer who never raised his

voice and resembled Lenny Kravitz. Five years ago, Eva gave birth to Josie, who, spookily, resembled me.

"Ben dropped Josie at Mom's, then he's going to a Lakers game with the West Coast partners of the firm."

I sighed. "A husband, a cute little girl, and a beagle named Bingo. I wanna be you when I grow up."

"I know a guy who'll give you all of that."

I sighed. "Mother doesn't approve of Adam."

Eva sucked her teeth. "What the hell does *Mother* know? She ain't been in the game since 1963. Oh, I ate the rest of that spaghetti you had in the fridge."

I made a face. "Mom made that two weeks ago."

"Delicious nonetheless . . . What is stigmata?"

TV Alex said, "Correct."

Eva said, "I should go on this show." When she rolled over to grab the snack plate from the table, she glanced at me and grimaced. "Damn, Sy. You work on an oil rig today?"

"Something like that." I nudged off my sneakers and placed my feet on the ottoman. "This Slayer case is getting bigger and bigger every week."

TV Alex answered, "He said, 'In what concerns you much, do not think that you have companions: Know that you are alone in the world.'"

Eva asked, "Who is Henry David Thoreau?"

TV Alex said, "Correct."

"You're not gonna ask me *why* this case is kicking my ass?"

She stuck two grapes in her mouth. "I'm off the clock, and I'm free of husband and child. I really couldn't care less why—"

"He killed another girl," I blurted. "This morning, while you and Lena were sleeping off the drunks, I was standing in an alley with a dead woman."

Eva stopped chewing and slowly twisted her head away from the game show. "What do you mean, 'standing in an alley'?" Those smoky eyes of hers now gleamed—she needed to understand madness more than I needed to write about it.

As a special agent with the FBI's National Center for the Analysis of Violent Crime, Eva filled her head with horrendous information about the nation's most violent criminals. Working out of Virginia, she met these monsters face-to-face to learn how they acted, how they thought, how they selected their victims, and how they avoided being detected.

I told Eva about the late-night text message from Tamar Haist. I told her about my early-morning trip to Western Avenue and finding the silver Neon parked in a church alleyway.

Eva plucked another grape from the vine. "And the victim?"

I told her that I had found Tamar sprawled on the asphalt, trash bag over her body. That she had been shot in the face.

"Did you know her?" Eva asked.

"No. She just texted me out of the blue."

"And you went to meet a stranger in a dark— Never mind. You wouldn't listen." Eva slipped the grape into her mouth and chewed as though the fruit could explode. "That's his second victim in two years. So now he'll disappear for four years just like he's done in the past."

"I guess."

Eva narrowed her eyes as she sat up on the couch. "An expensive weave and breast implants . . . Tamar Haist doesn't match the victim profile."

"But the text message connects this case to the others. That message, the location, and the shot to the face. Nothing's changed."

"He's the same, but she isn't, and that's bothering me." She tapped her French-tipped nails against her chin. "The Slayer has always shown control in his methods. One blast to the face and that's that—he doesn't hang around to play with the body. Did she fight?"

"Looks like it."

"Good for her," Eva said, nodding. "Still: He chose her. Why?"

"Don't know. But his MO is the same."

She sat back and cast her eyes to the ceiling. "But it's not about the MO. It's about the *signature*, the rituals he performs to satisfy his emotions."

"Like throwing filled trash bags over their bodies?"

"That, and even selecting his victims. And Tamar Haist—"

"May have been a sex worker," I said. "Just a cleaned-up one."

"Do we know that for sure?" Eva asked. "Does she have a record?"

"Don't know yet."

"Was she sexually assaulted?"

"No."

She grunted. "Maybe he became bored with the heroin addicts, with the women obviously in trouble. Maybe he wanted to cross class lines, target a professional escort, or . . ." She shook her head. "Maybe he knew her."

"Maybe."

"The Slayer is angry at all the women in his life," Eva said, eyes back on the television. "If that woman wasn't Tamar, then Tamar certainly represented her. He's in a dependent relationship with this woman and it pisses him off. He gets told what to do at work. Gets bossed around by this wife or girlfriend who constantly remind him that he's not making enough or being a good provider. Castrated male bullshit.

"He gets set off because he fought with her or had a run-in with his boss. Some event made him feel weak . . . Killing set the world right because then he has power and control again." She reached for the plate, but froze with her hand outstretched. "Did he leave anything behind? A bullet casing? A cigarette? A note?"

I shrugged. "Don't think so."

"Probably not. He hasn't yet. Keep me posted." She glanced at me. "I can say this: He's not gonna stop on his own. He'll either die, get caught by the police, or cataracts and arthritis keep him in front of the television." She slipped on her sneakers, then stood from the couch. "I better drive to Mom's."

"Yeah," I said, "before she starts thinking we're conspiring against her."

"Just keep your promise when dealing with this guy," Eva said as we started down the hallway.

"I won't make the Slayer larger than life," I said, my fingers in the Boy Scout salute.

"He'll start thinking that killing is the only way to get his fifteen minutes and an agent at CAA. Every sicko murderer wants Anthony Hopkins to play him in the movie."

"I want Angelina Jolie to play me," I said, opening the front door. "And Esther Rolle can be you."

"Esther Rolle is dead." Eva hugged me, tugged a lock of my hair, then headed to the driveway and to her rental car. "I had fun last night, even though I can't stand Lena."

I braced myself against the cold breeze. The leaves of the neighborhood magnolia trees rustled. The air smelled of sweet flowers that blossomed year-round. "She taunts you because you react. You have to treat her like you'd treat a bear: by standing very, very still."

"Promise me that you'll get some rest and have more parties and be young and beautiful."

I smirked. "Young? Ha. And I can't be the grasshopper all the time. I have a murderer to catch."

Eva sighed. "Working nonstop won't bring any of those women back, Sy. And I understand and appreciate your dedication—sometimes, I never see the sun or my kid and husband because I force myself to keep going. Because if I keep going, it will all work out. It has to. People will live and families won't be shattered. Unfortunately, it doesn't work that way."

"But don't you feel like shit if you stop and attempt to have a life?"

"Sometimes. Why am I having fun when there are people—children—being murdered?"

"So, what do you do?"

Eva said, "I'm working on this case where nine- and ten-year-old boys are being snatched in shopping malls. This monster kills them and dumps them off highways up and down the Eastern Seaboard. He's on his seventh victim now. I had been putting in sixteen-hour days, and right when I thought I had this guy's profile, Ben made me go with him to some fundraiser at the Smithsonian. I had fun but when it was time to drive back home, my heart ached—how could I have deserted those babies? What type of person was I?

"But being away had refreshed my mind. Opened it to new ways of thinking. And a few weeks ago, I developed a pretty accurate profile of this sick bastard. I know that I care, Sy, and I know that I'm trying. Sometimes that's all you can do." She narrowed her eyes. "Other than working on this case, how are you? Physically?"

"I'm good. No complaints. Did you see the doctor?"

She sighed, unlocked the car.

"Eva, you promised."

"I will, I will," she said, flapping her hands. "Work is crazy, and Josie's in karate, ballet, *and* piano, and I just don't have the time."

I assumed the Big Sister stance: folded arms, high chin, mouth set in a grim line, *I'm gonna tell Mom* on my tongue.

"I'll go," she said.

"Don't make me come to Virginia."

"What if the lump is . . . something bad?" she asked, her eyes bright with tears.

"Then they'll take it out."

"And then what?"

"If it's like mine, you'll get sewn up, bandaged, and attached to a pump that sucks out lymph fluids. Then, you'll drive to the Mercedes-Benz dealer and pick out the model you like. On the way home, you'll stop at Neiman Marcus and buy two pairs of Manolo Blahniks and a Fendi bag."

"It's more serious than that." She studied me now, waiting for my honest response.

"In between all the crying, all the panic attacks, and imagining worst-case scenarios, you'll tell yourself that the doctors caught it in time, that you won't die, that you're gonna be okay." I forced a smile. "And you'll be okay, Eva."

After my diagnosis, what surprised me most was this: Life had continued. Bills came. Laundry piled up. I made turkey lasagna on a Wednesday night. Nothing had changed except for the tumor that had been growing in my left breast.

10

After calling Lena and telling her about my reunion with Toni, I shuffled down the hallway, ready to work. My home office looked the same as it had when I left at dawn except that now, Eva was no longer asleep on the couch. The asteroid screensaver still blinked from my desktop computer. Stacks of newspapers still sat on my desk, waiting to be reviewed. Somewhere in that newsprint was a story about a strange death, a touching reunion, or interesting science—all future story ideas. Since my surgery, I had fallen behind on my scouring; now, with Lena's help, articles would soon be clipped and scanned to digital files.

I wandered to the window and glanced out to the backyard.

Something moved through the bougainvillea.

My face numbed as I stared at the space on the back wall.

No. There's nothing there.

Just leaves rustling in the wind, flowers trembling from the breeze. No Deon Jackson lurking in the shadows.

I'm acting like this is my first night living alone. Get it together, Sy.

I said, "Yep," then settled at my desk and wiggled the mouse to awaken the computer.

So who was Tamar Haist?

If the nineteen-year-old had existed up until one o'clock that Wednesday morning, then maybe I'd find her on the internet, on Myspace or Facebook. I'd find her name listed in a high school newspaper or a church newsletter. At least two hits on a search engine.

I typed "Tamar Haist" into Google's search bar.

Hit One: a picture and biography of Reverend Murray Haist, the young-looking pastor of Great Redeemer Church of God in Christ. Reverend Haist looked forty-something, maybe forty-five. He wore a purple and white robe, and stood over a trio of women: a brittle-looking woman captioned *His Wife Evelyn Haist*; a plump young woman named *His Daughter Noemi Haist*; and *His Youngest Daughter Tamar Haist*, before the weave and the breast implants.

Tamar was a preacher's kid.

A preacher's kid who had been murdered behind her father's church.

I hit "print" and the printer clunked to life.

I clicked on the second link: a PDF of a flyer created with fifty million fonts announcing the church's silver anniversary celebration. For ad details, contact Church Secretary Tamar Haist at 323-555-1317.

The five remaining relevant hits offered more of the same. Church retreat, call Tamar. Announcements for next week's bulletin, call Tamar. Want to join the choir? Call Tamar.

Church *secretary*?

I turned to my Death Wall. I had pinned photographs of every Phantom Slayer victim on that wall along with articles, timelines, and maps of the crime scenes. I grabbed the photo of the Haist family from the printer and stuck it in a blank space after 2007's victim.

Tamar Haist didn't seem to exist beyond the realm of the church. What would a preacher's kid know about dead sex workers and serial murderers? And when did she get all glam? *Why* did she get all glam?

What did Tamar have in common with the other victims?

I touched the mug shot of Paula Owens, a young woman plagued with chronic acne and a hare lip. She had been released from jail one day and shot in the face three days later.

My gaze moved to the next photograph—Denesha Jackson's lower jaw had been blasted off. Would Tamar even know someone like

Denesha, a working girl who had left a motel on Western and was found in a nearby alley two hours later?

Maybe Tamar was turning tricks after prayer meeting.

I had a friend back in college, Krystal Miller, who hooked on the weekends and attended Introduction to Sociology on Thursdays. Krystal hadn't been a preacher's kid, but she'd had a secret life. And Tamar, tired of the church's restrictions, could have led a secret life, too. Selling sex.

And if Tamar was a sex worker, maybe her john killed her.

Or maybe her father had found out and became so outraged that he murdered her.

Called *honor killing*, a woman's father or brother believes that she's disgraced the family's honor and he takes her life. It happens, even in America. In Georgia, a Pakistani father strangled his daughter after she ended her arranged marriage. In Texas, a father shot and killed his two daughters after discovering they both had boyfriends. In these two instances, religion had been the common link.

Would a Black minister of a conservative Los Angeles church kill his own daughter?

Why not?

But why did she want to talk to me?

Dennis Rader.

"Maybe," I said as the possibility cemented in my mind.

Dennis Rader, the BTK Killer, had a daughter, Kerri. Some claim that Kerri Rader gave the police a sample of her DNA. Some theorize that Kerri Rader had wanted to clear her father for killing all those people in Kansas. Unfortunately for Kerri, that DNA sample had proved otherwise.

Maybe Tamar had been attempting the same thing. Or maybe she thought her dad *was* the Slayer and wanted to give DNA but was too scared to go to the police. So she came to me, the messenger.

Made sense.

Or not.

I retreated to the bathroom. Spun the shower knobs and stood there as steam billowed around me. I peeled out of my T-shirt and winced as my stitches pulled. I pat my left breast as apology, then studied the white Steri-Strips poking past my bra.

Other than a few root canals, I had avoided surgeries until the biopsy and partial mastectomy. Prior to those procedures, I had been falling in love with Adam, sharing my life without much worry. Then, wham! I had become a single heroine in a *Lifetime* Movie of the Week. *Mother, May I Sleep with Cancer?*

That night, Adam had discovered the lump. "It's big," he had said, then switched on the lamp. He placed my hand on the spot. "You feel that?"

"Yeah." I had sat up in bed and poked at the lump. It rolled beneath my fingertips like a small dumpling. "It's been there awhile. Doesn't hurt, though."

The next morning, I had called my gynecologist's office—the next available appointment was six weeks away. Not thinking that there had been something actually *wrong* with me, I had taken the slot.

Sometimes, I'd forget my life-change until I glimpsed my bandages or a robust stretch sent sparks flying through my body. Sometimes, I'd find myself glaring at women with fake breasts, who had willingly stuck foreign objects into their bodies just to fill out a shirt. And I held my breath a lot. *Will I make it? What if they don't catch it the next time? Will there* be *a next time? What if it shows up in another place—my spine—and I have no clue until I can no longer stand?*

After showering, I retreated to my bedroom and settled beneath the down comforter. The room was dark and quiet. Outside, there were no police helicopters, no barking dogs, no creaking foundation settling into the earth. I lay there listening to the silence, my eyes fixed on the ceiling. Breath by breath, I slipped closer to sleep.

I'm following Toni Fortune down a grassy hill. She hands me an orange rose. I twist it into my hair. A thorn plucks my thumb. Blood streams down my wrists. She laughs—

The doorbell rang.

Yanked from sleep, I popped up and stared at the bedroom's entryway. Who would be visiting this late at night?

Deon Jackson. Did you get my fruit, Miss Syeeda?

The phone rang.

I startled again, then grabbed the receiver from the nightstand.

"Hey." It was Adam. "I'm standing on your front porch."

He shuffled past me and into the foyer, the smell of beer on his clothes.

"You scared me with all your late-night noise," I said, closing the door.

He stooped to kiss me . . . and kiss me again. His hands roamed my back, then landed on my butt. "Sorry it's so late, but I can't drive all the way to Silver Lake in this condition. Mind if I crash here?"

"Does it look like I mind?"

We kissed again.

"I miss you," he said, then nuzzled my neck.

I stroked his cheek and whispered, "I miss you, too."

"You don't have to."

"I know. I'm almost there."

I took his hand and led him to the bedroom. On nights like these, back when we were together, he would bring Thai food, DVDs, or cupcakes. I'd rub his back as he told me about his day. He'd massage my feet as I read him a draft of a chapter. We'd listen to Prince or The Roots, play *Left 4 Dead* on my Xbox, then fall into bed and onto each other.

"This day was just stupid," I said now. "Deon Jackson sent me a fruit basket."

He stopped in his step, his mint-green eyes now dark and hard. "Did he threaten you?"

"No. He called me the apple of his eye."

"I'm gonna fuckin' punch him in that eye. I'll pay him a visit tomorrow." He pulled off his leather bucks and strode to the bathroom.

"Any new information you can share about the case?" I asked, standing in the doorway, and watching him undress. "Like the topic of that very important phone call you got when we were in Spencer's office?"

"I'm off the clock, babe." He twisted the shower knobs and stepped into the tub. "No one can make me talk about work right now, not even you, and I usually bend to your will."

Three minutes later, he turned off the taps. Water raced down his chest and back, slabs of flawless golden muscle. He smiled drunkenly as he flicked the towel around his body.

My gaze followed those rivulets of water down to his greatest muscle of all. *Yeah.* I headed back to the bedroom, that fluttery feeling in my stomach, my skin prickly, my pulse quick.

Adam followed me. He took my hand and kissed my palm, my wrist . . . Pulled me closer with each kiss. I draped my arms around his neck. His tongue found mine—he tasted like beer and limes—and his hands slipped beneath my boxer shorts. Before I could say, *I had a hard time sleeping, can you help me out with that,* a flash of pain exploded from my bandages. I winced and snatched my arms from around his neck. "Oh, crap. What the *hell?*"

"What's wrong?" he asked, startled sober.

The sharp twinge in my chest continued to zigzag down to my hip.

I now experienced these random pains that came out of the ether and possessed my body as I performed arbitrary acts, like reaching for the lemon pepper in the cabinet. *Zing!* Or bending down to tie my shoe. *Zap!* Random pains that demanded that I never forget. And I never forgot because that sharpness killed my desire for lemon pepper and made me trade in my tie-up sneakers for slip-on Vans. And it made me fear another's touch.

"I'm okay," I told Adam now. "It's just . . . This weird pain . . ." I covered my face with my hands, forced back the tears, and muttered, "Sorry, didn't expect that, sorry, don't know how long this is gonna hurt, my range of motion is still crap, and I do the exercises, but still, sorry . . ."

He shushed me and gently pulled me into a hug. "It's okay."

The demon abandoned my body and left me limp against Adam. I tried to smile as I said, "You're a very patient man."

His turn to find a smile. "Only with you."

We climbed into my bed. I tucked my head beneath his chin and buried my face in his chest. Legs entwined, we lay there and our breathing slowed. He stroked my hair, kissed the top of my head, and whispered, "Get some sleep, love."

Within five minutes, he was snoring.

11

My eyes fluttered open.

Sunlight fell in slats across the comforter. The spot in bed beside me was cold and bare.

"Adam?" I sat up and drew my knees to my chest. "You here?"

No answer, just echo.

He was gone.

My heart sank—I had planned to cook us breakfast. We'd eat on the deck, and I'd grimace as he spread peanut butter on his toast, he'd wrinkle his nose at the hot sauce sprinkled on my eggs, and we'd read the newspaper, fighting over who got to read the crime section first. Just like we used to. Then, we'd give long goodbyes in the driveway. Goodbyes that sometimes forced us back to the bedroom.

Not that I had told him my morning plans. Not like I told him much.

I climbed out of bed and shuffled to the bathroom. The white wainscoting and mint-green tile were horrible sights for scratchy, exhausted eyes.

I'm gonna paint this weekend.

But it's been seven years' worth of weekends.

I filled the sink with cold water, then stuck my face into the bowl, eyes open.

The telephone rang, but I didn't move to answer it—the cold on my skin was working. My pores were closing, and the large bags beneath my eyes were shrinking into small carry-ons.

Two more minutes.

Five minutes later, I pulled myself away from the frigid water and dried my face. I considered my reflection in the mirror—brighter and tighter—then retreated to my office.

A Post-it note was stuck to the computer monitor. *I miss being here with you. Your bed's much softer than mine. Talk to you later. A. S.*

My hands clasped before my lips as I read the note three times. "I miss you being here, too," I whispered.

I grabbed the telephone to check voicemail and wandered to the window, Adam still on my mind.

The grass shimmered with dew. Yellow-eyed black birds hopped across the lawn in search of plump earthworms.

Spencer's voice drifted from the receiver:

Hey, Syeeda. Just wanted to let you know that the parents identified Tamar Haist this morning with Polaroids and fingerprints. They may need an advocate. They'll probably have some questions for you as well. Maybe even a few answers. Give them a call if you want. I hope you do. 323-555-9222.

Talking to the family was always the hardest part of any assignment. I'd done it several times before and it always made me hesitate. Because what do you say? *Hi, I'm a writer. Please share an anecdote about your dead daughter. How does it feel knowing that she was brutally murdered? Do you know anyone who would've wanted her dead?* Questions that made only a few reporters blush. As a twenty-something, I had no sense of shame in asking shit like this—the job required it. Through experience, though, my inquiries had become more nuanced and more respectful than the bald ones of my youth. Still, sometimes, I paused.

I sat at the breakfast bar and watched the morning news telecast on the television bolted above the kitchen sink. Lena had just brought over breakfast, a tradition she started after my surgery. Twice a week, she'd lug to my house a Canter's Deli bag filled with scrambled eggs, fried meats, and bagels. Then, she'd sit and watch me eat until I shooed her away.

And now, tiny Lena, dressed in a ruffled miniskirt, a tight T-shirt, and multicolored python stilettos rummaged through the refrigerator. Even in bare feet, Lena stood on her tiptoes, Barbie-style. "I just don't . . . *understand* the desire to wear flats," she'd say, nose wrinkled with disgust.

I don't remember the last time she wore flat shoes. Maybe back in college. Probably never.

Unlike the murders of the poorer victims, the murder of Tamar Haist did not go gently into the night. The news story on KTLA had cataloged her life into a fifteen-second blur. *Tamar was the daughter of a minister, she mentored inner-city girls, she sang soprano in the church choir, she organized food drives, clothing drives, and blood drives.*

Made no sense.

The prim and benevolent church secretary Tamar did not jibe with the DD-implant-having, weave-wearing Tamar murdered off Western.

The anchor shot us over to a press conference already in progress. Reverend Haist stood in Great Redeemer's parking lot, a bank of microphones before him. He wore a long-sleeved dress shirt, but no tie or cuff links. Dark circles couched his red-rimmed eyes.

"He looks more pissed than sad," Lena said as she poured coffee into a cup.

"He looks too young to have a nineteen-year-old daughter," I said, then sipped from my own mug.

"The cops don't ever stop looking for the murderers of white women," Reverend Haist was saying. "They seek vengeance for people who are better off or politically connected. People with so-called cash or class. I may not be a rich man, or a white man, and my daughter's skin may be the color of our slave forefathers, but she—*we*—matter. And I expect the LAPD to make the same effort for my daughter as they would for a daughter of Brentwood, for a daughter of Beverly Hills."

I muttered, "Amen."

"Tamar was a good girl," he continued. "A churchgoing girl who loved everybody, but loved God most of all. She was lost, but she didn't deserve to die."

After the anchor shot us to Burbank for a traffic update, I aimed the remote at the television and turned off the set. "No one mentioned the Slayer. Not Reverend Haist, not the news anchor."

"Maybe they don't know," Lena said. "The cops haven't even told the other victims' families that these are serial murders. Your articles only whisper it."

"Because the police chief would kill my access if I did. I'm crazy but I ain't stupid. But this may help—doesn't sound like Reverend Haist will be shutting up anytime soon."

"You'll be thrilled to know that I've completed my little investigation," she said. "Oh. My. *Lord.* I've never smelled so much urine in one—"

"Yeah. Okay. What did you find out?"

She crossed her legs—legs that had not seen hair since the seventh grade. "One girl—she said her name was Skittles. She swore that's the name on her birth certificate. *Anyway,* Skittles said she'd met Tamar before."

"So Tamar *was* a sex worker?"

Lena shook her head. "Tamar was doing needle exchange with the free clinic. Skittles said Tamar prayed with her and gave her a flyer about a drug rehab program run by the city."

"A do-gooder, once again. Maybe the Slayer confused her for a working girl."

"Skittles also remembered seeing a man sitting off Western in a minivan."

When Lena didn't go on, I said, "And?"

She shrugged. "He was Black. Clean cut. She thought he was a narc or a minister."

"And the minivan?"

Lena sighed, rolled her eyes, bored now with the conversation. "Tan. Gold. Yellow. I stopped asking cuz I was starting to feel oppressed.

I gave her two hundred dollars and that Hustler store gift card you gave me for Christmas.

"She kept staring at my shoes, but I told her: If she's on her feet all day, Louboutins are not the shoe to wear. She was a sweet kid, and . . ." Lena shook her head. "I can't believe I'm helping you with this case. It's so creepy. So macabre."

"Tell me: What should I write about? Puppies? Rainbows? Springtime in Paris?"

"Don't be so damned obtuse, Syeeda," Lena said as she licked cream cheese from her fingertips. "What about doing an in-depth report on the environment? Or how immigration is affecting Black people?"

"Interesting," I said, not interested at all.

"You need rest, that's my point. Seriously, we should fly down to Cancún and eat, sleep, and read trashy Zane novels. Stop chasing murderers and finding dead women in alleys and just chill."

"You plan this getaway, then. But if I'm reading Zane, I'm certainly not going to Cancún alone with you."

"Then we'll make it a foursome," she said. "You and Adam, and me and Sergey."

I squeezed her hand. "I'll frolic on the beach after I discover why the police are keeping a serial murderer secret. There could've been witnesses, Lee. Someone may have seen something, forgot that they did, and had no context for what they saw. Maybe if Adam sent his team around again asking questions. Like, has he even talked to this Snickers person?"

"Skittles. Taste the rainbow."

"Whatever." I dumped my coffee in the sink. "He's running the show. It's his fuckup, not mine."

"Didn't deserve to die?" Lena muttered. "I know Tamar's dad is upset, but who deserves death? Women who aren't in church every freakin' day?"

I understood the reverend's point—some people have it coming, some people live dangerous lives. I didn't *agree* with him, though. Far from it. Sometimes, you ain't gotta be bad to find yourself in a fucked-up situation.

But in the reverend's world (and those who thought like him), women like Tamar weren't supposed to be murdered. Women like her have never seen a penis or an R-rated film. They don't dance and they don't drink. They're virgins until marriage, their chastity pledged to their fathers, who they live with before moving into another man's (e.g., husband's) house. No drama except for a skirt hem .05 inches too short.

Mythological creatures. Pure, selfless, and solitary. Unicorns living in LA.

And I had found one. A murdered unicorn in a South Los Angeles alley.

The doorbell rang.

"I'll get it," Lena said and clip-clopped out of the kitchen.

My thoughts turned back to Tamar.

What had she done?

Who did she cross?

Why did she call me?

Lena returned with a basket of cupcakes in her arms. *"Pour vous."*

"Holy crap." I hopped off my stool and backed away from the counter. "What are those?"

Lena cocked her head. "Um . . . In America, we call them *cupcakes.*"

I gawked at the gift. "Who sent them?"

She stared at me as though I played clarinet in the Tinfoil Hat School Orchestra, but then, she sneered and slapped the bar top. Deon Jackson sent muffin baskets once a month. "I will hunt him down *today* if he—" She snatched the card from the cellophane. *"Hey, Sy. It was so cool seeing you yesterday. Glad we're friends again. Tell Lena 'hey.' See you soon. Toni a.k.a. Not Antoinette. Ha ha."*

I exhaled, muttered, "Okay," and settled back at the bar.

Lena tore away the basket's wrapping and selected a pink cupcake from the dozen. "Toni's our friend now? Did Joey dump her? Give her some type of STD again?"

"Sure for your first question. Nope for the second. And probably for the third." I chose a chocolate cupcake, then took the phone to the backyard.

My sister answered on the first ring. "Rescue me, please," she whispered. "We're watching another HGTV show."

In the background, Mom said, "Now that's just ugly. I can come up with something that looks better than that."

Eva groaned.

I laughed. "Do you have your computer?"

"I'm off duty, Sy."

"Fine. Have fun watching *Design on a Dime*, then."

She sighed. "What do you need?"

"Tamar's father, Reverend Murray Haist. Is he in the system for anything?"

Eva paused. "You think Tamar's *father* killed her?"

I shrugged. "Just a thought. Something's off about this situation."

"Everything's off for you. You don't know what's normal anymore. I'll call you back."

Eva was right—what was normal to me? I replayed my night with Adam—were we back on the road to love? Was I ready for that type of exposure? Literally, ready to show him all of me? Was this fear normal? And if I couldn't be comfortable with him, who would I be comfortable with?

After my diagnosis, everything had shifted—what I thought I wanted flip-flopped, and who I thought I was changed the moment I was wheeled into that operating room. It would have been easier for Adam to be with another woman—someone healthier, body and soul. But I didn't want him to be with anyone other than me.

The ringing telephone saved me from further introspection.

"Assault back in 1995," Eva said. "He served a year and was released on good behavior. He was arrested again for domestic assault in 2003. Nothing else since then."

"So he has a history of violence," I said.

"Him possibly beating his wife doesn't mean that he beat his kids," Eva pointed out.

"We don't know that. What if—"

"Sy, you need to take a break. You're still recovering from surgery, and—"

"Why is everyone telling me to relax?"

I sank into the Adirondack chair. The bones in my body creaked and the yard shimmied before me—a new thing since the surgery. I closed my eyes and pinched the bridge of my nose.

"You okay?" Eva asked.

"Stop worrying." I opened my eyes.

The world had not stopped its wiggling.

"I'm fine," I said anyway.

Yeah. A-okay.

12

I spotted one news van in Great Redeemer's parking lot. The female field reporter from KTLA, a skinny blonde with helmet hair, stood before the cameraman with a microphone clutched in her claws.

Noemi Haist stood amid a cluster of women who were hugging her, kissing her, and stuffing into her hands white envelopes most likely filled with money and condolences. Noemi wore a long-sleeved forest-green dress that hit her clunky shoes and added too much weight to her frame. Her hairline had receded—too much time spent in tight ponytails. Her well-wishers wore similar shapeless frocks, functional yet depressing shoes, and their hair had also been pulled into no-nonsense buns.

As I neared the group, the women turned to me. Their eyes flicked from my face, down to my slacks, and back up to my glossy lips. Then, they sneered at me: the worldly outsider.

Noemi's eyes were swollen and her nose was red and flecked with tissue lint.

I held her gaze and attempted to smile. "Noemi, I'm Sy McKay."

"The doctor at the coroner's office told me about you," Noemi said with a nod.

The other women didn't speak and kept giving me the sanctified stink eye. I expected one of them to pull out a tissue, wet it with spit, then wipe the *whore's paint* off my face.

"Dr. Brooks told me that you're writing a book about . . ." Noemi narrowed her eyes. "That you may think that Tamar . . ."

"I *am* writing a book," I said, "but it's not clear yet if Tamar's case is related. The police—"

"Don't care," Noemi said.

The women rolled their eyes, offered *mm-hmms*, and clucked their tongues in agreement. The Righteous Borg.

"They're saying sit and wait," Noemi continued. "They searched Tamar's apartment this morning, but they're not telling us what they're looking for. They're not telling us anything."

Tamar had her own apartment?

Noemi hugged herself. "How are we supposed to believe that they'll remember that we're here?"

Mm-hmm.

Why should we?

They don't care.

"Some crackhead broke into the church last year," Noemi continued, "but did the cops do anything? A few of our members got jumped in the parking lot back on Mother's Day. Did the cops come? Yeah, they did— three hours later. And now someone's murdered my sister, and I'm supposed say, *Let the cops do their jobs?* They've ignored us since we've been here. If we were West Angeles, this parking lot would be full of police."

West Angeles Church of God in Christ was located in a better section of town, and had rich and famous members, like Denzel Washington and Magic Johnson.

"I know the detective in charge of Tamar's case," I said. "He won't forget you. He wants to catch this guy, and he will. I'm sure of that. And if it'll make you feel better, I'll talk to him today, tell him your concerns." I considered the other women, then returned my gaze to Noemi. "Could you and I talk somewhere . . . ?"

Noemi turned to the group. "I'll meet y'all later, at the house."

She and I didn't speak as we wandered into the chilly church lobby. I peeked through the glass panes on the doors that led to the sanctuary. It was a large, impressive space with lavender-padded pews and matching carpet. An organ sat in one corner, and a baby grand piano sat in the other. A stained glass scene of Jesus in Gethsemane glistened above the baptismal pool.

"Are you a believer, Miss McKay?" Noemi asked.

I turned back to her. "Excuse me?"

"Are you a Christian?" she asked slowly.

"I haven't been to church in a long time, but I still try to be . . . good."

Noemi grunted, folded her arms.

Uncomfortable, I swallowed, then volunteered, "My mother fears for my soul. She thinks I've moved away from all that I was taught to believe. But I think, in some ways, my faith and my belief is stronger than hers." I glanced back into the sanctuary. "In my line of work, I have to believe that I'm protected. I have to believe that there's someplace better than this. I don't need to sit in a pew every week to convince me of that."

Noemi nodded, satisfied with my answer. "Tamar was the sweetest girl in the world. Never gossiped. Always helped others. Why would someone kill her?"

"I was hoping you could help me figure that out," I said. "Your sister knew something, and I think she was too scared to tell the police."

Noemi furrowed her brows. "Like what?"

I told Noemi about the Phantom Slayer, the types of women he murdered, and the text message that Tamar had sent me early Wednesday morning.

"First of all," Noemi said, "I ain't heard of no serial killer around here. Second of all, my sister wasn't no prostitute, and she didn't associate with people like that unless they came to the church for help. I'm sorry, but we don't live exciting lives. Secrets and intrigue and late-night meetings in dark alleys. I teach *kindergarten*, for Pete's sake."

"Guess I'm at a dead end, then," I said. "Thanks for talking to me."

She smirked. "You don't get what you came for, so you'll disappear?"

"What am I supposed to do? You say Tamar knew nothing about this case, so okay, she knew nothing. I have a job to do."

"Have you ever been ignored, Miss McKay?" Noemi's eyes darted from my face to my feet. "Looking at you, I doubt that you have. Even though my father is the pastor here, I'm still invisible. The other young women who aren't pretty and skinny? They're ignored, too. The men don't see us until one of them gets desperate and needs a wife and a mother for their children. I'm twenty-four years old, and up until today, nobody inside or outside this building has ever asked my opinion about anything. Until today, most people didn't know somebody like me existed. But now that my sister's . . . gone, some TV reporter had her microphone all up in my face, asking me how I felt? I wanted to smack her in the head and scream, *How do you think I feel?*"

"I understand. And you're right—we reporters can be stupid, insensitive creeps. And you deserve to be left alone, especially in your most painful moments."

"Wait." Noemi clutched my arm. "Just . . . wait." Tears shone in her eyes and her grip tightened. "If you help, maybe the world will pay attention to us for the right reasons. No one ever notices when young Black women go missing. At least with your voice, the world can't claim that no one said anything. You can testify that my sister existed and that she had a life and that there were people who loved her."

I squeezed her hand. "I don't know if I'd have the time—"

"One story about my sister," Noemi said. "Please, Miss McKay. Just write one story. It doesn't have to be big, and they can put it in the back with the weather or somewhere." A tear slipped down her cheek. "People should know. Even though Tamar strayed, she was a good person. She was so brave." She swiped the tears from her eyes and sniffled. "Wish I had half the courage she did."

"I can't. I'm already behind on covering other aspects of this story, and . . ."

She opened the doors to the sanctuary. "Come to Tamar's apartment later today. My parents will be there and you can meet them. You'll see what a wonderful person Tamar was. Please?"

I gazed at stained glass Jesus in the garden. Distressed, and hours away from arrest and crucifixion, He had been pleading with God to let this cup pass. *Yet not as I will, but as Thou wilt.*

The Righteous Borg had returned to their cube, and the news van had departed in search of other civic tragedies.

Before leaving the church grounds, I stopped by the alley where Tamar Haist had lain just a day before.

The yellow tape and plastic cones were gone, and in their place a shrine had been erected. A pile of countless teddy bears of every size and color hid the new patch of butter-yellow paint. Three Our Lady of Guadalupe votive candles burned even though Tamar had been far from Catholic. A stick of sandalwood incense smoldered in one of them, the aroma mixing with alley smells. There was a *Dora the Explorer* doll as well as balloons twisted into red and white flowers, *we miss you, baby girl* written in black ink on every petal. Someone had enlarged Tamar's high school graduation portrait into a poster—green cap and gown, wide smile, the promise of a future bright in her eyes. Two young Black women stood over the site. They clutched each other, their faces wet with tears.

I stopped short, and let them mourn in private.

A security guard in a blue cap and uniform stood near my car. He smiled as I walked in his direction. He looked like no one and everyone. One of God's templates. A broad nose but not too big. Brown eyes. Skin the color of graham crackers. The cleft in his chin was his only distinction, an afterthought in design.

"Nice car," he said, nodding at my Benz.

"Thanks. Where did everybody go?"

"To go take care of Reverend and Mother Haist," he said. "Hard to believe that Tamar's gone. I've known her since she was a little thing.

She used to climb on her daddy's lap during service. He'd hold her sometimes as he preached."

"Were you and Tamar friends?"

"Kind of. I've been a member since forever. Since the reverend started his ministry here. I'm really close to the family." He narrowed his eyes. "You're the one who found her, right?"

I nodded. "Were you working Tuesday night?"

"My shift ended around ten," he said, "and no one was here when I left. I talked to the detectives and told them everything. This part of town is dangerous, but not this bad. Well, that's what I thought."

"Are you usually here all day?"

"No. I work part-time with the county. Used to be full-time until the economy thing." He frowned as his gaze skipped around the lot and stopped at the alley.

"So she was a daddy's girl back in the day?"

"Yeah." He regarded the church. "People change, though. Situations change. For better or for worse. That's how it is, right? The reverend's a good man. A little stubborn, but so was Moses. And Jacob. And Peter. It's hard to have a ministry here, hard raising kids in the middle of a dangerous city. You have to stay vigilant, stay prayerful cuz if you don't, you lose all control."

I nodded, recalling my own parents' struggles to keep us safe. "I have to admit: When I first saw Tamar, I didn't think she was a preacher's kid."

He shrugged. "Like I said, people change."

"Do you think Tamar's change had something to do with her death?"

He pushed back his cap. "I'm no CSI guy, so I can't comment on that. And I can't tell you who would do something like this to such a nice girl. Why was Tamar meeting you here?"

I unlocked the car door. "She wanted to talk to me about a story I'm writing."

His eyes brightened. "About the church's anniversary celebration?"

I peered at him and paused before saying, "No. And you are . . . ?"

He stuck out his hand. "Jay Dennis. Nice meeting you . . ."

"Sy McKay," I said, shaking his hand. "I may come back if I have more questions. Is that cool?"

"Anything to help." He stepped away from the car as I climbed behind the steering wheel.

I checked for messages on my phone. No calls. I glanced around the parking lot.

The security guard—I had already forgotten his name—waved at me, then ambled back to the church.

13

Adam and his task force partner, Lew Hsieh, stood in front of 4406 Don Tomaso, a dingy-white two-story apartment complex a few miles west of Great Redeemer Church. Temperatures had soared into the high eighties, yet Adam wore a black Hugo Boss suit and shirt. Guess he wanted to channel Al Pacino in *Heat*. He and Lew were talking and chuckling, glancing back at the apartment building, then shaking their heads. As I approached, they fell into smirky silence.

"Well, if it ain't Miss Marple," Adam said with a smile. "What's happening, Renko?"

"Do you google the names of fictional detectives just to impress me?" I asked.

"Of course I do. Didn't expect to see you here. What's up?"

"Noemi Haist asked me to stop by. I grew up not too far from here."

"Up the hill or down it?" Lew asked. He was round faced and tall. Favored Drakkar Noir cologne and copious amounts of hair gel.

"Somewhere in between," I said. "Kinda like this place, only worse." I turned back to the apartments where some tenants had draped wet towels and underwear on their little balconies, and others had stowed hibachis, bicycles, and large potted plants.

Go west and up the hill, and you hit View Park–Windsor Hills. Big homes. BMWs and Benzes in the driveways. Black folks jogging on trails that dotted the hillsides. No trash. No tags. Everyone votes. Go east and you hit Chesterfield Square. Poor to working class, Black and brown. *Lavanderías* and liquor stores. More buses than Beemers. Walls covered with spray-painted names, many crossed out. Churches the size of the neighborhood KFC.

My family had lived in the Jungle. In the sixties, that name had referred to an area thick with begonias and palm trees. With the seventies came PCP and gangs, and the Jungle became synonymous with "scary-ass ghetto," a dangerous and violent part of Los Angeles where beasts shaped like men shot up drugs, shot at each other, and then raped and robbed in their spare time. Because of this, my parents had prohibited Eva, Kenny, and me from playing with the neighborhood kids. We couldn't even play outside. Guns and gangs were outside. Dope, beer, and teenage pregnancies were outside. Jail and death? Outside.

"Thought you guys searched Tamar's apartment earlier today?" I said.

Adam nodded. "We're just doing more follow-up."

"Find anything interesting?"

"Would I tell you if we did?"

I raised an eyebrow. *When you're in my bed, you tell me a lot.*

Spots of color found his cheeks and he smiled. *I do.* "We were officially assigned the Haist case this morning."

"As a Phantom Slayer case?"

The two detectives nodded.

Adam said, "We can't ignore the text message she sent you."

"And the signature is the same," Lew added. "Blast to the face of a young Black female left in an alley."

I reached into my bag for a notebook and pen. "So the bullet came from the same gun? The striations matched?"

"Ballistics are still out," Adam said.

I nodded. "And in addition to her being a church secretary—"

"Not at the time of her death," Lew said.

Adam threw a *shut up* glance at his partner.

"What do you mean?" I asked. "Was she fired?"

"Next question," Adam said.

"What about the church's security system? Was there a camera aimed at the lot? Or at the alley? There's a memorial there now. Does the camera get that view?"

"System was down," Lew said. "Somebody stole the two cameras from the parking lot. We talked to the security guard on duty that night. Said he saw nothing strange."

"And before you ask," Adam interjected, "he has an alibi—he drove Reverend Haist home that night. They were together."

"And the reverend confirmed?"

Adam nodded. "And we're monitoring that memorial."

"To see if anyone suspicious stops by?"

He smiled, said nothing.

"Reverend Haist has a history of violent behavior," I said. "Arrested for domestic assault, right? Is he a suspect?"

Lew looked to Adam. "Did you tell her?"

Adam shook his head. "She finds shit out. She's magic."

"Maybe you should talk to this sex worker named Skittles," I said. "She told Lena that she saw a strange Black man in a minivan just sitting and staring. She said he looked like a minister or a cop. He didn't belong there, in other words." And I told them about Tamar and the needle-exchange encounter.

Adam turned to Lew. "Wanna call Troy in Vice?"

Lew pulled his phone from his jacket pocket and stepped away from us.

Adam asked me, "What color was the minivan?"

"Gold or tan," I said. "She wasn't sure."

"You hear that?" Adam shouted to Lew.

Lew, phone to his ear, nodded.

"Will you be testing the Reverend's DNA against the Slayer's?" I asked.

Adam's expression hardened.

"Did you ask him if his daughter was a sex worker?"

"I have not asked that question yet," Adam said. "But I will."

"And maybe she wasn't your garden-variety prostitute," Lew added, joining us again, "but she was definitely into something. A freelancer, maybe."

I lifted an eyebrow. "Are there such things? Freelancing prostitutes? You say this because . . ."

Adam met my eyes and didn't blink.

"We found a thousand dollars cash in her purse," Lew offered. "We also found six condoms. And you saw the dress she wore—"

Yeah. I saw the dress. A used-to-be-pink bandage number very popular with curvy starlets who usually skip wearing underwear. You can buy a really cheap and uninteresting Hervé Léger for $700. I have an awesome scarlet version I found on sale for $1,000.

According to Spencer's autopsy report, Tamar had also worn a pair of $1,100 Manolo Blahnik jeweled slingbacks. Again, you can find them on sale for $800. I have three pairs—when you're wearing a $1,000 dress, you shouldn't skimp on shoes.

Throw in the pair of diamond silver studs in Tamar's ears, and the Tiffany charm bracelet, the former church secretary wore $2,500 worth of apparel.

"The boob job and the weave cost a grip," Lew was saying. "Hell, her hair probably cost more than what we bring home every month."

The detectives nodded, satisfied with their assessment. They turned to me. *Your move.*

I nodded, accepting the challenge. "A fake-boobed white girl in a revealing, expensive dress, with diamond earrings, a thousand dollars, and six rubbers in her purse sounds like I'd be describing Paris Hilton. But the Black church girl in the Neon is a ho. Possibly a freelancing ho. Is that what you're saying?" I squinted at them, tilted my head as a warning that they should carefully word their response.

Lew blushed and stammered, "Umm . . . Well . . . I know it sounds like we're being prejudiced . . . Or sexist . . . Or . . ."

Adam placed his hands on his hips. "Why are you here, then, if she's some innocent victim who just happened to be in the wrong place at the wrong time?"

I offered him a saccharine smile. "I'm here to keep you guys from screwing up. To ensure that you won't make wrongheaded assumptions, like who a woman is because of the dress she's wearing." With that, I killed the fake smile.

Adam glanced back at the apartment building and said, "Whoever Tamar Haist was, or whatever she did as her side hustle, the girl had serious issues. A confused freak, if you want my honest opinion."

"Confused freak. That's good." I placed pen to paper. "May I quote you, Detective?"

"Always nice seeing you, Sy." As Adam turned on his heel, his fingertips brushed against my hand, sending a jolt zigzagging up my arm. He sauntered to the Crown Vic, glanced over his shoulder, and winked at me.

"A pleasure, Adam," I said, calling after him. "I mean that. You, too, Lew. Nice haircut, by the way."

Lew nodded, cleared his throat, then followed his partner to the car.

I walked through the building's shaded entryway and arrived at a patio area with a kidney bean–shaped swimming pool no larger than three bathtubs. Someone was frying bacon, and the aroma of pork wafted through the air. A white man in a pea-green sweater used a push broom to gather leaves that had fallen from a sickly-looking eucalyptus tree. His chore had made his pink head dusty, and injury or age had caused him to stoop. He glanced at me, then shifted his eyes back to his heap.

"How are you today?"

He grunted a response as he kept sweeping. If it were possible, he would've slipped his head beneath his sweater's neck and waited until

I left him alone. Unfortunately for him, I have nothing to do all day except agitate turtle-men wielding push brooms.

"Are you the landlord?" I asked.

He swiped at his sweaty, hooked nose. "I am." He peered at me with beady black eyes. "You need help finding someone?"

"Tamar Haist's apartment?"

"Unit 2, second floor." He slowly shook his head and made *tsk*ing sounds. "That poor, poor family."

"Yeah, it's awful what happened."

His eyes darted to the second-story units. "Do you know what's going on up there? I mean . . ." He shrugged and smiled nervously. "The cops came this morning, then they came back again this afternoon. What are they looking for?"

I returned his smile. "Who knows? The police are funny that way. Looking for stuff and not telling you anything. Happens to me all the time."

"They had search warrants just like they have on TV." He leaned against the broom and scrunched his eyebrows. "It's hard to rent nowadays, with the economy and all. People losing their jobs, gas prices skyrocketing . . . Are they coming back?"

"The cops?" I shrugged.

"People get nervous seeing the police hanging around," he said. "Especially potential renters. They get the wrong impression, think that there's drug dealing or gang activity going on here. The other tenants are nervous, too. I'm already at thirty percent capacity. And if the cops keep coming back . . . Although I don't know *why* they would come back. Tamar wasn't killed here. What would they come back for?" He waited for my answer.

I smiled and shrugged again. Then, I used the toe of my shoe to sweep escaped leaves into the pile. That's me. Always lending a hand. Or a foot. "What kind of tenant was Tamar?"

"Quiet," he said. "Never much noise in that place. No destroyed carpets. Never even had to unclog a sink or the toilet. Paid her rent on time. She and her family are pretty religious people."

"Did she have many visitors?"

"A couple. Most times, it was her sister."

"Any male visitors? Like boyfriends or . . . ?"

He closed his eyes as he thought, then shook his head. "Don't think so. She wasn't that type of girl."

"The type to have a boyfriend or the type to have lots of men over?"

He opened his mouth, but closed it without answering.

"Did you talk much to her?" I asked.

"I invited her over for dinner once, and . . ." He narrowed his eyes. "And you are . . . ?"

"No one important."

"A TV reporter?"

"No."

"A detective? FBI?"

I shook my head.

He furrowed his brow, unable to think of other fields that weren't TV reporting and law enforcement.

"Were you . . . *interested* in Tamar?" I asked. "Did she accept your dinner invitation?"

"I have work to do," he said, blushing. "So if you'll excuse me." No longer trusting me, the scales fell back over his beady eyes, and he whirled away to sweep his leaves.

I made a mental note to ask Adam about the landlord.

Everyone was a suspect . . . until they weren't.

I found Unit 2 at the northern end of the complex. I rang the doorbell, my stomach already twisted into knots.

The theme music of *The Price is Right* drifted from behind the door.

A moment later, the door opened two inches, and a Black woman peered back at me. "Yes?"

She had a soft baby voice, like an eighth grader, and wore her hair in two styles: the front divided into several twists, then the end of those twists captured into a tight bun. Her eyes were bloodshot and swollen—crying as she watched a woman from Buena Park play Plinko. She wore the type of short-sleeved top favored by pregnant women, the kind that flared up front for the baby bump, and a floral skirt that grazed the tops of her shoes.

I couldn't predict her age—the clothes, the voice, and the hairstyle each suggested anywhere between thirteen and seventy-five.

Noemi Haist emerged from the shadows of the apartment and stood behind the woman. "Momma," she whispered, gripping the woman's shoulders, "this is the writer I was telling you about." Then, Noemi smiled at me. "Miss McKay, this is my mother, Evelyn Haist."

Really? This woman with that voice and perfect skin didn't look like she had started menstruating, yet here she stood, the mother of a nineteen-year-old and a twenty-four-year-old. I did the math—she had to have been a few years older than me. Or a few years younger.

Noemi took her mother's hand and said, "Let's sit down, Momma. Please come in, Miss McKay." She pulled her mother back into the living room and helped her sit on a fussy, floral couch. Then, she aimed the remote at the television. *Pop.* No more Plinko.

I stepped into the living room and gasped. Countless acrylic cases sat on every flat surface or had been fixed to the walls. Each displayed a posing collectible Barbie. Halston Barbie. 25th Anniversary Barbie. Bob Mackie Barbie. Barbies of every color and every profession. Nurse. Flight attendant. President of the United States. Tamar had converted the two-hundred-square foot space into a Barbie showroom. Hated to admit it, but Adam's *confused freak* comment had some foundation.

"My sister collects them," Noemi said, noticing my wide eyes and gaping mouth. "She has 135 in all, including one of the first Barbies ever made. We had the entire collection appraised last year. It's worth forty thousand dollars."

I glanced around the living room. The couch and armchair were covered in yards of generic English Rose fabric and thousands of throw pillows. Roses had been carved into the legs of the coffee table, and the entire place smelled of damp potpourri. Vertical blinds hung over a sliding patio door that led out to the balcony. A man stood out there, his back to us. His hands sat on his hips as he stared down at the tiny swimming pool.

I wandered to the Barbies closest to the big-screen television, an appliance totally out of place in this Laura Ashley Barbie Bunker. "I've never seen so many in one area," I said, settling into the armchair. "I had a Malibu Barbie, and I gave it to my sister. But I kept the town house—"

The patio door slid open.

Reverend Haist stepped into the living room and glared at me with unforgiving eyes. "What's happening here?"

The minister looked older than his wife only because of the salt and pepper in his mustache and at his temples. He wore a wrinkled dress shirt with no tie, and his pants had become a size too big since he had learned of his daughter's death twenty-four hours ago.

"Daddy," Noemi said, "this is the writer I was telling you—"

"I told you: no writers." The minister continued to glower at me. "You will not capitalize on my daughter's death." His baritone voice was as tight as a guitar string, seasoned from the fire-and-brimstone sermons he preached every Sunday from eight in the morning to two thirty in the afternoon.

"Daddy," Noemi said, "people should know."

"*Know?*" he boomed. "Know that she was living a life contrary to what we believe? That her life caused her death? Even the police think that."

Evelyn whispered, "I begged her not to move here."

"Tamar lived with Mom, Dad, and me up until six months ago," Noemi explained to me.

"We tried to protect her," Evelyn added. "We tried so hard."

Hard to do in this city. Despite my parents' vigilance in protecting us—*you have lessons, time for church, go to the library, don't look over there, don't listen to that, no you can't go to her house*—that Wicked Outside had still oozed through protective fingers covering our eyes. We had pregnant friends who were kicked out of school and never seen again. We attended funerals for friends who had been gunned down at bus stops. Our friends had brothers, uncles, and daddies who had disappeared into gangs, into jail, or into graves.

"She wanted to be worldly," Reverend Haist was saying, "and she succeeded. She got her own apartment. Wore clothes that . . . that . . . with those . . ." He cupped his hands in front of his chest. "Those . . . *things* hanging out like that." He shook his head, awed by his dead daughter's breasts. "She wanted to live a sinful life without having to answer to me or to God, so she moved here. And you see what happened? You see? Even though I did what I was supposed to. Even though I gave her all the tools she needed to live right. I kept her straight as long as I could."

"I begged her to stay home," Evelyn whispered.

"I moved out of my parents' house after college," I said, keeping my voice steady, ignoring the burn in my belly. "I just wanted my own space. That's all. Not because I wanted to sin, but because I wanted to decorate, cook . . ."

Reverend Haist glared at me.

"I'm not here to judge who she was," I said. "Really: I just want to find out what happened. Noemi asked me to come and . . ." I cleared my throat and glanced at Noemi.

Noemi offered a curt shake of her head, then shifted her eyes to Pirate Barbie, fiercely *fabulous* in her plastic case.

I attempted to smile. "Noemi asked me to come today to learn more about Tamar. So, I'd like to ask you all a few questions. I won't take much of your time, and I promise not to sensationalize. This will be a simple profile of—"

"If Noemi wants to talk to you," Reverend Haist said, "she can. She's an adult. But my wife and I have said all that's necessary to the police."

O-kay. I opened my notebook, and turned to Noemi. "When was the last time you saw your sister alive?"

Noemi took a deep breath and slowly exhaled. "At church on Sunday. After I greeted visitors at the door that morning, Tamar and I sat together during service. She came over later to the house for dinner." Noemi hugged herself. "She made macaroni and cheese. Remember, Momma? It was dry like always. Tamar hated using lots of cheese. Thought it was unhealthy."

"What kind of mood was she in that day?"

"She was a Christian girl," the minister said as he twisted the wristband of his watch.

I paused, waited for more. "Which means . . . ?"

"Tamar was filled with the Holy Spirit," Evelyn answered. "Always happy because she was so blessed."

I cocked my head. "She never experienced sadness or depression or anxiety?"

"Tamar knew Christ," the minister said with a final nod.

I was also a Christian, and on many occasions (especially since my surgery), I had been a sad Christian, a fretful Christian, a Christian on the verge of losing her mind. Because I was human, too, subject to pain and anguish, humiliation and loneliness. Was Jesus less Christian when He wept? Or when He tore down those tables set up in the temple?

"Tamar was a handmaiden of the Lord," Evelyn said, now a Chatty Cathy. "Holy and pure, righteous in His sight. Always obedient."

"Why did the church fire her?" I asked.

Silence from the trio. Angry eyes from the parents. Uneasy grimace from the sister.

"Was Tamar seeing anyone? A boyfriend, I mean."

Noemi said, "No." She shifted her eyes to the carpet, then glanced back at me.

I scribbled *secret lover* on the page. "When did you plan to see her again?"

Noemi's eyes filled with tears. "For Wednesday night prayer meeting."

Evelyn let out a weepy breath.

"Did you and Tamar get along? She was a few years younger than you, right?"

Reverend Haist leaned forward and pointed at me. "Sounds like you're trying to sensationalize, little lady. Watch what you say, understand?"

Little lady?

I offered him an innocent smile. "I'm a big sister, too, and my little sister broke all the rules my brother and I had to obey." To Noemi, I said, "It may have been a little tense, with her moving out before you. Or changing the way she looked. Regular sister stuff, you know? I'd just like to put Tamar's last days into context—"

"We were a happy family," Evelyn said, louder than necessary. "She was our daughter. We loved her."

"Tamar always rebelled against tradition," Noemi said. "Against the rules."

"Noemi is the calm one," Evelyn said. "The one who never strays."

"Tamar came out breech and stayed that way," the minister muttered.

"Tamar had a good heart."

"She was very generous."

"She was selfish," Reverend Haist said.

"Yes," Evelyn said into her lap. "She was selfish."

"I'm sure she was all of that," I said, forcing patience into my tone. Because *damn*, these people. "But did her . . . *lifestyle* cause any problems? For you, in particular, Reverend?" I offered another smile. "There you are, preaching that young women shouldn't wear pants or jewelry or live alone, and your own daughter goes out and does the complete opposite—"

Reverend Haist shot up from the couch and stomped to the tiny dining room. "I'm not staying here to be mocked by someone who thinks she knows all the answers. By some *female* who thinks she's better than us 'silly' Christians."

I stood from my seat. "Sir, I don't think that you're silly. I'm just trying to figure out . . ." I sighed. "Tamar showed a rebellious side. A quality that made her more human. Qualities that may have, like you said, contributed to her death."

Evelyn left the couch and joined her husband at the small dining room table. She gathered her purse and a floral-print dress that had been draped across a chair.

The couple started to the front door, but Reverend Haist turned back to me. "How do you think this feels, Miss McKay? To have my daughter die this way? She did whatever she wanted, never once stopping to think how her behavior would affect me. How the world would look at me. She seemed intent on destroying all the work I've done, and I can't understand why.

"I did all that I could for her and the worst still happened. How can I save people for God's Kingdom if I can't even save my own daughter?"

His nostrils flared as he pressed his lips together to regain control. "This isn't a game or some story in a newspaper for us. When you're gone, my daughter will still be . . . She'll be . . ."

"I didn't mean to upset you," I said.

"Then stay away from us." He squared his shoulders and pointed at me. "I'm warning you: If you come near my wife and me again, I will file charges against you for harassment. Understand?"

I nodded.

He strode out the door in angry silence with Evelyn trailing behind him.

14

As a journalist, I act as a tour guide for readers wanting a glimpse of someone else's tragic life. Woman burned alive in the trunk of her car . . . Culver City man gets forty years for threats to kill in-laws . . . All those years at the *Times*, I had rarely blinked an eye, rarely turned away. Witnessing Reverend Haist mourn his daughter while hating who she was hit too close to home, though. Reminded me of my own fragile relationship between my mother and me, and how I'd always find new ways to disappoint her without meaning to.

Never blinking an eye?

Can't do it all your life.

Noemi led me down a short hallway to Tamar's bedroom. "I apologize for my father," she said. "He can be pretty . . . *intense*. But it's been tough for him. Tough for all of us."

I pressed my hand to my heart. "If I'm frightening you, or harassing you, or if you just want me to go away—"

"I don't feel that way at all," she said, eyes wide. "I asked you to come."

"Because I can step away from this. I know what it's like to be harassed, and the last thing I want to do is make someone else feel threatened."

"No, I want to talk," Noemi said with a final nod. "You being here is important to me."

All young women just starting independent lives have bedrooms similar to Tamar's. The single floor-to-ceiling window behind vertical blinds. The low bookcase filled mostly with paperbacks. The cheap floral comforter from Sears, and the even cheaper pine headboard found at some mom-and-pop furniture store that still offered layaway.

Only one Barbie lived in Tamar's room—a blinged-out doll of dubious race. Her acrylic case had been fixed to the wall above the bed's headboard.

"Tamar's favorite," Noemi said, nodding to the case. "Kimora Lee Simmons Barbie."

The supermodel doll wore a faux full-length chinchilla coat and pink thigh-high boots. In one hand, she held a designer handbag, and in the other, the leash to her little dog Zoe. The real-life Kimora had married (and divorced) Def Jam Records founder Russell Simmons. She had also coined the term "fabulosity" and embodied everything that God-fearing, humble people loathed. Greed, noise, and me, me, me.

"Tamar watched Kimora's reality show all the time," Noemi was saying. "I think that's who she wanted to be."

Tamar had the hair and the boobs. All she needed was a lap dog and a music mogul.

"Your mother doesn't talk much," I said.

"My father speaks for her," Noemi responded. "He's the head of the family."

I said, "Hmm."

Noemi said, "It's biblical."

"Sure."

"Are you saying that my father's a sexist?"

"Not at all." I sighed, shook off my irritation, and pushed "restart." "Your father complained about Tamar's actions affecting him, yet he's the one with a criminal record. How do you think his arrests affected Tamar?"

Noemi's eyes bugged. "How did you know about . . . all that?"

"Crimes against the people of California are public record."

Embarrassed, Noemi offered a weak smile. "Tamar didn't like the way women were treated in the church and she told him that sometimes. Too many times. She stopped being scared of him. Well, she became *less* scared of him. Seems like she set out to be the type of woman he hates."

I wandered to the dresser and found two turquoise Tiffany jewelry boxes among bottles of perfume. I opened one box—tiny diamond studs—and glanced over my shoulder at Noemi. "Are they paying church secretaries Tiffany-money nowadays?"

She folded her arms and leaned against the doorframe. "My parents don't know about him."

"What's his name?"

"Christopher something. Tamar was very hush-hush. He's not a member of the church, so Daddy wouldn't have approved."

"You ever meet Christopher?"

"Once. He did a job at the church. He's old. Like your age. Tall. Hazel eyes. Gorgeous . . ." Her lip curled as the image of Christopher formed in her mind.

"Didn't like him?"

She jerked, surprised that her poker face had transformed into wild-eyed craps table. "Tamar was cute, but not cute enough to pull this guy. She never had a boyfriend, and now, all of a sudden, she gets *him*?"

"Why her, right?"

Noemi stood straighter and pushed out her chest. "He wasn't my type. He was too slick. Too *worldly*. And I didn't like him because he changed her. She never worried about her body or her hair before, but as soon as they started dating, she wanted a weave, wanted new clothes, wanted to move out. He wasn't worth it to me. *'For what shall it profit a man, if he shall gain the whole world, and lose his soul?'*"

"Was he married?"

"She said he was divorced. That she didn't see him all the time because he traveled a lot for his job."

I slipped the Tiffany box back on the dresser. "It's always the job. Or the wife."

Noemi wandered over to her sister's bed and stared at Kimora Barbie. "I talked to Tamar on Monday afternoon, after she got back from the hair salon. The shop is called Wholly Holy Hair. Anyway, Tamar got her hair done because she was seeing Christopher Tuesday night. She thought he was gonna propose because that weekend, they had . . . umm . . . They had . . ." She blushed.

"They had *sex*?" I asked, no longer the dainty flower like my new friend, the Virgin Noemi.

"It was her first time."

And she fell in love. Nothing new there.

"They had been together for six months," Noemi said, as though time and sex automatically resulted in a big white dress and a honeymoon cruise on the Mexican Riviera. "She didn't want a big wedding. Especially since Daddy would've flipped out—he had already picked someone else to marry her. She was so happy, though, and she swore that she wouldn't have a marriage like our parents'. If you couldn't tell, Mom and Daddy aren't friends. I've never seen them laugh together, or touch each other, and I can't see them ever having . . . sex. They did, of course, but they were teenagers when we were born."

"I'm familiar with the 'man is head of the household' thing," I said. "Even with that, I'd still say your mother's pretty quiet."

"Because Daddy . . . ." Noemi sighed. "Let's just say that he *tolerates* being with my mother. I've seen how some of the women at church look at him, and how he looks at them. He thinks that I'm blind because I don't talk much, but Tamar saw it all, and she hated it. She just wanted to elope and get away from the church, away from this neighborhood. She wasn't expecting to come back home on Tuesday night."

"Is that why she had a thousand dollars in her purse?"

Noemi nodded.

"She had saved for her escape?"

Noemi paused, shook her head.

I waited for her explanation, but got none. "She didn't save?"

"It wasn't her money. It belonged to the church."

My mouth opened but I had no words.

Tamar was a thief, too?

"Is that why she was fired?" I finally asked.

Noemi nodded and wrung her plump little hands. "She was taking a little every week and stashing it away. The treasurer caught her stealing and demanded that Daddy fire her or else he'd tell the entire congregation and have Tamar arrested. My father was so angry, but he agreed. He even forced her to date the treasurer's son. Tamar promised to pay back the money, but she never did. She told me that the church had taken so much from her that she was now taking something from them. It was her getaway money.

"She called me and told me that she loved me, and that I'd see her when she got back. She sounded so happy. But then, Tuesday night came, and she called me—Christopher hadn't shown up yet at the restaurant and she didn't know where he was. She said that she was gonna wait for ten more minutes, that she'd call me then and head home. She never called me back, so I thought that he was just running late, and that it all worked out. I was so happy for her. I couldn't wait for her to get back and tell me about all the wonderful things she'd seen, things that I'll never see. But now that she's gone . . ." Noemi closed her eyes and her shoulders slumped.

"Has anyone called Christopher to let him know that Tamar . . . ?"

"No."

"Does Detective Sherwood know about him?"

"Can you tell him?" Noemi asked with pleading eyes. "Because if I do, then my father will know that I knew about him, and—"

The doorbell rang.

Noemi spun away from the sound as though Reverend Haist had heard every word she'd said. She looked back to me, bug-eyed, hands clenching and releasing. "Please, Miss McKay. I know I keep asking you to do this and do that, but—" The bell rang again and Noemi moved toward the door with frightened eyes. "Stay as long as you need," she said, then disappeared down the hallway.

Cheese and rice, what a mess.

I kneeled before the bookcase and ran my fingers over the spines of *The Purpose Driven Life, Lies Women Believe,* Christian romance novels, books on prophecy, and stories about great women of the Bible.

I slid open the closet door and found plain frocks made of rayon and cotton blends. Unflattering, uninteresting, straight-out yikes. I peered into the back of the space and moved the last Dress Barn item to find a black Hervé Léger bandage dress, size zero. I pulled the dress off the rack and held it out before me. The price tag still hung from the bodice. A gift from Christopher? I'm sure if I searched hard enough, I'd also find a box of fancy La Perla lace undies hidden beneath a bushel of Hanes cotton briefs.

I lay the dress across the bed and opened the nightstand. A quick search through the top drawer resulted in a book of crossword puzzles, a bottle of eye drops, a box of tissue, and . . . *Brown Sugar: Erotica for Sistas.*

I opened the book to page 27.

I kissed him, then flung my head back. He tugged at my bra, and slipped off my panties. Our eyes met in the reflection of the full-length mirror. Brown, sexy bodies. Chocolate love. I watched his hands slide down my luscious, thick hips, and moaned as his fingers, thick and sweet as Twix, slipped into my moist—

Yep. That's Afro-erotica. Us sistas love us some sweet, thick Twix fingers.

The title page had an inscription. *To my wicked Angel. You are my Fire. You are my happily ever after. Love, Chris.*

"Shit." I closed the book.

With those few words, I saw Tamar Haist rushing off an airplane in the Bahamas, wearing that sexy black dress that showed off her legs and ass, wearing Manolos that hadn't been broken in. I saw her strolling along the shore, holding hands with Christopher. Saw her sip her first strawberry daiquiri, then dance the merengue as the sun kissed her bare shoulders.

"You almost made it," I whispered, studying that inscription again.

Wicked Angel . . .

Young Tamar would not live that life of love and bliss, and that violent theft of her happiness made my heart scream.

15

Sweat socks, exhaust fumes, mildew, desperation . . . He hates the smell of the old minivan. He's not a snob, but he prefers to drive newer cars with leather seats, automatic locks and windows, and clean carpets. He'd be a fool, though, to take a Lexus, a BMW, or even a decent Camry, to the ghetto. The crackheads, hookers, and winos don't have enough sense to succeed in school or on an honest job, but they'd remember any car worth more than $5,000.

Minivans work well in these situations. Police officers rarely suspect the guy driving one—guys with families and dead-end jobs, who eat chili Frito pie every Thursday night. And the girls see his plain, old car and think that he's like the other johns—an unhappy husband in search of an illicit BJ before returning to that stupid nine-to-five, to that succubus wife and to that chipped plate of Frito pie.

He's supposed to be mourning with his people, but he's tapped out. He has no more tears. Parked in the Auto Track store lot across from the Burger King, he rolls down the window and snaps a few quick shots of the Snooty Fox Motor Inn. The motel is a toxic dump. Black stains—old blood—have been stomped into the carpets, and dried, mustard-colored urine darkens the toilet seats. Random strawberries knock on your room door in the middle of the night, asking for crack in exchange for sex.

Western Avenue is quiet now—the sun won't set for hours and the working poor are still climbing on and off buses, carrying grocery bags or pushing overstuffed laundry carts down the block. On the sidewalks, heaps of burned aluminum squares and crushed glass vials pile next to crooked and crusted spoons. Puddles of blood dry beside week-old crimson stains. Wide-eyed, God-fearing people hurry down these streets to hide in their homes before the monsters come.

Once darkness settles over the city, the girls buzz out of their swamps like West Nile mosquitoes.

It's the women who started it all. The pimps, johns, and drug dealers all come because of the women.

And since the city won't take out the trash, he does it for them.

Now, though, he will pretend to enjoy his burger and wait for the one he's selected.

Even in his choosing, he is not like the others.

Deviant sexual fantasies don't drive him like they drove the BTK Killer. He doesn't kill to appease Satan like Richard Ramirez. He doesn't target children like John Wayne Gacy, *sick fuck, thank you, death penalty.* Cannibalism and Jeffrey Dahmer? What the wicked hell was that? No rape. No torture. No eating. No depravity.

He laughs—*no depravity.* More than one shrink would disagree with him on that.

Once he spots the "chosen one," he finds out more about her. A name. Any family. An arrest record. He stops by her place, most times a dump that should've been torn down after the riots. He keeps all his data on index cards stowed away in his garage. Some call this *stalking.* He calls it *information gathering.* When it is time for her to go, he gathers his tools—he only needs two: his camera and a .38. Efficient.

A cop car cruises down Western and slows near the Snooty Fox.

Who are they?

He has taken pictures of all the policemen who patrol this strip of Los Angeles, and he doesn't recognize the two young Latino officers in the black and white. Rookies? Transfers? *Can't take any chances. No more pictures today.* Nauseous, he shoves the rest of the burger into the bag and starts the car.

Two hours later, he pulls into his driveway.

Skin burning, he watches the garage door raise, then eases the minivan in between his mountain bike and an ancient elliptical machine. He turns off the car and sits. Listens as the garage door rumbles back down, listens to the engine tick as it cools off. He stares at the metal pegboard that holds saws, hammers, wrenches . . .

He enters the house from the garage. The curtains are drawn and the living room is dark and cool. The smell isn't too bad today. But it's there. Even with lime and time, he can still smell it.

He has no neighbors anymore. Not really. In this part of Southern California, seventy-five miles from the city, every other house has been foreclosed on. Nature is taking back the land. Thigh-high weeds grow in the yards. Coyotes roam the streets. Mosquitoes breed in neglected swimming pools. No working streetlights since thieves have stolen copper from every fixture in this ghost town.

His had been a nice home. Anonymous and generic in that Insta-House way. Cream carpets. High cathedral ceilings. A ridiculously large main bedroom.

But now, the carpets . . . Can't even see the carpets. Photo equipment and dirty dishes cover every flat surface. Cobwebs hang like dusty rags from the high ceilings. And that smell . . .

He steps over the piles of camera parts, crumpled photo paper, and fast-food bags. He stumbles over sandals and soiled panties. He had two cats, a gray tabby and a calico, but they are lost somewhere in the house. Something crunches underfoot—could be a used hypodermic needle. Or a cat.

He glances up the staircase, to the bedroom where she lies. He will visit Esther later. Let her rest for now.

He rushes to his computer desk in the south corner, finds the USB cable, and attaches it to the digital camera. As the photos download onto his hard drive, he closes his eyes and calls up the image of the writer.

Syeeda McKay is nothing like his girlfriend Esther. His angel is pure. She never curses. She never uses her tongue when she kisses him. He can finish her sentences because she is that predictable.

The writer, though. Vulgar. Far from a virgin. Obviously. Sherwood wouldn't buzz around her like that if she wasn't laying it down.

The photos flash across the screen. They're all pretty good, and he thanks his dead parents for sending him to photography lessons.

He selects the picture of Syeeda McKay standing in the alley just yesterday, alone, fear stark on her face. She had sensed someone watching her. He could tell by her wide eyes, by the way she hugged herself. She had seen the flash from his camera, but probably told herself that it had only been her imagination. He chuckles, traces his finger across her face. *Nope. I was there.*

He turns to survey the living room—it's a mess. He must clean before she comes. She's anal-retentive. Always buying paper towels. Always using napkins to blot her mouth and fingers. Never leaves a mess at the coffee shop. If he wants her to complete her chore, his home cannot be a hostile working environment. So he must make it nice. He'll drive to IKEA and buy some new furniture. An area rug. Fake flowers.

Yeah, that'll be good.

He hits "print" and the photo printer springs to life. He rummages through the mess on the floor and finds the right frame. So silver it's almost white. Metal. Cold.

The picture slips out of the printer. He waits a moment to let it dry. No smudges. He plucks the photo from the tray and slips it into the frame. Grabs his keys from the desk and steps over the mess to reach the basement door.

He unlocks the door and takes the stairs down to the cleanest room in the house. The stink of his dead ones is strongest here. He had pulled up the bloody carpet and bleached the walls and ground, and poured new concrete twice. Still, that smell . . . And that is why he kills them now in the alleys. To keep their filth with the filth.

He turns on the light and his throat constricts. *Beautiful.*

His collection almost covers two walls. Picture after picture, black and white, sepia, color, overexposed, hang in neat rows. Photos of the women before and photos of them after.

Angie Kane's is one of his favorites. She had been working when he met her in an alley not far from Great Redeemer. Watching her down there on the dirty asphalt, on her knees, made his stomach sour, and he had pulled away from her before she could finish him off. She had taunted him, called him "limp dick," had told him that he still had to pay her. That sneer on her junkie face had pissed him off as she kept teasing him about his withering manhood, and he had pulled the gun on her just like that, he told her that she was trash, nothing but a whore, and *boom!* Afterward, he had snapped his Polaroid—he had brought it with him for other reasons, but why not use it now? He hadn't waited for the picture to develop before throwing a few filled trash bags over her body. He had darted back to the car, and by the time he pulled back onto Western Avenue, the photograph had revealed itself.

The evening news never mentioned a woman murdered in an alley in South Los Angeles, and no one put up any flyers looking for her. Angie had been a No One. She'd never paid taxes. She'd never had a job outside of selling her rotting body. She hadn't contributed one positive thing to society. Who would miss her? Drunken johns? Violent pimps? The roaches and fleas that shared her mattress?

A church deacon found her three days later.

That had been eighteen years ago.

Then, there was LaTasha Owens, his 1991 mission.

And Denesha Jackson—1994.

Katrina Finney—1995.

Monique Vaughn: That had been more of a charity case. She hadn't even been on the streets for a year when she died. But she had been on the road to becoming another Katrina, another Denesha. So in 2000, he put Monique out of her misery.

Stevie in 2001 and Paula in 2007—he couldn't remember their last names. One had claimed that she hadn't been a working girl, that she had been dressed like that because she was going to a pool party. A pool party in that part of town? There weren't any private pools in the ghetto.

He grabs a hammer and drives a nail into the drywall.

Seconds later, Syeeda McKay's picture hangs in front of him. It is her before shot. And soon? Very soon, he will have the after.

And it will be beautiful.

16

I didn't leave Tamar Haist's neighborhood right away. As soon as I climbed back into my car, I grabbed the notepad from my bag and wrote down everything I had seen and heard—from the Barbie collection and dowdy decoy dresses to the Tiffany boxes and stowed-away erotica. I had taken pictures of her apartment with my phone, and now, slipped through each photograph to prompt my memory.

Toni had called during my visit with the Haists and had left a message inviting Lena and me to join her that night for dinner. *How about tapas at Cobras y Matadors? My treat. And I'll scoop you up so you won't have to drive.* Once upon a time, like the day before Dr. Yu called me with bad news, I would have ignored Toni's attempts to refriend me. Twenty years ago, she had called me a bitter dyke—you just don't forget insults like that, especially since I had been far from bitter. And just yesterday, she had implied that I was too old to have a baby, that without a husband I was in danger of becoming a nonperson, a bag of bones, lint.

But that was yesterday. Life was short and Toni was paying for tapas. I sent her a text—I'd love to. As Lena would say, *"Laissez les bons temps rouler!"* Let the good times roll, indeed.

Back to the photos. *Diamond studs . . . Kimora Barbie . . .*

My phone chimed: a text from Spencer. Meet me in the parking lot on lvl 2 @ 3:00.

That left me twenty minutes to drive to Mission Road.

I sent him a one-word response—Okay—then started the car.

I called Lena as I raced onto the freeway. Told her about my visit with Tamar's family, about the jewelry, and the designer dress hidden in the closet.

"Are you kidding me?" she screeched. "How could she afford a Hervé Léger on her salary? Is he designing dresses for Target now?"

"There's a rich, older boyfriend her father knew nothing about," I said. "Her sister Noemi let me take the dress."

"To do what with?" she asked.

"No idea."

"This is so sad."

"Oh, and Noemi wants me to tell Adam about Tamar's secret lover."

"Why are you getting involved?" she asked. "None of this is directly related to the Slayer project. I mean, yeah, Tamar's a victim, but you've never acted as an errand girl for the other victims' families. You have to stay focused, Sy. *Slayer, Slayer, he's our man, if we can't catch him—*"

"Did I hire you to keep me focused?"

"You hired me cuz you think I'm hot." She paused. "Grace called. She said that she's cool with the Tamar Haist angle but she'll still need your article no later than Monday night if it's going in Tuesday's edition."

I sighed. "I have no idea what to send her."

"And that's why you should pass on this side quest," Lena said. "Write the fluffy story about Tamar when there's a lull in the larger Slayer case. What's two weeks?"

"Yeah, I know, but . . ."

In the public's flabby minds, fourteen days was the equivalent of fourteen years.

"I still don't understand," I said. "Why did Tamar send me that message? And if she didn't send that message, who did?"

"Who knows?" Lena said. "Maybe the Slayer bought her those diamond earrings."

Mission Road's parking garage was dark and cold. The morning shift had ended, and nurses from Women's and Children's Hospital next door climbed into their cars, weary from caring for patients and their families since midnight. They certainly didn't notice Spencer and me strolling around the lot's edges.

Forensic investigators had found Tamar's black Motorola Razr beneath the Neon's passenger seat. "Her fingerprints were the only ones on the phone," Spencer said. "And we pulled her records. Text messages from a 'Chris' all Tuesday afternoon."

"Noemi Haist said that Tamar had a secret boyfriend named Christopher."

Spencer blinked. "A boyfriend?"

I nodded. "And the parents have no clue."

"Does Sherwood know?"

"Not yet."

He rolled this nugget around his mind. "This changes some things."

"How?"

He reached into his pocket and pulled out a folded square of paper. "Don't lose this. It's the only copy I could print out without someone asking why a medical examiner would need phone records."

12:25: Lets meet @ Houstons @8 for r Special nite. Chris

3:29: I luv u baby. Chris

7:02: Send me a pic so I can c ur prtty face. Chris

"No more messages after that last one," Spencer said. "No activity at all until she texted you early Wednesday morning."

"Did they trace the number that sent the texts?"

"The message came from one of those prepaid cell phones. No contract. No credit check. No deposit. We do know that whoever purchased it got it from one of those carousels set up in the middle of Fox Hills Mall."

"That's no help."

"Adam's still having his team scour through the contracts."

"To look for . . . ?"

Spencer shrugged. "I may have some good news later today. We're tracing the serial numbers on Tamar's silicone implants."

"You're tracing what now in the huh?"

"There's a barcode on every breast implant sold," Spencer explained. "Tracking numbers that connect the wearer to her medical records. For the medical staff, in case there's a problem."

"Maybe we can find out how she paid for them," I said. "Or *who* paid for them since they're what, at least five grand each? Definitely more than what a fired church secretary could afford. And if Christopher bought them, maybe we can trace the payments and get his full name and an address. Talk to him and find out what happened on Tuesday night."

"Exactly," he said. "But that doesn't answer the big question: Who sent you that message? Maybe this Christopher *is* involved. Maybe he broke up with her and it ended badly. Violently. Maybe he tried to cover his tracks, acting like the Slayer to throw us off the trail."

A twisted smile found my lips. "You sound like me."

He choked himself. "Kill me now!"

"I'll kill you later. But first: Can I have the number to that disposable phone?"

"Nope," Spencer said as we approached my car. "Don't think that would be a good idea. It would be obvious who gave it to you, and there goes our little arrangement. But I'll see what I can do."

As he headed toward the exit, I plopped into the driver's seat. I studied the transcript of Tamar's last text messages.

I luv u baby.

Didn't seem like Christopher had planned to break up with her. How could he go from a special night at Houston's at eight o'clock to "It's not you, it's me" two hours later? And worse: How could he shoot her in the face?

But that's how it goes: Love and hate fitting on the same cracker.

I stuffed the report into my purse and reached for the ignition.

A piece of folded green paper was stuck beneath my windshield wiper.

I opened the door and pulled the paper from the blade. My eyes fixed on the paragraph written in green ink:

> Dearest Syeeda,
> I hope you liked the fruit basket I sent you yestrday. We have not talked for a long time. I am sorry for that. Just wanted you to know that I'm still here and I care for you very deeply. I told the detective today. I would never never hurt you. Not never. Because I am a very caring person. Christmas will be here soon and I am looking at vaireous items for you. Do you like gold or silver? Please let me know. I care for you very very deeply and always will.
> Always and forever,
> Deon Jackson

I glanced around the garage to see if my stalker was still around.

A nurse in a yellow Camaro ate Cheetos and talked on a cell phone.

An old couple sat in a Buick and stared through the windshield.

A teenage couple in a souped-up Honda Civic made out as though no one else was around.

No stocky Black man sitting behind the wheel of a Ford Aerostar.

I slipped Deon Jackson's note into my bag, then called Adam.

He answered on the first ring. "What's up, love?"

"Guess who left a note on my car?"

17

After Kenyon had cashed his first big check as a film director, he bought my parents a modest two-story home in Baldwin Hills. My father died twelve years later, leaving the property to slowly waste away. Mom's neighbors, also retired but better off, said nothing about the disrepair, but their eyes always lingered on the peeling paint and the cracks in the driveway, on those crusty rain gutters and that crumbling brickwork. Pride and mourning made Mom refuse to let Kenyon or me pay for repairs. "I'm not poor," she'd say. "I'll get to it."

She still has yet to *get to it.*

Mom plopped into the passenger seat of my car, and we tucked into ten minutes of chitchat—*how are you, how's church, talk to Eva, talk to Kenyon, why didn't you call yesterday?*

"I had a nightmare last night," she said. "I dreamed that stalker broke into your house and beat you up. I couldn't go back to sleep after that. Almost got in the car and drove over to your place but remembered that the car was in the shop."

"Just a nightmare," I said with a shake of my head, deciding not to mention Deon Jackson's fruit basket.

She flapped her hands at her shiny face, then punched the air conditioner button to its highest setting. "I actually slept soundly when what's-his-face stayed overnight. Of course, it bothered me that you two were practically living together in . . . in . . ."

I smiled at her. "In sin?"

Mom checked her fingernails. "Yes, unless it's called something else now. Anyway, I was relieved that you weren't living in that big house all by yourself."

"Mom, you live in a big house all by yourself."

She flicked her hand. "Whoop-de-do. I've lived a full life. Had a great job, a wonderful marriage, talented children." She touched my knee and squeezed. "I want you to have all of that and more, and I don't want some ignorant nigger, excuse my use of the word, with a sick mind and a hatred of women messing everything up for you."

"Got it."

"But then you broke up with what's-his-name, just when you needed him most. But that's what you do when relationships get serious. Eva thinks you like dating people who stress you out, men who don't demand that you stay put. And I think she's right. Like that crackhead. He didn't ask you for anything except money to buy dope."

I rolled my eyes and sucked my teeth, sixteen years old all over again. "He wasn't doing coke when we were together."

"What about the one who stole from your checking account and used your car in that bank robbery?"

I gripped the steering wheel tighter. "I was never serious about him."

"Not that this policeman is any better," she said, shaking her head. "A cop, Sy?"

"Detective."

"Whatever. They're not stable enough to have healthy marriages. I read in the paper that more and more police officers are taking their own lives—"

"Adam's not that guy. And I'm comfortable with him. He's not the angry, jealous type, and when we were together, random women weren't calling his cell phone."

Mom whispered, "I guess that's something."

"If it makes you feel better, Spencer's talking to me again. Guess he's forgiven me for writing the rat story."

"Why can't you write Christian fiction?" she asked, reaching for another of her memes.

"Because I don't."

"And your doctor's appointment?" she asked.

"It's in two weeks."

"Do they know why you . . . ? How you . . . ? You know?"

I glanced over at her—she was tugging at her lower lip just like I did anytime I worried. "If you're asking me if my cancer was genetic, and whether you should be worried, don't be. It's pretty rare. Eva's lump is probably benign."

Her shoulders drooped some. Relief.

"At my last appointment, Dr. Yu mentioned putting me on tamoxifen. It's a drug that stops the production of estrogen, which then decreases my cancer risk. I'd have to take it for five years, though."

Mom frowned. "No estrogen for five years?"

I nodded. "I would be forty-three years old when I'd pop my last pill." I glanced at her, wondering if she understood all that I hadn't said—no estrogen, no pregnancy. No pregnancy, no grandchildren.

But she didn't speak and chose to stare out the windshield.

"In other news," I said, my voice weak, "a source for my story? I found her dead yesterday morning."

"What?" Mom shouted. Her hands clenched around the handles of her purse. "Where?"

I filled her in on Tamar Haist—I was all smiles and excitement now that I had gained more than twenty-four hours' worth of distance from standing in that alleyway.

"Oh my lord, Syeeda," Mom whispered. Then, she muttered about sex work, dangerous parts of the city, that I had a death wish, and *somethingsomethingsomething.*

I sighed, rubbed my forehead. "It's my job, Mom."

"I should've forced you to be a candy striper," she said, "instead of letting you do that internship at the paper."

"I still would've found my way to the psych ward."

"Or the morgue," she said, shaking her head.

"Life ain't as sanitized as it is in those Christian romance novels you read. And this Slayer case. It's the first time I've felt focused, anchored to something bigger, more important than sorority life and designer shoes. I can't give this up. Not for anyone."

She sucked her teeth, then looked out the window. "You keep me on my knees, Syeeda Michelle McKay. Prostitution? Stalkers? *Guns?* I only wish that you wouldn't go around looking for bad things—evil finds you on its own and needs no help." She shook her head and muttered something else. "Anyway, I talked to your aunt Linda today. She says hello and told me to tell you that you're on her prayer list. She wants to know when we're coming to Phoenix."

Mom's sister Linda kept me on her prayer list. I've been on it since she caught me holding hands with Alonzo Green at vacation Bible school when I was eight years old.

"Maybe we can visit for Thanksgiving," I told Mom. "I'll check my calendar to see if I have plans."

"Remember your friend Tammi from church?" Mom asked. "Found out that she's having twins."

I said, "Wow."

"And Joelle—"

"How is she? I need to call her."

"She's finally getting married."

"Wow."

"Her fiancé works for IBM," Mom added.

Then, silence.

"So are you still seeing that detective?" Mom glanced at me. "I know you keep telling me his name, but I can never remember."

"Adam Sherwood." I gripped the steering wheel tighter. "And I am. Kind of. It's complicated." Her gaze warmed my cheek—she wanted to hear more. I took a deep breath. "I met his family last weekend. They came down from San Francisco. Nice people. His father's a judge on the Ninth Circuit Court of Appeals, and his mother teaches ballet." I snuck a peek at her. "Adam wishes he'd met you before that day at the hospital. Maybe we can have him over for dinner one Sabbath."

"Is he Adventist?"

I said, "Nope."

Mom clucked her tongue and gazed out the window.

I swallowed a few times, irritated and prickly. "I got your email yesterday. I didn't have that form of breast cancer, though."

"I thought you'd find it helpful," she said.

"I did."

"You know how I am. I see something and I send it on."

"Yes. Thank you."

"What's that drug called? What your doctor was recommending?"

"Tamoxifen."

"Hmm." She opened her purse and pulled out a thick white envelope. "Before I forget . . . I clipped you some coupons. There's one in there for that yogurt you like." She stuck the envelope in the glove compartment and pawed through the space to hunt for condoms or Uzis. "Now that Eva's set me up on the computer, I can't get off the internet. I can buy all kinds of things without leaving the house."

I made a left turn into the mechanic's yard, then glanced at my mother. "But you need to leave the house. That's why the doctor said you have a vitamin D deficiency, which I thought was impossible since you live in Los Angeles. You have to take care of yourself, Mom. We have the trip in April. You can't be sick on the Champs-Élysées."

She nodded. "I do need to get out in that garden, but . . ." She glanced at me. "Your dad and I used to work in the yard every Sunday, remember? He'd lift those heavy bags of potting soil and fertilizer, and yank the weeds. Kenny's always on some movie set somewhere, not that he ever liked dirt. And since Dad died . . . There are just some things men are supposed to do around the house, you know?"

I pulled into a parking space, feeling like shit.

Earl, Mom's service adviser, waved to us and pointed to Mom's Volvo.

"He should be smiling," Mom mumbled. "Charging me a fortune. Brakes should not cost that much, and the car ain't even that old."

"I'll pay for it, Mom."

"Oh, sweetheart," she said, "I wasn't asking you to—"

"I insist." *That* I could do for her.

I reached to open the car door, but Mom found my other hand. "Syeeda, I want the best for you. All mothers want the best for their daughters. And I don't want you to be alone. Forgive me if I . . ." She touched her heart. "If I voice my opinions too much. I just want you to be happy."

"I am happy." I slipped on my sunglasses before she saw the tears in my eyes.

18

Mom pulled onto Crenshaw Boulevard in her repaired Volvo.

I waved to her, and headed back home and back to Tamar Haist.

In just twenty-four hours, I had filled more than half the pages of the notebook I had started for "T. H." And still, none of us—Spencer, Adam, or I—had yet to discover the real Tamar. The former church secretary had been a complex bird. She didn't completely match the profile of the Slayer's other victims, nor did she match the profile of an innocent who had accidentally stumbled in front of a gun.

She was like the rest of us—a little bit country and a little bit rock and roll.

Adam had left a voicemail message on my home phone, and I listened to it while sifting through the day's mail.

Hey, love. Just calling to check in . . .

Phone bill. Mortgage statement. *Vanity Fair* and *Essence.*

Talked to your friend Deon Jackson. Asked him if he had been contacting you lately, and reminded him about the restraining order . . .

I pulled out a large manila envelope that had been stuck between the pages of *Essence.* My name and address had been written with thick black marker. Didn't know the return address. *5438 Pacific Coast Highway, Santa Monica.* A Love stamp sat in the upper-right corner.

Anyway, be careful. If he comes around again, let me know and I'll personally arrest his dumb ass.

I plopped on the couch and tossed all but the manila envelope on the coffee table. *Who lives on PCH?* I tore open the flap and pulled out a two-page document. Stapled. Typewritten. Single spaced. "Finding Piece (Peace) of Mind." I flipped to the second page and found the author: *With all my love, Krystal.*

What. The. *Hell?*

Krystal Miller and Toni Fortune had been college roommates and best friends. In fact, we had all hung out together. A drunk and a chronic booster, Krystal had dropped out during our senior year. Between the DUIs and stints in jail for shoplifting, she didn't have time for Feminism in Chicano Culture and Twentieth-Century World Literature.

I last saw Krystal five years ago, the night of our ten-year college reunion. She came even though she hadn't graduated. Guess she remembered that, and wouldn't leave the bar to join our group. We spent that night looking at her over our shoulders. As she got drunker, her tiny white dress got higher in some places and lower in others. She eventually left the restaurant with a benchwarmer from the LA Clippers. I never saw her again.

And now, here she was, in letter form.

> Dear Syeeda:
> A lot has happened in my life. Some good. Some bad. Right now, I am faced with some challenges, and I need to resolve some issues. Some of these issues involve you. And although this will come off as negative, please keep in mind that I'm saying this with love in my heart. So, here goes:
> Syeeda, I didn't really like you. Even when we hung out at school, I had a problem with you. You thought you were so funny and so charming. You always pretended to be so nice and everybody's friend, but I'm not stupid. You used your words like swords to hurt people. Your constant put-downs and witty

retorts drove me to drink. Trying to be as cute as you and as smart as you helped make me the mess I am today because I never felt good enough.

Remember that night you and Patrick hooked up? After I had spent months doing his papers, cooking his dinner, washing his clothes and everything? I loved him like I've never loved anybody. But you slept with him anyway.

There was also the time you became secretary of our prepledge chapter. I wanted to be secretary, but somehow, you convinced the other girls that you could do a better job because you were a writer. I was a writer, too, Syeeda. I wrote that poem for the Black Alumni reception.

Yeah, I read your books. You still think that you're clever. You're not. (And yeah, I wrote those negative reviews on Amazon and I meant EVERY. SINGLE. WORD.) Who do you think you are, writing mean things about us? Saying that I had herpes or whatever?

Yes, I hooked and shot up and drank, but my heart and my love and loyalty were always purer than yours. You took so much from me in those four years in Santa Cruz, but no more. NO WEAPON FORMED AGAINST ME SHALL PROSPER!!!! (Isaiah 54:17)

I feel sorry for you, Syeeda. Either you have mental problems, or you're naturally evil. I don't appreciate you making fun of me, even if you change my name.

In Matthew 5:43–44, Jesus said, "You have heard that it was said, 'Love your neighbor and hate your enemy. But I tell you: Love your enemies and pray for those who persecute you.'" So, I will pray for you as I strive to be a better person. I hope my wake-up call helps you, too. You are pretty, but your heart needs work. Get to it before it's too late.

With all my love,

Krystal

Love?

What the hell *was* this?

I never set out to take anything from Krystal Miller, nor did I live to make her look stupid. And that chlamydia-having character in *Pledged* was a composite of my friends *and* me, with Krystal representing 1/16 of the "Dana" character. And the secretary thing . . . *sweet crap on a cracker.* I was the secretary of our group at the beginning of the pledge process and so it made sense that I remain secretary once we crossed. And Krystal never crossed because Alpha Kappa Alpha, Incorporated didn't cross dropouts.

Running into Toni. Getting a letter from Krystal. Was this some twisted version of *This is Your Life?* Who would show up next? The girl who had pushed me that day in '78 on the tetherball court? My piano teacher who had rapped my knuckles with her ruler?

Wounded, I lay across the couch, knees to my chest, exhausted from countering each of Krystal's accusations. Being called "evil" by a woman I had loaned money to and shared drinks with, who came home with me during quarter breaks because she didn't want to return to Compton and to her embarrassing, dysfunctional family? It hurt like hell. How could she write something like this? And then *send* it? And why send it now?

I drove her around Los Angeles.

I typed her papers.

I spoke to her when no one would.

When I left the house three hours later, I was still pissed. Had I imagined being a sister to Krystal? I would never be voted Miss Congeniality, but I *was* loyal, ride-or-die for those I loved. Krystal had been a part of that circle.

I had to force myself off my living room couch and into Toni's black Yukon. I had not found the will to change clothes.

Toni wore a tight, gray, scooped-neck dress and more ice than a rapper. Lena, wearing some *confection* of tulle and satin, had been waiting for Toni and me at the restaurant. As soon as they saw each other, Toni and Lena shrieked, hugged, hopped up and down.

That dress is wow!

I must own those shoes.

The girl who does my hair . . .

Hate, hate, hate.

We have to go.

Fabulous!

It's a serious matter.

Indeed.

Lena turned to me and eyed my black chinos, black *Star Wars* T-shirt, and black Cons. "Did you think we were going to a comic book convention? Having dinner with The Simpsons and Batman?"

Toni laughed.

I said, "Ha."

Lena cocked an eyebrow. "What did Adam do this time?"

"Wasn't Adam," I muttered as I sat at our table.

Couldn't share Krystal's letter right then. It stung too much to think about it, and it shamed me—someone in the world, someone I knew and had cared about, despised me enough to send hate mail.

On my third helping of paella, I pulled the envelope from my bag and I handed it to Lena without comment.

She said, "Is this why you've been so sullen throughout this, our glorious reunion?"

I stared at the pitcher of sangria as she and Toni read Krystal's letter. So much noise. Clanking glasses and dishes. Drunken shouts from birthday party guests three tables away.

Lena looked at me and shook her head. "This is wack."

"Wanna do a drive-by beating?" Toni asked. "It'll be just like it was in college."

Lena chuckled. "Good times. Sisters sticking together."

I slapped the tabletop, not ready to laugh. "How in the hell did I use words to hurt her? How can she even claim that I stole the secretary position from her—?"

"Way the hell back in college," Toni said, shaking her head.

Lena said, "Bitch was crazy in 1988. Bitch is crazy in 2008. *Ce n'est pas grave.* Whatever, Sy." Then, she raised her glass to her lips and took a long, greedy gulp.

I slumped in my chair. "It *does* matter, Lena. When I'm being mean, it's always with intent, always with purpose. But Krystal's saying that I leak evil like it's a hormone."

Toni's eyes skipped down the page. At one point, she laughed and said, "This is straight comedy." She plucked a bacon-wrapped prawn from the platter and laughed again.

Lena turned to Toni. "Your homegirl is sick."

"*Ex*-homegirl," Toni said as she rubbed a purple scratch on her forearm. "I haven't talked to Krystal in ten years, nor am I interested in talking to her now. She was a total time vampire. Just sucked all my energy. She's not like you, Sy. Krystal's . . . off."

"We saw her at the reunion," Lena said. "And Sy tried to get her to come over—"

"But she just grinned at me like an idiot and said, 'I will. I will.'" I tore at a napkin. "I went out of my way to include her and she sends me *this*?"

Toni took my hand and squeezed it. "You wanna know why? Because she needs help. Here you are, trying to save lives, trying to find a serial killer, and Krystal's writing *this* shit. Has she forgotten that *you* were the one who made us buy her books that semester? That you tutored her and tried to keep her lazy ass from dropping out?" She nodded to the letter. "That would scare me off opening manila envelopes for the rest of my life."

I blinked. "I'm not evil, am I?"

Lena said, "Oh, sweetie. Not all the time."

"Krystal was always jealous of you, Sy," Toni said. "You're pretty and smart. You grew up just as poor as she did, but you never stank of desperation. You're not an attention whore, you know?" She waited a beat, then said, "You know what she does for a living, right?"

"Let me guess," I said. "She writes greeting cards."

"She's still hooking," Toni said with a crooked smile. "She's charging thousands for it now instead of Big Macs and M&M's."

I screeched, "You've got to be kidding me."

Lena threw her hands in the air and called on the Lord.

"So being with Patrick would've kept her from going full-time?" I asked. "And somehow, her life choices are *my* fault? And for the record, I didn't *steal* Patrick from her. He hated Krystal, and he used her like all the guys did."

"Sy," Toni said, "all of this is beneath you. Enjoy your night out with friends who actually care about you, okay?" She pushed the plate of prawns in front of me. "Let it go. Eat a shrimp."

With my blood pressure jacked up to 175/100 from all the salty Spanish food, asking me to let go of anything was like asking a golden retriever to let go of a leather pump. "I'm gonna have to bail and go find a cave somewhere to chill out because all of this is becoming too much. Between the surgery, and this book, and another dead girl . . ."

Lena was staring at the pitcher of sangria, not saying much.

"What's wrong with you?" I asked.

"Just thinking about your dead unicorn." She gazed at me. "Homeboy killed her. What's his name? Christopher? He lied to her. He wasn't divorced. I bet you he was still married." She plucked two olives from the bowl and stuffed them in her mouth.

"Divorced men do exist," I pointed out. "Your ex-husband, for instance."

"What's up with the sister?" Toni asked. "I saw her on the news."

"Noemi?" I shrugged. "She's an old-maid-to-be who teaches five-year-olds and can't understand how her sister landed a rich, handsome man."

"Maybe she killed Tamar," Toni offered. "Jealousy makes people do stupid things, like shoot people in the face."

"Like Amy what's-her-name?" Lena said. "Long Island Lolita?"

"She jacked up poor Mrs. Buttafuoco," I said. "Lady can't even talk right anymore. But no—Noemi lived vicariously through her sister. She wouldn't kill her."

"Okayokayokay," Lena said, leaning forward. "So here's my theory: Tamar and Christopher, for whatever reason, are standing in the alley behind the church. They're talking about their relationship, and he tells her that he can't see her anymore, that he's married and that he still loves his wife.

"Tamar's shocked. *Shocked,* I say, because she had no effin' clue. He claims that he didn't mean to hurt her, that he's sorry, but Tamar ain't having it and threatens to tell the wife. Christopher doesn't appreciate her threatening him and warns her to stay away from his family. Tamar says that she's gonna tell it all—about the affair, about the jewelry and clothes he bought her, the vacations . . .

"She starts to get in her car, but he grabs her. She slaps him. He slaps her back. She hits him again, harder this time. He punches her in the face. They're going back and forth like this until he shoves her away and pulls a gun from his coat pocket.

"Tamar freezes, apologizes, swears that she'll keep her mouth shut. He doesn't believe her and he pulls the trigger. Shoots her in the face. After she collapses, he grabs a bag from the dumpster and throws it over her." Satisfied, Lena nodded and said, "The end."

"So, to make a short story long," Toni said.

"Well, I'm impressed," I said, clapping my hands.

"But Tamar had to know about the wife," Toni said. "At our age, if he was straight and successful, of course he'd be married."

I held up my hand. "My last boyfriend was successful, straight, and has never been married."

"Exception to the rule," Toni said. "And why did Christopher have a gun?"

"Maybe he's a cop," I theorized. "Maybe he had his service pistol on him."

"Cops are issued .40 calibers at *least*," Toni pointed out. "She wouldn't have had a head left if he shot her at point-blank range with a .40."

Lena nodded. "Maybe it was his personal gun. A smaller caliber, like a .22 or a .25."

"It was a .38," Toni said.

"You're the authority?" Lena asked.

"Between the three of us? Yes. My husband was SWAT. And I've seen what a .38 can do."

"Guess his expertise trickles down, then," I said, rolling my eyes.

"Have you ever fired a gun?" Toni asked me.

I nodded. "Just a few months ago. Adam took me to the firing range. I have a Glock."

"But not a .38?" she asked.

"Glocks are nine millimeters."

"Exactly," Toni said. "You still have less experience than me."

"Who cares?" Lena said. "Tamar Haist is still dead. Maybe Christopher was planning to kill her all along."

Toni narrowed her eyes. "And he shot her in the face because . . . ?"

"To make her murder seem related to the Phantom Slayer murders," I said.

"That's possible, but . . ." Toni shook her head. "Even if he did break up with her, he doesn't sound like a man who's bought this woman thousands of dollars in jewelry and dresses. So his wife finds out? Who cares? He probably shuts her up with a few Kobe Bryant specials, diamond rings as big as Sherman tanks. Unless he's the president of the United States, what does he have to lose? Why risk it all and kill his mistress?"

We sat in silence as people laughed and shouted around us. Finally, Lena picked up the pitcher and looked around for our server. "I need more sangria."

Toni smirked. "Guess you're not cut out for being a crime reporter like Sy."

"Don't wanna be," Lena said. To me, she said, "I still say that you need to find this Christopher. He's not the Phantom Slayer, but I'll bet that he killed the unicorn. It's a fact: It's always the boyfriend."

19

After she and Lena had exchanged numbers and arranged a time to get waxed together, Toni and I climbed back into the Yukon.

I didn't talk much as my old friend jabbered about college days and the difficulty in finding a good wax woman in Los Angeles. Twenty minutes later, she pulled into my driveway and only unlocked the car door after I had accepted her dinner invitation for Sunday night. "Seven o'clock," she had shouted from the Yukon's window. "Don't forget."

I trudged into my living room, reeking of garlic and spilled sangria that I didn't even get to drink. I found the phone on the coffee table—the antennae's red light was blinking. Voicemail.

Message one: background noise for ten seconds until the caller decided to hang up.

The second message played as I pulled off my T-shirt and headed to the bathroom.

Hey, Sy.

Spencer.

I stopped in my step.

I have more information about the Tamar Haist case. Do you wanna meet for breakfast to go over everything? I'll be at Canter's at eight tomorrow morning . . .

Guess I was having breakfast at Canter's.

After washing my face, I switched on the television and found *March of the Penguins* on cable. I grabbed my laptop from the dresser and climbed into bed.

Six emails since last checking. Five of them from my mother—prayers and poems, and messages about Sony Ericsson giving away new laptops to people who forwarded this note to eight friends.

I paused at the message sent from "rwraith411." Didn't know anyone with this email address.

> Dearest Syeeda McKay. You do great work. This is for your next article. I have so much more to send you. But thou shalt open thine hand wide unto him and shalt surely lend him sufficient for his need, which he wanteth. A Fan.

O-kay.

I clicked on the JPEG that had been attached to the message.

A Black woman lay in a dim alley. Her face was a mess of bone and blood. The asphalt beneath her was wet with dark liquid. The neck of her white tank top was soaked crimson.

I startled, cried out "Shit," and watched as my laptop tumbled to the floor.

What the hell is that? What the HELL?

I retrieved my VAIO from the floor—it was still working—and forced myself to peer at the photograph again.

I didn't know this woman. She wasn't on my Death Wall. But her scraggly hair and the keloids on her arms from burns and needles suggested the type of life she had led.

Call Adam right now.

I stared at the picture a moment longer. *This could be a hoax.* After the *Times* had published my first article a year ago, I had received all kinds of kooky letters and pictures from people. I had forwarded every tip to Adam, not knowing if any of it would be helpful. After the two hundred and fiftieth false lead, Adam had stopped chasing, and I realized that some folks saw what we did as entertainment.

My pulse slowed as reason worked its magic. Yeah. A hoax. I hit "reply" and typed:

> Thank you for the picture. Don't know what you want
> me to do with it, though. Or what it's supposed to be.
> Cheers, S. McKay.

The woman in the picture could be very much alive, an actress working for her auteur boyfriend who had sought to publicize his movie via viral marketing. My brother *was* a big-time film director.

I glanced at the computer screen.

A new message from rwraith411.

> Today, I visited your home. Your friend greeted me
> at the door and told me you were on an errand.
> She was very nice to me. You look a little tired. I
> hope you are feeling well. Please stay strong. This
> journey is almost over. I will pray for you, so do not
> be troubled. Truly, I am with you always, even in
> the end time.
>
> I AM who you want. And to answer your question: I
> want you to share it with the world.
>
> Jesus loves you,
>
> P.S.

P.S.?

Phantom Slayer?

"No," I said, shaking my head. "That's impossible. That's . . ." I popped the rubber band on my wrist, knowing that all things were possible.

Another picture file had been attached to the message, and this time, I didn't rush to click on the icon. I sat there, barely breathing, staring at those words.

I AM who you want.

My finger double-tapped the tracking pad.

There I was, standing in the alley behind Andy's Liquor Emporium, behind yellow tape bright like sunshine. I remembered this day. July 3, 2007. My first crime scene.

During my ride-along with Adam, a call had come over his radio. *10-54. Possible dead body.* Adam flipped a switch and the car's emergency lights exploded with life. We had reached the alley behind a liquor store. Patrol cars and people were everywhere. Adam had hopped out of the Crown Vic as it had rolled to a stop. I had opened the door, and the smell hit me like an asteroid to the gut. I had sunk back into my seat and waited for my blurred vision to clear. Adam had glanced back at me—*are you coming or what?* I had swiped at my eyes with a weak hand and pushed myself out of the car.

The two hastily gulped martinis Adam bought me later helped wash away the image of the victim's bloody arms (most of her had been hidden beneath trash bags). But the smell . . . That smell . . . Paula Owens stayed in my nose all week no matter how many times I flushed my nostrils with saline spray, no matter how much perfume I wore.

And now, I was gawking at a picture that had memorialized the day we discovered the Phantom Slayer's eighth victim.

My fingers launched across the keyboard. *How do I know if you are who you say you are?*

And what did he mean *share it with the world?* And he came *here?* What did he look like?

Waiting two minutes for A Fan's response felt like waiting two days.

And he's taking pictures of his victims? Why? And he's taking pictures of me? Why?

Ice slipped down my spine.

Because he's watching me.

"Crap." I glanced at my French doors—locked. Curtains kept me from seeing the dark backyard, and fear kept me from leaving the bed, pushing aside those curtains and peering out into the night. My bladder pressed against my abdomen, but I didn't want to leave the bed.

But I did leave the bed. I grabbed my gun from the closet, stuck the Glock beneath my pillow, then climbed back beneath the comforter.

I glanced at my email account: Inbox (1).

What's he gonna say?

What should I say?

Is he watching me right now?

I held my breath as I clicked on the link and read the message:

Undeliverable. The email account at *rwraith411* *@questnet.com* does not exist.

PART II

20

The Phantom Slayer had sent me email—the first communication of any kind from the city's most active serial killer. He had also sent me two photographs: one of an unknown victim shot in an alley and another of me at a crime scene from *last year*.

He was watching me.

I grabbed the phone from the nightstand and called Lena.

"We just saw each other," she snapped, "and I'm about to climb atop a very hot man who just called me his *petite papillon*, but in Russian. What could you possibly want right now?"

"Did someone come to the house today?" I held the receiver so tight that it cracked.

"Someone comes to the house every day. A man brings mail. A guy sticks a Thai food menu on your door . . ."

I shook my head. "I'm talking about a regular guy who didn't have mail or water bottles or flyers."

She paused, then said, "Oh, yeah. That guy. He asked to speak to you. I think he was a pollster or something because he carried this clipboard and wore a tie. If he hadn't been Black, I would've thought he was a Mormon."

I nibbled on my thumbnail. "Did he look strange? Did he have, like, any tattoos? Moles? A beard? Weird hair? Something to make him stand out?"

"No," she said. "Clean cut. On the short side. Skin as brown as yours." She waited a beat, then said, "Are you okay? Did something happen? Is that fur-wearing son of a bitch bothering you again?"

I exhaled and said, "No. My neighbor just mentioned a visitor."

"I'm coming over," she said.

"Why?"

"Cuz you sound funny."

"I don't need muscle, Lee. Seriously."

She didn't speak.

"Lena?"

"Yes?"

"I'm cool."

"And I don't believe you." Then she hung up.

I dialed her number again, ready to beg her not to comb the streets for Mormon-looking Black men with clipboards.

But she didn't answer.

Crap.

I dialed Adam's number next, but he didn't answer, either. "Hey, call me. It's important. Something strange just happened and I don't want to get into it on voicemail, so call me."

Minutes passed. Then an hour.

No call from Adam.

As I waited, I startled at house sounds. The clank of ice cubes dropping into the freezer bin. The knock and grumble of the hot water heater. The flash of weird lights in the world beyond the French doors. I ignored my laptop—didn't want to see the Slayer's pictures again even though the images had already snagged hard-drive space in my head.

Three hours passed, and I was still waiting for Adam's call.

Doesn't he care?

Does he think I'm crying wolf?

What is more important than calling me back?

I sat in bed, gun in my lap, a pillow over the gun, eyes trained on late-night sitcoms, ears listening for footsteps.

On many occasions, I felt myself jerk awake. Each time, the television was still on. The gun still sat on my lap.

No call.

At one point, I glanced at the clock: 6:28 a.m.

The sun had poked through the darkness, and now dull orange light filled the bedroom.

I climbed out of bed, my muscles resisting any efforts to stretch. I swallowed, but no spit came. I blinked—dry eyes, no tears. It was a new day, but I felt stale and ancient.

I decided to walk the one mile to my morning meeting with Spencer.

Is that safe, being out in the open like that? What about the Slayer?

If the Phantom Slayer wanted to hurt me, he could do it in my car. If he was smart enough, he could break into my house. Didn't matter if I lived in the "nice" part of Los Angeles, if women in long skirts, men in full beards, and *payots* were my neighbors. That the makeup of my environment was synagogue, synagogue, religious school, pet groomers. The number of safe places had diminished greatly since I had received that picture of me at Paula Owens's death place. No sanctuary anywhere.

I did slip a can of pepper spray into my jacket pocket before leaving the house (the gun would've been too extreme, too Dirty Harry). And I did leave a note on the fridge. *Walked to Canter's for 8 am mtg w/Spencer.* Just in case.

"So this is my life now," I muttered, peering up and down my block for something strange. Do this, then do that, *just in case.*

I quick-stepped down the block, past the public park and the *huffhuffhuffing* of early-morning joggers and their dogs. No cars pulled in and out of the Grove—too early for shoppers. A buttery draft smelling of fresh-baked pastries from Du-par's wafted past me. But I didn't stop in my step, not even for a hot, gooey cinnamon roll.

Spencer sat at a window booth at Canter's Deli, his eyes lost in the California section of the *Los Angeles Times.* The *San Francisco Chronicle* and *Oakland Tribune* sat next to his cup of coffee, their crime sections next to be scoured.

Canter's has not changed since the Eisenhower administration. Same old-school deli restaurant layout with vinyl booths and display deli cubbies filled with platters of potato salad and slabs of cured meat. Same baskets of bagel chips and pickles offered, even at seven in the morning, by the same peroxide-blond waitress who had served my parents back in the sixties.

Panting, I slid into the seat across from my old friend. "Morning."

Spencer looked up from the paper and offered a puzzled smile. "You walk here?"

I nodded and gulped from the water glass near my place setting. "Does it look like I'm about to pass out?"

He nodded. "You look gray."

I pointed to the newspaper as I tried to catch my breath. "Anything worth reading?"

"Not since you left the beat."

I flapped at my face to cool down. "Is it me or is it getting dark in here?"

"Maybe you should limit unnecessary exercise until the next election."

"Done."

He cast his eyes back onto the newsprint. "The police are still searching for that missing couple from San Marino. They're using sonar now because Clark Rockefeller or whatever he's calling himself may have buried them." He motioned to the waitress at the counter and said, "Another coffee, please."

Diners, mostly tourists wearing I <HEART EMOJI> THE PRICE IS RIGHT T-shirts, laughed, shouted, and ordered poached this and fried that. They craned their necks to peer out the window, hoping to spot a Bentley or Aston Martin roaring down Fairfax with Britney Spears or Paris Hilton behind the wheel, even this early in the morning. Sunscreen and heavy perfume mixed with the aromas of fried eggs, hamburger grease, and dill pickles. After the game show's taping, they'd clog the streets around the Grove and make the natives' drives home hell.

The waitress brought over two cups of coffee, and we gave our orders: corned beef hash and eggs for him, and an egg white spinach omelet with oat bran toast for me. Eight minutes later, we had our meals.

"So I met Reverend Haist yesterday," I said as I dumped three packets of sugar into my coffee.

"And what was your impression?"

"Not the warmest man, is he? So young, and yet so angry."

"He's very Old Testament."

"It sounded like Tamar was a disobedient little puppy who got the ultimate newspaper smack in the nose."

He leaned forward. "Do you think she died because she dishonored her parents?"

My lips twisted into a smile. "You're asking *me*? Dishonorable Daughter Number One who stopped attending church regularly and who sometimes slips and says the f-word in the presence of her mother?"

"Strike that question, then." He slid a folder toward me. "For your consideration."

I read the ballistics report as Spencer grabbed the salt and pepper shakers.

"That came in late last night," he said. "Tamar's bullet doesn't have the same signature scratches or the other ballistic marks found on the Slayer's bullets."

Slack-jawed, I stared at him.

He shrugged. "I know, right? Did the Slayer kill her or not? This report says that he didn't."

"Maybe he's using another gun," I offered. "Maybe his old gun broke. He's been using it since 1990."

"Maybe."

"What did Adam say?"

"Before or after he threw his coffee mug at the wall?"

"I left him a message to call me," I said, my eyebrow arched. "He didn't."

Spencer shrugged. "He's busy right now?"

I grunted, then flipped through the last sheets. "What about the DNA from beneath Tamar's fingernails? If it's the Slayer, her sample should match the sample from '90."

"Nothing yet," Spencer said. "The tests are on rush, but that still could take up to a month. As soon as we get a hit, I'll let you know."

My shoulders sagged. "This sucks."

"And in other good news," he said, "Tamar paid cash for her breast implants. The money came from her bank account. No links to a rich boyfriend."

I banged my head on the back of the booth. "Any other dead ends to share?"

He offered a sad smile and shook his head. "At least we know they're dead ends."

Out in the parking lot, the sun had burned through the fast-moving haze, promising another extreme weather day in the city—from thirty-seven degrees to ninety. Spencer and I walked in silence until we reached his city-issued Tahoe.

"Good breakfast," he said. "I'm glad you came." His sandy-brown eyes complemented his cranberry-colored polo shirt.

"I'll drive the next time," I said. "Nice shirt, by the way." I glanced at his feet—he wore a pair of brown leather bucks similar to Adam's. "And fancy shoes, too? You're all *Project Runway* today."

He pulled at his collar and dropped his eyes to the asphalt. "Thanks."

"What forced you out of your Cons and *Star Trek* T-shirt?"

He shrugged. "Guess I'm growing up. You getting sick made me think about my life."

I chuckled. "Cancer makes you do that."

"And I bought a suit the other day."

I nudged him with my elbow. "Okay, what's her name?"

He chuckled. "Georgia."

"Adventist?"

He nodded. "But not a good one. Which suits me fine."

"No premarital sex on the Sabbath, I'm guessing?"

He laughed. "Something like that, yeah."

I held up the ballistics report. "Thanks for this."

"No problem." His brow furrowed. "Everything okay? You seem a little distracted."

"Nope. Got a lot on my mind. But that's not so strange, right?"

"You have that look."

"Me?" I forced a broader smile. "Nope. No look here."

He said, "Please be careful, whatever's going on."

"I'm always careful," I said as my fingers stroked the can of pepper spray in my pocket.

Spencer stared at me for several seconds, then climbed into the truck.

I darted out of the parking lot, not sure if being careful was still possible.

21

Some sickos tape their murders.

Others record their deeds in journals.

A few write letters to the newspaper.

He takes pictures. For him, these missions are significant, and profoundly meaningful. To not photograph them would be a sin.

He's only shared two pictures with the outside to prove his existence.

It was not an easy thing, coming out of his burrow and sending those emails. It had taken an entire notebook to draft that first message to the writer. His words had sounded right in his head, but something happened once they landed on paper. Nothing had made sense. Everything had been . . . screwy. Even after he had scratched out the paragraph and started again, the words still made no sense. He had crumpled the paper, tossed it to the floor, and started a new sheet. Eighty attempts later, he had finished.

Then, after all that, she sends him a smart-ass reply. Don't know what you want me to do with it, though.

Didn't she know? Him contacting her . . . that was a big deal.

And he had only reached out to her because the Word had confirmed that she was the one. Before emailing her, he had taken his Bible and let it fall open on its own. He had closed his eyes and let his finger land on a verse.

Truly the signs of an apostle were wrought among you in all patience, in signs, and wonders, and mighty deeds.

Made perfect sense.

But then, he had thought Esther had also been the one.

The Spirit had told him, *No, not her*, but he had ignored the warnings because he had wanted her. Wanted her so much his veins ached. He is patient in some things but not in all. And after his desire for Esther had melted, he had to face the truth: He had been a disobedient sinner. He had been wrong.

This time, though. This time, he won't mess up. He will listen. *Not my will, but Your will.*

His lens zooms closer to the whore he will capture next.

Tisha Whitfield.

It was easy to learn about Tisha—only took a box of cupcakes for the lovesick clerk at work to print him a copy of Tisha's extensive profile. Hooking since 1983, the woman had spent most of her teens and all of her twenties and thirties on the streets of Los Angeles. And when she wasn't hooking, she took up precious space in the crowded county jail. Prostitution (of course). Shoplifting. Writing bad checks. Trespassing.

In addition to being an ex-con, Tisha is also a walking health hazard—herpes, genital warts, and asthma. She's been treated for all three maladies at various free clinics around the city. She's received countless vials of Valtrex, tubes of 5-fluorouracil, and Ventolin inhalers courtesy of Los Angeles County taxpayers. Does she take her free meds? No. Does she listen to her doctors? No. She rarely takes showers, and the johns that seek her services are too stupid to identify the sores on her lips and between her legs as infectious. These same horny idiots carry their filthy mouths and penises home to wives and girlfriends, spreading the filth, causing disease and death.

He starts the minivan and creeps down the block for a better view.

Tisha is leading a beer-bellied Hispanic behind KJ Sons Liquor.

He aims the camera in Tisha's direction again: She's slathered Vaseline and cheap fuchsia lipstick across her lips to hide the sores. She's even changed out of that grimy red tank top and those crusty black biker shorts for a floral sundress. It is her birthday after all.

The john hands her several dollar bills.

Tisha drops to her knees.

He snaps a few pictures, then tosses the camera onto the passenger seat. He blows through the stop sign as his blood races through his veins. He wants to turn the car around and run down both Tisha and her customer. But he won't end her life today. Let her enjoy her birthday. It will be her last.

He had fallen for one of their traps once and what happened next hadn't been very good. She had tried to hide her sour-fishy stink with baby oil and perfume. She had climbed on top of him and moved this way and that, grunting like an ape, smelling worse than a pigsty. It had been over very quickly. He shot her in the face, and then he bathed her, probably her first bath in months. He had snapped a few pictures—they weren't very good, either—then climbed atop her and tried again. He liked Benecia Martin this way. Warm but lifeless. Bloody but . . . not. He buried her in the basement, and then he took seven showers to get her nastiness off his skin.

He won't bury the writer in the basement nor will he desert her in some ghetto alley. No. She will reside in his master bedroom, where Esther now lives. But first, he will have to leave Syeeda McKay in the basement so that she can adjust. And when she is ready, he will move her upstairs.

He drives the seven miles to Third Street, and his heart pounds harder the closer he gets to the writer's neighborhood. He stopped by her house yesterday, but the tiny drag queen answered the door wearing some ridiculous skirt made with blue feathers. She had a bored look on her face, stuck-up, pampered bitch. She told him that the lady of the house wasn't home.

There she is!

His foot automatically hits the brake pedal as he spots Syeeda McKay walking along Third.

She is alone. She looks spooked. Her eyes are darting around her. She's frowning.

His heart sinks—he hadn't intended to frighten her with those late-night messages. She had no reason to be afraid of him. Look at her now, though. Trying to be so brave but failing.

He drives past her, and as soon as he is able, he U-turns and heads back. She makes a left on Vista. Walking quicker now since she's almost home.

We will be together soon.

Back at home, he unloads several bags from the minivan. He had stopped at Home Depot, the grocery store, and Staples. Checked his list, crossed items off.

But the next task before him . . . he has not looked forward to it but he cannot avoid it. Not if he is to have a life with the writer.

He climbs the stairs and unlocks the master bedroom.

The smell washes over him, and for a second, he gags. He shrugs it off, though. It is the most natural odor in the world. But the bugs . . . the bugs are worse than the smell.

"Esther?" He creeps over to the window and pushes aside the rotting linen curtains.

Dust motes dance in shafts of dying sunlight. That penny-colored light spills across the piles of soiled clothes heaped on the carpet, and across the body of his girlfriend reclining in the California king.

"Esther?" he says again.

She says nothing.

He walks over to the bed and looks down at her. Memory tells him that seven months ago, Esther had been a pretty Black woman with glossy, shoulder-length hair. Now, though, that hair has lost its sheen even as it fans across the pillow like an ebony corona. She's still pretty even with that cheesy, gray skin. And she looks bashed in, but then her organs have disintegrated. He takes her hand and perches beside her on the sheet soiled with insect decay and with . . . Esther. He plucks off two ticks attached to the dried skin, frowns at their invasion, reminds himself to spray the room with pesticide to kill the sick bastards. He swallows his rage—first things first.

His eyes prickle with tears and he bites his lower lip. "This is hard for me to say . . ."

She waits. *Yes?*

He takes a deep breath, then says, "The Spirit is leading me in another direction. This writer I've met . . ." He traces the fracture that zigzags from her forehead to her left ear. "She understands me, and she will help me fulfill my mission, help me do all that I need to do."

The sun has almost dipped beneath the horizon when he finishes burying Esther in the flower bed near the back wall.

So much to do.

He kneels before the door that separates the basement from the upstairs. He had purchased three padlocks to install on that door, but after an hour, he has only succeeded in installing two, and the second lock . . . It wiggles and the screws stick out some. He was never good with power drills, saws, and all that. And his hands hurt from trying.

He wipes the sweat from his forehead and stares down into the basement, mind somewhere else.

What is she doing now? Is she still scared? Did she talk to Sherwood?

He hates scaring her, but he will make it up to her. He has kept a running list of things she likes, and today, he bought most of them. Smoked Gouda cheese. Uniball pens, micro, not bold. That blue Lever shower gel. She loves venti nonfat caramel macchiatos. He bought that two days ago, and he stares at the Starbucks cup now sitting on the basement's little round table. It is good coffee and she likes caramel macchiatos.

And we will go on walks together.

She'll need the exercise to write well. He read about that in *Prevention* magazine. Clear minds improve efficiency and all that. He will have to bind her so she won't run away. Poke his gun in her back a few times so she won't scream. Gag her, maybe. That won't be so bad.

She will write his story, and the world will know the power of God. And maybe then people will turn from their wickedness and come to Him.

So she will need that exercise and her cheese and good pens. And walks.

Yes, but she will have to be bound.

22

The sun had scoured the blue sky of all color, and every moving thing on Crenshaw Boulevard lumbered like stegosauruses caught in tar. Even in an air-conditioned luxury car, my underarms still stuck to my T-shirt. Couldn't imagine being that mother of three stairstep toddlers, hoisting a double-wide stroller across the street. Couldn't imagine being one of the folks at the bus stop, my face glistening with sweat as I waited for a bus that would never come on time. Everyone was frowning, using the *Final Call* as a fan instead of a guide to Nation of Islam enlightenment.

Krispy Kreme's HOT DOUGHNUTS neon sign blinked. Who would want a hot, incredibly delicious doughnut right now?

No customers stood in line at Louisiana Fried Chicken. Spicy food without a Mason jar of cold lemonade? No thanks.

The Liquor Bank's parking lot bustled with activity. Customers were leaving the store with brown bags probably filled with ice-cold beer, 7UPs, and bottled waters.

The weather girl on Channel 11 had predicted that a tropical storm was now heading toward Los Angeles. Doubted that. Not with this sky. Not with that sun.

I needed to talk to Tamar's hairdresser. She had been one of the last to see the young woman alive. She may have also known more about Christopher the Secret Boyfriend. After searching for a listing of the shop and finding nothing, I had called Noemi Haist. "I can't find Tamar's hair salon on the web."

Noemi had laughed. "Oh, you're not gonna find it listed on the internet. It's a small shop. Like really *really* small." She gave me directions. "Make an appointment with Audrey."

And now, I was trying to find Wholly Holy Hair Salon located somewhere on Crenshaw.

If you drive too fast, you'll miss Wholly Holy Hair. I passed 11853 Crenshaw twice and still missed it. On the third time around the block, I parked on the street within the shop's vicinity . . . and missed it again. In one step, I had moved from 11849 to 11857. I backtracked and found 11853, a structure similar to those urban swap-meet buildings with tiny stores selling ten pairs of socks for five dollars and bootleg CDs. I scanned the business directory—Wholly Holy Hair, Store 7.

I wandered past separate stalls situated like the exhibit booths at a county fair. In one, a Black woman sold fake-leather-*G*'s-turned-the-wrong-way-don't-let-the-rain-hit-'em designer handbags. The shop across from her, manned by a lady with a short blond Afro, hawked homemade bath gels and candles. No customers loitered in either shop, and each vendor sat on her stool, eyes in an open Bible on her lap.

Up ahead, I spotted Wholly Holy Hair Salon. The shop's sign had been painted by an artist with more spray cans than talent. It was not a salon in the traditional sense. You know: ten stations manned by stylists, a separate shampoo room, a slew of hair dryers, customers with their hair in scarves or plastic bags, Frankie Beverly and Maze booming from the stereo. Nope. Wholly Holy Hair had operating room for only two stylists. Noemi hadn't been hyperbolic when she said *really, really small*.

A tall, skinny woman with Shirley Temple curls stood at one of the stations. She held a white Styrofoam container, and was eating something drowned in hot sauce. The other stylist sat in her styling chair and flipped through a magazine. She saw me standing there and said, "You looking for the bathrooms?"

"No," I said. "I have a one o'clock with Audrey."

Shirley Temple Curls asked, "You Syeeda?"

I nodded.

"You caught me eating lunch, but go 'head and sit." She pointed at her chair. "I'll be finished in a minute."

I smiled at the other stylist—the license on her mirror said CHERIE LAWRENCE—and glanced at Audrey's meal: fried red snapper and french fries baptized in hot sauce. My stomach growled. When compared to fried fish, eating an egg white omelet for breakfast that morning had been the equivalent of eating air.

Audrey took another bite of snapper, then closed the container. She wiped her fingers on a tired, greasy napkin and glimpsed my reflection in the mirror. "A wash and flat iron, right?" She opened a cabinet and pulled out a purple smock. She fluffed it out and draped it across my chest. "I wasn't expecting any customers today. Just got back from Tennessee last night. But I can't turn people down in this economy."

"You from Tennessee?" I asked.

"Yep. Right outside Nashville. My momma's still living there. She's been sick—I've been with her since Tuesday." She ran her fingers through my hair. "How did you hear about us?"

"From Noemi Haist," I said. "Tamar's sister."

Audrey said, "Tamar's a sweetheart. She came in Monday. I was on my way to the airport, but she begged me to hook her up real quick. She wanted it nice for her big date. So I said, come on in."

I studied the woman's reflection in the mirror—she was parting my hair and checking my scalp. No sadness in her expression—Audrey didn't know Tamar was dead.

"It's sad all that happened," I said, testing the temperature with my toe.

Maybe she *did* know. Tamar's death had been on the news, although I doubted that the story had reached east of the Mississippi. Or perhaps Audrey had already grieved for her customer and was now moving on.

The stylist was looking at me, though, waiting to hear more about the Sad Happening. But as I took a deep breath, and prepared to say, "Tamar died," she tapped my shoulder. "Come on over to the shampoo bowl."

Three steps away, I found myself reclined in a chair with my head in the sink.

Audrey ran the tap, waited for the water to warm. She sang Donnie McClurkin's "We Fall Down" softly as she stuck the nozzle in my hair. She grabbed a bottle from a shelf above the basin. Squeezed banana-scented shampoo at my crown.

"Was Tamar seeing Christopher back on Tuesday night?" I asked.

"Uh-huh," Audrey said as she lathered. "She usually comes every other Wednesday, but she wanted it done fresh. She loves that man. All she talks about is Christopher. *Christopher gave me this. Christopher took me there.* Tamar is all Christopher all the time."

"What does he do for a living?"

"He was a cop. But he got shot by some knuckleheads over in the projects, Nickerson Gardens, I think. He had to go out on disability."

"LAPD?"

"Uh-huh. A detective. Or maybe he was SWAT. I don't remember. All I know is this: He was a cutie. You ever seen him?"

"No."

"He came in with her once. Tall. Caramel skin. Good hair. Pretty eyes."

"Wow. He must've looked good in his uniform, with all those guns."

She laughed. "Girl, you ain't *lyin'*. Brother had it goin' *on*, you hear me?"

Yeah. I hear you.

"How could he afford all those fancy gifts being on disability?" I asked.

"I know, huh? Cuz he hooked Tamar up for real. He was supposed to—" Audrey gasped and stopped massaging my scalp. "Did he propose to her?"

"Audrey!" Cherie called. "Come on. They here!"

Audrey glanced over her shoulder and shouted, "Let me put some conditioner in!" She rinsed the shampoo from my hair, moving quicker than before. She grabbed a bottle of strawberry-scented conditioner—I'd smell like a banana split for a week—and worked the lotion into my hair. "I'm gon' let that sit for a few minutes." Then, she tapped my forehead and retreated to the stations.

My shoulders relaxed and I closed my eyes.

"Lord, we come before You in humility and thanksgiving . . ."

Huh?

"Bless our hands so that we may touch others and fill them with Your spirit."

Audrey, Cherie, and the two women who sold bath gels and fake Guccis stood in the middle of the shop with their hands and faces lifted to Heaven. *"In your name, we pray . . . Amen."*

Interesting. Afternoon prayer at work.

Audrey said, "So today's Bible study is about—" .

Umm . . . *Really?*

The women sat in the chairs and started flipping through their Bibles.

I clenched my jaw. On basic principle, I hated going to the salon. I'm not down with all the talking and overbooking and gossiping about the shop's owner. I lose four hours of my life with my head in a sink or left to rot beneath a dryer, waiting for my stylist to finish the two perms, the weave, and her red-snapper combo plate. And now, they were throwing in *Bible studies* on top of all that? What in the wholly holy *hell?*

I lay in that tilted-back position for twenty minutes, listening to Cherie read the flood story from Genesis, listening to the group's half-baked wonderings.

That must've been a big boat to have all those dogs on board.

They didn't have every breed on the Ark.

Then how did they come about then?

Silence.

I wanted to shout, "Evolution!" and freak them out with the notion that God could have taken thousands of years to create every breed of dog instead of seven days. He is God, after all, and He knew man wouldn't need poodles until the fifteenth century.

After a final prayer, the group dissembled, and Audrey returned to the shampoo bowl. "You should be ready now," she said as she twisted on the tap.

She rinsed out the conditioner and dried my hair with a towel. Then, we returned to her station. A customer who resembled a lion—tawny-skinned and snouty—now occupied Cherie's chair.

"You got some nice hair," Audrey said as she worked a comb across my scalp. "Tamar did, too, before she had me put that weave in. Her daddy was not happy about that."

I nodded. "That is a lot of hair on her head."

"She only got it cuz Christopher is a hair freak," Audrey said. "Anyway, Tamar don't care no more what her daddy thinks. She got her a man who'll take care of her. Who'll pay her rent just like Babyface wrote in that song." She sang, "Soon as I get home from work." She bobbed her head as she pulled a blow-dryer from her cubby.

"She never told her father about Chris," I said. "So she still must've cared."

Audrey shrugged. "She didn't want no drama. He was already stressing baby girl out—"

I couldn't hear Audrey over the blow-dryer, so I stopped talking until she finished.

"I love my reverend," Audrey said as she grabbed the flat iron. "He doin' the Lord's work and all, but that man is a control freak. Poor Mother Haist can barely say a word without him telling her what to say. I don't blame Tamar for leaving that house. When she told him she was moving out, he went *off*. Threw her stuff out on the lawn. Even her mattress. He pushed her out. Told her that she wasn't welcomed there no more. That she was dead to him."

"Cuz he wanted to be the only man in her life," Cherie chimed. "He wanted her to act like Mother Haist and Noemi who ain't ever gon' get married."

"I've heard some unflattering things about the reverend," I said.

"All that is yesterday's news," Audrey said. "He got a temper, but he ain't hit nobody since, when? Five years ago?"

"Guess I look differently at that," I said. "I'd never go back to a man who abused me."

Audrey's eyes widened. "The reverend ain't hit Mother Haist. Nuh-uh. Never that. He treats that woman with respect, like she's a precious jewel. He was doing some rescue work near the church and this woman needed a ride—"

"A woman?" I asked. "Who was she?"

Audrey shrugged. "They say she was one of them streetwalkers, but who knows. I doubt it cuz why would Reverend have a woman like that in the car with him? And Mother Haist is a beautiful woman—he don't need to go nowhere else. Anyway, whoever she was pulled a knife out on him and tried to rob him. So he hit her in self-defense. Basically, he got sent to jail for trying to save his life."

"And that other thing?" Cherie said, waving her hand. "He was arrested but they never charged him cuz it was all a misunderstanding. He was doing rescue work for the church when Vice arrested him for soliciting. But he wasn't soliciting. He was asking the woman if she needed shelter and all that. He wasn't even preaching to her about all the wrong she was doing. Just trying to help. You can't help nobody nowadays."

"He got rebaptized anyway," Audrey added. "Cuz it just looked bad. He and Mother Haist even renewed their vows. Had a reception with doves and all these little candles on the tables."

"That was so romantic," Cherie said.

"How sweet," I said, not thinking that at all. More *how convenient.*

"But Tamar got so upset with him," Cherie said. "She acted like he intentionally beat that woman. But the chick in Reverend's car with the knife? She had it comin'. Some women deserve a pop in the face sometimes. Tamar just didn't understand that. I loved her, but she didn't know how the real world worked. It ain't pretty."

"She knew enough about the world to get a man," Audrey said as she placed a segment of my hair between the two hot plates. "And now, the reverend's got himself a new son-in-law, so he's gonna have to get on his knees and pray about it. Make the best of life and wait for some grandbabies. What's done is done."

The woman with the lion face said, "Girl, Reverend ain't gotta pray about nothing. Tamar didn't get married."

Audrey slipped more of my hair between the plates. "She changed her mind?"

Cherie said, "Audrey, you tellin' me that you ain't heard?"

"I been in Tennessee for three days," Audrey screeched. "What ain't I heard?"

Lion Face considered my reflection in the mirror.

I didn't speak. Just cocked my eyebrow—*shall I tell her or do you want to?*

"Audrey, honey," Lion Face said. "Tamar's dead."

Audrey froze. She gawked at my reflection in the mirror.

I nodded. "She was killed Wednesday." Then, I eyed the flat iron that still held a section of my now-burning hair.

Audrey wailed, "Oh, Lord!"

The iron hit my left ear.

I yelped and hopped out of the chair.

The tool clattered to the floor and landed next to its weeping operator.

Cherie and the lion-faced customer rushed to Audrey's side. They told Audrey to calm down and muttered "It's okay" as Audrey continued to wail.

I watched them as my burned ear throbbed like hellfire.

"What . . . what . . . happened?" Audrey blubbered.

"She was shot," Cherie said. "Some reporter found her in the alley behind the church."

"I . . . I found her," I stammered.

The crying trio turned to me, wide-eyed and silent.

"She wanted to meet me," I whispered. "But I don't know why."

Audrey whispered, "Who killed her?"

I shook my head. "I don't know."

"Why? Why her?"

I said, "I don't know."

With that, Audrey returned to her grieving place.

The two women from the purse and bath gels stalls had heard the ruckus and now rushed back into the noisy salon. "What's wrong? What happened?" they both shouted.

"Audrey just found out about Tamar," Cherie shouted back.

"Oh, Lord, *why!*" Audrey screamed. "Not Tamar. Not her, Lord!"

Unable to stand the crying and yelling, I left sixty dollars on Audrey's workstation, offered apologies to the air, then slipped out of the salon unnoticed.

23

So. I did not leave Wholly Holy Hair Salon with bouncy, shiny hair. I left the shop with the right side flat ironed and my left ear singed. I pulled back onto Crenshaw, still grimacing from the burn.

A white Lexus rushed behind me.

I cursed and sped up so the driver wouldn't rear-end me.

My mind turned to the conversation in the salon. Who was this woman the reverend had beaten up? Was she a sex worker? Was she alive?

And: *Men with pretty, doting wives would never turn to women like that for sex?*

Ha ha, very funny. Snort.

I glimpsed in my rearview mirror.

The white Lexus was still behind me.

Is this guy following me or . . . ?

The car inched closer to my bumper.

I could now see the driver's face in my rearview mirror.

Reverend Murray Haist.

I glanced in my side mirror.

He smiled, but not because he was happy to see me.

I gripped the steering wheel tighter and drove a few more blocks.

He continued to follow me, inching closer to my bumper every time we stopped at a light.

Did he see me leave the hair salon?

Was he pissed because I had talked to Tamar's stylist?

At Wilshire Boulevard, the Lexus swerved from behind me and slammed into the right lane. Reverend Haist glared at me and uttered something that I couldn't hear. Those three seconds felt like three years. He hit the gas and made a right, racing east and away from me.

I sank in my seat and waited for the tremors to stop.

What the hell was that about?

Adam's Crown Vic was parked in my driveway. The detective sat on the car's hood with a bouquet of wildflowers in his lap. "Sorry for not calling you back last night," he said, handing me the flowers. "If I keep screwing up, you won't take me back, will you?" He brushed my cheek with the back of his finger and eyed my hair.

"The stylist couldn't finish," I said, sniffing the bouquet. "She found out that her client was murdered two days ago."

"You went to Tamar's hairdresser?" he said. "What the hell for?"

"Doing background for this small piece Noemi Haist asked me to write. And yes, I'll run it past you before I send it to my editor."

"I don't mind you playing Encyclopedia Brown—"

"Since it's benefited you in the past." I tilted my head. "Benefited you in many ways."

"True," he said, "but I still need you to find some other bright shiny object to follow for a while. Isn't there a boat show at the convention center today? I hear the Sea Bay booth is a hotbed of sex and murder right now."

I nodded a hello to the ancient Jewish couple turtling past, then turned back to Adam. "Why do you want me distracted?"

"So I can talk to people like the hairdresser without filtering you out."

"She asked me what happened, and I told her that I didn't know. And I don't know, especially since the bullet from Tamar didn't come from the Slayer's known weapon."

"You've talked to Spencer?" he asked.

I nodded.

"Doesn't matter. Move on for now. Seriously."

I folded my arms. "What do you want me to do while I'm waiting?"

"Find another aspect of the story to focus on that doesn't include the Haists." He shook his head and said, "Reverend Haist called to complain. He said people you're talking to have been calling him—"

"He's a lie."

"A preacher?"

"Since when are preachers infallible?" I asked. "Maybe instead of following me around the city, he should be trying to find out who killed—"

"Following you?"

"Just now," I said. "Riding my bumper. You know, trying to scare me. Anyway, I've only talked to Noemi and the woman at the shop. Who are all these people the reverend claims I'm talking to? He just doesn't want me to find out how much of an asshole he is. The girls at the shop confirmed that he's had 'episodes' over the last couple of years."

"Yes."

We stood there looking at each other until I started rocking on my heels.

Adam said, "I'm aware of his history, Sy, so step back and let me do my job."

"I'll let it go for now," I said. "But not for long. By the way, have you seen anyone strange at Tamar's shrine?"

"Nothing unusual so far."

"Tamar's landlord was a little strange," I said.

"Yeah, but he has an airtight alibi."

"You guys find Skittles?"

He nodded. "Netriece Mimms. And she's with the police sketch artist as we speak."

"And have you talked to Christopher yet?"

"Sy, this ain't a competition." He paused, chewed the inside of his cheek. "Who?"

"Christopher, no last name. He's Tamar's secret boyfriend. She saw him the night she died. Noemi Haist mentioned him during yesterday's tour of the Barbie Palladium. Then, the hairdresser told me that he's either a former detective or ex-SWAT. A cop, anyway. Tall, light-skinned, good-looking. Interesting, huh? Or not. Who knows? Maybe you should do some detecting and find out."

Adam clicked his teeth together as he thought. "I'll ask Noemi about him. But who says he was Tamar's boyfriend and not a pimp, or a john with a fake name? Maybe he was a security guard at the Toyota dealership in Carson but wanted to impress his rent-a-date with the 'I'm a big dick in SWAT' line."

I gawked at him, then marched to my front door.

"What did I say?" Adam asked, trying not to laugh. "I'm just being the devil's advocate."

Wild-eyed, I whirled back around to face him. "I know you're a failed lawyer, but must you argue *everything*? You find no hard evidence, yet the girl's still a ho?"

He shrugged. "Occam's razor. The simplest solution tends to be the best solution."

"No semen or saliva found on her body," I countered. "No record of arrests for prostitution, drugs, or even jaywalking. Occam's razor. Tamar's father is a dangerous man."

"And that's why I want you to keep your distance," Adam said. "Especially if he's following you. I'm very aware of Murray Haist and what he's doing when he's not preaching."

"What is he doing when he's not preaching?"

He shook his head. "Don't."

"I deserve to know if he's gonna be stalking me now."

"I wouldn't classify what he did today as stalking," Adam said.

I folded my arms. "Maybe I should return the favor and follow *him* around. See how he likes it."

"Don't, Sy. Please?"

"I'll leave him alone if you make a serious effort to check into Christopher the Secret Boyfriend."

Adam sighed. "Of course I'll make the effort—that's my job, Syeeda. It may take a while, and eat up resources that I don't have, but I'll look. Maybe this one will pan out and I won't have to wear snowshoes and a fur coat. Anyway: Stay away from the Haist family. The reverend's talking restraining orders."

"How long must I wait? I have an article to publish."

He shrugged. "Give me the weekend. That's reasonable, right? And if something good comes up, I promise to share it with you and no other reporter. Deal?"

I considered him for a moment, *no deal* on my tongue.

"Know what you can do for me that would help?" Adam asked.

I hopped up and down. "Put me in, coach!"

"Without disturbing Reverend and Mrs. Haist, do you think you can find more about Christopher the Secret Boyfriend? Again: without disturbing the reverend and his wife?"

"Of course I can. I'm magic, remember?"

I couldn't fault Adam for not wanting to chase another one of my leads. Listening to me, he had chased Marvin Trainer, the ex-Marine; Bernard Hogan, the ex-janitor; and George Papawell, the ex–Sunday school teacher. Each man had been guilty of something, but not for murdering sex workers off Western Avenue.

I slipped Adam's wildflowers into a crystal vase, then sat it on the dining room table. He gave me bouquets like these all the time. "Random and pretty," he'd say. "Like you."

I grabbed the telephone from the living room couch and punched in Spencer's work number. The line rang three times . . . four times . . .

On the fifth ring, he said, "Hey."

I hustled down the hall to my office. "Thought you had already left."

"Nope. I'm here. Working as always. What's up?"

I clicked on the desk lamp and glanced at the Death Wall now illuminated with golden light. "I know we just talked this morning, but I was calling to follow up on Tamar and the DNA. Any hits against the Slayer or anyone else in the database?"

"Nothing yet. And just in case we come up blank again, we've received permission from the attorney general to take another route."

Curiosity flicked in my mind, a spark in dry brush. "What's your big idea?"

"Going into CODIS to do some familial DNA testing." CODIS stood for Combined DNA Index System, a federal database that stored DNA profiles from crime labs across the country.

"Are you kidding me?" My cheeks burned and I covered my eyes with the crook of my elbow—just *talking* about peeking into someone else's gene pool without their permission gave me the heebs.

"Almost half of violent criminals have close relatives in jail," Spencer said. "The Slayer could have a brother in Folsom, or a father at San Quentin . . ."

"I know, but digging through other people's DNA? That's an invasion of privacy."

He snorted. "They gave that up when they were handed the orange jumpsuit."

I pushed away from the desk. "What about false positives? Or identifying someone who's not related? What about the fact that everyone in the family will be a suspect and will have to take DNA tests? And I won't even go into the racial implications—"

"Then don't," he snapped. "Do you want to know if we get a hit or not? I don't have time to take your Race, Ethics, and DNA symposium right now."

"Can I mention this in my article?"

"Maybe."

I twisted in my chair and tapped the pen against my lip. *Sleep in bed with Big Brother or stay true to my ACLU membership card and wait for information from a less insidious source, like . . . like . . . some other reporter's story.* "I want to know." I decided to also donate $1,000 to my local civil liberties affiliate to make up for temporarily switching sides. "Call me as soon as you get something."

24

It took me thirty minutes to flat iron the rest of my hair. I showered, then changed into a cranberry sweater dress, gray tights, and high-heeled boots. I resisted the urge to slick on lip gloss, swipe bronzer across my cheeks, and brush eye shadow over my lids. Nor did I dare to dab Chanel No. 5 on my pulse points. I considered my reflection in the mirror—modest enough for my visit to Great Redeemer but fly enough to boost my confidence. And I needed all the confidence I could get before entering the lion's den.

I didn't plan to talk to the reverend or his wife. I wanted to talk to that security guard, the one who had offered his help. He was an adult, and not a member of the Haist family. Fair game.

With Friday night traffic, it took close to an hour to reach the church. Angelenos wanted to get home before the alleged storm a'comin'. But the clouds hanging over the city didn't look menacing. I'd seen worse in this city—cloud cover that came straight out of Stephen King novels, with fierce winds that knock down hundred-year-old live oaks.

To my surprise, the grounds of Great Redeemer were brightly lit and the parking lot was filled with people. Folks were walking to the church empty-handed and leaving the grounds with foil-wrapped plates. There were no spaces in the lot, so I circled the block. Sex workers, dealers, and brown-skinned day laborers eyed my car, cruising in a neighborhood where liquor store cashiers stood behind bulletproof glass and motels charged by the hour.

I didn't completely halt at stop signs. I wasn't scared, just cautious. Everyone should be cautious.

Half a block away from the church, I slipped into a spot on the street vacated by a VW Beetle. As soon as I opened the car door, I smelled hot oil and fish. *Friday night fish fry.* The air was so heavy with grease, you could scoop it and dump it on a plate as a side. I smiled and anticipated buying my own Styrofoam container of fried snapper and potato salad.

I threw a few glances around to let those watching me know that I was aware. But the slinger on the corner was collecting money from a crackhead and didn't notice me. A middle-aged Hispanic man was peering into the open hood of his broken-down Chevy. He didn't notice me, either. Patrol cars cruised up and down the street, not stopping to make busts or to help a man fix his truck. I was invisible.

The police helicopter hovered over a neighborhood two blocks over, its spotlight trained on the tops of houses and apartment buildings. Gospel music blasted from speakers in the church's lot. A long line snaked from the sidewalks of Western to fold-up tables set up near the rear gates of the parking lot, ten feet from the alley where Tamar Haist had been shot and killed. The tables were loaded with steel trays stuffed with fried fish, Tupperware filled with loaves of Wonder bread and potato salad, and jumbo coolers jammed with ice and cans of soda. A long strip of white poster paper had been taped to the gate behind the food stations. Pictures of the slain woman surrounded painted words: TAMAR HAIST MEMORIAL FUND.

Business before mealtime.

I wandered the lot in search of the security guard and prayed that I wouldn't bump into Reverend Haist. People were smiling and laughing. Some wore picture buttons of Tamar on their shirts. Children sat on laps or were carried on hips and shoulders. Old people were herded into fold-up chairs, their eyes blank as though they had been lobotomized.

I glimpsed a blue uniform near the alley and weaved through the crowd until I could touch the man's arm. "Excuse me. Sir?"

"Uh-huh?" He turned his head—he wasn't the security guard I had met yesterday. This man was 100 years older. His features were pinched, moray eel–like, and he had a gap between his top front teeth. "How you doin?" he asked as his rheumy eyes swept over me.

I smiled, ready to flirt if needed. "I'm looking for the other security guard who works here. Thin. A little taller than me. And . . ." Couldn't remember anything else about him.

He nodded. "You talkin' 'bout Jay. He with Mother Haist right now. Had to take her home. She couldn't handle bein' here."

"I know about her daughter," I said. "So sad. So unexpected."

He surveyed the crowd, then clucked his tongue. "We havin' this here fish fry to help cover the funeral costs. We family, you know? Gotta watch out for one another, 'specially after a wolf comes in and snatches one of us away. Folks may be smilin', but they feel it, all this cold air where Tamar used to be. But she wit' the Lord now, and that's where we all wanna be, so . . ."

I looked past him to the alley. The shrine had grown. More helium-filled balloons bobbed against the church's outer walls. Stuffed animals competed for space against the sea of carnations and mums.

"There was a time when the church was safe," the guard said. "Not no more. Niggas. They just come in and ruin everythin'. That's what happens when they take prayer outta schools, so . . ."

"Do you have any idea what happened that night?"

"Who wanna know?"

I offered a small smile. "Sy McKay wants to know. I'm a reporter with the *Times*."

He smiled wide and stuck out his hand. "Pleasure. Miss or Mrs.?"

I said, "*Ms.*"

"I'm Clarence Dear. *Mister.*" He chuckled.

"So what do you think, Mr. Clarence Dear?"

He reached beneath his cap and scratched his scalp. "Who knows? She was arguin' with the treasurer a lot. That be Deacon Stone. He 'round here somewhere."

"I know this will sound crazy, but is it possible that the deacon had something to do with . . . all of this?"

He laughed. "That do sound crazy. But naw. He was angry with Tamar cuz she turned down his son but he ain't nothin' like that. See, she and Eli was supposed to be married. It was all worked out between the parents and everythin'."

"An arranged marriage, in other words?" I asked.

"Nothin' like what those Indians do, though," he said. "There was some talk, and the reverend agreed for Tamar to get to know Eli. Court him and all that."

"What did Tamar think of that?"

He chuckled. "Wasn't havin' it. No ma'am. Nobody told her who to love—that's what she told her daddy. Foolish girl." His smile faded. "I heard the whole thing that night. Her and the reverend fussin' in his office. Broke my heart hearin' her talk back to her daddy like that. Chil'rens just throw that commandment out the window. And it ain't like the boy is ugly. He got a job. And most importantly, he love the Lord." He craned his neck to survey the crowd and pointed. "There he is, over there. By the Mission Outreach table."

I followed his finger to a man with a low haircut and goatee, a pot belly, and a perspiration problem. Far from a boy. More like somebody's daddy. "He looks . . . older than nineteen."

Clarence Dear's hand dropped. "Oh, yeah. Eli, he 'bout thirty-seven, thirty-eight . . ."

I blinked at the guard. *Was he kidding?* He couldn't understand why nineteen-year-old Tamar would balk at being married to a man who had watched the Berlin Wall being torn down?

I parted ways with Mr. Clarence Dear—a homeless man had wandered onto the church grounds and the guard had to shoo him away. As I stood in line, I debated introducing myself to Eli Stone. Maybe he had been with

Tamar on Tuesday night. Tired of her rejection, he had cornered her in the alley and *pop!* "If I can't have you, no one can," and all that.

But I didn't—he was friends with the reverend, and would certainly mention my visit. No. I'd let Adam handle Mr. Stone.

Besides, the longer I stayed at Great Redeemer, the greater my chances of running into trouble. Sure as hell didn't want that.

So, I paid ten dollars for three pieces of red snapper, a scoop of potato salad, and a can of strawberry soda. I stuffed an extra five dollars into the donation jar, and as I left the lot, I glanced at the sky. The helicopter still thundered beneath the clouds. The faint whir of sirens competed with gospel music and the roar of traffic. The homeless man was screaming, "I'll sue you, I'll sue you" at Mr. Clarence Dear. No one noticed a thing.

Just another Friday night fish fry at Great Redeemer.

25

He slips the knapsack over his shoulder and looks up and down the street. Empty. He can't see the minivan parked down the block. He strolls into Syeeda McKay's courtyard as though he belongs there. A privacy wall shields the front door from the street, and now, no one can see him. Only the porch light burns and a gang of moths flutter around the bulb. She left on the living room and kitchen lights as well as the television in the kitchen to make passersby think that someone is home. To discourage evildoers from breaking in. But she isn't home. He saw her leave thirty minutes ago. He used the public telephone at the neighborhood 7-Eleven to call her landline three times, and there's been no answer.

He's wearing gloves and barely feels the key he had made earlier today, after the tiny drag queen had left the house. He had then summoned a locksmith to Syeeda McKay's place, had told the old guy that he had locked himself out of the house. That his wife had been in a car accident that afternoon and was still at the hospital, that his mind was all gummy with worry. The old guy had studied the address on his driver's license. *101 N. Vista.* The locksmith's watery eyes peered at him again, at his nice leather loafers and pressed chinos, the silver wedding band. No suspicion. No hesitation. He wouldn't know a fake ID if he held one in his hand. "You and the wife must be doing well," the old guy had said. "Pretty nice neighborhood."

Minutes later, the old man drove away in his truck, and Syeeda McKay's "husband" had his own key.

So easy to get someone else's something in this city. A fake driver's license from a guy at MacArthur Park. An address and phone number from the internet. Her itinerary each time she updated her Facebook status. Easy-peasy.

He slides his key into the lock and steps into the foyer. The alarm dings once—she left the house without arming the system. He shouts, "Honey, I'm home." He likes saying that.

His eyes drift back behind him, to the front door.

A mail slot.

Good.

No one will see mail piling up when she goes. And he can grab the newspaper every morning, no problem.

A breeze drifts through the living room. He smells her: apples, cigarettes, burned hair. Everything here is maroon or gray. Her furniture probably came from a catalog that showed smiling white people with their expensive dogs. Pens and notebooks clutter the coffee table, and a pair of Converse high-tops lay abandoned near the armchair. Dark wood beams run across the ceiling. No cobwebs.

He keeps off the lights as he tiptoes through the room. Such a beautiful home. He wants to go through and touch everything. No time, though.

He enters her bedroom, her inner sanctum, and sits on the bed. Runs his hand across the smooth down comforter, then sniffs her pillows. A long brown hair is trapped in the fabric. He plucks it away, studies it, then lets it drift to the hardwood floor.

He slips over to the dresser, opens the top drawer to find frilly things, cotton things, panties, bras, camisoles. He will buy her more of these undergarments. Lots of them since they will have to last, since she won't be shopping anymore. He finds a lacy pair of pink bikinis and fingers the crotch. His stomach tightens as his jeans strain against his erection. He closes his eyes, imagines the writer wearing these and nothing else.

He finds the kitchen. Stainless steel appliances shine even in the dark.

He grabs a few more items, just to make Syeeda's stay more comfortable. A glass coffee mug. A fancy-looking plate. Some crap novel by Caleb Carr. He grabs a T-shirt from the laundry hamper on the service porch.

He pauses in the dining room. A vase of mismatched flowers sit in the middle of the table. *From Sherwood?* He reaches to knock over the vase, but stops. Instead, he plucks off each petal, lets them drift to the tabletop.

He returns to the bedroom.

A car door slams.

He freezes.

He didn't hear the car pull into the driveway. Damned German automobiles.

He stuffs her belongings into his pack, in with the camera and the gun.

Maybe I should take her now. She's alone.

No. Not now.

The basement isn't ready. The futon and desk are in place but everything else . . . The paint on the walls is still wet. The area rug is still rolled up. And he didn't bring the binds, the Taser, or the Special K.

Soon.

He opens the French doors and the alarm *dings* as he slips outside. Almost immediately, the alarm chimes again—another opening door.

He stands on the deck, gripping the door handle, longing to see her undress up close.

Take her.

The cold air bites his sweaty skin.

Take her now.

Sweat plinks into his eye, but he doesn't dare swipe it away. She may hear his hand brush against his skin.

Footsteps . . . She's walking down the hall.

He shakes his head—the Spirit is telling him that this is not the time, that he is in danger.

He takes a step away from the French doors.

Silence.

What is she doing?

His cell phone in his back pocket rings. *Shit.* He grabs for his phone, hops off the deck, and dashes across the lawn. He fumbles for the "off" button and silences the phone in mid-ring. He ducks behind the shrubs farthest from the house. His teeth chatter. He wants to cry. He wants to vomit.

Did she hear?

The light in the bedroom pops on.

She's standing at the French doors. The doors open and she steps outside. The light shines behind her. His angel. She's holding a gun.

When did she get a gun?

The Spirit was right. Good thing he didn't make his move.

She says something but his mind is shrieking and he can't hear what she's shouting. The keening starts in his belly and works its way up his esophagus. He sounds like a mewing kitten. He wants to cover his mouth to muffle his cries, but if he moves . . .

A gun. Everything's different now.

26

I stood on my deck, paralyzed, my heart thumping wildly in my chest. Before coming outside, I had swiped my hand between the mattress and the box spring for my gun. And now, my hands gripped the Glock so tight that all feeling had left my fingers.

Anger flared in my gut—*fucking Deon Jackson*—and I shouted, "Hey! Who's out there?"

Chirping crickets. TV sounds. Hissing sprinklers.

"Come out! *Now!*" I lifted the Glock and aimed at the bushes with cold eyes, asking in advance to be forgiven for accidentally shooting any stray animal that scampered in front of me.

A dog barked. Another dog joined in. And another.

I stood there, arms and neck aching, mind screaming, *This is bad, this is bad, go back in.* Stared at the piece of yard before me, waiting for something to move so I could shoot it.

My arms quivered.

Nothing moved.

I didn't move.

Nothing . . .

I exhaled, then let the gun swing back down to my side.

The telephone rang.

I yelped and spun around to the house, gun held high, a second from pulling the trigger.

The phone's caller ID droned, "Sherwood, Ad, Sherwood, Ad."

I caught my breath and hustled back into the bedroom for the phone.

"Hey, hot stuff," Adam said. "Just got paid, it's Friday night, how *you* doin'?"

I sat on the bed, my knees too weak to support me. "I'm holding my gun and searching the house cuz it feels like someone's been in here. There's nothing broken or incredibly strange . . . Just . . . my door in the bedroom was unlocked. Nothing's missing, though."

But I didn't believe that. Why didn't I believe that?

"Need me to come over and look around?"

"No." I slipped the gun back beneath the mattress, the grip now moist from my clammy hands. I sank to the floor and rested my head upon my knees. "I'm probably just hallucinating. Had a strawberry soda, so I'm on a sugar high. But I don't wanna be here right now."

"I picked up some Thai food and *Purple Rain* is on cable," he said. "I'm feelin' lonely so come over."

I had just started to stand when I saw something move out in my yard.

No . . . Nothing.

Madness and exhaustion, for the win.

Adam said something else—don't know what—but his voice felt good. Made my pulse slow. "Well?" he said. "Are you coming over?"

I stared at the dark television—I'd seen every episode of *Cheers*, *The Nanny*, and *Roseanne* and did not wish to add *Home Improvement* to that list. I glanced at the clock: almost eleven. So, I said, "Yeah. See you soon."

27

Adam lived in Silver Lake, a schizophrenic, northeast burg of Los Angeles. Like most neighborhoods in Southern California, Silver Lake is a tale of two minicities existing within two zip codes. One section: primarily immigrant, poor, taquerias and *carnicerías*, Laundromats and Iglesias de Pentecostales. Three blocks over and up a hill, you'll find the second city: Adam's neighborhood and hipster-singer Beck's hometown. High-end grocery stores, trendy nightclubs, and million-dollar townhomes filled with yuppies.

Adam's Spanish-style duplex was close to the reservoir and restaurants that had cred even though they weren't on the Westside. An old woman who, once upon a time, had been a session singer for RKO Pictures lived in the unit next door. In the quiet, you heard her voice, captured on vinyl, bouncing off the hardwood floors. Nice lady. She had let Adam use the one-car garage beneath their units because she didn't want a nice police officer exposed to the cold.

As Adam and I exchanged a long hug, my hands roamed his strong back. He had muscles you could die on. Muscles that made you want to write a sonnet. How magnificent had they been when he was a wide receiver at Cal?

"You give good hugs," I said.

"I can give more than that."

"I know you can." I pulled away from him. "Before I become too distracted, though . . . I went to a fish fry at Great Redeemer tonight."

"You're supposed to be staying away from the Haists," he said, tensing beneath my hands.

"I didn't go to talk to them. I went to talk with the security guard who had been on duty the night Tamar was killed."

Adam wandered to the armchair and plopped onto the cushion. "And what did he say?"

I straddled him, wrapped my arms around his neck. "He wasn't there, so I talked to this other guard, Mr. Clarence Dear." I told Adam about the treasurer, the suitor, and Tamar's rejection.

"I'll call on Eli Stone tomorrow," Adam said.

I traced his lips with my pinkie. "So I did good?"

He stroked my arm and his eyes skipped from my shirt to my hips. "Mm-hmm."

"Remember that when I screw up."

"Can we stop talking about work now and enjoy each other's company?"

I hopped up and over to the couch. "You said something about Thai food and Prince?"

We sat next to each other on the couch and gobbled spicy beef and coconut soup. We laughed at Apollonia's atrocious acting, flapped our arms to "Jungle Love," kissed during "The Beautiful Ones."

With all of my issues, sex had been the farthest thing from my mind. Now, though . . . Now, my body welcomed Adam's large hands, the taste of his mouth, his scent of soap and gunpowder. At the spa party, a drunken Lena had told me (and our friends), "Sy sweetie, you need to get laid." Then, she had thrown a pack of pink, cotton candy–flavored condoms at my head. I had stuffed those condoms into the dungeon of my bag, not planning to pluck them out anytime soon.

That was then, and now, three nights later, I was glad to be here with this smart man who knew not to grope me in certain places, who knew that I loved kissing more than anything, who probably had fresh strawberries and cream in the fridge because he knew that's what I liked to eat before falling off to a deep, satisfied sleep.

I was ready.

"So, yeah?" Adam whispered.

"Yeah," I said. "Please."

He made a trail of tiny kisses on my neck as he pulled my T-shirt over my head. He eyed the Steri-Strips poking past my bra, then stooped to leave a soft, warm kiss above the bandages. "I'm glad you're okay now," he whispered.

And I was.

Naked and sweaty, I stared at the ceiling. Adam, smooshed beside me on the couch, and also naked, slept like the dead. The old woman next door would probably pen a strongly worded letter asking that, in the future, could he please prohibit his lady friend from cursing and taking the Lord's name in vain so loudly and so frequently.

I slipped from beneath his arm and wandered to the kitchen. His badge and Glock sat on the countertop. I tiptoed past the gun, just in case it decided to go off on its own, and opened the fridge. After a final nervous glance at that gun, I grabbed from the shelf a basket of strawberries and a tub of high-end Cool Whip. After gobbling a few berries, I tiptoed down the hall and into the bedroom for a cover.

An LAPD sweatshirt was on his bed, and I pulled it over my head. I started to leave the bedroom but stopped when I noticed a greeting card on top of the dresser. Two cartoon bears were walking into a heart-shaped sunset. I snatched the card from its spot and opened it.

Purple ink. Only women wrote in purple ink. Women and Prince.

> Baby, I miss you so much.
>
> I hate this job, all this traveling, because that means I'm not touching your beautiful face or feeling your heart beat next to mine. I know we've only been together for a few weeks, but I miss rubbing your

back, kissing you in the rain, taking walks around the reservoir, and making love afterward.

Until I see you again, I will dream about you (and do other naughty things, wink wink)!! Adam, I can't wait until I'm back in LA and we pick up where we left off. Give you what you like all night. You won't regret it. I adore you. I want you.

Roya.

Roya . . .

Okay.

I want you.

Well, that's just . . . Damn.

I placed the card back onto the dresser and tugged off the sweatshirt. The breath from my nose singed my lips. I'm sure if I had opened my mouth, the curtains would've caught fire. A part of me wanted to take the card, stomp back into the living room, and rouse Adam from his sleep. Throw questions like daggers at his head. *Who is she? Why is she? Why did I meet your parents? Are we a lie?* And on and on.

But I didn't. I couldn't.

Back in the living room, Adam still slept.

I grabbed my clothes from the carpet and dressed.

He turned over and noticed me pulling on my Cons. "Where you going?" He glanced at his wristwatch. "It's late, babe."

"Got shit to do," I said, double-tying, then triple-tying the laces.

He sat up and considered me as I grabbed my bag from the ground. "What's wrong?"

"I'm an idiot, that's all." I avoided his eyes. "I'll talk to you tomorrow, 'kay?"

"Why are you angry? Wait, Sy." He slipped on his boxers and followed me to the door. "Will you say something? Syeeda, stop. Why are you mad?"

You used me while your girlfriend was away.

Or . . .

You never even told me that you had *a girlfriend.*

Or . . .

You made me think that we were a possibility, that we had a future together, and I'm a fool cuz I almost fell for it.

"It's been a long night," I said. "I'm tired and I didn't bring any pain meds and . . ." I opened the door. "And it's raining."

The streets were wet, and the sky was silver with raindrops.

Adam tapped his fist against his lips. He didn't believe that I needed to leave because I'd left the Vicodin at home, but he couldn't prove that I was lying. "Call me when you get in, okay?"

I was already down the stairs.

He remained in the doorway, a dark figure silhouetted by the golden glow of lamplight.

The weather had worsened by the time I pulled into my driveway. Strong winds forced rain to fall sideways like drying bedsheets caught in a draft. A miniature river coursed down Vista, and clumps of fallen magnolia leaves, plastic grocery bags, and wads of paper blocked the sewer grates.

I grabbed the phone from the kitchen counter and dialed Adam's number.

He answered on the first ring.

"I'm home," I said. "Talk to you—"

"Will you stop it, Sy?"

I said nothing. Glared at a grease stain on the kitchen wall.

"If you're thinking that I only wanted you for a quickie, that's not true. Babe, you know that."

"I don't know anything."

"What did I do? Will you tell me?"

I held my breath as I slid my fingertips through a batch of crumbs near the toaster.

"Are you gonna say something?"

No.

"You're . . . You're . . ." He sighed. "I'm confused about a lot of things right now. I think we both are, but . . ."

I closed my eyes and willed myself not to care about anything this man said.

"I'd do anything for you," he said, softer now. "If you just ask. Baby, just say it and I'll—"

"Adam, it's late. I need to . . . find this article on the internet before I forget and—"

"Why do you do this?"

"Do what?"

"Back away. Run for cover. Never stay in one place long enough for me to . . . For us to . . . You're here and then you're not here. Even if I'm holding you, you still manage to slip away."

I closed my eyes and nibbled on my thumbnail.

"What do you need?" he asked, pleading now. "Please tell me."

"Sleep."

Quiet, then a disappointed "Okay."

"I'm not ready for anything more."

Another "Okay."

A teardrop slipped down my cheek and I swiped it away. "I'll talk to you tomorrow."

He grunted and ended the call without saying another word.

28

A sharp explosion blasted against the house. The windowpanes shuddered.

The noise yanked me from a deep, Vicodin-induced sleep.

The bedroom brightened with lightning, and thick drops of rain pounded against the windowpanes and the patio. The storm had reached Los Angeles.

I grabbed my extra pillow and stared at silver raindrops zigzagging down the glass.

The clock on the nightstand flickered: 2:42 a.m.

I climbed out of bed and shuffled out of the bedroom. The hallway was empty, and the security panel on the wall glowed green in the darkness—I hadn't armed the alarm. *I really need to start turning that thing on.* I padded down the cold corridor, a long and unfamiliar place in this storm, at this hour. I glanced at the skylight above me. Another blast of thunder made me jump. Icy lightning lit the hallway.

I crept to the guest bedroom on my right and peeked in.

Stacks of boxes filled with books. Shadows. The aroma of stale, damp cigarettes.

I glanced in my home office to my left.

Empty.

I stepped over to my desk and stood there. Thought about booting the computer or turning on the television—

I cocked my head.

What's . . . ?

Sounded like squeaking.

My underarms prickled and a thin sheen of sweat covered my arms and back.

I waited, listened . . .

There it is again!

That squeaking. Like a wet sneaker on dry floor.

Someone's here. I hear them. This is not a freak-out.

My Glock was beneath my pillow, as far from me as Nepal. I dropped to the floor, swiped my hand beneath the couch, and grabbed Dad's wooden baseball bat. I inched back to the hallway, bat clenched in both hands. *Please, God. Be with me.* I crept toward the living room, ignoring the rain, the thunder, the floor creaking with every step I took.

"Miss Syeeda."

I cried out and swung around.

Deon Jackson was standing in the doorway of my bedroom.

He looked serene, satisfied, smiling at me as though he belonged there.

"Get out!" I shouted, my hands, my face, all of me numb.

He wore that ratty chinchilla vest, and he stank of wet fur, sweat, and musky cologne. "Let's just talk," he said, walking toward me. "I ain't tryin' to hurt you. I love you, girl. We can find that phantom, just—"

I shrieked and swung the bat at Deon Jackson's head. The bat glanced his ear and hit the wall. The impact wiggled up the shaft to my arms and loosened my grip.

He growled, grabbed for my wrist, but missed.

I stumbled back, planted my feet apart, and swung again. This time, the bat found the left side of his head.

He bellowed in pain, staggered back, then lurched at me again.

I screamed, swung, and thwacked the other side of his head.

He fell to the floor like a bag of dirt.

One more hit on his back, and I dropped the bat and raced to the kitchen. Grabbed the cell phone and my car keys from the countertop and ran out into the rain and to my car. I dove behind the steering wheel, jammed the key into the ignition, and raced down the block. At the corner, I screeched into the 7-Eleven parking lot to call 911, and then Adam.

Adam didn't answer. His phone kept ringing without rolling over to voicemail.

I disconnected and tried again, ignoring the bloody fingerprints ghosting over the touch screen's numbers. "Please pick up. *Please.*"

No answer.

As the storm battered the city, I sat in my car, shaking, wearing only wet boxers and a bloody T-shirt.

A police car zoomed down Vista, lights swirling but no sirens shrieking.

I pulled out of the parking lot and headed home.

The neighborhood was as quiet as it was every morning before dawn.

Two officers turned to me as I rolled into my driveway. They eyed my drenched nightclothes and bare feet.

"You live here?" the blond cop asked.

I nodded. *This is a nightmare. I'm dreaming.* Thunder boomed and the sound hit me in the gut. Not a dream. Very real.

"What happened?" he asked.

I told him about waking up, wandering the house, Deon Jackson stepping from the shadows. "I hit him on the head with a baseball bat," I droned. "He hit the ground and I left the house and waited at 7-Eleven." Then, I told him about the restraining order that had already been filed against Deon Jackson, and that I was dating a detective in HSS just so they'd treat me better than the average citizen. And then, I vomited all over the cop's shoes. I apologized to him as I swiped my mouth.

He assured me that it was okay, that it would come off, that he was used to worse. Then, he and his partner walked toward the front door, guns drawn, shoulder radios crackling, utility belts clanking.

I waited near the walkway.

The light bars on the patrol car clicked and swirled red and blue.

I closed my eyes—the colors were making me dizzy.

Another patrol car pulled up. Cops Three and Four nodded as they walked past me. A light blue Crown Vic pulled behind the second patrol car. A chubby Latino wearing a trench coat and rumpled suit rolled from behind the steering wheel and waddled toward me. "You the resident?" he asked.

I nodded.

Without another word, he moved toward my porch, then disappeared into the house.

Cop One—his tag said B. CANTERBURY—returned to my side with my jacket in his hand. He slipped it over my shoulders, then guided me to the foyer. Detective Flores took my statement as the other officers tromped through the house.

Ten minutes passed and the blond officer—M. KINSEY—returned to the foyer. "He's not here. We searched the house and the backyard but no luck. He got through your kitchen door. Cut the mesh screen, jacked up the window, and climbed in."

The kitchen door had the only window in the house without an alarm sensor.

"He won't be coming back here tonight," Officer Kinsey said. "And we'll put out an APB to all the emergency rooms in the area. If you hit him as hard as you said you did, and from the amount of blood left on your floor, then he'll need a big bag of ice and some stitches."

"A forensics team is supposed to be en route," Detective Flores added. "But that may take some time."

"Does Detective Sherwood live here, too?" Officer Kinsey asked.

I shook my head.

"You try calling him?"

I nodded.

He wanted to ask, "Why isn't he here right now," and waited for my explanation.

But I stood there, quiet as a snail.

"Can you stay somewhere else for the night?" Officer Kinsey asked.

I nodded. *But where? Mom's? Lena's? Adam's?* Didn't like any of those choices.

The officers waited in my driveway as I drifted to the service porch. I pulled clothes from the dryer and stuffed them into a plastic grocery bag. The window screen flapped against the doorframe. Cold air surrounded me as though I was standing at the edge of the world.

"Call your alarm company tomorrow morning," Detective Flores instructed as he loaded me into my car. "And have bars put on that window. That seems to be your most vulnerable point of entry." He gave me his business card, then said, "Need anything else, Miss McKay?"

I whispered, "No. Thank you."

The police officers continued to loiter on my land as I backed out of my driveway and headed to the Sunset Marquis Hotel.

29

I will take her now.

At five in the morning, he is awake and ready to start his day.

There is no sun, and rain falls upon the women on Western Avenue. They wear tiny biker shorts. The wet hides the scabs and scars that cover their legs and filthy, calloused feet. They don't care about the weather as they wiggle up and down the street in grimy summer gear, as they beckon passing cars this early in the day.

He spots Tisha, glassy-eyed and snot-nosed in her purple halter top. A gold heart pendant dangles from her neck. She stands alone in front of a dollar Chinese restaurant. She swipes at her nose, then scratches her scalp.

He forces back his disgust and pulls up to the curb.

She leans into the minivan. "What's up, baby?" She reeks of phlegm and cheap beer.

He does not breathe through his nose—he'd vomit if he did. "Down for whatever. Got any rainy-day specials?"

She laughs. "You a funny one. I'm gon' hook your fine ass up." She slinks toward the alley, throwing a few glances over her shoulder. She smiles, pleased that she lucked up on a customer so early in the day and in such crappy weather.

His hands, protected by tight leather gloves, grip the steering wheel as he follows her to an alley off the main street. "Fine ass, yeah right," he mutters. Women will lie even when they don't have to.

The minivan's headlamps shine on the graffiti-covered walls, on the trash bins and telephone poles. Broken glass sparkles on wet asphalt like diamonds. Past the golden shafts of light, he sees the shadows of other hookers and johns. He hears their noises.

Tisha is waiting for him near a dumpster.

He clicks off the lights and climbs out of the car. By now, he is used to the stink of alleys. The camera and the gun weigh down his coat pockets. Something beneath his shoes crunches. He looks down—cockroaches as big as his thumbs cover the alley floor.

Tisha grins and beckons him closer to the trash bin. She holds out her filthy hand and smiles. "You need to pay me first."

He gazes past her—the others are deserting the alley, and now, he and Tisha are alone. Perfect. He hands her a fifty-dollar bill.

Tisha's eyes widen and she sticks the money into her top. Immediately, she drops to her knees, down there with the roaches, and reaches to unzip his pants. She smiles as she gazes at him, but her grin falters. Face-to-face with a .38. She flashes hot eyes at him. "Why the hell you got a—"

Her face explodes in a shower of blood and bone. She crumples to the ground.

The shot sounds like a quick *pop*, and that is dampened by the rain, by the barking dogs, and the faraway drone of a police helicopter.

He moans and his legs weaken and the clothes rubbing against his skin make him twitch. He turns his face to the sky, to the rain. The weight on his chest lifts, the loud roar in his head quiets. He waits until his hands steady. Then, he plucks the camera from his coat pocket. *Beep.* One picture. The flash is quick, bright white. He zooms in for a tighter shot of her neck, perfect and long as a gazelle. *Beep.* One less whore in the world and one more picture on his wall. If he succeeds, his pictures will span the length of the Great Wall of China.

He stoops and considers the dead woman's pendant, but he leaves that and the money. He's not some petty criminal. He grabs a filled trash bag from a nearby dumpster and tosses it over Tisha's crumpled body. Then, he climbs back into the minivan.

He will go for his tattoo later today. "T. W." will go beneath his left underarm, the place where he sweats the most. He will dress like a thug. Sagging blue jeans, blue Dodgers sweatshirt, dark sunglasses, sneer. He'll drop his *G*'s and use *ain't* a lot. Boast about smackin' hos and cuttin' niggas.

Yeah. He will fit right in.

30

All night, I dreamed.

Of Deon Jackson's hands wrapped around my neck.

Of the hotel room door being kicked in and being pulled out of bed and into the darkness.

Of running blindly in fog that stings my skin, tripping over roots of trees, scraping my palms and knees, a trail of blood behind me, screaming wildly but no one around to hear.

Those times I didn't sleep, I sat up in bed, startling at strange hotel noises. Voices murmuring down the hall. The crash of crushed ice into buckets. Footsteps. Lots of footsteps that sometimes paused at my door.

Morning did come.

I aimed the remote at the television and found the weekend local newscast.

Blond news anchor Amber Andersen chatted about the economic crisis, about who was voted off *Dancing with the Stars, blah blah blah.* After my own dance with the devil, I didn't give a damn about foxtrots or foreclosures.

I yawned, then regarded my surroundings. *Noguchi rice-paper lamps, white linen curtains, tan carpet.* On any other weekend, this hotel was my favorite place to hang. Now, though, it was a designer prison with a minibar.

I grabbed my cell phone from the nightstand and dialed Adam's number.

No answer. This time, his recorded voice told me to leave a message.

"Hey," I said. "Something awful happened last night . . ." Between long pauses to keep from crying, I told him that Deon Jackson had finally broken into my house.

I padded to the large bathroom and stripped. The cascade rain forest showerhead forced me to shower longer than environmentally acceptable, but the beat of water against my body loosened my tight muscles. Cleared my mind. Made me feel stronger, more in control. Brain washed.

I returned to the bedroom.

Lena had left a message on my cell. *Where the hell are you? With your detective? Please, please, please say yes. How can you be with him every day and not want to tap that, like, all the time? Anyhoodle, call me as soon as he pries himself off you.*

Yeah. Not so much.

Amber Andersen had switched to reporting local stories. *LA officials clear the way to hire more police.*

As I slipped a T-shirt over my head, I heard her say, "We now have breaking news about a string of murders around Los Angeles, some dating as far back as 1990."

My eyes fixed on the television screen.

Amber Andersen continued: "Early this morning, police apprehended this man . . ."

A mug shot of a Black man filled the screen. He had coffee-colored skin, a mustache, and big, sleepy eyes. He hadn't looked straight into the camera as the booking officer had taken his picture. Either he had found something more interesting to focus on across the room or he had simply been too ashamed to look the camera in the eye.

I crept closer to the television.

"Herschel Halley," the newswoman said, "is being questioned in the shooting of a young woman found this morning in an alley off Western Avenue." A shot of an alley flashed onto the screen. The high school portrait of Tamar Haist followed. "Halley is also being questioned in the murder of another Southland woman found three days ago in an alley off the same South Los Angeles street. Police have not released the name of this morning's victim, but she is described as an African-American female in her thirties."

Tape rolled for an on-the-street reaction.

A gap-toothed woman wearing a pink do-rag—Corliss Jones, Resident—said, "This is a tragedy. A real tragedy. Just don't make no sense."

Another tape interview began, this one with Betty Cadaret, Resident.

"Why would anyone do this?" Betty wondered as tears soaked her wrinkled face. "She ain't never done nothing to nobody. She ain't never hurt a soul."

In death, everyone was nice, everyone was harmless, and everyone went to Heaven to live with the saints and Jesus.

Back to Amber Andersen: "The victim is in critical condition at an undisclosed—"

My knees weakened and I plopped on the bed.

She's alive?

The anchor announced the scheduled press conference at Parker Center, then said, "And now for an update on that water main break in Sherman Oaks . . ."

Did she see Halley well enough to describe him?

Did she get his license plate?

Could she describe his car?

After checking out of the hotel, I sped through the slick streets of Hollywood and to my neighborhood for my laptop and a change of clothes for the press conference. I called my security company as I drove and told Customer Service Rep Oscar that I needed someone to immediately install an additional alarm on my kitchen window.

"It's Saturday," Oscar said. "We only do a few installations on the weekends, and I don't have anyone to send out. I can for sure have a guy come out first thing on Monday morning, though. Between nine and twelve."

Since I had no choice, I took the appointment.

My street looked the same as it always did on rainy Saturday mornings. Families were sloshing through puddles on their way to temple. Mr. Mendelbaum was standing in his driveway in his blue bathrobe, stooping for the newspaper.

I grabbed my bag from the passenger seat and dashed to the front door.

"Miss McKay?"

I spun around. My keys clattered to my feet.

Reverend Murray Haist bent over. He plucked the keys from the ground, but he did not offer them to me.

I stepped away from him and bumped against the closed front door. I held my bag of clothes in front of me like a shield.

"Didn't mean to scare you," he said, his baritone as smooth and rich as coffee. He stepped back to give me space. He looked rested today. Shaven. No dark circles or splotches on his skin. A pinstriped tie and cuff links.

I threw a glance down my walkway—no one could see us because of the privacy wall that separated the courtyard from the front yard. "How did you get my address?" I whispered.

He nodded. "Internet."

I waited for more explanation.

He looked at me and said nothing.

"How can I help you?"

He held out my keys.

I hesitated, wondered if this was a game, then snatched them from him. No hassle.

"I wasn't very nice to you the other day," he said, "and I'm sorry about that. You probably think I'm an awful person. Selfish. Hypocritical . . ." He paused.

My fingers flexed around my keys. Was he waiting for me to say, *No, not you, you're sweet as sugar*? Ha.

"I'm just a servant of God," he said. "I'm a father whose daughter was violently taken from this world. It's been very difficult for my family and me, Miss McKay. The phone hasn't stopped ringing. We haven't slept in days. And the pain of . . ." He choked, then looked away to hide eyes silver with tears. "I miss her so much."

My grip on the keys weakened. "I know, and I'm sorry if I came off as—"

"No," he said. "You were very polite. Very sensitive to our situation. And God is certainly using you as a comforter to Noemi. She loved her sister so much." He took a deep breath and his shoulders relaxed. "I don't expect respect from strangers, from those other reporters who intrude on our privacy. But you . . . You're not a stranger. You're from the community. You were raised here. From what Noemi told me, you were brought up in the church, so you understand . . . *things*."

What *things* was he referring to?

"All I ask of you," he said, "from *family*, is that you just give us time. Time to grieve. Time to bury our daughter. And then, we'll tell you all that you'd want to know about Tamar."

"In other words, put off publishing my article?"

He held up his hands, palms out. "Just until life settles down some. There are *issues* that will add fuel to the fire. Issues that will distract from her death."

I removed an imaginary piece of lint from my shirtsleeve. "Like the embezzlement? Or the failed engagement to the treasurer's son?"

He nodded. "Among other things that I can't share with you until the right time. Can you do that for us?"

Lena's silver Range Rover screeched into my driveway.

Reverend Haist and I watched my little friend teeter up the walkway with a tray of coffee cups and a clear container of cinnamon rolls.

"I'm still waiting for you to call me," Lena said, kissing my cheek. She then gave the minister the up and down.

He returned her gaze with a lesser sneer.

She shot me a look. "What's going on? And why do you look like crap?"

"Lena," I said, "this is Reverend Haist, Tamar's father."

Nonplussed, she said, "Huh," then used her key to open the front door.

"So about the story," I said to the minister.

"What the hell happened in here?" Lena shouted from inside the house.

I took a deep breath, then tried again. "I have to think about it. I've already promised my editor a story."

"Totally understandable," he said, smiling and bobbing his head in agreement.

"Because my job is to report the truth."

"And the truth shall set you free," he said with a chuckle and an even wider grin. Then, he clapped once, the sharp sound making me jump. "So, it looks like I'm keeping you from your day. Thank you again for listening. And I apologize for startling you and . . ." He took a step back and offered another smile. "Let's talk again next week, yes?"

I nodded. "I really am sorry for all that you're going through."

His smile froze, and he looked at me as though I had transformed into a can of corn. And as quickly as it came, the trance ended and his eyes brightened again. He muttered, "Thanks," turned on his heel, and headed to the white Lexus parked at the curb.

Lena stood in the hallway, eyes wide, arms spread. "Why is there blood on the wall?"

My gaze found the flecks of darkened crimson on white paint. Someone had cleaned the blood from the hallway floor. "Deon . . . Deon . . ."

She took a step toward me and grabbed my hands. Even though her eyes shimmered with tears, her nostrils flared. "What did he do?"

I told her.

Her grip tightened, then she released me. She swiped at a tear that had tumbled down her cheek. She shook her head, then met my eyes. "Where was the cop?"

"At home." And I told her about my night with Adam.

She exhaled, ruffled her hair, then glanced at the blood again. "So . . . So . . . I have things to do today."

"Yeah. I have a press conference that . . ." My words trailed off.

She hugged me. "Don't worry, dearest. You know I got your back." She offered a reluctant smile, then marched to the front door.

All the innocence had been sucked from my house. The air stank of wet fur, cheap cologne . . . and him. I could have every square foot of my home steam cleaned, and would probably do so, but Deon Jackson would still be there, in the house with me.

But he's not here. He'll never come here again.

A receipt sat on the dresser in my bedroom—the forensics team had taken possession of the baseball bat. Great.

The Glock was still beneath the pillow. Okay.

The doorbell rang.

I plodded back to the foyer. Kept the chain on as I opened the front door.

A Black guy in a blue uniform smiled. "I'm Sean with ASC."

The security company.

I exhaled and slipped off the chain. "Thought you guys couldn't make it out today."

Sean wore a goatee, and braces covered his teeth. He stepped past me, his heavy work boots echoing through the house. "We had a few cancellations, so here I am."

"Let me show you, then." I pivoted and headed to the kitchen.

"Now, I won't be able to do anything," he said, "but I can get a sense of what we'll need to do on Monday."

I stopped before the kitchen door—the cops had used strips of duct tape to hold down the screen. "He came in through here. Cut the mesh, jacked up the window, and crawled through."

"Were you home at the time?" Sean asked as he studied the window.

"I was asleep in my bedroom. I have a restraining order against him and everything, and still . . ." My words sounded dull, flat.

The kitchen smelled like wet dog, Obsession cologne . . .

"Was the alarm armed?"

I tapped my fists against each other and tried not to breathe in that stink of stalker. "I forget sometimes." All the time.

Sean tugged at his cap and sighed with exasperation. "That would've given you a heads-up." He nodded at the door. "This shouldn't be too hard. Just another sensor. Something to keep that window from being opened from the outside. Shouldn't be too expensive."

"Wonderful." I hugged myself, not really caring anymore.

Sean considered me for a moment, then said, "Sorry this happened to you. I hope they catch him."

I thanked him for his concern.

"Need anything else?" he asked, sorrow in his expression.

I shook my head, then led him back to the foyer.

"So you'll be here Monday?" he asked.

"Me or my friend," I said. "Between nine and twelve, right?"

He nodded, then headed down the walkway. "I'll try to get here sooner, though."

"Thanks for coming," I shouted after him.

He looked back over his shoulder. "See you Monday."

Four minutes later, I grabbed my laptop, armed the alarm, and rushed out of the house.

31

The rain had stopped, but heavy clouds the color of battleships still hung over Los Angeles. Since "weather" complicates every task in this city, it took me ten minutes to find a parking space at Parker Center, the Los Angeles Police Department's headquarters. But I lucked out and beat an old lady in a station wagon to the last spot in the lot. She shook her fist at me, but I didn't care. After last night's drama, the Universe owed me. It could start by offering me a freakin' parking space.

Spencer was standing near the entrance to the building, his eyes lost in his BlackBerry, his thumbs tapping away at those tiny silver keys. He didn't look like a physician, at least the type who announced it everywhere he went, MD tattooed on his forehead and tongue, wearing scrubs to the post office, a stethoscope always coiled around his neck as though it gave him life. With those wire-framed glasses, that button-down shirt, and his slight frame, Spencer looked more dot.com than doctor.

He looked up as I approached, not seeing me at first, and then smiling as those blinders lifted. "I was just emailing you. Didn't know if you'd wrangle your way in. Just wanted to make sure that you did."

"My name's still at the front desk," I said. "And I'd pay a million dollars to sit in today."

He touched my shoulder. "You okay? Don't take this the wrong way, but you look like crap."

"Long night," I said without blinking. "Had a hard time sleeping."

"You sound stuffy. Maybe you're catching the flu."

"Maybe."

Reporters started to crowd around us—the press conference about the arrest of Herschel Halley was starting in five minutes. A cameraman jostled past me, sending me into Spencer's arms. I glared at the madness swirling around us.

Spencer took my hand. "Guess we should go in before you're trampled."

"A routine traffic stop on Western Avenue led to his arrest," Adam announced. "He was driving erratically, and the arresting officer who pulled him over quickly determined that Mr. Halley was under the influence of drugs or alcohol."

We were all huddled in the press room. Some of us held notepads and pens; others held digital recorders and video cameras. Our faces were turned to Adam, who stood at the bank of microphones, his small task force beside him. The mug shot of Herschel Halley loomed large on a screen that had dropped down from the ceiling.

Since his honorable discharge from the army, Halley had worked as an auto mechanic. He was also hiding a growing drug and sex addiction. In fact, a baggie of cocaine and a sex worker named Savannah were in the car with him at the time of this morning's arrest. Cops had also found a .38, its barrel still warm to the touch and still stinking of gunpowder.

The picture of Halley clicked away, and was replaced by a shot of an alley off Western. Less than a mile from Tamar's church.

Didn't know how to feel. Relief since they had caught a documented bad guy? Wariness since part of me refused to believe that Halley had murdered Tamar Haist even if he had possibly tried to kill the woman now being discussed?

"We found Mr. Halley near Motel Row," Adam was saying. "A search of the suspect's car also resulted in the discovery of an engraved heart pendant that belonged to the victim."

I held up my hand, but Adam called on Connor Sullivan, the police reporter at the *Times* who had replaced me. "Who found her?" Connor asked.

Adam said, "A homeless man searching through the dumpsters for cans. He also claims to have seen Mr. Halley removing the money as well as that chain from the victim's person."

"Is she talking yet?" Sullivan asked.

"She slipped into a coma before we could interview her."

"What's her name?"

Adam said, "We will not be releasing that information. With today's arrest, though, we hope to start bringing closure to those families affected by these murders."

I raised my hand again. No luck.

Genevieve Bellman, reporter from the *Sentinel,* said, "Has Halley confessed?" She wore a pink headband that matched her pink J.Crew shirt dress. That was her "thing." Headbands. So original.

Adam shook his head. "Halley insists that he is not the Phantom Slayer."

Genevieve asked, "Did he kill Tamar Haist?"

Adam said, "We will let you know if he did."

She batted her eyelashes. "Thank you, Detective."

Frustrated, I thrust my hand into the air again.

Adam said, "Syeeda?"

"Where's the mayor?"

"Out of town. But he has been briefed on this morning's events."

"And why isn't the police chief here?"

Adam said, "He's involved and aware. We're continuing to work with Vice and Homicide detectives as well as local sex workers to alert them of the danger."

Meaning: The higher-ups could give a damn. No surprise there.

Spencer and I ambled toward the parking lot as synthetic-looking humans with helmet hair stood before bright lights emitted from video cameras. *Reporting live from Parker Center with late-breaking news.* I had left the conference room with more questions than answers. The constant drone of helicopters and the blurp of sirens had also given me a headache. And my arms and healing breast were sore from beating Deon Jackson with my father's baseball bat.

I felt like a champ.

"Did Halley do it?" I asked Spencer.

He didn't respond.

I stopped in my step and turned to him. "His DNA won't match what you found on Tamar. Am I right?"

"We haven't even swabbed the man's cheek yet, Sy. What do you want me to say?"

"What about Reverend Haist?"

"What about him? He has an alibi, Sy. Why do you still think he—?"

"He has a history of violence against women," I snapped. "In particular, sex workers who do business around his church. And who says the security guard is telling the truth? Maybe they're going around town together, beating up women after prayer meeting."

Spencer blinked at me. "Sy—"

"Is Reverend Haist's DNA being tested against the Slayer's?"

He sighed, but said nothing.

I took that as a yes. "How did this morning's victim live when the others didn't?"

"Luck," he said. "The bullet hit the right side of her head. Ripped apart her jawbone and severed her carotid artery. Honestly? She's supposed to be dead."

Adam was waiting by my car. He didn't smile as I approached, nor did he call me Jessica Fletcher. Instead, he said, "What do you know about Halley?"

I stopped in my step. "Who are you talking to, Detective? Me? And can you say hello first?"

"Hello. What do you know about Halley?" He took a step closer and stood with his hands on his hips, his feet spread apart. The cop stance.

"I don't know anything about him."

"Is he one of your sources?"

"Did you not hear me? I don't know the man." I sighed, then said, "Did you get my message?"

He shook his head. "I've been busy."

I faked a smile. "You're always busy."

"You can't keep doing this to me. Pulling me in and pushing me away."

I said, "You're right."

"And I'm getting tired of it, Syeeda." He paused, then said, "No. I *am* tired of it. I can't do it anymore."

I blinked at him. "Okay."

He nodded.

We were done.

"So you left a message?"

"Yep. Wanna listen to it before we go any further?"

He pulled the phone from his coat pocket. As he listened, his face crumpled. He found my eyes and kept whispering, "I'm sorry, babe," until my message ended. He closed the phone and said, "Shit, Sy. I'm sorry. I didn't know. I was pissed off after you left, and I didn't feel like talking to you and . . ." He shook his head. "Forensics come out?"

I nodded.

"Who was the detective?"

"Flores, I think. He gave me his card. Told me to stay somewhere else for the night."

"Where did you go? To your mother's? Lena's?"

"Nope. Stayed at the Sunset Marquis."

He shoved his hands into his pants pockets. "You didn't wanna stay at my place?"

I squinted at him. "You wouldn't answer the phone."

He dropped his eyes. "Did you call the security company?" He sounded weak, defeated.

"They're coming Monday," I said. "A guy stopped by this morning, though, just to see how Deon Jackson got through."

"Damn it, Sy. I'm sorry. I should've—" He reached for me.

I stepped away from him.

"Don't," he said, shaking his head.

"You're tired of it, remember?"

"Sy." He closed the space between us.

I moved away again.

"I'll make it up to you," he said. "I swear."

"No. That's okay. About the Phantom Slayer . . ."

Adam swiped his face with a hand. "What about him?"

"I need to show you something." I pulled the laptop from my bag, sat the computer on the hood of the car, and opened the first message from the Slayer. "I got this late Thursday night."

Adam double-clicked on the icon and his eyes flicked across the screen. He frowned and took a step back. "Who the hell is she?"

"I sent a reply and got this back." I opened the second message.

"What the . . . ?" Adam clicked on the JPEG. "This is you. Wait . . ." He glanced at me. "This was last year."

"Paula Owens."

"Why didn't you say anything?" he said in his uppercase voice.

"Don't yell at me, first of all. And I left you a message, but you didn't call me back. That's your 'thing' now, ignoring me. Hope you treat Roya better than that."

His eyes widened. "Roya? Sy, what—?"

"And second, I didn't say anything because I thought it was another hoax. And on the off chance that it wasn't, I was hoping that he'd send me something else."

"For your stupid book?"

"No. For your stupid case."

"And has he sent you anything else?"

"No."

Adam stared at me, waiting for a better answer.

"He hasn't," I said, "and his email address no longer works."

Adam paced a bit, then turned to me. "I need your computer. We need to trace the emails. Examine the pictures and those messages."

"What if I say no?"

"You have a desktop at home."

"I need to be mobile. Can't do that with a desktop."

Adam's eyes darkened. "I'll get a warrant for it, then. I'm either getting your computer now or three hours from now. It's your choice."

Defeated, I handed him my beloved VAIO.

"I promise to get it back to you as soon as I can. I'll even have the tech guys back up your hard drive before diving in."

I muttered, "Yeah."

"Anything else I should know?" he asked. "Anything else you're not telling me?"

"No."

"Would you be willing to take a polygraph?" he asked. "To verify that you don't know Halley?"

My mouth opened again, but I couldn't speak.

"Is that a no?"

"It is what it is," I said, reaching past him to open the car door. "I'm not lying, and I'm all kinds of offended right now because how dare you, but I'll take your stupid test if that makes you feel better."

"It's not about me feeling better or you being offended," he snapped. "It's about finding the lunatic killing women in this city. It's about coming down on someone who knows more than what she's saying—"

"Halley is not my source," I said. "Other than you and Spencer, I had one other contact and she was killed before she could say one word to me. When do I take the test? We can do it today. My lawyer will be happy to schedule a time."

He snorted. "Lawyer? It's like that now?"

I spread my arms. "Is it? You're the one threatening people with search warrants. You're throwing me under the bus, Adam."

We glared at each other without speaking.

"Roya and I aren't together anymore," he said. "She thinks there's something between me and her. And she's right—you're between us."

"And what am I supposed to do with that?"

"Nothing." He turned on his heel. "I'll be over later to fix your window."

"Don't bother."

He looked back over his shoulder. "You need it fixed."

"I *needed* my friend last night, but he wouldn't pick up the phone."

Before he could respond, I slammed into the driver's seat and hurled my bag to the floor well. I closed my eyes and belted out the strongest "*Fuck!*" ever. My hands clenched the steering wheel as I gulped air and forced back tears. After my pulse had slowed, I opened my eyes.

Adam was gone.

And I was alone. Again.

32

Before heading back home, I stopped at Home Depot. Bought a wooden plank, two long sticks of PVC pipe, five security-bar door jammers, two security chains for the French and kitchen doors, an electric saw, and a power drill.

I dumped all of it in the middle of the living room, not knowing what to do with 90 percent of the crap I had just bought. Saws terrified me, and how-to instructions made my brain bleed. So I did all that I could, tasks that didn't threaten my limbs or sanity: I jammed the security bars beneath the doorknobs, then rolled five-gallon water bottles at the foot of the bars for extra resistance. Then, I armed the alarm before retreating to my office.

Detective Flores had left a voicemail message: The Long Beach police had arrested Deon Jackson at a hospital emergency room. He had been beaten far worse than what I had described. Broken ribs and a broken arm as well as a concussion.

Was that Lena's work?

No remorse for the ailing thug. Didn't want to think about what he would've done to me had he caught me still asleep in bed.

I plopped in the chair in front of the computer and snapped at the band on my wrist. *What now?*

I opened the Slayer's emails and studied the first picture again. Who was this woman in the alley? Like the others, she was Black and looked to be in her late twenties to mid-thirties.

And where was this picture taken?

I had visited several dark, narrow streets around Los Angeles. Unfortunately, the alley in this picture looked like every alley in the world. Broken glass, overstuffed trash bins, graffiti, pools of mysterious liquid on potholed asphalt.

I grabbed the phone and punched in Eva's number.

"Auntie!" Josie, my niece.

"Hey, sweet potato!" I said, forcing light into my voice. "Happy Sabbath."

The five-year-old launched into her day: church and a lunch of macaroni and turkey meatloaf. I saw her in my mind, rocking two Afro puffs with some decorative bauble on each, two spaces in her bottom row of teeth. "My mom wants me to take a nap," she said, "but I already slept at church."

As a kid, I, too, used to snore during eleven o'clock service. "Hey, Josie. Is your mom around?"

"She's on the couch. Hold on." The phone rustled, and Josie shouted, "Mom, Auntie wants to talk to you."

As my niece walked the phone to her mother, I debated telling Eva about Deon Jackson, then decided against it for now.

"Did you go to church today?" Eva asked, sarcasm in her tone.

"Uhhh . . . I'm gonna hit the evening service," I said. "Yeah. That's right. The evening service. Is Josie still in the room?"

"She's outside with Ben. Why?"

I took a deep breath, then said, "There's been a new develop—"

"It's the seventh day. No working."

I frowned. "When did you become so observant?"

"I'm trying to be better. For Josie. You'll understand when you have kids."

"Can you break the law this one time?" I asked, irritated. "And who says I want kids?"

She sighed, now pissed at me. "What do you want, Sy?"

I wandered over to the window and gazed out at my rain-drenched backyard. "Two days ago, the Slayer sent me pictures and two email messages."

Silence . . . More silence.

"Did you hear me?" I asked.

"Why didn't you tell me?"

"At first I thought it was a hoax, and then, freakin' Deon broke in—"

"What?"

Crap. I told her about the break-in and then about the Slayer's messages and pictures. "I had to leave the house, and Adam took my computer, and . . . I'm having a midday crisis combined with the slowest nervous breakdown ever experienced by one woman." I rested my head against the cool windowpane.

"Send me a PDF of the barcode on Tamar's dress," she said. "Maybe I can move this along somehow. Keep you from losing your mind for a few hours. Is Adam sending the pictures and messages to my office?"

"I guess."

"I'll call him on Monday," she said.

"Why would the Slayer take pictures?"

"Mementos," Eva said.

"Souvenirs of his murders?"

"Yep. He can look at the photographs of his victims and be reminded of the thrill of stalking them, of killing them."

I closed my eyes, my stomach twisty and sour. "This is getting sicker and scarier."

She chuckled. "You're lucky he didn't send you video. Now *that's* some sick, twisted . . . One time, this monster sent me a DVD that showed what he did to his victims. I won't even describe it. I didn't go near my DVD player for two weeks."

On Eva's end, I heard Josie shrieking, "Spider! *Spider!*"

"I'll let you get that," I said.

"Keep me posted," Eva said, hanging up before I could respond.

I returned to my computer and to those messages. I considered the photograph's file name—06113551.

Couldn't be a date. One digit short to be a Social Security number.

The doorbell rang.

I hopped out of my chair, hoping that it was Adam.

The bell rang again. "Sy, you home?" A woman.

I left the chain on and opened the door.

Krystal Miller stood on my porch, all smiles, like a neighbor selling Mary Kay. "Bet you didn't think you'd ever see me again."

Stunned, it took me a few seconds to respond. That response: lots of blinking.

Could the day get any stranger?

Beneath her jacket, she wore a tight JESUS IS THE ANSWER T-shirt, a different style from the last time I'd seen her five years ago. That night at Houston's, she looked like a boozy working girl, all heavy makeup and perfume, fetid from spilled Rémy Martin and sex. Tonight, she had scrubbed the makeup off her cinnamon-colored face. She had freed her scalp of weave tracks, and now, she wore her long, coiled hair in a low ponytail, just as she had in college.

"It's raining out here," Krystal said. "Are you gonna invite me in?"

I looked past her to my driveway—a cherry-red Maserati was parked next to my car. I slipped off the chain and gestured for her to enter.

She held a bouquet of yellow roses. "Your house is beautiful," she said, her eyes flitting to the foyer's stained glass window and crown molding. She flicked me a smile, then searched for something else to compliment. Her eyes landed at my feet. "Hardwood floors. Nice."

We retreated to the living room. She slipped off her jacket, then sat on the couch with a sigh, as though she visited all the time, as though we were still homegirls. I sat on the sofa across from her, my legs crisscross-applesauce beneath me. A good hostess would've offered her a cup of tea or hot cocoa to chase the chill, but I didn't. Instead, I folded my arms and slowly exhaled.

"These are for you." She handed me the flowers. "And . . ." She reached behind her and pulled a gun from the small of her back.

I sat up. "Krys . . ."

"Don't worry." She placed the tiny, pearl-handled pistol on the coffee table. "I'm not gonna shoot you. I carry it for protection. The world's been a scary place lately."

Word.

She wore no fake nails and no colored contacts like she used to. She couldn't do much about the tattoos on her wrists and biceps, or the ink on her lower back. If it were possible, she would've cut out the implants that made her tee tighter than what a religious shirt should've been. She had been the prettiest of our group of twelve, but she had never believed it. No self-confidence. Even less self-esteem. She'd do anything to please a person, to be accepted.

And now, even though she was obviously trying to "be good" with the Jesus tee, the clean face, and sober hairstyle, it was also obvious that she still wanted to fit in.

"So why did you come?" I asked. "Are you orating part two of your letter?"

She clapped her hands once and rubbed her palms together. "I don't have a lot of time left here, and I need to resolve some issues before . . . before I go. Sending you a letter helped me tie up some of those loose ends. By the way, you weren't the only person to get mail." She grinned. "I'm more popular than ever."

I had stuffed Krystal's letter into my purse two nights ago, when Toni, Lena, and I had eaten at Cobras y Matadors. I hadn't read it again, nor had I taken it out of my bag. Because what do you do with something like that? File it? Burn it? Scrapbook it?

"I haven't had a drink in three months," Krystal announced.

"Congratulations."

"It's not about that. It's about achieving sobriety, one step at a time."

"Well, now I know," I said, rolling my eyes.

"You can't right wrongs when you're drunk. As I was making a moral inventory of myself, I realized that I've also hurt people, and that I've allowed people to hurt me because I saw myself as worthless." She tilted her head and offered a crooked smile. "Believe it or not, I sent that letter out of my love for you."

"Yeah. I saw the LOVE stamp." I glanced at the gun and decided to dial down the smart-ass.

"Maybe the program will help you with your struggles with alcohol," she said.

I sat straighter, now interested in the conversation. "I'm not struggling with—"

"The first step to recovery is to admit that you're powerless over alcohol, that life—"

I laughed and peered at the ceiling. "Is there a hidden camera somewhere?" I whipped around in my seat as I searched above me. "Is this the moment when the person who's caroused and fornicated all of her life finds God, then tells her former friends how wrong they are?" My heart beat wildly in my chest as I turned back to consider Krystal with narrowed eyes. "Or is this the *Ricki Lake* episode with the bully tricked into coming on the show to be confronted by some pathetic whiner who's still nursing a grudge."

Krystal held my gaze. "I see you haven't changed."

"We haven't talked in five years. I've changed a lot." I snapped the rubber band on my wrist and gritted my teeth.

She nodded. "You know what, Sy? I forgive you. I forgive you for every single thing you've done to me. Let go and let God—that's what I'm doing from now on."

"I've never done anything to you," I said. "And the last time I saw you, I kept pleading with you to come over, to be a part of the group. But you may not remember that—*you* were the one drunk that night. And that's not being mean. That's being observant."

"I drank because I was ill," she said. "Same thing with sex. I was sick, body and mind. Thought I was okay because I had all the material things a woman could ever want."

"Like the Maserati in my driveway?" I asked.

"But I'm more than that. I'm sad that it's taken me all these years to realize this, but I'm a child of God, blessed and highly favored. I'm not trash. I'm not a whore."

I shrugged. "Fine." Because what does one say to "I'm not a whore"? *The hell you are?*

She leaned forward, her eyes wide and greedy. "Come to a meeting, Sy. Before I go, I wanna help your body recover, help you experience what I've achieved. The rehab places you've been to don't—"

"I've never been to rehab," I said, too loudly. "I'm not—"

"An alcoholic," Krystal said, rolling her eyes. "Let's be honest, Sy. You drank a lot in college."

I made an exaggerated sigh. "Everyone drinks in college. And everyone bounces a lot of checks and falls in love with losers who—"

"You lied to your mother about drinking," she pointed out. "And you'd black out—"

"Krystal, what are you talking about?" I asked, confused. "*Who* are you talking about? I lied to my mother about a whole bunch of crap, like every other college kid in the world, and I passed out one time during those four years and . . . You know what? I don't have to explain *shit* to you. I know who I am."

Krystal exhaled, so patient with the alleged alcoholic sitting across from her. "Syeeda, the image you have in your mind isn't the one the world sees. We're all good, sober people in our imaginations. Really: I'm not here to put you down. I'm just being honest."

My neck muscles were bunched beneath my skin. "And I honestly don't remember being mean or spiteful to you."

"Of course you don't. You were drunk most of the time."

I hopped off the couch and strode to the front door. "Good seeing you again, Krystal. I hope you'll be happier wherever you're going."

"Why are you being so defensive?" Krystal followed me into the foyer with the gun in her hand. "We were all scandalous bitches back in college. Some of us were just sneakier about it."

"Me, for instance?" My eyes skittered to that pistol and back to her face.

She stepped toward me. So close that I could smell the Columbian roast AA coffee on her breath. "Sleeping with friends' boyfriends?"

"Like?"

"Derrick."

"Who?"

"I was in love with Derrick, and you slept with him and you don't even remember?"

I crossed, then uncrossed my arms. "Krystal, that was almost twenty years ago."

She took another step, trying to crowd me in my own house. "I bet Toni wouldn't care if it was twenty years ago or twenty minutes ago. You slept with her husband."

My stomach dropped, and my mouth filled with spit. I placed a hand against my clammy forehead, and said, "Toni and I . . . we're cool now. And Joey wasn't her husband when all that happened. And it didn't mean anything anyway."

Krystal smirked, pleased that she had forced a reaction from me. "They were still dating."

My eyes burned into hers, and I straightened to my full height. "What do you want?"

"No, Syeeda. What do *you* want? Don't you wanna live the way God wants you to before it's too late?"

"According to your rules? No, I don't." I opened the door, tired of her mash-up of evangelism and extortion. "Good night, Krystal. Thanks for stopping by. Good luck with everything. I mean that."

She didn't move. Tears filled her eyes, and as she opened her mouth to speak, a sob escaped. "I've had so much pain in my life. Pain that you'd never understand . . . I just need . . . I need a friend right now."

My anger died some as damp air washed over me, as Krystal (obviously not well) wept in my foyer. With a gun stuck in her pants.

"I'm sorry I hurt you," I said. "Even though I swear that I don't remember what I did." My mind raced—*what else can I say?* "If I'd known—"

She stomped out of my house and tramped down the walkway. She froze midway, swaying as though she stood on a boat. She turned back, her face in shadow, her eyes dark holes. Ghost eyes. "This isn't turning out how I had expected."

"No?"

She swiped at her face. "Things always sound worse on paper than when someone says it. Sounded better in my head, too. Kinda like using the all caps key in an email, not because you're angry but because you're not thinking. But the other person has no idea and they just see the capital letters, and that's what happened with the letter I sent."

I said, "Fine."

"And I'm sorry for that letter and for coming here and upsetting you." She covered her eyes with a hand and chuckled. "So much is going on right now. It's like I'm living that stupid Rockwell song from the eighties. The song about somebody watching me."

"Who's following you, Krys?"

She chuckled. "Wives who have found out about me. Private investigators who are trying to bust unfaithful husbands. The IRS. The whole state of Kentucky."

I stood there, mute.

She eyed the security bar and the water bottle. A sad smile found her lips, and she shook her head. "You can't keep out people who really want to come in."

My turn, now, to look at my security measures.

She placed her hand on her heart. "You think that we can move past all the drama and be friends again?"

I shrugged. "You're the one who sent the letter."

She stared at a spot behind me. "Yeah . . . I guess what's done is . . ." She sighed, too tired to complete the phrase. She glanced over her shoulder, then turned back to me with worry in her eyes.

"Are you okay?" I asked.

"No." She paused, then said, "Later, Sy."

My nerves crackled beneath my skin like candy wrappers as I watched her climb into the Maserati.

Moments later, the car's high-profile tires squealed out of my driveway, and its four-hundred-horsepower engine roared up Vista like a cyclone.

I paced the living room as I tried to understand Krystal's reasons for her "come to Jesus" visit, for her sudden desire to be friends again. Had I been that mean and vindictive without ever realizing it? Had I been Krystal's Phantom Slayer from 1988 to 1992, slowly killing her with bon mots and by bedding the boys she loved?

And Derrick? Yeah, I remembered Derrick. Basketball body, cocky as hell, drove a black Volkswagen GTI, couldn't kiss worth shit. Since freshman year, he had ignored and teased Krystal. In our junior year, he finally came after me. I slept with him. Once. After a Saturday night Pajama Jammie Jam. I didn't call him again, rarely acknowledged him if I saw him in class or at a party, just so he'd know how it felt to be ignored. I was the Robin Hood of Love.

And Joey . . . I had wanted him, and I had had him. An awful friend, I admit, for the second time in my life.

Back then. A long time ago. College. Truckloads of stupid crap happened during those four years. Drinking too much. Having unprotected sex. Using your financial aid money to buy lingerie for Pajama Jammie Jams.

As an adult, you already had to forgive yourself for being such a freakin' idiot. Why hold a grudge against someone else who had acted just as stupid?

33

After my old friend's departure, I grabbed Tamar's dress from the hallway closet and dashed out the front door. My eyes flicked up and down the wet street. Some families were walking back from temple. A few teenagers were skateboarding through puddles on the sidewalk. I dove behind my car's steering wheel, turned the ignition before strapping the seat belt, and threw the car in reverse. Too much gas. I squealed out onto Vista, almost hitting Mr. Mendelbaum's Oldsmobile.

Ten minutes later, I pulled into a metered parking space off Rodeo Drive.

The sidewalks were bereft of shoppers and tourists. Rain and the economy had created the worst-ever shopping conditions. Cars on Wilshire Boulevard were passing through Beverly Hills, heading to Target and Marshalls instead of Neiman Marcus and Gucci. In a few stores that lined the swanky street, security guards stood by the doors with no customers to scrutinize. Bored salespeople chatted with each other as their jewelry and handbags went untouched.

The women's apparel section of Saks Fifth Avenue was as busy as a swimming pool in the Antarctic. The few women at the racks browsed, searching for that marked-down St. John suit, half-off D&G blouse, or clearance pair of Rock & Republic blue jeans. They'd glance around to see if anyone was looking their way, then they'd check the price tag. Their eyes would widen in shock, and they'd bite collagened fish lips—*charge or not?* Most chose not, and stuck the shirt/suit/jeans back on the rack, returning to the escalators, misty-eyed and empty-handed.

With Tamar Haist's dress on my arm, I headed in the opposite direction. Some women glanced at me with a glint in their eyes. *Who did she screw to score a dress like that in times like these?*

The saleswoman in women's apparel hummed beneath her breath as she sorted skirts and slacks that had been left in the dressing room. She wore a hijab over her hair, a dusty-pink scarf with sequins and embroidery. Her badge said MARTI, and she smiled at me as I approached. Her heavily lined eyes sparkled with the prospect of a sale.

I returned the smile and hoped that she would be bored and stupid enough to help me.

Marti frowned as I placed the dress on the counter. "Oh no. You didn't like it?"

"I love it," I said. "Unfortunately, it's the wrong size *and* it may have been purchased with a stolen credit card."

Marti scrunched her exquisitely drawn-on eyebrows. *Go on.*

"I was dating this guy," I said, "and I thought he was The One. But his wife—"

"He was married?"

I poked out my lip. "Married with three kids, one of them with muscular dystrophy."

"What a douche."

"It gets better. He bought me this dress—by the way, a size zero? Has he seen me naked?"

Marti laughed. Laughed a little too long and too loud. *Homeboy must be blind.*

"Anyway," I said, kicking away annoyance, "I confronted the wife and told her that her husband was a dog. But she broke my heart with the kids and her recent cancer surgery, and then she told me that Chris had stolen her credit card."

Marti gasped. *That douche.*

"She hasn't seen the credit card statement that comes in the mail," I continued, "because he's hiding them from her. But she remembered that he came home with a Saks bags on a day she was at chemo. He's shopping and she's at chemo, can you believe that? She's divorcing him as soon as she goes into remission and as soon as her little boy starts occupational therapy and gets his leg braces. I'm gonna help her get all that she can from that cheating bastard. She deserves more than half. She deserves all of it."

Marti nodded, touched her heart. "Women gotta stick together."

I leaned forward on the counter. "I know you can't give me the credit card number he used, but I'm hoping that you could scan the tag to find his name or her name somewhere. Just to prove that he bought it."

In the car, I had outlined my story, but just as it happened with my writing, I had veered into another direction. Every word after "married with three kids" had been so melodramatic—*shopping during chemo?*—that I held my breath, waited for Marti to call bullshit and then call security.

The saleswoman held the dress up for inspection. "I don't know if I can do that. It's against store policy to give names of our customers . . ."

"Anything you can tell me will be helpful," I said. "I haven't even worn it. And his wife—she couldn't fit into a size zero if Jenny Craig paid her to." *Why am I snarking on a cheated-on wife battling ovarian cancer?* Didn't she have enough to deal with without me making fun of her weight?

Marti grabbed her scanner and aimed the laser at the tag's barcode. The register beeped and she consulted the monitor. "He bought it here on September 19. So a few weeks ago. And he did use a credit card. An American Express. There's nothing else I can tell you. Sorry, sweetie."

"You're a doll. That's still more than what I knew before. She doesn't even have an AMEX card." I offered her a sad smile as I took the dress and started toward the escalators.

"Are you on our mailing list?" Marti called out to me. "Cuz you'll get something from us in a couple of days. We're having a sale next weekend. Forty percent off all Juicy Couture!"

As though I needed another velour sweat suit with Juicy on its ass. Gilding the lily, indeed.

I retreated to my car, unsure of my next steps. A group of giggly Japanese tourists passed, all huddled beneath a giant, Burberry-plaid umbrella. Only one woman in the group clutched a Louis Vuitton shopping bag.

Now that's a store that never has sales . . .

Sale.

Sale on Juicy Couture.

Sale.

An unformed idea flitted around that word like a moth around a campfire.

Sale.

I sat still, barely breathing, waiting for whatever it was to fully realize into a true thing.

If the store is having a sale . . .

Then . . .

Then, they announce the sale.

Okay . . .

With mailers.

So?

. . .

The idea sat on a rock, refusing to flit any further if I continued to be this dense.

. . .

I sighed and reached to start the car. "Oh!" The idea hit me so hard my vision blurred.

I called Noemi Haist.

A man answered the phone.

"Is this Reverend Haist?" I asked, praying that it wasn't.

"No. It's Jay. Who's this?"

Who? "Sy McKay. I'm trying to reach Noemi Haist."

"Hey, Miss McKay. We met at Great Redeemer. I do security . . ."

Oh, yeah. Reminded me of . . . no one and everyone. "Yes, I remember now. I was actually looking for you last night."

"Oh, yeah?" He sounded pleased. "What do you need?"

"Well, right now, I need to speak to Noemi."

"She's right here," he said. "Are you stopping by the church?"

"Not tonight. I just need to talk to—"

"No problem," he said, still bright. "Anything you need, just let me know."

The phone rustled, muffled voices, more rustling, and then: "Hello?" It was Noemi.

"How are you?" I asked.

"Can I ask you something?" She hesitated before saying, "Why are the police following my father around the city?"

Caught off guard, I opened my mouth and a strangled "Erumwhat" moved past my lips.

"Do they think . . . ? Is my father . . . ? Did he do something wrong?"

Not sure what to say—Adam had not mentioned this to me—I cleared my throat and ran my fingers through my hair. "I think they're trying to see if the Slayer will approach your dad at some point." Yeah. That's it.

Noemi exhaled. "Oh. Okay. I thought . . . Okay. I feel better now. Jay said the same thing, but . . . That's good to know."

"The article on Tamar is being published on Tuesday," I said, knowing that I still had yet to write one word.

"I can't wait to read it," she said. "I really appreciate this."

"Well, you may not when all this is over."

She grunted in disagreement. "If it's an honest portrayal of my sister, then I will."

"Have you kept any of Tamar's mail?"

"I'm keeping all of it," she said. "So when we're ready to handle her affairs, we can go through everything at once."

"Mind if I browse through what you have?"

She paused. "Why?"

"Because I think I've found Secret Boyfriend Christopher."

The office of the 320 Task Force was located in Room 320 of the Parker Center, and it was the size of three broom closets. Mounds of paper piled high next to empty Styrofoam coffee cups and Krispy Kreme boxes. Plastic crates filled with stuffed envelopes were stacked in corners, moments away from toppling. The sound of ringing phones was constant, and lines blinked red and green like traffic signals. Two detectives studied a wall plastered with photographs of dead women. It looked just like my Death Wall at home.

Adam sat at one of six messy desks. He was gnawing on a pizza slice and sipping a Coke as he flipped through the pages of a thick murder book.

He glanced at me and said, "You can't have your computer back yet."

"Fine. Have you talked to the treasurer's son?"

"Yep." His eyes remained lost in the book.

"They arrested Deon Jackson," I said.

"Yeah. I heard. Was Lena around when Deon Jackson slipped down that flight of stairs?"

I swallowed, then said, "No."

Silence.

"You didn't tell me that you're trailing Reverend Haist."

"Because it's supposed to be a secret," he said, still avoiding my eyes.

I wanted to slap the book out of his hands, then stomp away. Instead, I cleared my throat, then asked, "Did you find anything on my computer that helps the case?"

He shook his head. "Just eyeballing it, I couldn't learn anything except that the dead address and the messages were sent Pacific Standard Time. I was told that I needed a court order to look at Internet Protocol addresses. So right now, I can't look at the network he used or where the message oriented. And I can't get the court order until Monday." Adam tossed the pizza slice back in the box and wiped his fingers on a napkin. "Doesn't matter anyway. It's all just piss in the wind."

Besides being angry with me, he was in a mood.

"And how's the victim?" I asked. "Is she still alive?"

"Yep, and still in a coma." He tossed the binder on his desk and finally looked at me. "And I know you have a hard-on for arresting Reverend Haist for murder but the DNA tests for him came back. His sample doesn't match the Slayer's."

Disappointed, I slumped against his desk. That was that—the minister was innocent of these murders, no matter my distrust or dislike of the man.

Adam watched me closely and waited for me to explain away the DNA results. *Bad science. Sloppy lab work. It* has *to be the Reverend.*

But I didn't believe any of that. The man was innocent . . . at least in this.

I said, "I've been trying to figure out why the Slayer named the first picture file the way he did. It doesn't seem random."

Adam brought up the file on his computer. He rubbed the back of his neck as he stared at the JPEG's file name.

"It's not a phone number or a Social Security number," I said. "Why that sequence?"

He sent his fingers to the number pad of the keyboard. "Let's look in the database. 06113551."

A picture filled the monitor—a booking shot of a Black woman wearing a tank top. She held a black board at chest level. There were white numbers on that board: 06113551.

"Is she the woman in the photo he sent?" Adam asked, already knowing the answer.

Frizzy hair. Skin the color of wet cinnamon. Bare shoulders covered in crisscrossed scars.

I nodded.

"Earleen Thompkins," he said. "Booked on October 1, 1989, for prostitution and possession of narcotics." Adam turned in his chair to face me.

We stared at each other, not wanting to say it aloud.

"Guess you have a new one for your wall," he said.

I nodded at the wall behind us. "You do, too."

He groaned, then rubbed his face. "I can't do this anymore," he whispered through his hands.

I touched his shoulder. "Yes, you can. Did he kill her in '89?"

Adam scrolled down the page. "Nothing here says that she's dead."

"So she was buried as a Jane Doe. How would the Slayer know her booking number?"

"He must have access to our computers somehow. Maybe you're right. Maybe he is a cop—"

"Or a clerk. Or a city official." I took a deep breath, then slowly exhaled. "You're gonna hate me for saying this, but maybe you should—"

"Swab every city employee's cheek, then test their DNA against the Slayer's?"

I nodded.

He twisted in his seat, pen tapping his teeth.

I didn't bother him about his pen-tapping habit. The thought of organizing a citywide DNA drive would force me to smoke six cigarettes at once.

My eyes wandered back to the detectives standing before the Death Wall. "Do you think the Slayer has something like that?"

Adam shrugged. "Dennis Rader kept his sick shit on index cards and in binders. Dahmer kept pictures of his victims before he killed them, as he killed them, and after he killed them. Hundreds of—" He looked at me with surprise, as though he'd forgotten that I stood there. "Maybe you should stay somewhere else for now. Like at your mother's."

"And put her in this sick bastard's sights?" I folded my arms across my chest. "Nope."

"You can crash at my place," he offered. "Until the security company comes."

"He may not contact me again if I'm staying with the detective in charge of finding him. As much as I hate to, I should probably stay put."

"I'll have a team monitor your house a few hours a day, then," he said. "Like, after Lena leaves and when you're alone. Don't know how long I can afford to do that, but I'll justify the cost. You're the only one the Slayer's contacted. Can't let anything happen to the messenger, right?"

"I didn't come here about my computer. I wanted to give you this." I slapped two Saks Fifth Avenue mailers in front of him: a fall catalog and a slick postcard announcing a sale in women's shoes and accessories. "I thought they would help us somehow."

Adam studied the mailers. "I gotta buy you something from Saks for you to fall in love with me?"

"Not at all," I said. "No falling in love. We're through, remember?"

"Sy—"

"The mailers, Detective."

"What am I looking at?"

"The mailing address."

Adam studied the backs of each mailer.

I stood back, self-satisfaction warming my body like peppermint schnapps. "I searched through five trash bags of Tamar's mail to find those."

Noemi and I had met in a McDonald's parking lot off Slauson Boulevard. Jay the Security Guard, dressed in uniform, had been with her. She had apologized for the location, but her parents still didn't appreciate me poking around. Also, she hadn't gotten around to telling them about Christopher. I had glanced at Jay, the reverend's right hand. Noemi had said, "He won't say anything." Jay had smiled at me as confirmation of his complicity. I had spent close to an hour plowing through bags of mail in the trunk of her ancient Aries K.

Adam said, "The name printed on these mailers . . . Christopher Johnson."

I nodded. "That's Tamar's boyfriend. We talked about him, remember? But I didn't know his last name. Anyway, I took one of Tamar's dresses that came from Saks back to the store, and I told the saleswoman that . . . Never mind what I told her."

"You lied."

My cheeks burned. "A little. It was for the greater good."

Adam just blinked at me.

"Anyway," I said, "she mentioned mailers, and it made me think about Tamar receiving something from Saks. Figured it was a long shot but . . ."

"And it is."

"Does it matter if it's a conventional lead if you get the information you need? I'm a reporter, not a private eye."

He tilted his head and offered a lopsided smile.

"So, these mailers were sent to Tamar's apartment, but with that name. Christopher Johnson. Why he'd have his mail sent to her house, I don't know. Maybe he doesn't want the wife to know. Maybe he had planned to move out. Whatever. And it doesn't matter anyway. The mailers were in Tamar's mail, and I found them. So, now you can find her mystery man and ask him questions. Do your thing. Solve the case. And you're welcome."

Adam blinked at me. "A Christopher Johnson in Los Angeles. Well . . ." He sat back in his chair. "I do enjoy a challenge."

"It won't be too hard," I said, pulling away cheese from his pizza slice. "How many African-American Christopher Johnsons who shopped at Saks in Beverly Hills on September 19 and used an AMEX card to buy a black Hervé Léger originally priced at $1,500 but marked down to $700 could there be?" I popped the cheese in my mouth.

Adam stared at me until his eyes darkened into shiny onyx. Shark eyes. "And Herschel Halley?"

I shrugged. "He doesn't fit the description that Noemi or the hairdresser gave me. Maybe Halley tried to kill the woman now in a coma, but he didn't kill Tamar Haist."

35

I sucked in my cheeks as my fingers flew across the computer keyboard. Felt like a smoldering, five-pound dumbbell sat atop my left breast—low and intense pain that urged me to stop and pop a Vicodin. Or two. But Lena was home and waiting to proof the Tamar Haist article before leaving Los Angeles with Sergey the Russian.

My cell phone rang from its spot on my desk but I didn't answer it. No distractions.

"Almost finished," I said to Lena through the landline's speaker. "I just need to proof it one more time."

"Sy, just stop," Lena said. "I'll proof it. That's what you're paying me for. Well, not paying me for. Whatever."

"I don't wanna keep you from your trip." My eyes scanned the words on the monitor—looked like black hash marks against the white screen. "Okay, I give up. You can take it from here?"

The ignored cell phone chimed—whoever called had left a message.

"Yep," Lena said. "You go self-medicate and get some rest. You're not sinning by popping a pill."

I pushed away from the desk and rubbed my eyes. "You're right. Maybe I'll have a cup of tea, watch an old episode of *Golden Girls*." I closed the document, then attached the file to an email. "Thanks for doing this."

I tossed the landline receiver on the couch, then wandered to the kitchen. I opened the cabinet and reached for my favorite glass mug.

Except that my favorite glass mug wasn't on the shelf.

I checked the dishwasher.

It wasn't there, either, and the sink was clear of dishes.

I didn't care enough to keep looking, so I grabbed another cup, then stuck peppermint tea leaves inside the teapot's strainer.

Three minutes later, I returned to the office, mug in hand. I grabbed my cell phone from the desk and retrieved the message.

Sy, it's Krystal. Sorry about my strange visit today. I didn't mean to be such a bitch. I don't want you to hate me, Syeeda. I have too many enemies already.

I grabbed the vial of Vicodin from my bag and shook one onto my palm. I chased the pill with a sip of tea, then wandered to the window.

I have to talk to you again. I need your advice. I'm scared and I have no one else to turn to that I trust. I told you that I think someone's following me . . . Maybe you can help. You know people on the police department, and you've always been good at solving problems . . . Well, you were back in college. Call me, okay?

I opened the window. The rain had stopped, and the moist air smelled of magnolias and wet grass. No crickets chirped, no neighbors' televisions blared. So still. So quiet.

I stood there for a long time, listening to nothing, strangely relaxed.

Maybe it was the Vicodin. Maybe I had hit my fear threshold. Or maybe I was too tired to be scared. And really, what more could happen? I had faced Deon Jackson and survived. I had faced cancer and survived that, too. Nothing in the world was scarier than a madman in fur and a life-threatening disease.

Minutes before eleven o'clock, I sat back at the desk to complete a final task.

Toni answered the phone on the first ring, as though she had been waiting for my call. "What's up, sweetie?"

I sank into my chair and placed my feet on the desk. "Remember when you offered the services of Fortune Security?"

She said, "Of course. What's up?"

I told her about my trip to Saks with Tamar's dress, and my search through Tamar's mail. "If I give you the price tag with the SKU number, you think you can pull buyer information? I know it's not a lot to go on, but it's all I have."

"Hmm . . ." Then: "Yeah. I can do that. Just bring the dress with you when you come for dinner tomorrow. Anything else happening in the case?"

I doodled Adam's name on a legal pad, then threw my pen at the computer. "The Slayer sent me two emails and a picture of a victim we didn't know about."

Toni said nothing at first, then whispered, "He's taking pictures of them?"

"Think so."

"What a sick son of a bitch," she said. "What did he say in his message?"

"Just a bunch of nonsense sprinkled with Bible verses. This guy's a religious freak."

"Those are the scariest kind," Toni said. "You know, Fortune Security can help you with this. Our bodyguards are all ex-military or ex–Department of Defense."

"I'm probably safe," I said. "I'm not his type."

"Oh! This morning, I had a wonderful idea and I hope you say yes. When your book is published, I want to throw you a party at the house. Wine, caviar, celebrities . . . You want a stripper? I can hire a stripper! Yes, that's what I'll do."

"Toni, you've gone around the bend," I said with a chuckle.

"*And* we'll rent one of those chocolate fountains! And eat strawberries as big as your head."

I smiled. "I have to finish the thing first."

"I have a feeling you're close to your ending," she said. "Especially now that I'm helping you."

I rubbed my eyes, then said, "Let's talk about it when I have a contract in hand."

She chirped, "Yep. I still think a stripper would be fun. Think about it! See you tomorrow, sweetie."

I aimed the remote at the television and found *Jaws* on a cable station. I eased into bed and pulled the rubber band on my wrist. Hypnotism was working—I hadn't smoked a cigarette in eight weeks. *Gold star for Sy!*

The Vicodin and tea combo was working. My body had loosened, my fists slowly unclenching. I stared at the television, not blinking even as the great white shark attacked little Alex Kintner on a sunny July afternoon.

My cell phone chimed from the nightstand.

My eyes popped open.

On the television screen, *Jaws* had been replaced with *Animal House.*

How long have I been asleep?

I glanced at the clock before reading the message: 1:13 a.m.

REALLY NEED 2 TALK 2 U. K.M.

Why is Krystal texting me at 1:13 in the morning?

The phone chimed again as though I hadn't heard it the first time.

Could I ignore Krystal until a more reasonable time of day? When I wasn't so tired and achy? I didn't have the thumb strength to text Krystal. Still, I grabbed my cell phone and tapped across the touch screen keyboard.

OK WHERE R U?

I lay with the phone on my chest, with that gun beneath my head. Didn't feel like talking, listening, or commiserating. I just wanted to sleep.

The phone chimed again.

2 LATE. COME 2 MY AUNT'S. 42ND & ST. ANDREW BY UHAUL @ 6AM MOVING@8.

Drive to her aunt's house in *that* neighborhood at six in the morning?

Is she kidding me?

I sighed, then sent my response.

C U @ 6.

36

No rain or storm clouds on this morning. The sun hadn't broken yet over South Los Angeles as I turned from Saint Andrew's Place, a residential street lined with well-tended bungalows, onto Forty-Second Street, still a part of the neighborhood but close to a traffic signal and a U-Haul store. I had not fully awakened when I parked a stone's throw from the moving company.

Crap. Krystal didn't give me an address.

I squinted at the houses nearby. Did her aunt live in the white duplex with cocoa trim? Or in the house wearing Christmas lights on its eaves? I powered my cell phone and sent Krystal a text message. **Krys, whats the address??**

I glanced inside my bag one last time—the Glock sat among my notebooks and pens. This part of Los Angeles had so many sex offender blue dots on the Megan's Law map that it looked like the Pacific Ocean. Not that I'd win a gun battle with gangbangers or rapists with guns, but I sure as hell planned to go out with my finger pumping the trigger.

I crossed the street, stopping in front of the Christmas-lights house, the closest building to the U-Haul. I prayed for protection and hoped that Krystal saw me standing there.

A black Impala blasting Snoop Dogg crept down Forty-Second, in my direction. The car slowed and the driver's-side window rolled down. The pungent stink of marijuana drifted from inside the car. The driver—a Black kid, about twenty or so—poked out his head. "You know how to get to Manchester?"

I touched my bag, felt my gun there. "Make a right at the end of the block and keep heading south."

He turned down the stereo. "So, umm . . . How much?"

I blinked at him.

"You deaf?"

"I'm . . . I'm not working."

He nodded. "Right, right. Listen, I'm gon' drive around some. Go buy some Doritos and shit. Give you time to clock in. Then, I'm gon' come back." He rolled to the end of Forty-Second and screeched around the corner.

Okay. Time to find Krystal.

I zipped my parka, then hustled toward the truck rental company. As I passed the alley, I spotted Krystal's Maserati. I strode toward the car, ready to end this meeting before the kid in the Impala returned.

I reached the rear of Krystal's car and stopped short.

The driver's-side window had been blown out. Glass sparkled on the asphalt.

"Krystal?"

Silence.

I took a step. Glass crunched beneath my running shoes.

Another step.

The cabin was empty. The stereo had been wrenched out of the dashboard. The leather seats had been slashed.

"Krys?"

The car's headlamps were on.

My gaze followed those beams of light to the enormous dumpster near the front bumper. I couldn't feel my feet as I tiptoed toward the bin. Could only hear my pounding heart. And flies. Hundreds of flies.

"Yo, Shorty!"

The kid in the Impala had returned to the street behind me.

I ignored him and took another step.

"Bitch, you hear me talking to you?"

The Impala pulled into the alley. Its wheels crunched against gravel and glass.

I spotted an abandoned platform heel by the car's left tire.

"I'ma get out of this car and beat your Black ass if you don't answer me!"

A foot, its toenails painted Day-Glo orange . . . brown thighs . . . a filled trash bag . . .

And Krystal's face blasted apart.

I sat on a grassy curbside, twenty feet from the crime scene. Hypnotized by the swirling red and blue lights, I stared straight ahead as a cigarette burned between my fingers. Adam and the medical examiner on call talked on the edge of the crime scene. Men and women in black bustled back and forth beneath the bright sun, twisting under taut yellow tape that never bode well for the person behind it.

So much noise.

The pop and whir of cameras. The drone of the police helicopter. The buzz and chatter of spectators and people there on "official business."

Krystal still lay in the alley, her paisley-printed dress dark with dried blood.

The sun climbed above me, and I glanced at that white disk in the eastern sky. Swiped my sweaty forehead, then tugged at my damp T-shirt. I stank—sweat, vomit, and tobacco clung to my skin like lotion.

I took a long drag from the cigarette and held the smoke in my lungs.

After a half hour of vomiting, hyperventilating, and rocking back and forth on my haunches, I had yanked the cigarette case from my bag. I had picked one of four Newports there, held my breath as the lighter flickered, as the paper burned. I took a drag and winced. Tasted like volcano. Third drag and it hit me—that lightheaded calm that makes your knees buckle and your body relax.

So much for better living.

Adam found me sitting on the curb. "You okay?"

I grunted, scared that I'd cry if I opened my mouth to speak. I shot smoke into the air. The cigarette wasn't working—unless it was. My hands and knees were still shaking, and my stomach felt like it was being mauled by a combine. Nicotine: It's a helluva drug.

"Any idea what happened?" he asked.

I stared at the concrete—an ant was trying to navigate around my shoe. I moved my foot to let it pass.

"You'll have to give your statement again," he said. "The officer you talked to couldn't understand a word you said."

I closed my eyes, my brain still as soft as Malt-O-Meal.

He kneeled in front of me and tapped my knee. "Hey. You there?"

"She said that she needed my help. She said that she was moving." My voice wavered, and I stopped speaking. My shoulders twitched. Shivering even though I sat in direct sunlight.

Adam perched beside me. "You know what street is on the other side of this alley?"

I blinked at him.

"Western Avenue."

My head lolled—Krystal had been murdered in the Slayer's territory. "I drove from Saint Andrew's," I said. "There was this guy in an Impala and he thought I was a sex worker, and I wasn't thinking . . ." My voice sounded small. Whoville small. I tamped out the cigarette on my shoe sole, disgusted with the taste in my mouth. "It can't be Halley," I said. "He's still in custody, right?"

Adam didn't answer and glanced over to the Maserati.

My phone chimed.

I didn't reach to answer it.

The phone chimed again.

Adam lifted an eyebrow. "You gonna get that?"

I pulled the phone from my pocket. "It's a text message."

I come like a thief and you will not know at what time I will come to you.

Beneath those words: a picture of slain Krystal Miller.

The sun shone bright on the bohos, soccer moms, businessmen, and jocks at the coffee shop. They had no clue that a woman had been murdered just a mile away. In the outside lounge area, old Black men with gnarled roots for hands played chess and smoked cigars. Younger men loitered at tables and benches and watched fly girls wiggle back and forth from the parking lot, drinks in hand, cell phones to ear.

I had settled at an outside table with coffee that had gone untouched. My hands had only stopped shaking long enough for me to cart the cup from the counter to my seat.

Adam, with his own cup, plopped in the chair across from me. "Did you get one of those mocha latte soy chai iced things you like?"

"Nonfat caramel macchiato." I reached into my bag and pulled out my cigarette case and lighter. I snagged a Newport and slipped it between my lips. My hands shook as I lit up.

Adam's eyebrows lifted. "Why do you carry a cigarette case if you wanna stop?"

"My dad gave me this case," I said as smoke curled from my mouth like asps.

"He didn't mind you smoking?"

I shrugged, tapped ash onto the pavement.

"You don't talk much about him. Why?"

"Both of your parents are alive," I said.

"Yeah. So?"

"So, you wouldn't understand why I don't talk about him."

Adam waited for more, but there was nothing else for me to say. "The tech guys said that the picture and text were sent from Krystal's

BlackBerry. We can't find that BlackBerry, but we can triangulate the area where the message originated."

"Does it matter?"

Adam shrugged, said, "It may." Then: "Before we begin, is there any doubt that Krystal Miller was a sex worker? Are we gonna debate this or can we move on?"

"I know what she was."

"When did she start?"

"During our junior year."

He stared at me, waiting for more. When I didn't speak, he said, "Some people are asking, 'Why is Sy McKay getting messages from women and discovering these same women once they've been murdered? Maybe *she's* the Slayer.'"

I startled, and my chair scraped against the concrete. I opened my mouth to speak but couldn't. Was he kidding?

Adam's mouth was a thin gash across his face—he wasn't kidding. "That's silly, right?" he continued. "Because the question should be: Does Sy McKay *know* the Slayer? Why is he sending her pictures and messages now? Does she have some kind of deal with him?"

I killed the cigarette on the concrete. "Adam, I told you—"

"I mean, I get it," he continued. "This guy wants his deeds written down. He sees himself as a historical figure, a man who's stumped the police all this time. And who better to record it all? The pretty writer who cares, who has a history of working with the dark side to land an explosive story. She'll finish her book, make a lot of money. Maybe this time, she'll even win a Pulitzer."

I blinked at him in disbelief, then laughed. *Okay,* now *he's kidding.*

Adam's eyes remained hard. "Is there some type of arrangement, Sy? He tells you everything and you publish and then . . . what?"

"I've never exploited victims for personal gain," I said. "You know that. And I couldn't care less about awards."

He avoided my eyes.

"What is going on with you?" I asked, bewildered. "Why are you treating me like—?"

"What led Krystal to prostitution?"

I snapped the rubber band I had already forsaken for a smoke. "Sometimes, she needed money for tuition."

"Most of us work at the Gap."

"Krystal didn't want to. Hell, I didn't want to. And she wanted crap she couldn't afford on a Gap salary."

"She grew up poor?"

"I don't think that mattered," I said. "Krystal would've wanted more had she been rich, and would've done anything to get it. We knew what she was doing, and some of us wrote her off. I tried not to, but . . ."

"Why didn't you?"

"I wanted her to snap out of it, I guess. I wanted her to realize that she was more than that. But then, that didn't work because that meant she was nothing if she never realized it." I rubbed my mouth. "So I just shut up and tried not to think about her."

"When did you last see her alive?" Adam asked.

"Yesterday afternoon. We had a scene."

"What kind of scene?"

"She blamed me for being a bitch to her back in the day."

"You? No. I refuse to believe—"

"Personal or professional right now?" I asked with a raised eyebrow. "She had a gun."

"Why?"

"For protection. It was small. Pearl handle. Maybe a .22."

"You talk to her about the Slayer?"

I shook my head. "No."

"Think she read your articles?"

"She didn't say. I didn't ask. I don't think so—she would've mentioned it. She ragged on my books in this letter she sent me a few days ago. But we made up, so I guess that no longer mattered."

"Was she high? Drunk?"

"She seemed sober. She said she hadn't had a drink in three months."

"You believe her?"

"Yeah, I did. She was very proud of herself."

"And she visited you out of the blue?"

"No. She sent that letter first. She wanted to get some things off her chest before she left LA. Before the letter, I hadn't seen or heard from her in five years." I stopped talking, not sure what else to say. "But she was my friend up until she busted me out, and she needed my help so I came. Since I wasn't thrilled about being in the middle of the hood so early in the morning, I brought my gun."

His expression froze. "Why?"

My nostrils flared. "After all that's happening with me, you're really asking that question?"

He nodded. *You're right.*

I sipped coffee—it tasted sour. Didn't mix well with the ash in my mouth.

"You said she asked for your help?"

"She left a voicemail a little past eight thirty last night. Then, she sent me a text around one fifteen this morning. She thought someone was following her. You saw the messages."

"Who was following her? A pimp? A john?"

"She said the world was following her. Wives, investigators, the government . . . We have a lot in common." I paused, then said, "*Had* a lot in common."

He narrowed his eyes. "Why did she want you to meet there?"

My stomach turned twisty. "I don't know, Adam. She wanted me to meet her at her aunt's house."

"No one on Saint Andrew's or Forty-Second knows Krystal Miller," he said.

"She said she was moving."

"The guy at U-Haul says there were no trucks reserved in Krystal Miller's name."

I slouched in my chair. "Then, I don't know what to tell—"

He snorted, scribbled into his steno pad.

"I'm not lying to you," I shouted.

"I'll need your gun."

"What for?"

"Neighbors said that they heard gunfire."

"In *that* neighborhood? No shit."

"Your gun has to be tested."

I waited for him to say, "Ha ha, just kidding," but he didn't. "Adam, I didn't kill Krystal. We didn't slam back shots and do each other's hair the last time we were together, but I'd never want her dead. Why are you acting this way?"

"Acting what way? Like a cop?"

"You know me."

"Yes, I do, but I also have a job to do, Sy. Your friend was killed. You found her. You have a gun. Krystal Miller was killed by a gun. Am I supposed to ignore all of this because we were lovers?"

Wild-eyed, I said, "Yes."

He rubbed his face. "Shit, Sy."

"Are you going to knock on every house on Saint Andrew's and make everybody hand over their guns?"

He said, "If I have to? Yes, I will." He stood from the table. "Where's the gun?"

I led him back to the parking lot.

"When was the last time you fired it?"

"When you took me to the shooting range three weeks before my surgery." I pulled the Glock from beneath the seat and handed it to him without saying anything else.

He unloaded the magazine, sniffed the muzzle for gunpowder. "I promise to get this back to you as soon as I can."

I stared at him, my vision blurred from tears.

"Oh," he said. "One more thing. Since 1992, there hasn't been a Christopher Johnson on the force. Not a patrol cop, a detective, or SWAT. Not in fifteen years."

37

How the hell did I end up here?

In less than twelve hours, my college friend had been murdered in an alley off Western, and I had received an email touting her death. But I still didn't know why the Phantom Slayer was sending me messages. To tell the world, he had said. But I had already done that. Why direct contact with me *now*? And did Adam really believe that I would collaborate with evil for a book deal? Tristan Small the drug dealer was no serial killer.

And had Adam been right about Tamar after all? Like Krystal, had she also been a high-priced call girl? Had Krystal mentored her? Were there such things as "mentors" in that business?

And now that I didn't have my gun, what would I do if the Slayer dropped by? Throw my laptop at him?

Couldn't even do that.

Adam still had my laptop.

I glanced in the rearview mirror—Adam's Crown Vic was behind me. He trailed me for a few blocks, then pulled into the next lane. When we both stopped at the red light, I glanced over at him. He hit a switch—*blurpblurp*, siren, police lights—and blasted through the intersection. I banged my head against the headrest.

How the hell did I end up here?

Krystal's letter still lived in my bag, waiting for me to do something with it.

I yanked out the envelope, now stained with lip pencil and scented with the Tommy Girl sample that had spilled in my bag months ago. *5438 Pacific Coast Highway.* I punched Krystal's address into the car's GPS and raced to the I-10 West.

Don't know what I planned to do when I reached her house. Pay my last respects? Find out why I'd been the one to find her? Learn why was she leaving the city?

Toni called as I poked along the congested freeway. "I'm at the grocery store," she said, "shopping for our dinner tonight. Do you prefer Absolut vodka or Belvedere? Not to drink straight, but to mix for martinis."

"Huh?"

"Dinner at seven, remember?"

"Maybe we should postpone."

"What's wrong?" she asked. "Are you okay? You better be sick as hell after all this cooking I've done."

I gripped the steering wheel tighter.

"What, Sy? What's wrong?"

"Krystal Miller's dead."

Toni gasped, then whispered, "Oh no. Oh *shit.* What happened?"

My eyes burned with tears, and I took several deep breaths before saying, "I was supposed to meet her this morning, and there she was . . ." Then, I backtracked—told her about the alley, told her about the car, about the shot to Krystal's face.

"Why did she want to meet you?" Toni asked, her voice shaky.

"No idea." My stomach cramped as though I'd done a hundred sit-ups.

"If you don't feel like coming over tonight, we can plan for some other—"

"No," I said, drying tears on the back of my wrist. "I need a good meal. It's only noon, but it's already been a long day."

The Pacific Ocean twinkled like sapphire in the sunlight, so close that if I draped my hand out of the window, my fingers would skim across cold water. Surfers glided across waves caused by the weekend storm. Toddlers shiny with sunscreen and sweat scampered from shore to sea, hauling buckets of sand, throwing inflatable balls and drinking cans of Sunkist soda.

GPS led me to 5438 Pacific Coast Highway, a rectangular beach home a mile from the Santa Monica Pier. The house had been painted lemony yellow, a foreign hue among wind-whipped whites, tans, and woods. I pulled into the driveway and parked next to a prehistoric gray Cadillac Eldorado with ripped black seats. Fifty pine tree air fresheners hung from the Caddy's rearview mirror.

I slipped my press tag around my neck and opened the car door. Took a deep breath—salty ocean air, fumes from speeding cars and trucks—then climbed rickety stairs to a salt-worn porch.

A Black man hung out at the open front door. He held a crumpled pack of Camels in one hand and a cell phone to his ear with the other. He was a male, roughneck version of Krystal, with the same ginger skin and freckles dusted across his nose. He wore his hair in intricate cornrows that swirled like crop circles. His tan Dickies hung past his hips, and his XXL white T-shirt almost hit his ankles. A thirty-seven-inch flat-screen television sat between his spotless Air Jordans.

He ogled me even as he called the person he was talking to on the phone "baby."

"What you need, Shorty?" he asked me, then told "baby" to hold up just for a minute, shut the hell up and hold up just a damn minute, damn, stop trippin'.

"Heard about Krystal," I said. "Sorry about your loss. We were friends."

He gave me the up and down. "You don't look like no ho."

"Because I'm not. Krys and I went to college together."

He sneered, then said, "Ohhh . . . You one of them stuck-up bitches. One of them Oreo hos."

By the way he eyeballed me and licked his lips, I could tell that he liked Oreos. "And you're her little brother, right? Gary?"

"The one and only."

"Mind if I go in? I'm putting together an obituary and I wanted to get a feel of . . . things."

"Don't take none of the shit in this house," he warned, pointing his tobacco-stained finger at my chest. "This here belongs to family. I'll call 5-0 if something comes up missing."

I seriously doubted that Gary would call the police. From what I knew about him, he had been in and out of jail since his sixteenth birthday. And now, at thirty-one, Folsom State Prison had become his Club Med—once a year, all-inclusive. Call the LAPD? Yeah, sure.

As I stepped over the threshold, he warned me again. "Keep ya hands to ya'self."

I glanced back at him. "Don't worry. I have three televisions already."

In the living room, two full-sized women rifled through the drawers of the entertainment console, too busy plucking CDs and DVDs from the shelves to notice me. Three trash bags stuffed with clothes sat at the foot of the tan suede couch. A Versace corset. A pair of bejeweled True Religions. A Chanel quilted jacket. Fancy things these two creatures could only fantasize about wearing. A shoe box—size seven Jimmy Choos—and a mirror Louis Vuitton bag sat on the coffee table.

The red-boned one—a poorer, plumper version of Krystal—froze in mid-swipe when she saw me standing there. She blushed, and the freckles on her nose disappeared.

"Hey, LeTanyah," I said.

She yanked at her YES, WE CAN T-shirt. "Why you look so familiar?"

"Sy McKay. Krys and I went to college together."

LeTanyah offered a sly smile. "Oh, yeah. She hated your ass."

Krystal also hated LeTanyah, a chronic booster, a chronic chronic-smoker, a chronic evildoer. From check fraud to stealing identities, from assault to bench warrants for unpaid traffic tickets, Krystal's sister had committed a smorgasbord of crimes against the people of California.

LeTanyah's buddy had stopped shopping and was now leaning against the TV stand . . . the *empty* TV stand since Gary had already emancipated the Panasonic to the front porch.

"We was just getting stuff for Krys's funeral service," LeTanyah claimed. "Since the cops took all they wanted this morning."

I wandered to the large picture window. A bank of fog sat offshore, waiting for the right moment to steal onto land and erase the world.

Behind me, LeTanyah and her friend rustled their bags and whispered to one another.

I don't see it.

You ain't looked hard enough.

You look then.

I understood my reaction to Krystal's death—*how sad and tragic, but I need to write my story*—but I couldn't understand Gary and LeTanyah's reactions. If either of my siblings had just died, I'd be wacked out on Valium and collapsed in a corner, just as I had been on the day my father died.

"How long has Krystal lived here?" I asked.

"For about three years," LeTanyah said.

"It's beautiful. Why did she want to move?"

"She didn't wanna move."

"Krys mentioned not being here anymore," I said. "She told me that."

LeTanyah folded her arms. "You callin' me a liar?"

"Of course not. I'm just trying to understand . . . She have any enemies?"

"Other than you? Hell no. Everybody loved my sister."

"If that was true, then why did someone kill her?"

She cocked an eyebrow. "I don't know. You tell me."

I chuckled, then shook my head. *Whatever, dude.*

"Laugh all you want," she said, her ham-hock fist on her hip, "but the cops asked me who her enemies were, and I made a nice long list. They got your name and all the names of your little stuck-up buddies, including that bitch Lena who thinks she's better than everybody cuz she got a little cash. I'ma get down to the bottom of this once we, you know, finish mourning."

"I look forward to you being on the case, then," I said. "What about her clients? Think any of them could've done it? Or maybe one of the wives of those clients?"

"What you mean, 'clients'?"

I folded my arms across my chest. "You know what your sister did for a living."

"She hosted parties," LeTanyah said.

I gaped at her, then shrugged. "Fine. Did any of the *clients* who attended her *parties* have something against your sister?"

"They some powerful men," LeTanyah said, as though she had stock in their fame. "They ain't gon' risk going to death row."

"They risked going to jail by paying her for a blow job."

"My sister wasn't some ho workin' Hollywood and Vine."

"You're right. She wasn't. Do you know who she worked for?"

LeTanyah puffed out her chest. "My sister ain't had to work for nobody. She was an independent contractor." She said this without embarrassment, like she had just said, "My sister is a Nobel laureate who discovered the cure for cancer."

Arms crossed, I leaned against the window ledge. "When did you and Krys become close? She didn't speak to you at all during school. Even up until five years ago, she said y'all were a bunch of leeches."

LeTanyah glared at me. "Blood is thicker than water."

"Especially to a leech."

"Who you calling a leech?"

I smiled. "No one. When did you see her last?"

"Christmas a year ago," LeTanyah said. "But she called Momma all the time. Sent her checks every Friday. That's who we takin' the TV to. Krys would want Momma to have it."

I nodded, then eyed the designer gear stuffed into trash bags.

LeTanyah's eyes followed my gaze, then she yanked at her shirt again. "Krystal don't need none of this shit no more."

I offered a small smile. "Guess not. Please give your mother my condolences." I glanced out the window back to the ocean and spotted a cruise ship in the distance. I closed my eyes and wished that I was relaxing on the promenade deck with a Bloody Mary and a plate of mozzarella sticks instead of standing in a dead woman's beach house.

LeTanyah and her friend gathered their trash bags of couture and clomped to the door, swinging it open so hard that even Gary said, "Damn. Why y'all tryin' to break shit up?"

I pulled open the desk drawer. Pens, lip balm, condoms, a travel-size bottle of hand sanitizer. An airplane ticket stub from a January flight to Cancún. First class.

The kitchen smelled of bleach and Mr. Clean. No scuffs on the tile. No random Froot Loop or dropped grape beneath the stainless steel refrigerator. Another bottle of hand sanitizer sat on the sink.

There were two magnets on the fridge. One was shaped like a foot. ONE STEP AT A TIME www.AA.org. Someone had used black marker to write on it: PAUL GALLASHAW 555-5469. The other magnet was a red and white square also from Alcoholics Anonymous. I yanked off the PAUL magnet and stuck it in my bag.

There were no wine bottles in the wrought-iron rack or in the undercounter chiller. No highball or martini glasses on the shelves. The only mess here was the AA literature spread across the kitchen table.

The hallway walls were lined with framed photographs. Our group of friends cheering and hopping at a college basketball game. Krystal and Toni vacationing in Jamaica before the start of senior year. Black-and-white artsy shots of a younger Krystal on a leopard-print rug, with big hair and a trough of makeup on her face.

Krystal's bed was covered with a red satin comforter and a small army of throw pillows. No messy piles of clothes were heaped in a corner. No empty water glasses sat on the carpet or dresser. A few generic prints of leaves hung on the wall.

The window boasted a view of the ocean and the southern coast. The pier's Ferris wheel stood bright against the milky-blue sky. One patio chair sat on Krystal's tiny balcony.

I imagined my old friend sitting there, composing her letter to me as Labrador retrievers off leashes bounded on the sand beneath her, as slick-as-seal surfers caught the last waves of the day.

One wall held shelves of DVDs and CDs. No gaps. Guess LeTanyah hadn't made it to the bedroom yet.

I ran my fingers over the titles. *Annie Hall. The Purple Rose of Cairo. Hannah and her Sisters* . . . Krystal was a Woody Allen fan. Hmm.

Her small closet was neat, organized, nothing on the floor, clothes arranged on hangers by color. Three garment boxes sat on top of a closet shelf.

I pulled one down and opened it.

Red, cinnamon-scented sachets sat atop latex pants, leather bras, six different wigs, and a pair of Lucite platform heels. Working clothes. The other two boxes held theater programs, glossies, and dried corsages.

Back to the bed.

I glanced beneath the box spring and found a plastic storage box. Container in hand, I sat on the edge of the bed, accidentally knocking a few pillows to the carpet. I pulled off the box's top and found arrest reports for prostitution, drug possession, trespassing, DUI. Hospital reports dating back to 2001 diagnosing contusions, concussions, fractures . . . Krystal had stayed in and out of county facilities just like her siblings. I shuffled through the pages, stopping at one document generated just three weeks ago.

"Adult HIV/AIDS Case Report for Krystal A. Miller." An *X* was placed in the box for an AIDS diagnosis.

My veins filled with ice as my eyes found a text box:

You have tested positive for HIV (human immunodeficiency virus).

Breathless, I read that sentence three times . . . four . . .

Shit, Krystal.

And that's what she had meant. Tying up loose ends. That's why she sent me that out-of-the-blue letter and then stopped by, full of anger and apologies. She had been diagnosed with a life-threatening disease and she had freaked out. I now understood—in my haste to cope with my own diagnosis, I had broken up with Adam and had purchased a luxury car that, in this economy, I probably shouldn't have bought. I had been angry many of those days, and had spat awful things to my friends and family that I didn't mean. I couldn't think straight, though. My life had changed.

And so had Krystal's.

My gaze fell on a framed photograph sitting on the nightstand.

In the picture, Krystal is embracing a man, not wanting to let go lest she drown. Easy to see who loved whom the most here. The tightness of her embrace makes her breasts spill over the seams of her yellow bikini top. His brown skin sparkles from sun and drink. His eyes glisten like the clear tropical waters behind him.

I grabbed the frame. I knew this man. Those eyes, that gap-toothed smile.

Joey Fortune, Toni's husband.

Well, goddamn.

I sat there, picture in hand, case report on my lap, my pulse thundering in my chest, my neck, my fingers.

Krystal and Joey.

My thoughts skittered around my brain like a wet cat. *What the . . . ? When did . . . ?* Damn.

My cell phone chirped, and I yelped, startling from the noise. I stuck the photograph deep into my bag. My hands shook so much I could barely hold my phone to read the message.

You should come down ASAP. Spencer.

38

Before heading downtown, I stopped to talk to Krystal's neighbors—a couple who lived next door and a trust-fund hippie who lived two doors down. They didn't know Krystal well enough to cry upon hearing of her death, but they did have a reaction to what she did for a living.

"She never told me straight out," the blond woman sniffed, "but I could tell by some of those outfits she wore."

"Did she have visitors?" I asked.

"A lot of men came and went," the blonde's potbellied husband said. "Too diverse to pin down a type per se. She was equal opportunity when it came to clientele."

Then, the blonde ranted about sex, drugs, nice neighborhoods, Section 8, and a woman's right to choose. Or something.

"Did you see anything or anyone suspicious the last few days?" I asked, my head spinning from her diatribe.

"They all looked suspicious," the blonde said. "They knew what they were doing was immoral. A blight on society. We worked too hard for people like that to move next door." The woman's cheeks reddened, and she fell silent. Her eyes shifted to her husband and the hippie, but both men had suddenly become interested in their sandals.

The blonde threw startled eyes at me and stammered, "I . . . I don't mean Black people, I . . . I mean . . ."

"She did have a regular guy," the husband offered. He turned to the hippie, now rearranging his dirty blond dreadlocks into a ponytail.

"The big one who blocked your driveway that time. Looked like a linebacker? You know . . . ? Big?"

"Oh yeah," the hippie drawled. "That jerk. Like I was wrong for having his shit towed."

"We all have Range Rovers, buddy."

"Bet he has a ten-year lease on it."

They all laughed since ten-year leases *were* ridiculous things.

"How did he look?" I asked.

The trio exchanged nervous glances.

The husband ventured forth first. "Big. Tall."

"Good-looking."

"Definitely good-looking."

"Bald."

"Great dresser."

"Mustache. Beard."

We were dancing around it.

"A Black guy?" I asked.

Anxious swallows, red cheeks, reluctant nods.

I smiled. "It's okay. He is what he is. I'm Black, and I'm pretty cool with that."

"I'm not saying that he has a ten-year lease because he's African-American," the husband said. He turned to his wife who took his hand. "Some of our closest friends are—"

"Yeah," I said. "I know." Before the trio could show me their membership cards to the NAACP and subscription notices to *Ebony*, I thanked them and dashed to my car. They all cheered up then, and waved as I pulled back onto Pacific Coast Highway.

Spencer was sitting behind his desk when I rushed in. He glanced at his watch.

"Accident on the freeway," I said, dropping my bag to the linoleum floor.

He nodded. "They gave me your friend's case."

I slipped into a chair and leaned forward on his desk. "So, she's Slayer related?"

"Possibly." He rose from his seat and closed the office door. "We have ten minutes before my boss is out of his meeting." He returned to his desk and opened a thin folder. "This is what he's talking about right now."

I glimpsed a color photo of Krystal before her death. In college, she had wanted to be a model. She had even called Barbizon and a few other scam agencies, but they had all wanted too much money up front. Instead, she'd found a small photography studio near the Capitola Mall where the owner told her that escorting was the backdoor way to the catwalk. She had believed him because he owned a fancy Nikon and a bag of expensive-looking lenses. He had snapped a few quick photos of Krystal on leopard-print rugs, then gave her his business card. A day later, she called him, and that was that.

"Your friend ate at El Torito last night," Spencer said. "Around eight o'clock. The hostess said she noticed Krystal because of what she wore. A short bob wig, Buddy Holly glasses, a seventies-style paisley-print dress. Spent most of the night having drinks with another woman."

"Krys told me that she was on the wagon."

"She was," Spencer said. "Got the toxicology reports back—no alcohol in her system. The hostess was outside on break when she saw Krystal and the woman leave in a black SUV."

"Could the hostess describe the woman in the truck?"

Spencer nodded. "She's with the police artist now. All we have is African-American, mid-to-late thirties. Expensive looking. Adam's team is looking at tapes from the security cameras, too."

He browsed through the folder's contents and selected one photograph: Krystal on the alley ground. She wore the same outfit Spencer had just described, but the wig had blown off the top of her head and was plastered to the asphalt. He slid this picture and the summary autopsy report toward me.

"She had HIV," I said, my voice weak.

He nodded. "I know."

I thought of telling Spencer about the picture I had found of Krystal and Joey.

Adam should know before anyone else.

I glanced at the close-up of Krystal's shattered face, one eye left intact, slightly open and peering at the morning sky.

Spencer flipped through his binder of glossy death pictures with a flat expression. As though he was searching for a recipe or checking the scores from last night's Lakers game.

"Do you ever get sick of looking at all of this?" I asked. "Like, physically repulsed?"

He glanced up at me. "Excuse me?"

"Does it bother you?" I said, louder now. "Being around dead people all the time?"

He blinked. "Does writing about dead people all the time bother you?"

"Lately? Yeah." I sat back in the chair as far as I could without toppling over. "My oncologist would be upset if he knew I was here. Stress doesn't help with the whole cancer recovery thing."

"We don't have to talk about this," he said.

"I'm fine. Keep going."

"You sure?"

I nodded but avoided peering closely at any more photographs. "Is it possible that someone other than the Slayer killed Krystal? Your honest opinion."

Spencer considered me but didn't speak.

I shifted in my seat and yanked at the band on my wrist. "Is it possible that a customer or a pimp got upset, or someone's wife did it? Totally unrelated to the Slayer?"

"I can't say right now," Spencer said.

I nodded, then dropped my eyes to the report.

"There were no defense marks or scratches on her hands," he said. "She didn't fight."

"Unlike Tamar."

I skimmed the summary report: Spencer had noted the time of death between 10 p.m. and 12 a.m. LeTanyah Dubois had identified Krystal through Polaroids, then, three hours later, she had gone shopping in her dead sister's house.

The external examination was just a confirmation of the pictures Spencer had shown me. Krystal had bled out almost completely—her left internal jugular vein and thoracic artery had been hit. *Linear surgical scars found beneath right and left breasts, two inches in length . . . Slight vaginal swelling . . . Traces of semen . . .*

"Semen?" I said.

"I'm doing a kit," Spencer said. "Won't know what that will mean, though. Could be a customer."

"Could be the Slayer," I said. "Back to having sex with the victim."

"No fingerprints other than Krystal's were found in her car," Spencer said. "They're still doing trace evidence work."

"This case seems to fragment every freakin' day."

"I hear the mayor's talking about having a closed-door meeting with the victims' families. I'll let you know. You should be there."

The sound of a man's shoes tapped down the hallway.

Spencer closed the file and sat back in his seat.

I held my breath and waited for the door to open.

The heels moved past the office, and a moment later, the copy machine roared.

"You don't seem too upset seeing your friend in my file," Spencer said.

"I was," I said, remembering how I had curled into a weepy ball in the back of a cop's patrol car. "And I'm sad that she was killed, but . . ." I shrugged, unable to identify my current emotion. *Purple.* That's what I was. Not blue, not pink . . . purple.

"The heart feels what it feels," he said, then stood from his chair. "You should get out of here before my boss asks why the door is closed and a beautiful reporter is sitting in my chair."

I didn't immediately leave the parking lot. Just sat in my car, in the dark, wondering what to do next. I blinked to clear my vision, but those photographs of Krystal's destroyed face had seared into my mind's eye.

Who had been drinking at El Torito with Krystal?

Who had Krystal slept with?

Why didn't she fight back?

If Krystal had died between ten and twelve, who had texted me at 1:13 a.m., luring me to Forty-Second Street and Saint Andrew's Place?

I called Adam.

"Hey," he said, "let me call you—"

"I found something you should see. It's a picture—"

"I need to call you back," he whispered. "The chief is standing in my doorway." He hung up.

I slumped in my seat. "Crap."

My cell phone rang—American Security Company.

"Miss McKay, this is Oscar at ASC. Sorry to tell you this, but I need to move your appointment time to the noon to four slot. It's just really busy right now."

"I thought you all had cancellations."

"Nope," Oscar said. "We're busier than ever."

"But your guy told me—"

"What guy?"

"The technician. Sean. He came by yesterday morning."

Oscar said, "Umm . . . We didn't send a tech to your house yesterday."

My mouth went dry. My grip on the phone tightened.

No technician?

Then who was Sean?

PART III

39

Toni and Joey Fortune lived a few blocks away from my mother, in one of those remodeled McMansions that existed in neighborhoods everywhere: those houses with the tacked-on ceramic-tile roof, with random dormers and cupolas everywhere; sculpted hedges that lined the flagstone walkway and led to a porch with Roman columns. Toni's bright-white house also boasted a weather vane, useless in a climate consisting of Hot, Earthquake, and Brushfire. The Fortune Manor stood out on the block of ranches, Spanishes, and Cape Cods, a drag queen in a klatch of soccer moms.

This part of Los Angeles was a Negro Mayberry with old people walking their dogs, teenagers washing their parents' cars, and stay-at-home moms tending rose beds. Everyone smiled and shouted to each other. A few waved at me as though I belonged.

At this point, I didn't know if I'd ever have a sixteen-year-old with my eyes and cheekbones, asking me for the keys to the Benz *cuz Dad says it's okay.*

Toni wore so much perfume that I smelled it even before I reached the porch. She also wore poured-on purple satin capris, a high-end Lakers jersey (No. 24 for Kobe, a good friend, I'm sure), and high-heeled Chuck Taylors.

I wore Gap. Didn't matter which pieces when compared to high-heeled sneakers.

We hugged.

"You okay?" she asked, stroking my hair.

"Yep. How are you?"

"I'm doing better." Her face looked tight. Like she had tied it on with piano wire and had used plaster of paris as a moisturizer. "I called Krystal's mother right after I talked to you. I sent her a fruit basket."

"Maybe I should send something, too," I said. "Flowers or a plant . . . Something."

"Anything you do shows that you care. No matter who Krystal was, she was someone's daughter. And she was our friend."

My cheeks flushed, and for a moment, I was back in Santa Cruz, sitting in my living room, knowing something about Joey that Toni needed to know but too scared to tell her. Sixteen years later, I stood before her again, stomach in knots, but not as knotted as my tongue, wanting to tell her because that's what friends do . . .

I'll tell her after dinner.

I held out Tamar Haist's black dress. "Here it is."

Toni's lips twisted and she fingered the fabric. "You can have a million dollars but you can't buy class."

"I have a Hervé Léger."

She laughed. "I'm sure yours isn't as revealing as this thing." She took the dress from me and found the price tag. "Marked down. Of course." She grabbed my hand and said, "I'll get on it after dinner. But now, let me give you a quick tour."

Boxes from Laser-Tech, EnviroNet, and ProtectSecure marched down the hallway alongside boxes from Overstock.com, Sephora, and Neiman Marcus.

"Mail day," Toni said, then turned and pointed above the doorway. "Say 'Cheese.'"

I glanced over my shoulder and saw the security camera bolted there. "Cheese." I offered a small wave.

"Joey's testing a new product," she said. "It's a safe room system. He wants to make it affordable for middle-class families. With the recession, crime's going up and parents will pay anything to keep their bad-ass rug rats safe. We'll make a—"

"Fortune?"

She giggled, then playfully shoved me.

My eyes darted back to the surveillance camera. "So can I see the room?"

She gave an impish grin. "If I did, I'd have to kill you."

I laughed. "Good one."

"Seriously," she said, straight-faced, "I can't right now. Industry secrets and all that. You *are* a reporter."

"Worried that I'd blab?"

"It's a great story down there. You'd be crazy not to. On with the tour."

The living room faced east, making the room dark and cold, Nosferatic. The only light came from the red beams of surveillance cameras capturing every step we took.

Toni led me to a media room. She touched a panel, and light filled the space. A Jumbotron-sized television had gobbled the north wall. Ten leather theater-styled chairs awaited occupants. Two Gibson Les Paul guitars encased in Plexiglas hung on the wall.

"You and Joey play?" I asked, nodding to the instruments.

"No, but the red one is worth seven thousand dollars. Do you like the floors? They're bamboo." She pivoted on her heel and waved her hand for me to follow her.

A crystal chandelier too big for this dining room hung from the ceiling. A dinner table the size of a redwood sat beneath it. Toni ran her hand across its surface, then checked her fingers for dust. "You own your house, right?"

"Yeah," I said, eyeing the glass menagerie above me. "Got it before the market went crazy."

"And you like living there with all those strange Jews?"

I didn't blink. "No stranger than the weird Baptists in your neighborhood."

She led me up the stairs to the four bedrooms, one master suite, three bathrooms, and a loft with a view of San Pedro. There was thick cream carpet throughout, not a stain anywhere. "My bedroom's a mess," she said, nodding at the closed double doors. "It was the only room that Rosa couldn't get to today. Joey can be such a slob. He leaves pieces of himself all over this house and it drives me nuts."

"Men," I said.

She took my hand and led me back down the stairs. "Dinner will be served out on the deck."

I noticed two Julius Shulman framed photographs hanging on the walls. Both were signed and numbered. "Cheese and rice, Lena would *love* to have these in her collection. I didn't know you were a Shulman fan."

"A who what fan?"

"Julius Shulman." I pointed to the first photo. It was of the Stahl House, a home built into the hills above Sunset Boulevard. Women in white dresses lounged on living room couches, living the Hollywood dream. "He's, like, the Michael Jordan of architectural photography."

She considered the pictures and shrugged. "I won them at an auction. They were pretty. Thought they'd look good in the hallway. Guess I was right."

Pretty. Yeah. That, and the sand-glazed vases tucked in cubbies, and the vintage Gibson guitars hanging on the wall. Each "thing" purchased without having a connection to it or what had led to its creation. And that was the problem with Toni's home. More than the stupid weather vane and the Transylvania castle–sized dining room table. She had filled it with cool stuff, TGI Fridays style. The rooms had flair but each lacked soul.

"So will I be seeing Joey tonight?" I asked.

"I ask him that every night," she said. "He works a lot. Travels all the time."

I cocked an eyebrow—couldn't help myself.

Toni rolled her eyes. "No, he's not cheating on me."

"I didn't say anything."

"A wife knows."

Last, usually.

"Well, if I'm being honest, he *was* cheating," Toni explained. "But we're past that now. Don't say anything to Lena."

"Chauncey cheated on her, too," I said.

"Yeah, but he was gay. It was inevitable." She tried to smile. "I told you the truth because you're not the type to rejoice in other people's failures. Lena would mock me for the rest of my life, in English and in French."

We found our way to the redwood deck and to a nighttime view of Los Angeles. The airport sat over there, Marina del Rey was over there, my favorite BBQ place was right down there. The patio had been filled with wicker furniture and throw pillows that matched but not obnoxiously so. A pair of crusty flip-flops sat at the foot of the couch. A pot of pink hydrangea died in the northernmost corner. It was the most honest place in the house.

A black scrapbook sat on the coffee table alongside a silver martini shaker and a bowl of spinach artichoke dip. A Bobby Brown song from our college years played on a hidden boom box.

"Hope you don't mind the music," Toni said, plopping onto the couch. "I felt like listening to old-school slow jams. Songs from the time when everything was high and firm." She grabbed the shaker and poured yellow liquid into two glasses. "You like lemon drop martinis?"

"Love them." *But I'm not drinking until Christmas*, I wanted to say, but didn't. When in Rome . . .

She handed me a glass and I took a quick sip. Cold. Lemony. Smooth.

Toni sat back with her own drink. "I don't get to cook much for Joey anymore." She watched me, waited for me to ask, *Why not?*

But I sipped my martini. "Did you find out about that reality show? Will I be seeing you on the TV next season?"

She grimaced. "The producers wanted to go in another direction, so . . ." She twisted the bracelet on her wrist. "What can I say? I'm disappointed—it was my one shot, you know? But you can't always get what you want."

"Sorry."

She flicked her hand. "Don't be. I have one more iron in the fire, as they say."

Over a dinner of chicken marsala, we talked about college and old friends, parents and politics.

Toni didn't give to the alumni association.

I gave $1,000 a year.

Of our group of school friends, she had only reconnected with Lena and me.

I regularly emailed, chatted, and hung out with most of our sorority sisters—everyone except Krystal and Toni.

"Joey and I vote Democrat even though we have Republican money," Toni said as she pushed roasted potatoes around her plate. She hadn't eaten—a nibble of chicken here, a bite of mushroom there.

The vodka had loosened my tongue, and I asked, "When are you and Joey gonna have kids?" A question I would have never asked a woman had I been completely sober.

Her smile dimmed as she gazed out at the city. "He wants a son, but . . ." She shook her head. "We're going through it right now, but all couples fight over nonsense, know what I mean?"

I sighed. "Love is a battlefield, and I'm tired of bleeding."

"It is stressful, isn't it? Being with someone is one heartbreak after another. This house? Joey actually bought it for me after one of our big fights. As a surprise gift. *Please baby I'm sorry* and all that. He messed up, and I told him I was on my way out. I packed my bags and everything. Threw all kinds of shit in suitcases. Books. Remote controls. Soap. Crazy, huh?" She stared into her drink. "I wasn't going anywhere. I just wanted to scare him."

I tweaked the diamond link on her wrist. "Was this a please-baby-I'm-sorry gift?"

"Yep." She twisted the bracelet, then yanked her fingers away as though the diamonds were barbs.

"Why stay in a relationship that breaks your heart?" I kept my gaze on those beautiful stones. *Will I ever get diamonds?*

She looked at me as though I had asked her if Santa Claus was real. "Because that's what love is, sweetie."

"Love is suffering?"

"Yes." She shook her head and continued to look at me. *Poor Syeeda.*

"I still can't believe what happened to Krystal," I said, uncomfortable with her pity.

"She stopped by yesterday," Toni said.

"To tell you what a horrible person you were?"

She pulled her legs beneath her. "Yeah. You don't seem surprised."

"I received a similar visit," I said.

"Did she do the whole confession thing?"

"Kind of." Wide-eyed, I sipped my martini. "What did she say to you?"

Toni brought her own glass to her lips but didn't drink. "She told me that Joey was cheating on me. Which I knew. I didn't know that he was cheating on me with *her.*"

I held my breath and waited.

She sat her glass on the table. "I was shocked. Krys claims she broke it off. Guess I was supposed to forgive her."

"Did you?"

"Hell no."

"Why not?"

"Because she intentionally set out to take what was mine," Toni said. "She knew we were married. She had no excuse to do what she did."

"And what was Joey's excuse?"

Toni didn't speak. She shook her head as her eyes filled with tears.

We sat in silence as my mind worked. Tell her about the photo? Offer supportive words? You know: *Leave him, girl,* and *Drop that zero and get with a hero* bullshit we all hear from a friend at some pathetic point in our lives? Or just shut the hell up and let her do the talking?

"Does Joey know that Krystal's dead?" I asked.

"Who the hell knows what Joey knows," she said. "We're not speaking right now."

"Understandable."

"I don't know what Krystal thought I was gonna say. *Let's chat over tea and scones about you screwing my husband?*" Toni sucked her teeth and flicked her hand. "Stupid drunk bitch." She pulled the strings on her face to make it smile. "Dessert?"

I also forced a smile. "Yes, please."

Something bothered me, though, and I couldn't pinpoint what it was. Toni's hostility was appropriate yet misdirected. Then again, women punish the mistress more than the man who had pledged his fidelity before God and two hundred guests.

We settled on the wicker couch to attack our wedges of crème brûlée cheesecake.

Toni asked, "What's happening with the story?"

"Nothing new," I lied. "The Phantom Slayer is as mysterious today as he was last week."

"That auto mechanic they arrested ain't the Slayer," she said.

I glimpsed at her, then wiped my mouth with a napkin. "How do you know?"

"Fortune Security knows all and sees all. I have access to reports, top-secret documents, information that you'd want that I can easily give you."

"And what would I have to do for you in return? Split my book money with you?"

"I don't need money. No . . . I want you to make me coauthor of your book."

I laughed but stopped since Toni hadn't even cracked a smile.

She pulled the scrapbook onto her lap and flipped through the pages. "I've saved every Slayer article you've written."

I pointed to Genevieve Bellman's piece. "I didn't write that."

Toni shrugged and kept flipping. "She's a hack, but it's related."

Her statement wasn't hyperbole. She had clipped every Slayer article published—from the clip announcing the serial killer's existence to a flattering profile on Adam and the 320 Task Force. Seeing all this together, and in order, made me bristle. *So freakin' macabre.* No wonder Mom was so concerned.

"The cops are acting like they're not interested in this case," Toni said, "but they are. They're giving your boyfriend more money because they're on to something."

"My boyfriend?"

"Girl, please. I know you're screwing Detective Sherwood. Everyone knows, including the police chief. Speaking of the police chief . . . I heard that your detective was called in yesterday. They think that he's letting his reporter girlfriend determine the way the Slayer murders are being investigated. They think you have too much influence over him. That he can't be objective because of your relationship. They're thinking . . . maybe he should be put on some other case."

My heart pounded. "How do you know that?"

"One of the Task Force wives is in my Pilates class."

They couldn't. He was close, too close to solving this thing. From the outside looking in, it may not have seemed so, but I had this feeling . . . Like knowing who it is before picking up the ringing telephone. Like knowing you're about to rear-end the Saab in front of you moments before it happens. That sixth sense.

I swiped at my damp forehead. Couldn't do anything about the knots in my stomach.

Toni still waited for my response, a Cheshire-cat grin on her face.

"Why do you want your name on my book?" I asked.

My question pulled her back into her own dark place and the grin disappeared. "Because I have nothing, Sy. No job. No identity. I can't even get picked to be on some crappy reality show. Females come up to my husband all the time and flirt with him like I'm not there. People at parties talk to him and completely ignore me. And what would I have to add to conversations anyway? It's not like I have an interesting career. If I got abducted by a UFO, no one would know because no one noticed I was standing there in the first place. It hurts like hell to say that. To admit that my entire existence relies on Joseph Fortune. His star got bigger, and I became a black hole . . . No. Black holes have power."

She took my hand. "Working with you would give me an identity, you know? Writer. Investigative reporter. Champion of poor women who only have their bodies to sell."

"Back on Wednesday, you said sex workers had a choice, that it was their fault for being exploited."

She blinked at me, then sat back. "What can I say? Change of heart. I know what it's like to be powerless, being taken advantage of. I've read all of your articles again, thought about it from your perspective, and you've converted me. Isn't that what you set out to do? Affect the reader?"

"Yeah, but . . . Yeah."

"Isn't Lena moments away from following some bright shiny object? Who'll do her job once she gets bored and deserts you for some Hong Kong businessman? Sy, you need my insight and my access to resources to take it to the next level. If you agree, I guarantee that you'll have an ending to your story *and* more money than you'll ever need."

I smirked. "All I have to do is buy these magic beans, right?"

"The original victims were poor and Black," she said, ignoring me. "Heroin addicts. But Krystal and Tamar weren't poor nor were they junkies."

"But they were both shot in the face," I pointed out. "And found in alleys off Western."

"The person who killed them is making a statement. That's why you received that email and picture of Krystal."

"Don't they all make statements?"

"The killer was drawn to their beauty," Toni theorized. "And the killer wanted to destroy that. Hence, the shot to the face."

I nodded and waited for more. When Toni didn't speak, I said, "That's it?"

Her eyes narrowed. "The killer was balancing the scales."

"Balancing for whom?"

"For women who can't compete against bitches who use their bodies to steal another woman's man."

"Interesting theory. Anything else?"

Her shoulders slumped. "You don't seem impressed."

"A serial killer with a theme."

"And that bores you?"

I shrugged again.

"The report says that Krystal didn't fight."

My pulse jumped. "Okay," I said, holding up a hand. "How do you know all this? None of these reports are public yet, inside connections or not. Joey wasn't HSS when he was on the force. And Fortune Security is successful but you all aren't the NSA."

"People talk. And I told you already: I'm practically invisible."

"Still," I said. "You're as good a profiler as Eva."

Toni brought a shaky hand to her forehead. "I'm not intuitive at all—I just pay close attention. And I also have the luxury of doing nothing all day except think about murder."

"You missed your calling."

"The report also says Krystal had sex a day or so before she was killed. Guess who she slept with."

I paused, then said, "Joey?"

"The report didn't say that, did it?" she asked. "That's not intuition, and I didn't need a degree to figure it out. I learned that the old-fashioned way."

"He told you?"

She nodded. "He told me a lot. Anyway, I don't think the murderer set out to kill Krystal, and Krystal obviously trusted this person. Something happened, and Krys didn't see it coming."

"Person," I said. "Joey, for instance?"

"I doubt that."

I lifted an eyebrow—*you sure?*

"Krystal had already confessed to me," she said. "Why would he kill her? After yesterday, their secret wasn't much of a secret."

"Maybe he killed her out of anger."

"Not Joey." Her eyes shifted back to those city lights. "He could never do something like that." She shook her head. "I know him."

Don't we all *know him*? *He'd never do that* falls off your tongue one moment, and the next moment, he's on the news, covered in blood as CSIs discover remains of humans he had buried in your backyard. Yeah. You know him because he sleeps beside you.

As Toni walked me to my car, I noticed a gray Crown Vic parked across the street. Didn't recognize the white guy behind the steering wheel, but he looked as though he reeked of gunpowder, coffee, and arrogance. Definitely a cop.

"So you'll think about it?" Toni asked as she watched me open the car door. "I promise not to boss you around. You're the lead on this. You're Sherlock Holmes and I'm Watson."

"I'll let you know." I threw an irritated glance at the detective in the car.

"Next time, stay the night," she said. "And we'll make Lena come."

We hugged.

I climbed into my car and waved at Toni before backing out of the driveway.

The Crown Vic didn't follow me down the block.

Was he one of Adam's guys that had my back? Or did he have his sights on Joey Fortune?

40

As soon as I got home, I collapsed onto the couch in my office, still not sure what to do about the security tech that didn't exist but who had shown up at my house. I thought my mind would've arrived at a solution by now, but my mind's hard drive had run out of space. Also, it was past ten o'clock, and I had been up since five that morning and my body felt as heavy as a truckload of bricks. The image of Krystal slain beside her Maserati looped, and my brain couldn't process anything else without a serious reboot.

Paul, Krystal's AA buddy—did he know she had been killed? Did he know who she had been with the morning she died? Had *he* been with her?

I scooped my bag from the floor and slipped over to the computer. I found the magnet with Paul's name and phone number. I typed his name into Google's search bar and got several hits. Paul Gallashaw was a former linebacker for the Oakland Raiders and he owned a nightclub in Hollywood.

I grabbed the phone and called the number on the magnet.

After two rings, a man answered, "Who dis?" His deep voice was tinged with anger.

I trembled as though he could pop me through the phone. "My name is Sy McKay, and I'm a friend of Krystal Miller's." I waited for his response.

Silence.

"I saw your phone number in her kitchen," I continued. "On an AA magnet, and I thought—"

"I don't know no Krystal—"

"She's dead," I blurted.

Silence on the other end. No background noise.

"Hello?"

"What do you want?" he snapped.

"I just want to talk to you."

"About?" House music now played in the background. A crowd roared. A door slammed.

"About Krystal's last days," I said. "You helped her with her drinking problem, and . . . well . . . I'm a writer, and I'm drafting a profile on her."

"The police already talked to me. I ain't got nothing to add."

"Still, I'd like to ask you a few questions, not necessarily crime related. I'll come to you. Right now if you want."

He hung up.

I called Lena.

"Bonjour!" she chirped.

"Listen. I'm trying to interview a friend of Krystal's." I told her about Paul Gallashaw and the AA magnet. "He owns this club called Trix. Do you know him?"

"Like Sonny knew Cher," she said. "I'll call you right back."

I hopped off the couch and dashed down the hallway to my bedroom. I opened the closet door and eyed my wardrobe.

The phone rang: Lena.

"When was the last time you told me how awesome I was?" Lena purred.

"It's been about a week. You reach him?"

"Of course."

"And when can I meet him?"

"Right now. At the club. Hollywood Boulevard."

"How will I recognize him?"

She chuckled. "He's just the biggest Black man in the Western Hemisphere. Warning, though: no wires, no tape recorders, no strange shit. And wear something that shows off your boobs."

"Why are you calling me at two thirty?" Eva asked.

"I didn't expect you to pick up the phone," I said. "It's only eleven thirty here. Still early."

"For raccoons. Where are you?"

"Sitting in Hell's parking lot." My car was just one of six hundred jamming Hollywood Boulevard. "It's pretty late for you to be at work."

Eva snorted. "The FBI never sleeps."

"A break in the kidnapping case?"

"Can't say. But I can tell you this: I made a doctor's appointment for next Monday."

"Oh, sweetie! I'm happy to hear that."

"And Ben's going with me, so if I freak out, I don't have to drive back home." She exhaled, then said, "Back to the question: Why are you out and about at eleven thirty? Can't you make Adam come to you?"

"Adam and I . . . We aren't together. Not that we were. But we won't be."

"Oh, Sy—"

"Don't wanna talk about it. And that's not why I'm calling."

"I'm still sorry."

I said, "Thanks," then told her about the murder of Krystal Miller. "I'm on my way to meet one of her friends. Paul Gallashaw. He owns this nightclub called Trix on Hollywood Boulevard."

"Never heard of it. And you should be resting at home and not hanging out in nightclubs."

"Resting? What's resting?" I glanced in the rearview mirror and startled at seeing my reflection. I had forgotten to spackle on makeup, and the hollows beneath my eyes looked cavernous. "Since you're up—"A Honda cut in front of me, and I punched my car horn. "I know you're busy, stopping the axis of evil or legion of doom or whatever, but can you look this guy up? See who he is before I go bumbling into his coke lair."

"Hold on." Eva's fingers tapped across a keyboard. "Paul Gallashaw. Former linebacker for the Raiders. Arrested for auto theft, assault, disorderly conduct, driving without a license . . ."

"So, a good guy, then."

"One of the best. His last arrest was two years ago. Domestic abuse. He beat a woman in a parking lot at the Hustler Casino. Guess who the woman was?"

"Krystal Miller?"

"And you said he's her AA buddy? With friends like that . . ."

"Maybe he found God during that last stint in county."

"Like Daniel in the lion's den, right? One more thing before I hang up on you. So this Christopher Johnson?"

"He's Tamar's mystery man."

"He's no longer a mystery," Eva said. "I followed your Saks Fifth Avenue tip and pulled that credit card. Got a Social Security number, ran it through our database, and got a hit. Grand theft auto, breaking and entering . . ."

"He's a felon?" I shrieked. "Why isn't his DNA in CODIS?"

"Those felonies aren't violent. They aren't rape. They aren't assault. Cops don't swab your cheek because you're stealing Toyota Corollas and VCRs." She rustled papers on her desk, then said, "His last known place of employment? Fortune Security."

I had never partied at Trix before. Not that I would have been allowed to enter.

The club was one room with booths that faced each other. With a maximum capacity of a hundred guests, the bouncer would never let some random word nerd pass through those doors. In fact, the valet won't even park your car unless he's absolutely certain you're getting in.

Trix was also known for its "no cameras, no press" policy. The paparazzi were forced to hang out on the sidewalks for their quarry. And on this night, young Hollywood waltzed into their private clubhouse, fluorescent creatures caught in bright light. High, drunk, and lusty. Who would still be here, on earth, next year this time?

I pulled in front of the club's entrance.

The valet asked my name, then took my car—guess I was on the list.

Photographers raised their cameras in my direction but hesitated before snapping. *Who's that? What show is she on? If she goes in, then she has to be someone, right?* A few took my picture just in case.

The noise level in Trix was the equivalent of an airport's. A Notorious B.I.G. song blasted from the club's speakers. Females shrieked and shouted to each other and into their cell phones. Martini shakers crackled with ice while corks burst and glasses broke. Not one pocket of silence existed in that building.

I found a white-haired waitress willing to stop and talk—after I hopped in front of her. "I have an appointment with Paul," I shouted over Biggie.

She pivoted on her platform heels and strode across the club.

I followed her and spotted that guy who's famous for not having talent, that girl known for flashing her lady bits to the guys outside with the cameras, and those siblings who were only famous because their daddy and momma could never tell them no.

Never seen so much weave, Botox, and silicone in one room. I felt crunchy, a Berkeley bohemian even in $200 jeans and $500 stilettos. There's always more excess, right?

A starlet hoisting a martini bumped into me and spilled vodka all over my sweater. She giggled, said, "I didn't see you," and slinked away to a booth and to a Lakers guard holding court with women who were not his wife. I swiped at my ruined cashmere and vowed never to watch her lame-ass show again.

The waitress led me to a closed door guarded by two men the size of grizzly bears. "She gotta see Paul," she said, then stomped away.

I smiled at the duo. "My name is Sy McKay."

The guard with the Afro mohawk muttered into a walkie-talkie. He turned to his partner, a white dude with a rock-'em-sock-'em-robot jaw. White Dude opened the door and said, "Go."

A bald Black man with a full beard and mustache sat behind a massive glass desk. He looked like Mount Everest stuffed into a leather throne. A spotlight shone on him, while leaving the rest of the room in darkness. Six different cell phones sat on the desk blotter—I had called one of them. He pointed to the much-smaller chair I should occupy.

"Thanks for talking to me," I said. "I've never been here before."

"Of course you ain't. You only here cuz of Lena." He gave me the up and down, then stopped at my breasts hidden behind my damp sweater. "Since when do hos get obits?"

"Krystal was a friend of mine," I said. "I've written several articles about a serial killer in Los Angeles, and her death may be related."

He extracted a cigar from the cedar humidor at the corner of his desk. "The cops think I know something. They probably think I did it."

"Did you?"

He eyed me as he lit his cigar, his cool expression still managing to convey *Bitch, you wanna die today?*

I winked. "Had to ask. So, I'm writing a book now, and my brother—you may have heard of him. Ken McKay, the director?"

"Yeah, I know his name. He's been here a couple of times."

"Well, he's already planning to do a movie based on this case."

Paul stopped puffing his stogie. "Movie?"

I nodded. "It's pretty much a done deal. He's talked to a few big names . . . Will Smith, Halle Berry . . . I just have to finish the damned thing. Find out who's important. Who really knew the victims. Who—"

"Krys and I was real tight," he volunteered. "She was closer to me than to her own family." He considered the cigar between his two sausage fingers. "I do a little acting on the side, you know. Got my SAG card and everything."

No surprise there. We all want to be famous for something. We'll sing before millions, be filmed living in a house with strangers, eat a scorpion or two just to get our fifteen minutes and a chance at winning a million dollars. And this isn't just an LA thing. I've seen those episodes of *American Idol* when they hold auditions in Lincoln, Nebraska, or Nashville—the lines wrap four times around the auditorium. And here was Paul Gallashaw, master of the most exclusive club in town, wanting to eat chicken tenders and score Snapples from the craft services table.

"When was the last time you saw Krystal?" I asked.

"At the AA meeting on Friday afternoon. She drank some coffee, I had some tea, we talked, that was it. I came here afterward."

"Were you and Krystal lovers?"

He clenched his cigar between his teeth. "She was my employee."

I paused. "She waitressed here?"

He laughed. "I managed her clientele, if you understand my meaning."

Meaning: pimp.

"Alcohol was messing up my life," he continued. "My business acumens and shit was being affected. So I joined AA." He puffed his cigar a few times. "And Krys. Clients was complaining about her showing up to appointments drunk as hell. Men who come to me for my services don't wanna deal with no real-life problems. Last thing they need is a drunk ho. They can go to Century Boulevard off in the hood if they wanted that." He tapped his cigar against a crystal ashtray. "I was losing money, so I forced her to go to some meetings."

Huh. A tea-sipping pimp. Only in LA.

"Did she have a client last night?" I asked.

"No, but I plan on killing the bastard who did this." He paused, then smiled. "Figure of speech, Miss McKay."

"Of course."

"Krys was my Number One. She brought in mucho dineros."

"Like how much?"

"She paid cash for that Maserati."

My eyes widened. "That's a hundred thirty thousand dollars."

He nodded. "Me and Krys was having problems cuz she was letting personal shit affect business. She was seein' some pinhead. One of my former clients."

"Joey Fortune?"

"Nigga think he hot shit now and ain't got to pay for ass. Krys got it into her thick head that he was in love with her cuz he took her places, bought her shit. Bought those fake titties she had put in. She thought it was fate cuz they bumped into each other after fifty years or something." He snorted, shook his head. "He ain't loved her. He just didn't wanna pay for her. That way, though, he ain't got to since they a couple or what the hell ever."

"Did you warn Krys about him?" I asked. "About his real motives for being with her?"

"Hell, yeah, I warned her. But she didn't believe me. And he dropped her ass for some other ho, and that's when she started drinking again."

"Did this other woman work for you?"

He shook his head. "Nah. But it messed Krys up. She stayed drunk until I stepped in again. Then, she went back to Joey's ass and begged him for another chance." He leered at me through the curtain of smoke. "You cute, Miss McKay. Got that neurotic, Black American Princess thang goin' on."

"Thanks." I guess.

"Need a job?" he asked. "Folks gots to get they hustle on in this fucked-up economy. A lot of writer girls are working for me cuz of the strike. I charge niggas extra for that—bitches that can spell and watch CNN and shit."

I cleared my throat and shifted in my seat. "Thanks, again, but no. Did you talk to Krys at all last night?"

"Around nine," he said. "I told her that she better stay away from alcohol cuz I was gonna come down to El Torito and beat her ass if she got drunk. Did it before. I'd do it again."

"Why did you do it then?"

"You ain't need to know that."

"But that's why the cops came here—"

"Time is money. Bitches can't be actin' up, understand? Too much competition in this town so you gotta put the smackdown on a ho every once in a while. And the cops—"

"Think you may have smacked her down for good."

"I got an airtight alibi—I was at a fundraiser with a whole buncha people who saw me sitting and eatin' fancy chicken and *haricots vert*, so I'm no longer a suspect." He waved his beefy hand, dismissing my concern. "And I'm not a stupid man. Why would I kill my moneymaker?"

"Maybe because she was HIV positive?"

Paul gaped at me, and his cigar dangled from his mouth. "Bullshit."

I shrugged. "I found the report at her house this afternoon."

He slumped in his throne. "You for real?"

"Other than Joey Fortune, could another of your clients be the bad guy?" I asked. "Maybe he found out about her health and . . ."

Paul shook his head.

"Did you give the cop any names?"

"Hell no," he said. "Protect the customer."

"Even if it lands you in jail?"

He shrugged. "What's bad about that? I could get my third degree, find Jesus again, and get this cavity fixed."

A woman shrieked out in the club area. People started shouting.

I looked over my shoulder at the closed door. "Is everything okay out there?"

Paul smirked. "Some bitch fighting another bitch. Gon' be weave tracts and shit all over the damned place. Blond hair hanging off my bar like Christmas tinsel." He tapped his fist against the desktop. "If Krystal gave somebody that AIDS shit, then I don't know what to say."

"Do you think she deserved to die?" I asked.

He glanced at a yellow Motorola that was now vibrating on his desk. "Yeah," he whispered. "Seems like she was gonna die anyway."

I rose from my seat to leave, nauseous and oily from my tête-à-tête with a misogynist. "One more question," I said. "Do the cops know what you do on the side?"

He chuckled as he grabbed the vibrating telephone from his desk. "I'm an upstanding businessman, Miss McKay. A member of the West Hollywood Chamber of Commerce and shit. And some of my best clients are cops." He opened the vibrating phone. "Who dis?"

41

The shrill cry of the telephone forced my eyes open. The office bloomed with copper-colored sunlight that offered no heat. Dust motes danced in the sunbeams. Already a gorgeous day in Los Angeles. My sleepy gaze landed on the television screen and Lucille Ball . . . *I Love Lucy.*

Morning already?

Could barely remember coming home after my Trix visit. Didn't remember undressing and collapsing on the office couch.

Getting too old for this crap.

I stood and stretched, and my bones *clickedclickedclicked.*

The phone rang again.

I ignored it and stared at the television.

Lucy and Ethel were stealing John Wayne's footprints from Grauman's Chinese Theater.

The doorbell rang. Furious knocks followed.

I trudged down the hallway to the front door. "Who is it?"

"It's me," Lena shouted. "Open the damn door."

I rolled away the water bottle, removed the door jammer, and slipped off the chain.

Lena stood on my porch, a vase of red roses in one hand and a Canter's Deli bag in the other. She wore a micro miniskirt, a tiny-tiny T-shirt, and red stilettos (what most women wear on Monday mornings). "Why the hell aren't you answering the phone? I've been calling you all morning." She brushed past me and stomped to the kitchen.

"Doing this thing called 'sleeping,'" I said. "Forgive me."

She sat the vase on the breakfast counter.

"I was hoping for a bottle of wine since you were in Temecula," I said, "but roses will do."

"They're not from me. While I was standing on your porch, being ignored, a delivery guy came. I'm assuming they're for you."

I hesitated—*they can't be from Deon Jackson . . . could they?* I pulled the card from the bouquet.

Can't stop thinking about you, Sy, and I'm sorry about everything. Love, Adam.

My hands were shaking. I looked up—Lena was staring at me, waiting.

I read her the note.

She crossed her arms. "Well?"

My head dipped to my chest. "I don't know what to do."

"What is your problem?" she whispered. "Sweetie, what are you scared of? He's seen your scar. Hell, he helped you with all those drainage pumps. And you're not gonna die, so you aren't sparing him from tragedy. And yeah: He's an ass sometimes, but bees buzz, bears shit in the woods, and men are assholes."

"He doesn't need me," I said.

"How much crack have you smoked this morning?" Lena snapped. "I've seen how that man looks at you. Those freaky eyes of his get all bright and stupid. Even when he's angry at you, he's still freakin' *worshipping* you."

I gazed at the roses.

"He pissed me off with the whole Deon Jackson thing," Lena said. "Not being here for you. And I told him—"

A flare shot through my gut. "You talked to Adam?"

"Hell yeah, I talked to him," she said, her eyes hot. "I stomped into his messy little office last night and freaked him out. He told me that Roya was a rebound, a temporary solution to his Syeeda problem. And I told him that he messed up by keeping that bitch's card in his house. And that he *really* messed up by not picking up the phone and getting over here and that he needs to spend the rest of his life making it up to you, and that you *do* love him, it's just that you're crazy. And then, I said a whole bunch of other shit that I don't remember." She shrugged. "I had been drinking. A lot."

I groaned, then muttered, "I need to get dressed."

"And Adam?"

"Can't deal right now."

She frowned. "When will you deal?"

"Soon," I said. "Flag Day, maybe."

"Do you love him or not?"

I had started to the door, but stopped. "Yes, I love him." I paused, then said, "I'll be in the shower."

"What about breakfast?" Lena shouted after me. "You need to eat."

No time to eat. I needed to visit an old friend.

Fortune Security was located in a Culver City industrial park with planned trees, planned paths, and cookie-cutter buildings with mirrored-glass facades. The lobby had been designed by someone with a brushed-steel fetish—everything shone dully like a fancy kitchen that would never see spaghetti sauce splotches or bacon grease spatters. Modern furniture, also gray, also stiff as steel, suggested that one should keep moving to her destination, not to loiter *cuz we got our eye on you.* The receptionist, keeping with the building's theme, wore a silver pantsuit that had been poured on then dulled with scouring pads. She directed me to the fifth floor, the offices of Joseph Fortune.

"Fortune" and the company's logo—a gun sight for the *o* in Fortune—had been nailed to anything that could hold brushed-steel letters. Corridors, desk fronts, elevator lobbies. *Don't forget where you are . . . Fortune Security.* I'm sure the tampon machine in the ladies' bathroom had also been branded with the Fortune name.

I waited in Joey's reception area as attractive females wiggled past in clumps of threes and fours, with bags of Fatburger and Popeye's chicken in their skinny hands. There wasn't a homely one in the bunch, and not one had hit thirty years old or 125 pounds yet. They could eat that high-fat crap without worry.

Just wait, I thought, smiling at them. *Just wait until your high metabolism is raptured away to Jesus and your thighs start rubbing against each other.* That made me chuckle.

Joey's redheaded secretary ended her phone call, then smiled at me. "I'm sorry, but Mr. Fortune isn't available. Mr. Norton, the vice president of the company? He's coming over now to talk to you." Her green eyes were unblinking and Frisbee big.

"Do you know if Christopher Johnson came in today?" I asked.

"Uhh . . ." The pretty ginger hesitated. "Mr. Norton will be here any—"

"Miss McKay?"

I turned to the man who had said my name.

He smiled. "Mitch Norton." He was US Marine Corps big, with a blond crew cut and Herculean arms tense against his dress shirt. As we shook hands, he took great care in not crushing mine.

"Thanks for seeing me," I said. "I just asked if Christopher Johnson was around."

Mitch glanced at the secretary. She offered a barely there shrug.

"Does he not work here anymore?" I asked.

"Chris was one of our tech guys," Mitch said. "He died three years ago."

"Christopher *Johnson*?" I said.

The secretary swiveled back to her computer monitor and pretended to check email.

"And you and Joey are friends?" Mitch asked.

"We went to college together," I said. "I'm working on this story, and I bumped into Toni a few days ago. She told me to talk to Joey, but I still haven't caught up with him yet. Haven't seen him in years."

Mitch grunted. "I haven't seen him in days."

I paused, unsure of his meaning. "Is he on a business trip?"

He tapped the counter. "We'll let Joey know that you stopped by."

"I have a few questions," I said. "Maybe you can—"

"Piper," he said to the secretary, "make sure you validate Miss McKay's parking."

Piper nodded. "Miss McKay, you said you needed to stop at the ladies' room?"

I looked at her. *Huh?*

She pushed away from the desk. "We use security key cards, so I have to let you in."

Mitch said, "Great," then offered me his hand again. "Pleasure meeting you."

We watched him stride down the hallway.

Piper led me in the opposite direction and stopped at the door to the women's restroom. She waved her key card before a black lockbox. *Click.* She pushed open the door and waved me in.

She checked the three stalls—all empty.

I glanced at the tampon machine on the wall. Surprise, surprise, no Fortune logo.

Piper anxiously regarded me with her bush-baby eyes. "I've only been here six months, and I'm talking to you cuz I just got engaged and what may not have bothered me in the past . . ." She inhaled and puffed out her cheeks as the air left her lungs. "The only way to get ahead at this company is to give the bosses . . . special attention." She tugged at her engagement ring. "I don't wanna do that. I can't . . ."

I offered an encouraging smile. "You shouldn't have to."

"They don't think I know a lot cuz I'm just a secretary," she said. "Mitch and Joey and the guys always talk around me like I don't exist, and I actually preferred that. But today, Mitch said something strange and . . . Maybe I can help you."

"Which may then help you?" I asked.

She glanced back at the door. "We should hurry."

"So do you know where Joey Fortune is?"

A smile played at the corners of her mouth. "He may be in Cancún with one of his . . . *clients*. But you didn't hear that from me." She leaned against the sink. "Why did you ask for Chris Johnson?"

"He was dating someone I knew. She died recently, and I'm telling a few of her friends. I saw Chris's name in a book he gave her, and on a credit card slip—"

"A credit card slip from three years ago?"

"No. From last month."

She narrowed her eyes. "What's your friend's name?"

"Tamar Haist."

She paled, and her hands gripped the sides of the sink.

"Did you know Tamar?"

"Kind of."

I shook my head. "Okay, I'm confused. Chris and Tamar were dating. They saw each other last Tuesday. Are there two Christopher Johnsons working here?"

"Only one, and trust me: He's dead." Piper met my gaze in the mirror. "Someone else is using his name."

"Someone . . . Joey?"

She responded with a single lifted eyebrow.

"How did Joey and Tamar meet?" I asked, trying not to sound surprised.

"We did the security system for her father's church," she said. "The crew was short one person that day and Joey went along, for old time's sake. He met Tamar, gave her a fake name—Chris Johnson—and that was that. He didn't think it would last that long."

"But it did. Sounds like they were serious."

Piper nodded. "I started noticing strange credit card transactions with Chris Johnson attached. Saks. Gucci. Tiffany. And I asked Joey about it, but . . . It's not my company, you know? I'm just a secretary. He was already using that card to pay for all the guys to party. They'd take some of the girls here to Vegas. I never went, but Mitch asked me this morning if I wanted to go and . . ." Her voice trailed off and she hugged herself. "Joey always had a new girl, but this Tamar. He was crazy about her."

"Mitch said he hasn't seen Joey in days."

Piper nodded. "He hasn't been in the office since last Tuesday." She rubbed her face, then released a long sigh. "Wait. Why are you here again? For real."

"I'm writing a story about serial murders in the city," I said. "And Joey may be able to shed some light on the subject since Tamar may have been killed by this lunatic. Tamar and Joey had a date last Tuesday. The next morning, she was dead."

Piper didn't speak.

"I think shit's about to hit the fan, Piper. All that's going on here with the pretty girls, the identity theft, strippers in Vegas being tipped with a dead man's credit card."

She flushed. "I think people should know. Aren't I protected by the whistleblower law?"

I shrugged, then said, "Did Tamar know Joey was married?"

She squirmed and futzed with the buttons on her blouse. "Joey loved Tamar because she didn't demand anything from him like the others did. They didn't even sleep together at first—she was pretty old-fashioned, and he thought that was sweet. He was planning to take her to Mexico—I booked the tickets—and that's where I thought he was all week. He planned to tell Toni about Tamar when he came back. He wanted a divorce."

"And you know all this because . . . ?"

"Sometimes, Joey doesn't close his door when he's on the phone with Tamar, or when he's talking to Mitch. Sometimes, he tells me to order flowers for her. And a divorce lawyer called him three weeks ago."

"Do you think Toni knew about Tamar?"

"Toni's an idiot," she said with a smirk. "Joey cheats right in front of her, and she's still clueless. He's slept with most of the girls working here, but Toni waltzes in with her furs and diamonds like she's the damn queen bee. Guess she is. But instead of buying a fur she needs to buy a freakin' clue."

"What about Krystal Miller? I hear Joey dated her, too."

"Dated?" Piper tried to keep a straight face but couldn't. "You don't *date* prostitutes," she said, giggling. "Sorry, but that's the truth."

"And how did you know what she did for a living?"

"I heard Joey telling Mitch about her, about how much she used to charge until they started officially . . ." She hooked her fingers and said, "Dating."

"She's dead, too," I said.

Her smile melted into slack-jawed awe.

"Yeah. Joey's in serious trouble. Two of his girlfriends are alive one day and dead within a few days of each other. Strange, huh?"

Piper stared at her reflection in the mirror. She opened her mouth to speak, but decided not to.

"Did you ever see Joey and Krystal fight?" I asked.

Piper sighed—she knew the ending to this story and probably wondered if she'd have a job a year from now. "All the time. She came here about two weeks ago, threatening to tell Toni everything. She said that she knew he was seeing someone else, and she had started following him around, checking his cell phone when he was asleep. You know, the kind of stuff wives do when they think their husband's cheating on them. Joey freaked out, dragged her into his office with her screaming all the way. I couldn't hear what they talked about, but she left looking spooked as hell.

"I asked him what happened, and he kinda smiled at me. I didn't think he'd actually . . . Joey cheated on his wife, but he's not a murderer. He's doing good work here. Keeping folks safe in their homes and businesses. He was a cop."

I nodded. "Using a dead man's name to lead another life while cheating on his wife with multiple women? A real American hero."

"He gives Toni whatever she wants," Piper said, regret now auburn splashed across her face. "The cars, the house, the clothes . . . He works his ass off building this company, and she can't even give him a kid."

"Guess she's getting what she deserves." I pulled my bag onto my shoulder. "Thanks for talking to me, Piper. Don't be surprised if a detective stops by today. He may be looking to talk to Christopher Johnson, too."

◆ ◆ ◆

Piper wouldn't have to wait long for that visit from Adam. The detective was in the Fortune parking lot, leaning against my car. Today, he wore a blue Oxford shirt, gray slacks, and black leather bucks.

"What are you, a youth pastor?" I jangled my keys and motioned for him to move.

He didn't move.

"Detective Sherwood, are you following me?"

He stood to his official height. "What can I say? You're irresistible, Sy. Did you get the flowers?"

I nodded. "They were beautiful."

"Lena visited me last night," he said. "She's . . . complicated, isn't she?"

I nodded, shrugged, smiled. Complicated.

"She cursed me out," he said.

"Did you deserve it?"

"Yeah. I did." When I didn't speak, he sighed and said, "What brings you to Fortune Security?"

"I'm visiting Joey Fortune. He's an old friend of mine."

"Was he there?"

"In an existential sense? Yes, he was."

Adam blinked at me. "Was he in the building? Physically in the building?"

"No, he wasn't."

He reached in his pocket and pulled out a folded piece of paper. "Thought you'd like to see this."

I plucked the document from his fingers. "What is it?"

"We're releasing this sketch today."

The Black man in the picture was almost featureless: skin the color of walnuts, almond-shaped brown eyes, full lips, low haircut, early forties. "This could be any Black man in America," I said, shaking my head.

"Skittles couldn't determine his height or weight since he was in the minivan," Adam said. "And we showed her different minivan models—she thinks it's a Nissan Quest." He shrugged. "It's more than what we had, right? Hopefully, someone will recognize him."

I slipped the paper into my notebook. "What's going on with Herschel Halley?"

Adam placed his hands on his hips, aware of the game. "The gun we found on him—"

"Doesn't match the gun used by the Slayer."

"Nor does his DNA match the sample found beneath Tamar's nails or on the victim back in '90. Halley isn't the Slayer, but we're keeping him for other things, including soliciting sex workers and beating them up afterward."

"Have you thought more about the DNA test for city workers?"

He nodded. "Still trying to figure out the logistics for something that big."

"What about my gun? I'd like it back now."

He reached for his jacket holster and pulled out my Glock.

"We tested the bullet that killed Krystal," he said as he handed me the weapon.

I slipped the gun into my bag. "And?"

"The striations matched those of the bullet that killed Tamar. Whoever killed Tamar also killed Krystal."

Joey Fortune?

I looked at him and didn't blink. "Maybe you should test the DNA that came from beneath Tamar's nails against the semen found in Krystal."

"I'm planning to do that . . ." He narrowed his eyes. "What aren't you telling me?"

"Christopher Johnson worked here."

Adam nodded. "I know that."

"And he's been dead for three years."

Confused, Adam narrowed his eyes. "So . . . ?"

"So who was Tamar Haist dating, you ask?" I pulled the framed seaside photograph of Krystal and Joey from my bag, then handed it to Adam.

"This is Krystal Miller," he said, studying the picture.

"And that man is Tamar's Christopher."

"Tamar and Krystal were dating the same guy?"

"And that guy is Joey Fortune. He's been using his dead employee's name. Poor Tamar had no clue. And Joey was Krystal's client and one-time lover, but he broke it off with her when he started seeing Tamar."

Adam rubbed his jaw and glanced at the building behind us. "And Joey Fortune?"

"Is missing. *And* he's an ex-cop. And he's tall and handsome. And his secretary hasn't seen him since last Tuesday. She thinks he's in Cancún."

Adam glanced at the picture again. "Can I have this?"

"I'll think about it."

He frowned.

I winked at him. "Kidding. Keep it. Find him."

Adam kept staring at the picture.

"What's wrong?"

"You know that text message you got yesterday? The one of Krystal that had been sent from her BlackBerry?"

I nodded. "You guys were gonna triangulate . . ." I swallowed. "Oh, no."

"Oh, yeah. Whoever sent it, sent it from this business park. That's why I'm here." He glanced in the distance, to Fortune Security. "Krystal's phone is here. Somewhere."

42

The black Yukon was parked in the Fortune driveway next to the purple Bentley. Had Joey Fortune returned from Cancún?

Maybe I should talk to Toni later.

I sat in the car, debating my next step.

Wait.

What's the benefit of waiting?

Come back with Adam. Cuz what if Joey's here and tries to leave?

Two minutes later, I rang the bell.

The door flew open.

Toni stood there, eyes wide, slack-jawed.

I smiled. "I should've called first. Sorry."

She blinked. "No. It's . . . No. Come in."

The house smelled of garlic and butter. The low murmurs of music came from the kitchen—Anita Baker or Miki Howard, some songbird from our past.

"I'm still working on the SKU from Tamar's dress," Toni said as she led me into the living room. "It's taking longer than I thought."

I dropped onto the ridiculously stuffed couch. My feet barely touched the ground.

A framed photograph sat on the coffee table—a black-and-white wedding portrait, *Toni and Joey* inscribed in white print at the picture's corner, in case someone forgot.

"I stopped by because we need to talk," I said.

"You're right," she said. "We do. Friend to friend. Sister to sister." She sat back on the couch and twisted her wedding band.

We studied each other, neither of us wanting to start. My right foot bobbed so much, it could've generated the room's electricity.

She leaned forward. "Okay, I'll go first." She futzed with her shirt-sleeve, then said, "Krystal told me something the other day, and I need to know if she was telling the truth. And I hope you don't get upset with me for asking."

I shrugged. "Whatever you wanna know."

"I know I'm being stupid, but it's been chewing away at me, and . . . Krys said that . . ." She chuckled and shook her head as if to apologize. "She said that . . . she said that you and Joey slept together."

My mouth opened and closed like a ventriloquist's dummy.

"Did you?" she asked, eyes bright with worry. "Please tell me the truth, Sy. Please. Did you?"

"Yes," I said, my voice weak. "Once. A very long time ago, if that matters."

Toni shrank before me, her jaw clenched tight.

"It was the past," I whispered. "Back in college, before you and I became good friends. Joey slept with a lot of girls. That's why none of us wanted you to marry him. Because we knew he'd keep cheating on you. And he did. With Krystal. And with Tamar Haist."

"Yes. Tamar." Toni folded her hands in her lap and stared at her wedding band. "He was the only man I ever slept with. The only one." She looked at me. "I'm a fool. That's what you're thinking, isn't it?"

Every muscle in my body tightened. "You trusted him. You trusted us. And we all let you down, and I'm so sorry."

She glared at me with hard, toffee-colored eyes. "How did it make you feel?"

I blinked. "How did what . . . ?"

"Was it worth it? Sleeping with him?"

"I was a kid, Toni. I would never do that now."

"How do I know you're not lying?"

I searched my mind for a way to prove it. I came up with nothing.

"How do I know you weren't sleeping with him last month?" she asked. "Or last week?"

I shook my head. "I wasn't. I haven't. I swear—"

She kicked the coffee table and shrieked, "But how do I know?"

I sat up now and shouted, "I haven't seen Joey since graduation. I'm telling you the truth."

Toni rolled her eyes. "Oh. Okay. You're telling me the truth now even though you've been lying to me all this time, pretending to be my friend. You don't know how to be honest. And you think because you warned me a long time ago that you're off the hook?" She stood from the couch and stomped to the doorway. She turned back to me. "Remember how I wouldn't let you see Joey's safe room?"

"Toni, please. Just listen. I need to tell you something—"

"I don't care about industry secrets now," she said, ignoring me. "And I don't care what you have to say. The door is open. Like I said, it's a great story down there. Thanks for nothing, Syeeda."

After she disappeared up the staircase, I grabbed my bag and returned to the foyer. Guilt dogged me as though my night with Joey had ended just an hour before. *What kind of friend, or person am I?* played in my mind like a recording even though that record had been broken a long time ago.

It's a great story down there.

I paused as I reached for the doorknob, but turned back to face the long hallway.

A great story.

I sighed, shrugged. *Why not?*

I crept through the dim corridor and found the cracked heavy steel door. I swiped my sweaty palms on my pants, then started down the narrow flight of stairs. Somewhere nearby, a hot water heater pinged. The air was thick, still and bomb-shelter quiet. And there was something there, a smell on top of that air current.

Bleach, citronella, and . . . and what?

The step beneath my foot creaked, and I reached for the handrail. I placed the toe of my shoe on the next step . . . then the next . . . I reached the bottom of the staircase and stood before another heavy door.

I pushed it open.

The door swung easily on its hinges.

I stepped into a well-lit room filled with television monitors, computers, and fancy consoles with important-looking lights. It was hot in here—the equipment had heated the room. Boxes of food, blankets, and bottles of water lined the walls. A man had been tied to a high-backed mesh chair. His skin was the color of blueberries and dog food. His chin had dropped to his chest and his fingers had frozen as they clutched the arms of the chair. His long-sleeved tee had been ripped apart and the black hair on his chest was crusted with dried blood. Dark liquid pooled around his bare feet.

My hands covered my mouth. I wanted to scream, wanted to look away, but I couldn't.

Acid bubbled at the base of my esophagus. I took another step forward. "Joey?"

I saw it coming at me from the right, in my peripheral vision. A flash of black, a burst of white, and then . . . nothing.

I lay on the cold stone ground, my legs tangled beneath me. My bag had cushioned my torso against the fall to the concrete, but my mouth tasted like I'd been sucking pennies—blood. Pain rocketed through my body with each breath I took. Something wet oozed down the side of my neck. My vision seesawed, and my head felt like a balloon filled with hot coffee.

Toni stood over me, her gaze on the dead man in the chair. She pulled her eyes lazily to me and said, "Change of plans. I want you to write a book about all of this. Just like you were gonna write a book about the Phantom Slayer."

I squeezed my eyes shut, then attempted to sit up. My hand pushed against the bag and touched something hard. *My gun.*

Toni held a .38 in her hand. Its barrel was trained at my head. "People need to know that I existed. That my life is just as compelling as anyone on those stupid-ass reality shows. That Joey made me look like a fool my entire adult life, and that I got him back in the end." She grinned at her husband, then at me. "Thank you, Syeeda."

"For what?"

"Your articles about the Slayer covered almost everything," she said. "I used them as a guide for this project. It was . . . *fun.* Interesting. Killing's easier than I thought. You gotta admit—you didn't think a woman could do something like this."

I leaned away from the pistol and held up my hands. "Toni, listen—"

"People need to know that the little church girl was a slut," she said, the smile gone. "The way you talked about Tamar Haist drove me fucking crazy. You make her sound like a lovesick virgin who did nothing but kiss puppies and catch butterflies all day. That bitch stole my husband and tried to ruin my marriage."

"Tamar didn't know about you," I whispered.

Her sneer deepened.

Wrong thing to say.

"Behind every successful man is a woman like me," she said. "He didn't become great by himself. He wasn't smart enough."

"He lied to Tamar about who he was," I said, selecting my words more carefully.

"But Krystal knew who he was."

"And she apologized to you."

"Only after I confronted her about it. And you—you couldn't stay away from him, either. Am I so insignificant that you don't even . . . even . . . ?"

"Toni, what happened between Joey and me was a long time ago." I shook my head and the room rocked. I closed my eyes and waited for the world to right itself.

"Know what he gave Tamar for her birthday?" she asked. "That hair and those breasts. He gave Krystal a set, too. Know what he gave me for my birthday? Nothing because he forgot. And when I reminded him?" She flicked at the diamond in her ear and waggled her ring finger. "These baubles, this coat, and a disease that's three letters long. Who did he get HIV from? Tamar? Krystal? You?" She squared her shoulders. "But guess who's gonna win in the end? Guess who the world will talk about? Me."

"You'd kill me for fame?"

She threw her head back and laughed. "Kill you? Sweetie, I don't wanna kill you. I mean, not right away. You're the Storyteller. That's why I sent you that text from Tamar's phone after I shot her ass. She didn't know who the hell you were. That bitch never read a newspaper her entire life. And I followed you all that morning after you found her in the alley, and I purposely bumped into you at Whole Foods. Same thing with Krystal. I sent you that text and picture of her. Brilliant, huh?" She wiggled her nose, impressed with herself.

"This is how it will work: I'm gonna tell you everything and you're gonna write it all up and make it . . . What's the industry word? *Unputdownable*." She paused, then said, "And I didn't do this for fame. I did this because I'm tired of being dogged. Tired of being mocked. I'm getting them back for everything they did to me." She shrugged. "Put simply: It's all about revenge. But you'll make it more interesting than that."

I swiped my mouth—my fingers came away bloody. "Toni, I can't."

She snorted. "You can't? What the hell? Sanctimonious now? You've written about other people's sordid lives, but when a friend asks you for help, you say no? Don't get all holy-holy writer with integrity now that you're caught up in it as one of the villains. And don't tell me you're not curious. Don't you wanna know how I got Tamar and Krystal in the alley? Don't you wanna know what we talked about before they fell to my feet like the trash they were?"

"You need help, Toni."

"You're right," she said. "I do need help. We've come full circle." She clapped her hands and grinned. "You're gonna stay down here and you'll write my story. About how I used betrayals from my husband and my friends to empower me. Even when faced with a life-threatening disease, still I rise, *blah blah blah*. And you're all about that, aren't you? Speaking for those who have no voice? Being a backbone for the weak?"

She considered her husband. "And after you're finished, we'll send the story to your agent, and I'll throw you a little party, just as I promised. No stripper, though. Or strawberries. Then, the cops will come but they won't find me. And you. You'll be . . . gone. You'll write the story, Sy." She smiled at me, then pushed Joey across the room.

I shoved my hand into the bag and rummaged around for the gun.

"You owe me," she said, rolling Joey near the bottled waters. "Consider it penance for sleeping with my husband."

I pulled my bag onto my lap to hide the Glock. "And what if I refuse to write?"

She turned back to me. "You'll die, and I'll find another writer. I know you have a huge ego, but you must know that you're not the only journalist in the world."

I stared at her as my mind raced. *How do I bluff my way out of dying?*

"I never thought this would be my life," she said, her voice cracking. "I never thought that we'd be down in this basement, with my husband . . ."

Was she backing down now?

"No one's life is perfect," I said.

"Says the woman with a man who's crazy about her, who knows that she exists and wants her around. You haven't committed to him because *you* don't want to, not because he wants his freedom." Her eyes darted to my bag. "We were friends, Syeeda."

I nodded. "Yeah."

She took a side step. "But that was a long time ago. We were different people then."

I slowly pulled my hand from behind the bag and aimed the Glock in her direction. "I don't want to shoot you, Toni."

Toni lifted her gun. "And I . . . can't say that."

An explosion, and then another, filled the room.

Toni's head jerked forward as her body fell back. The gun ripped out of her hand as she crumpled to the concrete. She fell back on the floor, her chest a mass of flesh and bone.

Cops milled around the Fortune front lawn as investigators searched inside the house. The morgue attendants from the coroner's office loaded a stretcher holding a body bag into the back of their van. Neighbors stood on the other side of the yellow tape. The cell phones were out, but there was no glee, only tears. These people knew Toni and Joey Fortune.

I thought of calling Lena, calling my mother or my sister Eva. But I didn't. To say what? *Guess what awful thing happened in Toni's basement?* No. Right then, I could only communicate the superficial. No words for that profound sense of loss that leaves you as dumb as driftwood. And there was so much loss. Joey, Tamar, and Krystal. My old friend Toni . . . by my hand.

Toni had convinced herself that she was invisible, that no one valued her. And it had become gospel: Joey had ignored her. Krystal had disregarded her. *I* had disregarded her sixteen years ago. Tamar had not even known that Toni existed.

And if Toni had suffered—a woman with diamonds, furs, and a Bentley—how awful was it for women with less? Woman who were faceless, nameless, who were considered statistics, blights on society, problems in the community . . . women who were not considered at all.

Women so different from my best friend and my sister, both who made people duck their heads and run for cover. Throwing perfume bottles. Chasing monsters across the country. Demanding to be heard. Demanding to *be*. Dimming Lena's and Eva's lights would be like blocking the sun with your thumb.

Who am I? A phantom or a cowboy?

I was something in between, a creature that slipped in and out of both worlds to tell each that the other existed.

Adam found me crying on a stretcher in the back of an ambulance. He said nothing as he hugged me.

Don't know how long we stayed like that but I wanted him to hold me forever.

He kissed the top of my head before breaking our embrace. He opened his mouth to speak, but no words came. He looked away, swiped his hand over his lips, then said, "I know it's a stupid question, but . . . you okay?"

I shook my head, unable to tell him that I felt thin, there but . . . not. Like a slick of milk at the bottom of the glass. I considered the cold compress the paramedic had given me for my head wound, then shifted my attention to the crowd. "I didn't want to," I whispered. "But I had to."

Adam cupped my face in his hands. "I know, babe."

I moved my head to kiss his palm. Closed my eyes. Saw Toni there. "I just . . . I wanna go home."

"I'll have a car take you."

I shook my head. "I can drive. I just wanna go."

He studied me and stroked my cheek.

I nodded. *I'm okay.*

"I have to stay here," he said, "but I'll come home as soon as I can. I'll take some days off and we'll go somewhere, okay? Get away from all of this. Just you and me."

"Yeah?"

He kissed my forehead. "Four Seasons Santa Barbara?"

I touched his jaw. The stubble on his chin bristled beneath my fingertips.

He whispered, "I love you, Sy."

"I love you, Adam."

And I did.

43

I stood on the walkway, a few steps away from my front door. Somewhere in the neighborhood, someone barbecued. Smoky, sweet air tweaked my nose. *Ribs.* I wanted ribs. And grilled sweet corn. And a pitcher of sangria. And Adam.

My skin crawled—I didn't want to go in, even though the house hadn't done anything to me except . . . *exist.*

Why didn't I want to go in?

The house was quiet and cold. The living room smelled of my perfume and Adam's roses now sitting on the dining room table. *Hope they last longer than the wildflowers.* A tech from ASC had come—an alarm sensor was now screwed above the kitchen door window. Security bars had also been installed on the outside.

I popped a Vicodin, then took a long, hot shower. Cooked eggs and rice for dinner, but I couldn't take more than a few bites—my mind kept turning back to Toni.

Poor Toni.

Poor Tamar.

And Krystal . . .

I retreated to my office, stood at the window, and pushed aside the curtains. Stared at the bougainvillea lining the walls of the backyard. Somewhere in the neighborhood, a German shepherd howled, ruining the quiet.

I settled at my desk and wiggled the mouse to awaken the computer. The Four Seasons Hotel in Santa Barbara had suites available for the weekend. I typed in my credit card number, then clicked "confirm." I sat back in the chair and closed my eyes. Imagined splashing in the turquoise waters of the Pacific, Adam beside me. Grilled lobster for dinner. Crème brûlée for dessert. Showers together. Clean sheets . . . No guns. No murdered sex workers. No Phantom Slayer.

"Come home now," I muttered, staring at the telephone, so close to picking up the receiver and calling him and telling him that I needed him, that I needed to leave this place and just . . . *be*. With him.

Instead, I grabbed the cigarette case and lighter from my bag, then stepped out onto the deck. The cool air made my skin prickle and my head wound throb. I closed my eyes, savored those flickering feelings of being alive, then sank into an Adirondack chair.

Don't know how long I sat in the backyard, watching plumes of cigarette smoke shift into airplanes and hippos and hearts. When I had first sat, the sky had been the color of melted Popsicles. Orange, cherry, grape. The moon just a fingernail sliver in space. But the darkness had come, and now the only light in the yard came from my office window and from the lit end of my cigarette.

The air had bite, but I didn't want to go back in. I wanted Adam to find me out here. I wanted him to take me out here. So I stayed in that chair, eyes on airplane and helicopter lights in the sky, waiting for Adam as my breathing slowed and my eyes closed.

A warm hand brushed against my neck. My eyes fluttered open—I had fallen asleep in the backyard. "Adam?" I smiled and reached for his hand. "Baby, I'm . . ."

The hand didn't belong to Adam—it was too small.

I froze with my hand over this stranger's, with his hand gripping my neck.

This is not Adam.

God help me.

A shock jolted my body. My fists clenched tight and my teeth slammed together. Couldn't move. Something sharp jabbed my neck and ice filled my veins.

All that time, the sky didn't change.

That fingernail-thin moon looked so far away.

44

Hearing that name, not his name, had made him tighten his grip around her neck.

Her eyes had widened with surprise—he was not Adam.

And now, he ties the cotton kerchief over her mouth even though she'll be unconscious for a while. It had taken longer than he'd planned to bring her down—she is tiny but strong. Chemistry is stronger, and as soon as the ketamine kicked in, she had collapsed in his arms like a rag doll.

He covers her eyes with another kerchief, then pulls from his pocket the plastic binds cops use to arrest rioters and slips them on her wrists. He throws her over his shoulder and returns to the house. Grabs her keys from the kitchen counter and hustles to the driveway. He peeks around that privacy wall to ensure that no one else is there.

The patrol car that drives by every other hour is gone.

Clear.

He opens the Benz's back passenger door and lays Sy on the floor. He checks her pulse—slow but steady. Still alive. His own pulse races—he wants to have her now, but she's not dead. Just unconscious. It's not the same thing. That heartbeat changes everything.

He climbs into the driver's seat and catches his reflection in the rearview mirror. He's smiling. His eyes dance. He's never been happier in his life.

It takes forever to drive home. The Golden State Freeway is always crowded at this hour, but the Benz makes the drive pleasant with its satellite radio and leather seats. An hour later, he exits the freeway and drives for another thirty minutes until he reaches the ghost streets of Lancaster, seventy miles north of Los Angeles and a stone's throw from the Mojave Desert.

He reaches the La Cuesta Verde development. A phalanx of tall palm trees flanks the entrance to this "Oasis of the High Desert." No one is shooting hoops on the basketball courts. No one is playing bocce ball on the lawns now dead from heat and neglect. No one is walking their dog or riding their bike. The earth creeps across the sidewalks and windows, taking back land that had been stripped and cleared for 3BD+2BA+loft. It will remain a ghost town until the end of time.

He drives slowly and makes a right on Ave de Contessa Court. His house sits in the middle of the block. A two-story home painted Egyptian Papyrus. A turquoise banner flies above the front door with a graphic of a dove in its center. The only other residents still living on this street are five houses down. They are home—the newish Honda Accord is parked in the driveway next to a dusty Buick Regal that hasn't moved since the Falklands War.

He reaches in his back pocket for the garage's remote control. Once the door lifts, he eases the Benz next to the minivan. He didn't have to drive to Sy's house. Many Angelenos refuse to believe it, but the city really does provide remarkable public transportation.

He removes the kerchief from her eyes.

She's awake. Her pupils are dilated. It takes her some time to focus, and when she does, she startles.

"We know each other, don't we?" He touches her leg. Feels her flinch and her muscles tense. "Be good and you'll be okay. Okay?"

She nods.

"I'm glad you're here, Sy, but I'm gonna have to put you out again. It's easier that way." He makes a show of tapping another syringe filled with ketamine.

She closes her eyes.

Has she already given up? Hope not.

He sticks the needle into her neck. Gently this time.

She doesn't struggle. Just lets him in.

He waits two minutes, then checks her pulse again—slower than before.

No more Special K.

She's no good if she's high.

Or dead.

Well, she's no good dead . . . yet.

45

I awakened to a bright burst of light.

Where am I?

I tried to move my arms—couldn't. My legs were heavy, as though they had been sandbagged. My throat burned. Tried to swallow, but no spit came.

I was floating above a futon with cold air streaming beneath me. Angels, each the size of a rice grain, drifted past me like stardust.

Am I in Heaven?

I shifted, and my bones clicked, skeleton-like.

Tiny golden doves joined those angels. *So pretty.*

I tried to move again, and this time, a silver hand flew in front of my face. But that couldn't have been my hand. This . . . *thing* was as large as a baseball mitt. And my hands were still behind my back.

I sniffed.

The room stank. Paint fumes, pine cleaner, and something sour. Something dead.

The rag in my mouth tasted bitter, acidic, vomit caught in cloth. The muscles in my neck ached. I squeezed my eyes shut and tried to will my hands to my neck.

Beep.

A burst of light.

Blinded.

I blinked to clear my vision.

There was a wall across from me covered with rows of picture frames.

Another beep. Another flash.

What the hell is *that?*

I squinted in the direction of the light's origins.

He stood in the shadows near a door. "You're awake." He stepped forward, a stupid grin on his face.

I knew this man.

Jay, the security guard from Great Redeemer.

Sean, the security tech who had come to my house.

Clean cut. Short. Nothing special to look at or to make you remember him. But I remembered him now.

"Welcome to your new home," he said. "This is where you'll be for now." He held out his arms. "Well?"

My eyes darted around the room. Was I supposed to be impressed with the cheap furniture and the puke-green walls, the fake Turkish area rug and the room's stench?

"Over there?" He pointed to the south corner, to an object that resembled a toddler's potty chair. "That's where you will go. I will empty it three times a day."

I stared at the camping toilet.

"Don't think you can hold it," he said. "And don't worry about offending me. I'd do anything for you. I'll do everything for you. Except let you go."

He stood over me now.

I closed my eyes, squeezed them shut. *I'm hallucinating. This isn't happening.*

"No one will hear you shouting down here," he said, his mouth near my ear, his breath hot against my skin. "I have no neighbors. I've taken precautions so that you cannot escape. The door has two dead bolts and two padlocks, and it's lined with metal sheets." He reached behind me and untied the gag. He kept his face inches from mine. "How are you, Sy?"

"What do you want?" I croaked.

"Let's talk about all that tomorrow. I brought you a few things." He nodded to the small round table near the picture wall. There was a glass mug filled with orange juice on that table along with a plate, a paperback book, and a large Starbucks cup.

He said, "You like nonfat caramel macchiatos, right?"

I didn't answer.

He grabbed my chin and forced me to look at him. "You like them, right?"

I tried to pull free.

His hands clamped both sides of my head and pressed.

My headache reawakened and pain burned through my skull and down my neck. My eyes filled with tears but I refused to cry, to give in. *The pain will wake me up. I'll wake up. You can't die in your dreams. You can't.*

"Have a snack and we'll get to work tomorrow," he said, calm in his tone. "It's been a long day for the both of us. I will uncuff you now. If you fight me . . ." He smiled and gave a half-hearted shrug. "You don't wanna do that, okay?"

This time, I nodded.

He released the plastic binds.

I brought my hands forward. The restraints had cut into my wrists. The more I rubbed the welts, the more my skin burned. But I couldn't stop.

He kissed my forehead. "Good night, Sy. See you in the morning."

I wanted to push him away, rip off parts of my skin he had touched, scream to the heavens and demand God strike this monster down and finally end this nightmare.

The door slammed. The locks clicked. The padlocks rattled.

Quiet.

I stood and immediately fell back on the futon. I tried again, standing slowly this time. Once my legs gained confidence, I took one step, then another . . . until I stood before the door.

Progress.

I twisted the knob.

Locked.

I wandered to the small table and stared at the Starbucks cup, the mug of juice, and the Oreos on the plate. Didn't touch any of it. He could've drugged it.

What had been in that syringe?

And had he used a Taser?

What did he want?

What would he do to me?

Those puke-green walls were closing in on me. My ears burned and my stomach cartwheeled. The room swayed like a pendulum, and the walls sucked in as though a vacuum had formed near the futon.

If you lose it, you can't think. And if you can't think, you're dead.

I sat on my haunches and hid my face in my arms until the panic attack ebbed. "Okay," I said, massaging my temples. "I'm okay."

I drifted over to the picture wall. There was a woman in every photo. Sometimes, the same woman. I recognized several of the faces in those shots. Denesha Jackson, Paula Owens . . . I covered my mouth with a hand and muttered, "Oh, shit." There were pictures of me. Grocery shopping at Whole Foods. Buying coffee at Starbucks. Standing in line for red snapper at Great Redeemer. I glanced back at those pictures of Denesha. In two shots, she had smiled for the camera. In two others, she had been tied up, fear bright in her eyes. In the final shot, she was lifeless, faceless, bloody.

He's the Phantom Slayer.

I spun around and scanned the room. The plate with the cookies. The glass mug of juice. *The Alienist* by Caleb Carr . . . All of this had come from my house. He had broken into my home and stolen these things. He had not kidnapped me on accident or on impulse. He had planned everything.

God help me.

Would Adam call my home phone and cell phone and get suspicious if I didn't answer either of them?

What if he didn't worry? What if he figured I was chasing some story and didn't want to be bothered?

My heart was beating too hard and too fast. My mouth filled with spit and bile. The back of my throat closed.

The room seesawed again.

I closed my eyes and waited for it to right itself.

Cry and die.

I shuffled to the futon and sat. Kept on the desk lamp light— didn't want to be in the dark with a monster so close. And I didn't want to sleep.

I curled into a tight ball and stared at a spot on the floor to keep me focused, to keep away the crazies. My lips started moving on their own.

The Lord is my shepherd; I shall not want;

He makes me lie down in green pastures;

He leads me beside still waters,

He restores my soul . . .

. . . pulse slowed . . . eyes . . . closed.

46

A cool breeze brushed against my cheek.

I opened my eyes, certain that I had finally returned to my bed with its down comforter and Egyptian cotton sheets, certain that I had nightmared everything. That the hit on the head at Toni's had knocked a screw loose and had sent me to a scary place that didn't really exist.

He was sitting in a chair, on the right side of the futon, watching me. He leaned forward on his elbows. "Rise, shine, give God the glory."

I sat up and moved away from him as far as I could without falling off the futon. Drew my knees to my chest.

"You were talking in your sleep," he said. "Are you okay?"

I refused to respond, in word or in gesture.

"You should probably answer my questions," he said. "It will only make life here better than it can be."

"What do you want?"

"The same thing as you, Sy."

"I want to be let go," I said. "Just drop me off in the middle of the desert somewhere. I don't know where I am so I'd have no idea where to find you."

He stared at me.

"Let me go," I demanded. "You know he's looking for me, and if he finds you . . ."

He smiled, but didn't speak.

"What's your name?" I asked.

"You call me the Phantom Slayer."

"What did your mother call you?"

His eyes darkened. "I told you the truth the other day, when I came to check your door. You probably don't remember that."

"You had a goatee. And you wore braces."

"But the other times. You never noticed me. I'd watch you at the grocery store. At the coffee shop. I was insignificant to you then, but now . . ." He glanced at his watch. "You should eat something before we start working."

"I don't want to eat. I want to go home."

He laughed. "You can't be serious, Sy. Here I am, the Phantom Slayer in the flesh. Don't you wanna know more about me? About my difficult childhood and my heroin junkie mother? Don't you wanna know my motivations? My so-called psychopathy? I will tell you everything." He leaned forward, a crazed grin on his face. "You're my apostle, Syeeda McKay, and you'll record it all, and then we will share it with the world. '*For the wrath of God is revealed from heaven against all ungodliness and unrighteousness of men, who hold the truth in unrighteousness.*'"

I blinked at him—*what the hell does that even mean?* "If I write your story, you'll let me go?" I asked.

He didn't respond.

I glanced around the room. "I don't have any writing materials."

He stepped over to the desk and pulled out a drawer filled with notebooks and pens. He tossed one of each on the futon.

I picked up the notebook, turned it over in hands that hadn't stopped shaking since the moment I arrived. "I can't use this notebook. It's spiral-bound and wide-ruled."

He said, "So?"

"I need college-ruled legal pads. Recycled paper." I tossed the notebook back on the bed, then cocked an eyebrow. "You didn't notice that when you were sneaking around my house, stealing shit?"

He slapped the desktop and stormed over to me.

I screamed, held up my arms as protection.

"You will *not* use that language here!" he shouted. "This is holy ground and I will not have obscene language—" He waggled his head, then smacked his forehead. He took several deep breaths, then said, "And if I don't get you these special pads?"

Still hidden behind my arms, I whispered, "Writer's block."

He stared at me.

I turned away from him so that he wouldn't see the tears shimmering in my eyes.

"I will get you the notepads," he said, "but only because I love you."

Oh, shit, no, not that, not love.

"Did you hear me, Sy?"

I said, "Yes."

He was standing over me now and bent toward me. He smelled of citrus and fresh linen, of Adam's cologne. He slipped his fingers into my hair. "I know it will take some time, but you will love me, too. I made this room just for you. And I will be telling you my deepest, darkest secrets. We will get close. You *will* love me." He scratched my scalp, then kissed the top of my head.

I closed my eyes, whispered, "Locking someone in a basement and holding them against their will is not love."

His grip on my hair tightened.

I held my breath, waited for the blow sure to follow.

But his fingers left my hair. He stepped back.

The air felt lighter. Could no longer smell his cologne. Just the stench of decay.

I kept my eyes shut, praying that he'd go away, that the impossible would happen and the earth would swallow him whole.

"I'll be back with your notebooks," he said.

A moment later, the door opened and closed.

47

He drives the minivan to the Office Depot ten miles away. He thought of taking her car—it's so clean and quick, and now that they are together, he has that privilege. But people would look at him because the car is so fancy. He doesn't need attention.

He wanders the aisles and finds the college-ruled, recycled-paper legal pads.

How did he miss this?

So stupid of him.

These pads are better. A little more expensive even though they are used paper.

He dumps into his basket three five-packs of these pads, Post-it notes of every size, and more packs of pens, micro, not bold.

She didn't even thank him. She didn't compliment him once, not on the paint job, not on the down comforter, not on anything. She's spoiled and petty. Expects men to just do shit for her because she's pretty. Because of the power she *thinks* she has between her legs. No wonder the detective refuses to marry her.

But he will change her. There will be a time when she is grateful to him, when nothing but *thank you, thank you, thank you* will spill from her mouth.

The skin beneath his underarm burns—he hates the pain that comes with new tattoos. But two weeks from now, the swelling will be gone, and "T. W." will look just like the others.

His cell phone vibrates in his pocket. He pulls it out and glances in the display.

Noemi Haist.

Now he has to talk to this simple bitch.

He forces a smile as though she can see him. "Hey, sweetie."

She proceeds to talk about shit he couldn't care less about. Funeral for Tamar. Dinner afterward. Community meeting.

Just shut up already.

Noemi prattles on, hinting about how marriage would heal her parents' broken hearts.

He says, "One day soon, sweetie."

She chirps, "Guess what I cooked you for lunch?"

She does this now: guess what I cooked, guess who called, guess what I did.

This guessing game doesn't make her interesting, and he could give a damn about anything she does. But he says, "Don't know. What did you cook?"

"Your favorite," she says. "Shrimp scampi."

"Wow. I love your scampi."

Just one shot to the face, and a picture to capture the memory.

Maybe he'll do it tonight.

Maybe he won't.

She did cook his favorite meal.

Noemi rambles on about something else, then says, "Remember the reporter who was covering Tamar's death?"

He freezes in the aisle. "No."

"Syeeda McKay." She laughs. "Don't pretend that you don't remember her. Any man who meets her remembers her."

He grunts and says, "Oh, yeah. The writer."

"She's missing," Noemi says. "Detective Sherwood came by this morning. Asked me if she had contacted me. He's so worried. He'd been crying—you could tell by his eyes."

He laughs.

"I don't think this is funny, Jay," she says. "Something bad could've happened to her."

"I'm not laughing at her being gone," he says. "I'm laughing at the weepy detective. Cops have no feelings, and if Sherwood loved Sy so much—"

"Sy? So you do have a crush on her." She sounds disappointed.

He rubs the back of his neck. "She's not my type. Too . . . stuck up. You're my type, Noemi. Sweetie."

Ten minutes later, he returns to the van. Anger has replaced humor. He will kill Noemi Haist for mocking him. For making him say shit he doesn't mean.

But Noemi's phone call hadn't been all bad.

Sherwood knows Sy is missing—*that was quick*. Not even twenty-four hours had passed. No matter. The cop won't find her.

And he won't tell Sy that the detective is looking for her.

Don't wanna get her hopes up. That would be mean.

48

I raced around the basement—I had to find a way to escape.

Breath hot in my chest, I tapped at walls, listening for the hollowness of cheap plaster. No give beneath my knuckles. Solid.

What time is it? How long has he been gone?

The room had no windows and only one door. And that door was heavy with locks and sheet metal.

How long do I have?

My eyes dropped to the concrete floor. In the corner near the camping toilet, the floor was cracked and crumbling away. I kneeled and swiped at the debris.

I can tunnel my way out of here.

What would I use as a shovel? And how would I keep him from noticing?

Crap.

I needed a weapon, something to gash his eye or slash his throat, stab and run.

My eyes skipped to the desk: pens, sticky notes, pads. Nothing like a letter opener or even a stapler.

I turned to the small table: the Starbucks cup, the plate of Oreos, my glass mug.

The padlocks rattled and locks squeaked.

The monster had returned.

I took one last look at the glass mug, then hurried to sit on the futon.

The door opened, and a whoosh of cool air spilled into the room. I drank it in before it turned as stale as the air I now breathed.

He stepped into the basement with several bags of office supplies. He placed the pads, packages of sticky notes, and packs of pens in the desk drawers. "There you go," he said with a smile.

He waited as though I should thank him.

"How long have you been watching me?" I asked instead.

A frown flashed across his face and quickly disappeared. "Four, five months. It's been difficult, wanting to be with you but having to wait. Seeing you with other . . . men." He balled up the plastic bags and stuffed them into his pocket. "Should we get to work now?"

"I am working." I nodded to the wall. "How many are there?"

His gaze followed mine. He narrowed his eyes as he studied the pictures there. "With or without you?"

I swallowed. "Without."

He said, "Fifteen."

"And . . . and how many are buried here?"

He looked at the concrete. "Three here. One in the backyard."

My mouth moved but no sound came—I had not meant "here" as in "this room."

"Shocked?" he asked.

I had no idea there were so many. No idea.

"You won't kill me," I said, tears welling in my eyes.

He tilted his head. "Why do you think that?"

"Because . . . Cuz I'm not like the others."

He laughed loud and shrill, like a hyena. "You *are* like the others, Sy. You just have a little money. A fancy college degree. Nice clothes. You may drink hundred-dollar wine instead of bottles of Cisco, but you are like the others." His amusement faded and his eyes darkened. "Adam Sherwood was not your husband, and yet you gave him all the privileges of marriage. Guess what that makes you?"

"You can't kill me," I whispered.

The monster's nostrils flared and he grinned at me like the devil. "Why do you fear death? If you're as good as you think you are, then you shouldn't worry. Don't you wanna leave this place? Be with the Father? Isn't that what we all want? To go to Heaven?"

I dropped my eyes to the cracked concrete. *Yes.*

"Now," he said. "Why don't you have a seat at your desk and we'll get started?" He pulled out the chair. "Don't make me ask again."

I settled at the desk—it resembled my setup at home. Pens over there. Pencils over there. Post-it notes within easy reach. Except there was no desktop computer and no tin of wintergreen Altoids. The two picture frames held photographs of happy white people instead of my niece Josie and my father Frank.

The monster stood behind me and massaged my shoulders.

My body tensed. Held my breath to keep from crying out. Gripped the edges of the desk to keep from pushing him away.

He pulled the second chair to the desk and sat on my left. Then, he turned my chair to face his and took both of my hands in his. He bowed his head and said, "Dear Father . . ."

He started to pray. Something about me being a vessel for his truth and the spirit guiding my pen.

I sat there, sneering at him, offended that he dared pray to the God I worshipped.

He said, "Amen," and squeezed my right hand, indicating that I, too, should say "Amen."

I said, "No."

He grabbed my left wrist and twisted it.

Something popped and heat rushed through my hands and up my arm like lava. I shrieked and fell to my knees. Hit my head on the desk, opening the wound Toni Fortune had caused just a day before.

He brought his scowling face an inch away from mine. "I will not tolerate blasphemy. Do you understand?" He shoved me.

My head hit the edge of the desk. My teeth bit down on my tongue, turning my spit metallic and thick. My body convulsed with sobs as I clutched my broken wrist. Tears and blood impaired my vision but not enough—I could still see my arm. A bone, tiny and white, slick with blood, poked past my skin.

Wide-eyed, the monster backed away from me and wrung his hands. "Oh, Sy . . . I'm . . . I didn't mean . . . You shouldn't have did what you did. You . . . You made me . . ." He smacked his forehead and waggled his head. He kept moving away from me. Backing away until he reached the door.

I pulled myself over to the wall next to the desk. Placed my bloody cheek against the puke-green drywall as white heat radiated throughout my body, as warm blood trickled down my temple and into my eye, as blood trickled from my wrist down my forearm, plopping off my elbow and onto my thighs.

My lips moved, driven by despair.

The Lord is my shepherd; I shall not want . . .

I thought about Mom, about Kenny and Eva. The family trip in April to Paris. Christmas dinner. Teaching Josie "Chopsticks" on the piano. And Adam. Sitting beside him on the couch, watching him play *Gears of War* on the Xbox, touching him . . .

Would I ever see them again?

The Phantom Slayer would kill me. The photographs on that wall proved that he would.

It was only a matter of time.

49

As he set my wrist, I bit down on a leather belt. Bit down so hard, I chipped a tooth.

"Sorry this hurts," he whispered, "but this is the only way." He paused, then said, "Don't be so disagreeable next time."

He did something else to my wrist that made me see stars and then gray.

"Almost done," he said, wrapping an ACE bandage around my wrist. He forced three pills between my lips, then used a wet hand towel and cotton balls brown with Betadine to clean my head wound. After he was done, he took away the belt, then sat in one of the chairs.

I didn't move from the wall and curled back into my tight ball.

I had been taught by my mother and the church that hatred was a sin, that hatred would damn me to Hell. But I hated this . . . *thing* sitting across from me. Hate burned in my heart like wildfire. I would surely perish unless God showed mercy.

But being "disagreeable" would not help my cause, and would, instead, hasten my death.

And Adam needed as much time as possible to find me.

"How did you learn how to set bones?" I croaked.

He sat up. "Police training."

"You're a cop?"

"I left the academy under my own will."

"What do you do now? Full-time security guard?"

"I work for the county. Department of Mental Health."

I had no energy to chuckle at the irony. "How do you know Adam?"

"I didn't know him. Not until he started looking for me."

The inside of my mouth had numbed. My left arm felt heavy. There were still twinges of pain but nothing like before. "What were those pills?"

"Two Demerol and a Valium."

I closed my eyes—my knees relaxed out of that hold, and my head rolled forward. Heard myself snoring.

Beep.

The room burst with bright light.

He was taking pictures again.

Didn't care.

I shivered.

Peeked and saw my bare belly, my bra, bandages . . . No shirt.

His hand brushed against my shoulder. "Oh, Sy."

So cold.

His thumb rubbed the scoop of my neck, the place where my pulse lived. "Sy?"

I opened my eyes, hating that he called me by my nickname. He hadn't earned the right and yet he used it like "the" and "me."

"What are the bandages for?" he asked.

I blinked at him but said nothing.

His finger jabbed at the gauze covering my left breast.

I didn't respond, not this time. My bandage, my scar, my cancer was none of his business.

"Did someone hurt you there?"

I said nothing.

He left his chair, perched beside me. "Did *he* hurt you?" His finger trailed from my throat down to the gauze.

I held my breath, steeled myself for pain.

He stood, nudged my leg with his foot. "I'm sorry for whatever happened to you. Okay, Sy? I'm sorry."

I closed my eyes, said, "Okay" even though I knew better.

Psychopaths feel no emotion. They pretend to be human for our benefit in order to advance their mission. They are never sorry. Not ever.

"I'll let you rest," he whispered. "Anything before I go?"

I opened my eyes. "I need fresh air. I can't breathe. That smell . . ."

He stuck his hands into his pockets and leaned against the wall. "Yeah. It is annoying."

"Just five minutes," I said. "I'm already working with a broken wrist."

He tilted my head back so that he could see my face. "I apologized to you for the wrist. Said I was sorry."

I closed my eyes—didn't have to look at him. "Please. Just five minutes."

He lightly thumped the back of his head against the wall. Then, he looked at his watch. Thumped his head again. "It will have to be at night."

"Okay."

"So no one can see you."

"Okay."

"And then, you will start the book."

"Yes."

"No more postponing. No more putting off."

He nudged me again with his foot.

"No more postponing," I said.

He grunted. "But it will have to be at night."

I didn't wait for him to leave before falling asleep.

I awakened, and tried to move, but couldn't. And not because he had tied me up. No. Both my hands and legs were free.

He had carried me to the futon and had dressed me in another T-shirt—the *Empire Strikes Back* shirt I thought I had left at Adam's. And now, it was soaked through with my sweat. My injured wrist had swollen twice its size. It felt thick and warm.

The locks clanked. The door opened.

He entered the room holding a tray of food. He sat it at my feet. "Your favorites," he said. "Rib-eye steak, asparagus, and jasmine rice."

I lay there, silent, motionless, eyes glazed, hair plastered to my damp forehead.

"Are you gonna say, 'Thank you, Sean'?"

I whispered, "Thank you."

He touched my clammy skin, then grunted.

I whispered, "I need a doctor."

"No," he said. "Your body's fighting it off. You need to eat."

"Not hungry."

"Yes, you are."

He helped me sit up, making a show of being very careful of my wrist. Then, he cut the steak and fed it to me, piece by piece. Tasted rancid—*when had he bought it?*

But I ate it all—I *was* hungry.

"Told you," he said. "Feel better?"

I nodded.

"Ready for fresh air?"

"Yes."

He placed a black kerchief over my eyes and slipped the gag back into my mouth. He led me up the stairs where the air was ranker than the basement's. Rotten food smells. Animal smells. Urine. That stink of decay. How was that possible?

I stumbled a few times on objects on the floor.

"I should've cleaned more," he muttered.

A door slid open, and this time, good air, cold air washed over me. I shivered—felt like I had fallen into an ice-cold river on a hot day.

Once we stepped outside, he removed the kerchief from my eyes.

The sky was white with stars.

Unremarkable backyard overgrown with weeds.

The rooftops and backs of surrounding houses looked familiar. Not because I had visited this place before. No. Familiar because there were thousands of neighborhoods like this in Southern California. Every first, third, and fifth house painted Sandstone; every second, fourth, and sixth house painted Moroccan Sun. Dream homes in the desert worth nothing now. For Sale signs dotting abandoned lawns.

Was this Palmdale? Lancaster? Moreno Valley? They all looked the same.

The monster stood behind me, his fingers lost in my hair again. "We're not far from the mountains. Maybe one day, when the world moves on, when Sherwood replaces you with another whore and doesn't care about you anymore, maybe we'll go on a drive to the mountains. Just you and me. Have a picnic. You like picnics. We'll bring that wine you like, and the Gouda cheese."

I took another deep breath of clean air.

"What do you think?"

"That will be good," I said.

He scratched my scalp. "Esther, my last girlfriend . . . She wasn't much for picnics. She preferred sitting and just . . . talking." His fingers froze. "I'm wrong. What I told you earlier? I was mistaken . . . There are two out here now. Two." His fingers started scratching again.

I pressed my lips tight, not wanting to whimper but failing.

"We'll take your car," he said. "I drove it here. It's a good car. A Benz. Never thought I'd own a luxury car. Not with my salary. It's better than the black Explorer you used to drive. It's very comfortable."

I'd almost forgotten about the Ford after buying my car . . . The fancy sedan with its seat warmers, wood interior, the satellite radio and . . . and the SOS system.

My heart tripped in my chest.

The SOS system.

Oh my God, thank you.

I shut my eyes so that he couldn't see the flicker of hope there. Because if he did, he would know, and I would die as soon as we returned to that basement.

50

The locks rattled and the door opened.

He entered with a tray of food and sat it on the ground. "Breakfast."

I lay on the futon—I had been staring at the desk, drifting in and out of sleep. Shivering then kicking away the comforter.

"I have to go," he said. "I have errands." He sounded sad, depressed. That worried me.

He left the room without saying goodbye.

The door slammed and the locks rattled.

I groaned as I rolled onto my back. The sheets were damp and my T-shirt clung to me like a second skin. My joints ached—the fever was worsening. I pulled myself to stand but fell back onto the futon. The room swayed and I hid my face in my hands until the dizzy spell passed. Even then, I sat there, holding my head in my hands.

Did he take my car to run his errands?

Didn't matter.

The GPS tracking capability in the car's SOS system would provide the police with the Benz's precise location.

But what if Adam doesn't realize the car has SOS until three days from now?

Would I be here in three days?

I couldn't wait for Adam.

The monster had left me coffee, eggs, and bacon as well as three pills on a paper towel. I dumped the pills into the camping toilet, then studied the clear glass mug.

It had been my favorite, and I had been looking for it just . . . a day ago? Two days? How long had I been here?

No matter. Time to go.

I chugged the coffee, hoping that he hadn't drugged it, then slipped on my Vans. I pulled the pillowcase off the pillow, then took the empty mug to the corner near the camping toilet. I stood there, wondering if this was the right thing to do, knowing that I had to do it or else.

Do it.

I wrapped the mug in the pillowcase, making sure that I could still hold the handle. I gritted my teeth, turned my head away, and struck the mug against the ground.

Even muffled, the crash of glass exploded in my eardrums.

I held my breath and waited for the door to bust open and for the monster to storm in.

But nothing happened.

With my heart in my throat, I shook the broken glass onto the concrete. I sifted through the shards. *There it is!* I plucked the handle from the mess. It was long enough and jagged enough.

I left the glass on the ground—he'd see that I had dropped it and wouldn't expect that it had been anything more than an accident.

I hope.

I climbed into bed, worried that fever and sweaty hands would keep me from holding my weapon.

Too late to do anything else.

No turning back.

Balls out.

That's what Adam would say.

◆ ◆ ◆

The locks rattled.

I sat up in bed, mouth dry, pulse racing from fear and infection. I hugged myself, my right hand gripping the glass handle and hidden beneath my left underarm.

He stepped into the room. "How are you feeling?" His eyes looked flat, emotionless.

"Not so good."

His eyes flicked to the corner of the room. "There's broken glass."

I nodded. "The mug slipped out of my hands. I was taking my pills and the fever's making my hands . . ."

He blinked at me.

"I'm sorry. Please don't hit me. I'm sorry."

"I won't hit you," he said. "I'd never do anything like that. Okay?"

I nodded. "Okay."

"This is not fulfilling," he said. "How we are now."

I swallowed, stammered, "And how . . . how are we now?"

"Friends." He shook his head. "It's no good. This is not how it was supposed to be. This is not why I brought you here. We're wasting time. It's my fault—with your wrist, I lost sight. But now I see."

I dropped my eyes. "So . . . what . . . ?"

He sat near my knees and placed his hand on my thigh. "You're shaking." He lifted my chin. "Don't be scared, Sy. It won't be bad. You won't feel a thing."

A hot tear rolled down my cheek.

He brushed the tear away and stroked my hair. "Sy, baby."

I whispered, "Don't call me that."

His eyes darkened and he slowly took back his hand.

My grip on the glass handle tightened.

He stood from the bed. "It's time for you to go upstairs now."

My heart pounded. I didn't want to go upstairs. Didn't know what was up there, in those bedrooms, but I knew that I'd never see my family again if I went upstairs.

He smiled down at me. "Will it make you feel good to know that you are the prettiest one on my wall?"

I took a deep breath, then muttered, "Fuck your wall."

He lunged at me.

I screamed and kicked him in the chest.

He grabbed my leg and pulled me toward him.

I struggled against him. Used my knees to try and keep him from lying on top of me.

He grabbed my broken wrist as he reached for my right arm.

An explosion of pain blinded me. My head throbbed.

Now!

But I couldn't see.

Do it now or die!

My right hand swung from beneath me.

The handle sank into flesh and stopped at bone.

He screamed.

Hot blood splattered on my face and neck.

The glass handle slipped out of my hand. I kicked him in the chest.

He crumpled to the floor, his hands covering his bloody face.

I jumped over him and raced to the door.

Ran up those stairs, not stopping—I knew he was behind me.

He shouted, "You *bitch*!"

I kept running. Ran out the front door, out to the walkway.

I squinted—blinded again, this time by bright sunlight.

Hadn't seen the sun in days.

No one was around.

I ran past abandoned homes, past empty parks, past towering palms.

Don't stop. Don't you dare stop.

I reached a highway. Parched asphalt and desert all around me. No traffic signals. No traffic. Nothing. No one.

My body was on fire but I still ran toward the sun.

I stumbled and hit the ground. Heard the scar on my breast pop. My bra became wet and thick against my skin. My broken wrist no longer existed.

My knees stung. Pieces of gravel had lodged into my palms.

I forced myself to stand. Stuck one foot in front of the other. One foot. Next foot. No running now. Marching in place.

So hot.

I stumbled again, and one of my sneakers popped off. Gravel in my eyes, in my mouth. The blacktop burned my skin, burned through my bloody shirt and nylon pants.

Get up.

Can't.

I lie there, clutching my broken wrist. The pain had returned, and icy sparks shot through my body with each breath. Tears and spit pooled beneath my cheek on the blacktop.

Get up.

No. I'm done.

I closed my eyes and waited to die.

The sky was cornflower blue. Soft wind kissed my cheeks and lifted my hair. Long blades of grass tickled my arms. I sat in a field of candy-colored poppies. In the distance, hot-air balloons drifted across the horizon like dandelion seeds.

A man was walking through the field toward me.

I narrowed my eyes. Couldn't see his face.

He came closer . . . closer . . .

My father wore khakis and a crisp white shirt. His eyes were bright, and his skin—the color of Maui earth—radiated in the sunlight.

I held out my arms.

He sat beside me, then kissed my forehead.

I threw my arms around his neck. "I knew we'd see each other again."

He held my face in his hands. "Wake up, Sy. Go home."

I lay on my back, on a random highway somewhere in the desert.

One lazy cloud drifted in the sky. That bright white sun beat down on me. A tiny airplane soared high above . . .

"Sy. Baby."

The monster had found me. He would take me back to that basement. He would take his pictures of me, then he would kill me . . .

I caught air, floating now. Light as cotton. Light as that lazy cloud.

The world rocked.

Lips brushed across my forehead.

"Sy."

I closed my eyes.

It would be over soon. No more pain. Not ever.

Heaven.

51

I opened one eye, and then the other. Above me, ceiling panels of corkboard, white and endless, stretched far beyond my view. The caverns behind my sockets ached and pinged.

I licked my lips and rough skin scraped my tongue. I tried to move but couldn't—I had been tucked tight beneath a blue blanket. One arm, my right, was pinned beside me. My left arm, wrapped in a hard white cast, sat atop the blanket with as much life as a log.

Something sharp pricked my thigh. Seconds later, coolness ran through my leg up to my torso. The muscles in my body relaxed.

My vision dimmed. My eyelids grew heavy as ice slipped through my veins.

My head lolled to the side.

Heavy pink drapes hung open on each side of the window. Outside, the sun prepared to set. The sky was the color of autumn leaves, of fire and orange juice. I licked my lips, imagined drinking orange juice.

Adam was sitting in a chair by that window. The butt of his Glock stuck from his jacket pocket, and another gun stuck from his ankle holster.

My gaze returned to the window.

The sky had darkened. Purples and blues, bruises and dragons.

And I slept.

Each time I opened my eyes, Adam was there, at my bedside.

Visitors came—Mom, Eva, Lena, and Spencer—but Adam did not leave that chair.

On the third day, I awoke to see him staring at me.

I moved my mouth, struggled to speak. Finally: "You find him?"

He nodded, left that chair, and stood over me.

"Go," I whispered. "Rest."

He kissed my forehead. "Can't rest. Not with you here." He nuzzled my healthy hand and placed it against his cheek. "Hey, baby."

"Hey." I gazed into his eyes—he was so beautiful.

He said, "Strangest thing happened a few days ago."

"Yeah?"

"I'll tell you about it later, okay? Sleep for now."

"Yeah." And I closed my eyes, still holding my love's hand.

AUTHOR'S NOTE

In 1985, a young Black woman named Debra Jackson was found shot to death in an alley in South Los Angeles. A year later, Henrietta Wright was found murdered in another alley in the same part of town. By 1988, four other women had been killed. The victims were similar: young Black women who lived in South Los Angeles. The bullets found in the victims shared similar markings that suggested the same gun had been used in each crime. The murderer had left behind DNA, but there have been no matches in state and federal databases.

The public didn't learn of these murders until Christine Pelisek, a reporter at the alternative newspaper *LA Weekly*, broke the story. Even then, city officials threw the detectives working on the case meager resources to catch the man deemed as "the most persistent serial killer in California history."

There was no uproar. No marches or rallies with galvanizing speeches from the city's leaders. No breaking news reports on local channels—just car chases, brushfires, and more newsworthy murders.

And the victims? They haven't received the attention granted to prettier, blonder, lighter victims. No—these women were poor and Black, several of them prostitutes, living dangerous lives in a dangerous part of the city. Their families have no voice or political power to demand answers, and until the *Weekly*'s reporting, their daughters went faceless.

It's as though these murdered young women never existed . . .

But one woman survived. The Grim Sleeper shot her in the chest and sexually assaulted her. She passed out, but a bright flash awakened her. The murderer had taken her picture with a Polaroid camera.

When I first wrote this book back in 2008, the death toll was at thirteen—all Black women—and detectives in the Los Angeles Police Department had yet to find the killer. The mayor's office had acknowledged that these murders were related, and the City Council offered a $500,000 reward for information that led to the arrest and conviction of the elusive murderer.

Even then, the Grim Sleeper hadn't sent letters or left behind clues like the BTK Killer or the Green River Killer. No DNA. No witnesses except for the lone survivor. The Grim Sleeper was as elusive then as he was in 1985.

Until his arrest in 2010, which was made possible through the utilization of familial DNA searches.

In May 2016, Lonnie David Franklin Jr. was convicted of murdering nine women and one teenage girl. He received ten death sentences and was sent to San Quentin State Prison, where he was found dead in his cell in March 2020.

No One Knows You're Here was inspired by those unsolved murders. Like the real Grim Sleeper case, no one knew the Phantom Slayer's identity—he could've been anyone. Neat. Tidy. Kind of geeky. The Slayer takes pictures of his victims and eludes the authorities. The real Grim Sleeper had been considered a great neighbor, someone who could fix your car, get you a great deal on a stolen television. He'd worked for the city of Los Angeles—including the police department. A little weird, but you know . . . hiding in plain sight.

Syeeda McKay is not Ms. Pelisek, yet she shares that same doggedness and determination. In many ways, Sy is me, born and raised in South Los Angeles, with parents who demanded only the best from my siblings and me . . . despite the surrounding violence, poverty, and hopelessness. Flawed yet emphatic, vulnerable yet brave, Sy represents that connection between the haves and the ain't-gots, a witness to both worlds, a community that only gets attention after the monsters come . . . and sometimes, not even then. This story offers a glimpse of another Los Angeles, a city where klieg lights aren't always used for movie premieres, and police helicopters land in the middle of the street. In these same neighborhoods, kids, moms, and dads make the best of life and love. Soccer and basketball games. Church potlucks. Spelling bees. Even in the madness, they are there. They are us.

—Rachel Howzell Hall

Photo © 2023 Andre Ellis

Rachel Howzell Hall is the *New York Times* bestselling author of *Mist and Malice, Fog and Fury, The Cruel Dawn, The Last One, What Never Happened, We Lie Here, These Toxic Things, And Now She's Gone, They All Fall Down*, and, with James Patterson, *The Good Sister*, which was included in Patterson's collection *The Family Lawyer*. A two-time *Los Angeles Times* Book Prize finalist as well as an Anthony, International Thriller Writers, and Lefty Award nominee, Rachel is also the author of *Land of Shadows, Skies of Ash, Trail of Echoes*, and *City of Saviors* in the Detective Elouise Norton series. A past member of the board of directors for Mystery Writers of America, she has been a featured writer on NPR's acclaimed *Crime in the City* series and the National Endowment for the Arts weekly podcast. Rachel lives in Los Angeles with her husband and daughter. For more information, visit www.rachelhowzell.com.